Say Cheese
and
Murder

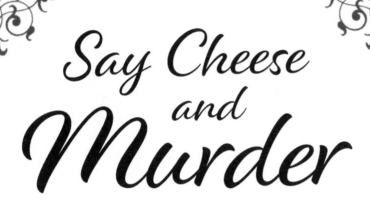

Say Cheese and Murder

A Lemington Cheese
Company Mystery
Book 1

12/19/22 Michelle Pointis Burns

Happy Sleuthing!

M Burns

Scrambled H Publishing
New York

Book Cover Design & Formatting
by JD&J Design

Dedication

To my daughter Abigail, who, for her eleventh birthday, requested a murder mystery party. Failing to find a ready-made kit that suited, I set out to write one.

In ten days, the characters and their web of secrets sprang to life at the celebratory event. Three years later, the characters begged to appear in a comprehensive narrative suitable for all audiences, yet more thrilling than "the dog stole the cake." And so, my novel-writing journey began.

Abby, you were so disappointed at not solving the case at your party, but now your character shall use her sleuthing abilities on your behalf.

Contents

MAJOR CHARACTERS

Birch, Jack..Head gardener

Chamberlain, Fredrick ....Jeweler

Dalton, Arabella (Bella).....................Cassandra's best friend

Fairchild, Flora...................................Head housekeeper

Fartworthy, Archibald ....Head butler

Fletcher, Poppy ....Piano player

Haywood, Cassandra..........................Lady Lemington's niece

Lemington, Lady Lily ....CEO of Lemington Cheese/
owner of Dutch Hill Manor

Lightfoot, Ruby...................................Photographer

Savage, Owen ....Guitar player

Spooner, Alexander............................Pharmacist

Turner, Robin ....Lady Lemington's sister-
in-law/Roland's mother

Turner, Roland ....Lady Lemington's
nephew/Robin's son

Von Pickle, Baron Rupert...................CEO Somerdale International
Cheese Company

York, Hamish ....CEO/co-owner of Rosewood
Cheese/married to Mimi

York, Mimi..Co-owner of Rosewood
Cheese/married to Hamish

MINOR CHARACTERS

Ahmed...Cabdriver
Eliza ....Housemaid
John..Butler
Lady Gwendolyn Bilford ....Lady Lemington's friend.
Nathan..Butler
Rose Forest.......................................Head cook
Sean Johnson....................................Valet

DETECTIVES

Detective Chief Inspector Carter ....Head detective
Detective Sergeant Jenkins ....Second-in-command to Carter
Detective Constable Baker.................Red-headed, female detective
Detective Constable Greenfield ....New detective
Detective Constable Henslowe
Detective Constable Penwarden

Chapter One

Ta-ta-ta-ta-ta-ta.

Helicopter blades whirled through the frigid air. The pilot guided the aircraft for a third time in an hour high above the icy, treacherous roads to Dutch Hill Manor. British law enforcement officers were aboard, responding to a servant's urgent telephone call. The situation called for immediate action, even in this dismal, New Year's Day weather.

Inside the manor, yellow tape marked off the crime scene. Detective Chief Inspector Carter and some of her team gathered near a body lying facedown. Detective Constable Greenfield, a recent graduate from the detective program, took notes.

Carter pointed. "Continue, Greenfield, and watch that you don't step in that fluid near your foot." She fixed her disposable glove with a snap. "What else do you see?"

"The victim lost at least a liter of blood." The new detective crouched, and his white, Tyvek oversuit crunched. "What I can see from this angle, there's a significant gash on the victim's head. I'm not sure where it ends under the body. This could have been an accident. Another possibility, someone was angry and slammed the victim's head into—"

"We need facts before developing theories. Don't make early assumptions. It'll limit your thinking." Carter turned to the coroner.

"What's your initial analysis?"

The medical examiner let out a deep breath under his face shield. "This happened several hours ago based on the temperature, the color of the body, and the large, viscous blood pool. And where it happened, the number of people who went through here beforehand might have muddied some evidence."

The head detective nodded. "I concur. We need to get photos before we shift anything to see the other side. With all this mess, we may have a bullet or stab wound we can't see yet. Is the photographer on the next helicopter? I'd like to crack on."

Nearby, Detective Sergeant Jenkins, Carter's second-in-command, scrolled on his mobile and shook his head. "No. They couldn't find anyone at this early holiday hour." The near-retirement-aged man looked up at his mid-forties' female superior. "Now what?"

Detective Constable Penwarden, who also stood away from the corpse, studied the papers on the clipboard he held. "Hold up. We may be in luck. A Miss Ruby Lightfoot stayed overnight as a guest. We've used her photography services before." He lifted the yellow caution tape, intending to come inside the boundary of the crime scene.

"No, I'll come to you. You're not suited up." Carter's blue overshoes shuffled across the floor.

"Lightfoot is who they were looking for," remarked Jenkins.

The head detective yanked off her gloves, tugged her face mask down past her mouth, and took the clipboard. "Is that the list the servant gave us?" Penwarden nodded as Carter flipped up the sheets.

DS Jenkins pointed at the list. "According to the head butler, this is everyone, and no one has left the manor since the storm last night."

"All of these people are still here? Holy crow!" The hood of her white coverall crunched noisily as she nodded. "Yes, locate Miss Lightfoot. She should have her camera since she was on call last night.

It's possible she's a guest and not the photographer. Find that out first. Second, if she had a close relationship with the victim, we need someone else. If not, make sure she's questioned before seeing the body. Everyone is a suspect until they're cleared."

DCI Carter pointed to the paper. "Let's do this." She took a pen from her pocket. "We'll divide the guest list into three groups. We'll call this group 'A.' DC Henslowe and DC Baker will question them." She circled a section on the sheet and added letters. "Penwarden, you take the ones we'll call 'B.' These people are the staff." She moved on to another sheet. "And I'll take group 'C' with Jenkins and Greenfield after we're done here." She held the paper away from her. "Yes, good plan. Now move out."

Penwarden took the clipboard, pivoted, and looked over his shoulder. "Detective Chief Inspector?"

Carter removed a fresh set of gloves from her pocket and pulled one on. "Yes, Penwarden?"

"Happy New Year."

She sighed. "Yes, that. Same. Go."

*   *   *

Twelve hours earlier . . .

Cassandra Haywood drove her decade-old Honda Accord up the steep hill to her aunt's lavish mansion for the New Year's Eve gala. A gossamer, ivory-colored scarf knotted under her left ear held back her long, golden-brown hair. She spoke on her hands-free device to her best friend, Arabella Dalton. "Have you decided?"

"I'm still in my closet. Help me," Arabella whined as her phone crackled.

"Arriving in minutes, Bella. Let's figure this out if you want my assistance." She waved a hand around. "Wear your black-and-pink dress. You look stunning in that."

"Which one?"

"The black, velvet top with the matching bolero jacket and the baby-pink, silk bottom with rhinestone accents." Cassandra turned down the heat in the car.

"I'm blanking."

"The Holy Grail of dresses. The one with the pockets."

"Yes! Here it is. You have such a fantastic memory, Cassie. I have the perfect hair accessory to wear. It's a prototype."

"Intriguing. Are you going to share some insider information on your latest design?"

"Not a chance. You must wait until you see me. I want your un-filtered response. The gala will be the perfect place to gauge reactions."

"Fair enough."

Arabella made shuffling noises on her end. "What are you wear-ing tonight?"

"A cream-colored, silk, peasant blouse and my long, peach, chiffon skirt. The one with the tiny, multi-colored flowers."

"Nice. How many scarves? Seven? Eight?" Her friend laughed.

"Three, Bella," said Cassandra, using the nickname her friend allowed only her to use.

"You're the one person I know who can pull off the bohemian look, wear a dozen delicate scarves, and still look elegant and not like a 1960s hippy throwback."

"Three is shy of a dozen." Cassandra turned the steering wheel to avoid a dip in the road.

"It's still quite a bit. What colors?"

"Raspberry, ivory, and lilac. I'm getting closer, and it's almost time for me to go. I'm looking forward to tonight's soiree."

"Such an elegant affair." Arabella cleared her throat. "There, I'm dressed, thanks to you. Getting ready to leave. Any fireworks expected for tonight?"

"Very funny. Actual fireworks are only for the summer garden party. As for the virtual pyrotechnics, we'll see. I hope Aunt Lily will conduct herself properly today."

Cassandra's aunt, the brilliant businesswoman, Lady Lily Lemington, owned Dutch Hill Manor and the Lemington Cheese Company, a corporation that supported the estate.

Arabella said, "Recently, I heard an angry local complain again that the replacements were all from out of town. Terrible."

"They really need something new to discuss in the village. Aunt Lily did that years ago before I came to live at the manor. Not all the grapevine talk can be true. I know for tonight, she extended an invitation to everyone with whom she has business or personal dealings. Even some locals."

"But why include rivals and stir up trouble?"

"I don't know. She's a riddle and must have her reasons."

"How can you defend her?" asked Arabella.

"How could you not? She's your best customer. How many headpieces and hats has she purchased from you? Dozens? And you accepted the invite for tonight's party."

Cassandra turned left onto the half-mile long, winding, up-hill, gravel driveway lined with giant oaks every thirty feet on either side. She clicked on the high beams. "I don't like these trees in the dark. At other times of the year, this drive is awash with color and life. Now they look like ogres with gnarled arms, ready to grab anyone coming to visit our estate."

"I'm telling your aunt! I'm telling her! You called it 'our' estate." laughed Arabella.

"Hush, now." Cassandra smiled. "I know it isn't mine, but

it's easy to get used to thinking like that when you live here most of the year."

The car wheels crunched on the gravel, making it difficult to hear. "The manor should really be yours someday."

Cassandra turned up the Bluetooth volume. "I doubt it. Roland will become CEO of the company, and I assume he'll get the estate, too."

"Cassie! How could you be fine with that? You should fight for it."

"The estate or the company?"

"Both."

Cassandra sighed. "I've told you a thousand times, Roland has an eye for the cheese business. Stop harping on this. I'm content to be a cog in the company."

"Don't you want more control?" Arabella huffed.

"That's too much pressure for me. I give advice."

"Yes, you do, and you've helped me tremendously with my business. You have a keen sense of industry and finance. The job of running the entire cheese company should be yours someday. I hate to see you settle."

"It's not settling." Cassandra tapped the steering wheel. "These trees are creepy. Aunt Lily should put some white fairy lights on them for this annual party or maybe the whole winter. It would be less dreary." Her car's headlights cut through the foggy, shadowy night.

Her friend sighed. "Fairy lights would be extraordinarily pretty, Cassandra."

"I'll talk to Mr. Birch about putting them up."

"Good luck with that. You would think a head gardener would be happy to have such a cushy position. Yet, every time I see him, he's ill-tempered."

"Yes, he tends to yell often at his grounds crew. I get along with him, though, and Aunt Lily tolerates him. Few people do. He has a hard time relating, and since he's in his late middle age, he won't change. I feel bad for the gentleman. To me, Mr. Birch seems to wish the choices he made in life were something different."

Arabella grunted. "You mean someone who settled for less than their potential?"

Cassandra bristled. "I . . . I guess so." Her car reached the end of the tree line. "So, I've arrived. Need to go."

"See you soon, Cass. We'll talk later. Bye now."

"Bye." She disconnected the call. *Why does she say that? I'm not settling.*

The car came out of the tunnel of doom and into a spectacular vision, like the opening of a stage curtain, revealing a lavish musical set. Dutch Hill Manor, a panorama of luminosity, stood regal and elegant against the bitter night. Three stories of cocoa brick, English tradition loomed with twenty-four windows on the front of the building. A real evergreen wreath, lit with white lights and trimmed with a magnificent, golden bow, hung across each window from the exterior, white molding.

A mixture of festive and ordinary lights from the interior illuminated the windows on the first two floors. Guest room renovations had not been completed before the holidays, and the third-floor windows remained darkened. Two dwarf pine trees flanked the tall, gray, stone steps. These evergreen centurions, festooned with additional white lights, had grand, red bows adorning the crown of their white, marble pots.

The estate had stood for generations. Twice, the BBC wished to use it for Jane Austen movie adaptations—with the last offer six months ago—and twice, Lady Lemington refused. Cassandra tried to persuade her aunt that a short movie production using the exterior, the gardens, and the parlor would help offset the expenditure of running the manor. General operating costs for customary upkeep, and the ongoing, expensive, guest quarter renovation, made the film proposal attractive. Five million pounds for several days of inconvenience was a fine bit of pocket change. Exposure through the BBC could have the potential to generate tourist interest, which would be a further source of income, Cassandra reasoned. The Austen fan tours of mansions used in other productions proved lucrative to other struggling estates. The answer from Lady Lemington continued to be a firm no.

Cassandra pulled her car around the circular, gravel drive and stopped. The head valet rushed to open her door. She stepped out of her vehicle into the sudden burst of frigid air.

Sean Johnson greeted her. "Good evening, Miss Haywood. Happy New Year to you! Chilly night for the party, innit?"

Cassandra handed him her keys. "Mr. Johnson, wonderful to see you. It's a little frosty. Are you and your team staying warm out here?"

"Yes, ma'am, we are. The fine, new torch heaters you got us are delightful." He twirled her keys around his finger. "And they light things up pretty bright."

"How do you know I ordered the heaters?" She wrapped her violet, wool coat around her, pinching the collar around her neck.

He gave an impish wink. "Eh. We know who takes care of us. Thank you, ma'am." He retrieved her plum-colored suitcase from the car's boot. "The weatherman said light snow, but I think he don't know nothin'. I feel it in my bones. We're in for more than a few flakes tonight. How was your visit to your mum?" He shut the boot lid.

"Lovely and mercifully short. You're right about the weather. It does feel like a storm is on the way. Have a Happy New Year!"

Sean moved to the front of the car. "With you lookin' out

for us, we shall." He tipped his Pershing hat and pointed in the car. "You forget somethin', ma'am?"

She turned around. Her large, patchwork travel purse sat on the left passenger seat. She sighed. *Typical.* "Thank you, Mr. Johnson. You keep an eye out for *me*, too."

Cassandra had dozens of ideas in her head for multi-million-pound projects, improvements to her aunt's company, and even her friends' business ventures, but she couldn't remember her accessories. She had a dreadful habit of leaving her purse, gloves, umbrella, and especially her scarves, behind. No self-imposed reward system or memory trick could shake this unfortunate failing left over from childhood. The indefensible quirk forced Cassandra to keep a ready supply of replacements and people who pointed out her oversights.

She retrieved the multi-colored shoulder bag from Sean and picked up her suitcase.

Sean pointed. "Let me get one of the other blokes to do that for you."

"Thank you, Mr. Johnson, but I don't need someone carrying my bags. I did it all my life before coming here. Have a good evening."

"You, too, ma'am. Enjoy the party." Sean hopped into her car to move it around the manor to the parking lot.

She climbed up the worn, stone steps. *I know everything about the manor and the people living here. I couldn't own this place or run the company. I'm not settling. Bella is mistaken.* Cassandra frowned. *Don't be moody. Enjoy yourself.* She quickly dissolved the irritable look, and a warm smile bubbled up to the surface.

Another member of the valet crew opened the century-old, Italian, double doors.

The young valet who greeted her stood straight. "Welcome back, ma'am."

"Thank you, sir. I'm glad to be home." She sighed. "I see the doors have returned from their restoration in time for the party." She caressed a carved scene and the wrought iron decoration. "It's exquisite. Ready for later?"

"Yes indeed, ma'am."

"Excellent." Cassandra walked through the antique front doors as the first wisps of snow drifted down from the sky.

Chapter Two

Dutch Hill Manor bustled with activity. Staff members, focused on their personal assignments for the party, crisscrossed the highly polished, white, oak floors in the great hall. The women servants bobbed a quick curtsy, and the men touched the side of their foreheads, greeting Cassandra.

A massive Christmas tree, encrusted with delicate, blown-glass ornaments, golden bows, glittering snowflakes, and fairy lights, made an impressive display. The silver-and-gold sparkling evergreen competed for attention in the large space with the grand, twisting, oak staircase.

Cassandra put down her purse and suitcase, shrugged off her heavy coat, and glanced at the mahogany grandfather clock against the wall to her right. *It's 7:34. Not late.*

The head butler, Archibald Fartworthy, strode in, carrying a gleaming, sterling silver tray full of crystal champagne glasses. "Miss Haywood, glad to see you have returned to us. Welcome."

An underbutler entered the great hall from the dining room. Fartworthy pointed to him and then to the luggage. "Take Miss Haywood's bags to her room."

"Yes, sir." Butler John tipped his head in Cassandra's direction.

She smiled and handed him her purse. "Thank you." She strolled over to the full-size closet under the grand stairs.

"T-minus ninety minutes." Fartworthy moved with calculated speed.

Cassandra suppressed a giggle. Even the staff had adopted her aunt's peculiar terminology borrowed from the American space program. She hung up her coat and followed.

She picked up her pace to keep up with the English "ninja" butler, calmly dashing to his destination. He deposited the crystal flute glasses on a side table and was off on another mission. The staccato clicks of his highly polished shoes on the wooden floor were his musical accompaniment. Fartworthy's manner suggested a man much older than his thirty-five years. His jet-black hair, clipped short and smooth with a slight wave across his forehead, barely moved as he pivoted toward the dining room. His livery, perfectly crisp and starched, had no trace of a renegade thread or crumb. The head butler's thick, black, rectangular-rimmed glasses gave him the appearance of a computer programmer.

"Glad to be back. Everything ready for tonight, Mr. Fartworthy?" Cassandra clasped her hands together. "Anything I should be aware of before the manor is teeming with guests?"

"One thing." His words were as disciplined as his movements. "Your aunt instructed me to leave paperwork on the dresser in your room. She wants you to look it over before guests arrive."

She really does consider me part of the household staff. Cassandra matched Fartworthy's strides. Her scarf tails flew behind like flags waving in the breeze. "Great. Put me back to work the second I come home."

"That isn't her intention, ma'am. It's a few items she wanted you to see regarding company matters."

Lady Lemington trusted her butler to assist in the cheese

business. Cassandra thought this an odd job for a butler, but it had been this way since her aunt took over running the company a few years ago. A nasty lawsuit and an unidentifiable leak of information made the lady of the manor suspicious of most. She trusted Cassandra and Fartworthy.

"She realizes it's a holiday, right?" Cassandra threw her hands up. "I don't mind helping with the party, but a work-related assignment? That's ridiculous."

"She knows what today is, ma'am. It shouldn't take long." Fartworthy stopped to adjust a flower arrangement.

"How do you know?"

He looked over his shoulder. "Didn't I ever tell you that a good head butler can predict the future?"

Cassandra sighed. "Often. We should sort things out during regular business hours, not today." She followed Fartworthy out of the room.

For the gala, the staff of the manor had an impressive list of tasks to complete that would make the most loyal servants cringe. Lady Lemington was legendary for her habit of adding last-minute preparations. Even a detail-oriented planner like Fartworthy couldn't anticipate the extra jobs she wanted her staff to complete before start time.

The fast-walking pair arrived in the dining room. A delightful grand table, laden with hors d'oeuvres and canapés, stretched out before them. Fartworthy paused to move a platter of pastries placed too close to the edge and flatten a slight wrinkle in the starched, bright-white tablecloth.

"Is Mr. Birch around?" Cassandra picked up a mini strawberry tart and bit into the confection. The sweet treat chased away her irritability. "I wanted to ask him something. I had an idea about the trees in the driveway."

The corner of Fartworthy's mouth rose. He neatened the arrangement where Cassandra poached the delicacy. "I haven't seen him for hours. Birch disappeared earlier with his blasted mobile." The mask of efficiency, duty, and indifference dropped for a moment. "Ahem. His phone."

"Not a fan of Mr. Birch?" Cassandra smirked. *I've never heard any emotion from Mr. Fartworthy in all the years I have known him.*

"I'm keeping a weather eye on him, Miss Haywood. For now." Fartworthy headed to the middle of the table to move another sloppily deposited tray.

"He's harmless. Grumpy, but harmless." She swallowed the last crumbs of the tasty tart. "These are superb. Mrs. Forest has outdone herself again. Anyway, yes, he's on his phone often and protective of his hothouse. He's like you. He does his job, and no one can measure up to his own standards."

"In that way, true. However, he's one to be wary of." Fartworthy repositioned the bowl of punch on the magnificent table. "I don't fire my staff on a whim as he does."

Cassandra ran a finger along the tablecloth. "I agree. It's maddening that there's a revolving door of groundskeepers. Yelling at anyone who enters the hothouse without permission is an extension of his perfectionism. Why are you annoyed?"

Fartworthy tugged on the cloth, straightening a wrinkle she created. "I'm not. Everyone should complete their assignments in a timely fashion." He rearranged two silver platters symmetrically beside the floral centerpiece. Large, white roses, hydrangeas, lilies, and bell-shaped blooms, punctuated with a scattering of crimson roses, reached high and wide. Tiny, red-and-white flowers mixed with greenery and cascaded over the sides of a marble urn. Scattered throughout the room, identical, smaller arrangements graced side tables. "Birch finished these bouquets before he left." Fartworthy pointed around. "I was concerned he wouldn't complete the job. His crew brought them in."

A petite, young housemaid appeared in the dining room with a sizable, transparent, plastic box. "Mr. Fartworthy, beggin' ya pardon, sir. Where should we place these New Year's Eve things? Miss Fairchild sent me and said ya would 'ave a spot."

"I do, Eliza." He pointed to the locale. "Take the horns, whistles, and hats and put them in the two baskets on the sideboard. Move both containers to the coat closet under the stairs in the great hall. I'll get them from there later. We don't wish for people to get a hold of the noisemakers until right before they need them. Some adults turn into little children with a shiny horn in their hands."

"Very good, sir. Thank ya, sir. 'ello, Miss 'aywood." Eliza curtsied.

Cassandra grinned. "Hello, Eliza. Are you looking forward to midnight?"

"Yes, ma'am. Very much so." The diminutive maid hurried off to do Fartworthy's bidding.

Cassandra touched a white rose. "These hothouse flowers are magnificent. Mr. Birch keeps us in exquisite botanicals all year long. The extra money he brings in by selling flowers to locals is a good thing. And don't forget the heirloom seeds he cultivates and sells online. The income he generates helps keep this place running. Besides, he can be sweet." She smiled and tilted her head. "He brings Aunt Lily fresh flowers to her room every evening and arranges them himself. Mr. Birch has a talent for that sort of thing."

"Yes, he does, Miss Haywood." Fartworthy paused for a moment from his butler responsibilities, his intense, green eyes focused on her. "Be careful around him, ma'am. I hate to see you—" He exhaled. "Just be careful."

Cassandra paused and then whispered, "I will."

"Good." Fartworthy resumed moving nimbly through the manor. Cassandra followed from the dining room downstairs to the basement level.

With Cassandra in tow, Fartworthy strode into the boisterous kitchen like a commanding officer walking into barracks. The beehive of activity quieted in an instant with all eyes on the head butler. "Platters brought into the dining room need to be placed neatly upon the table. We have time, so there's no excuse for sloppy execution. Understood?"

"Yes, Mr. Fartworthy," the staff chorused.

"Please." Fartworthy motioned for them to continue.

The bustling in the vast room resumed with fervor. Clanking dishes, pots, and other kitchenware rivaled the noise of a hectic, expensive restaurant. Steam rose from vats of food in different stages of completion, making the kitchen noticeably warmer than the rest of the house. Immaculately kept, professional grade, stainless steel appliances and counters ringed the room. The scent of rosemary, cumin, sage, and oregano filled the air. A wave of chocolate, cinnamon, ginger, and strawberries from the dessert prep tables wafted by Cassandra's nose. Sauces bubbled and released notes of lemon, garlic, or tomato, adding to the symphony of aroma.

When staff members noticed Cassandra, they gave her a nod or a smile. Mrs. Rose Forest, the head cook, waved.

Flora Fairchild, the head housekeeper, holding a clipboard with a collection of lists, approached Fartworthy and Cassandra. Although in her early forties, Miss Fairchild had the figure and look of a nineteen-year-old. She removed a pen from the pocket of the starched, white half apron she wore over her black dress. Her blonde hair, neatly wrestled into a low bun, completed her signature look. "Good evening, Miss Haywood. Welcome back. Did you have a happy Christmas?"

Cassandra smiled. "I did, and I'm pleased to be back. How is everything here?"

"We're fine." Miss Fairchild jotted something on a page attached to her clipboard. "We had a few minor issues earlier, but all fixed." She turned to Fartworthy. "I'll go over party protocol with the staff tomorrow. A post-event review is always an excellent idea. Did Eliza find you?"

"Yes, she did. Situation handled. Flower arrangements are in place and so is the tableware." Fartworthy rubbed his forehead with the back of his thumb. "Hot food and more champagne glasses are needed. We have time. When are the musicians expected?"

Miss Fairchild finished writing. "They're set to arrive within the hour. Miss Ruby Lightfoot should also be here soon. Maybe."

Fartworthy pointed up. "Ah yes, Miss Lightfoot. She takes excellent pictures but tends to run late. We need table photos, and Lady Lemington wants candid shots of the guests throughout the party. Tell the musicians and the photographer they'll eat downstairs in the kitchen on their staggered breaks. Text Miss Lightfoot to give her a heads-up about Lady Lemington's desires." Fartworthy scanned the room. "Regular staff members need to be at their stations in an hour."

"Noted. Appetizers and main courses are in progress. Mrs. Forest and the baking staff completed the desserts." Miss Fairchild flipped through the sheets. "We might even have a moment before the guests arrive to catch our breath or a cuppa." She looked up with a twinkle in her robin's egg-blue eyes.

Fartworthy chuckled. "Doubt that."

Fairchild and Fartworthy were the Ginger Rogers and Fred Astaire of the manor. They performed their tasks with ease, understanding and anticipating the other. The rest of the staff fell into line effortlessly with such in-tune leaders. Three years of working together created a rhythm that kept Dutch Hill Manor running smoothly, even when Lady Lemington challenged that cadence.

Lady Lemington entered the kitchen, and the room fell silent again.

Chapter Three

All eyes fixed on Lady Lemington as she glided through the busy room. "Fartworthy, Fairchild, I do hope this little break means we're ready for tonight's event." She waved her hand in a circle. "Everything needs to be perfect. No excuses."

"Yes, ma'am," replied Fartworthy and Fairchild in unison. The rest of the staff, surprised by the sudden arrival of the lady of the manor, remained hushed.

Lady Lemington's youthful, hourglass figure had left her long ago. She now dressed in black clothes, not because of mourning, but for the slimming effect. A plush, black, velvet shawl with fine fringe hung from her shoulders, draping over her black, silk blouse. The shawl fastened in the front by a large, intricate, diamond brooch in the shape of a flower. She wore a long, black, chiffon skirt. The attire gave her the appearance of a moving shadow. A pop of color emerged on her head in the form of a fascinator. On the headwear, large plumes of dark-purple feathers stuck up and swayed like field grass in a breeze whenever she moved.

"Cassandra, when did you return?"

"Good evening, Aunt Lily, nice to see you. I arrived a short time ago." Cassandra smiled. "Happy New Year."

Her aunt gestured to her. "Look at the paperwork, Cassandra. We'll need it tonight. And for heaven's sake, don't leave any personal items of yours around. It's unbecoming and makes you look irresponsible. We have a family image to maintain."

"Yes, ma'am." Cassandra's smile flickered for just an instant. *Does she realize when she reprimands me, I feel like I'm eleven years old?*

Fartworthy interrupted the admonishment. "We're reviewing the last few things. Almost everything is complete. Staff will be at their stations shortly, ma'am."

"Good." The lady in black pivoted and headed out of the kitchen. The head butler, head housekeeper, and niece followed. Cassandra looked behind her and watched the kitchen crew breathe a collective sigh of relief.

The "white stairway," as it was known to the occupants of the manor with its bright, wainscoted walls and white, painted steps, only went up one level to the first floor. This passageway made for easy access of food deliveries to and from the dining room. Lady Lemington held on to the white, metal handrail as her knee and the stairs creaked. With her other hand, she pulled out a sheet of paper from a hidden pocket. She handed the list over her shoulder to Miss Fairchild. "I have a few things I want completed before the guests arrive."

Behind Lady Lemington, Fartworthy gave an I-told-you-so smirk to Miss Fairchild. The head housekeeper smiled and looked at the list. "Ma'am, beg your pardon, but why are we preparing for overnight visitors? The guest bedrooms on the third floor are unusable since the contractor hasn't finished yet."

"Look at the list, Fairchild. Prepare the bedrooms on the *second* floor. The weather forecast shows a chance of foul weather after the guests arrive. The last thing I need is for someone to die on their way home and to be sued by angry relatives because I didn't accommodate inebriated guests for the night. I have finally recovered from the last lawsuit and don't wish to repeat that financial nightmare."

As the group arrived in the dining room, Flora shook her head. "There aren't enough bedrooms on the second floor to lodge all our guests. Oh, I see you noted to double up servants. Very good, ma'am." She attached the paper to her clipboard.

Lady Lemington huffed. "Make sure you read through all my notes before you comment, Fairchild. This is only a precaution, as I don't want anyone to stay. We know my sister-in-law will. She always finds an excuse."

"For Mrs. Turner, we made up her room on the second floor to her usual specifications." Flora tapped the papers together. "I personally changed the lightbulbs to a higher wattage."

"Anything else, ma'am?" Fartworthy smoothed a wrinkle in the cloth his boss created when she brushed up against the table.

"Yes, Fartworthy, I need to discuss something with you later. Find me before the guests arrive. I need to talk to Miss Haywood alone now." Lady Lemington waved her hand in dismissal. "Fairchild, go upstairs with Fartworthy to assess what needs to be done."

"Yes, ma'am," replied the servants whose hopes for tea before the festivities had just vaporized. They retreated from the room.

"Things are never finished around here. Follow." Lady Lemington glanced around and nodded in satisfaction. "How was your trip, and how's my sister?"

"My trip was fine, and Mum is the same. She still questions why I'm living here and not with her. I use my recycled answer every time."

"That she's stubborn, and you can use your business skills with my profitable company?" Lady Lemington smirked.

"Just the last part. I thought it best to leave the rest unsaid." Cassandra grinned.

"I'm glad you're home. I missed you." She gave her niece an affectionate, motherly hug. Lady Lemington released her and gently held Cassandra at arm's length. "My sister doesn't see who you really are." She smiled. "You and I are like tea bags. We find our strength when we're in hot water. Remember that."

"What?" Cassandra whispered, stunned by the uncharacteristic embrace. Before her aunt could explain, the underbutler, John, came into the room, followed by a tall, young man holding a black guitar case.

"Excuse me, ma'am. I can't find Miss Fairchild. Do you know where she is?" asked John. "The guitar player is here. I found him wandering on the second floor."

The lady of the manor stepped away from Cassandra and inspected the musician from head to toe. "What's your name, and what were you doing upstairs?"

"Your 'ome is big, and I got lost. Owen Savage, ma'am. Guitar player. Miss Fairchild told me to meet 'er in the kitchen. I told 'im," he said, pointing to the underbutler, "but he didn't believe me. Thanks for 'iring me again. I'm needin' this job. Me mum's medications are super expensive and—"

"Kitchens are rarely on the second floor." Lady Lemington's stare drilled into the musician. "Next time, go directly downstairs and don't sneak in a tour. Otherwise, your engagement will be terminated on the spot." She spoke to the servant without taking her eyes off Owen. "Take him downstairs and stay with him. Fairchild will be there soon."

"Very good, ma'am. Come this way." John gestured for Owen to follow, and the pair exited the opposite doorway. From the same entrance, another maid appeared and approached Lady Lemington with a piece of paper.

Before the young lady could reach them, Lady Lemington said, "Cassandra, we'll talk later. Go rest and then get ready for the party." Her niece, still reeling from the hug, didn't utter a word, left the dining room, and headed upstairs.

At the top of the main staircase, Cassandra found the second floor as hectic as the kitchen. Several male servants transported single beds. Up and down the hallway from open doorways, starched, Egyptian cotton sheets snapped. Maids, in black uniform dresses and white half aprons, rushed through carrying stacks of navy-blue, wool blankets. Other maids moved baskets of light-blue towels into each room. Some held the baskets over their heads to get past the bed movers and blanket carriers. The passageway looked like a bustling outdoor market.

Miss Fairchild called from the other end of the hall. "Miss Haywood! Can we assume Miss Dalton will stay with you if needed?"

"Yes!" answered Cassandra over the heads of several servants.

"Thank you." Miss Fairchild wrote something down and spoke to a maid.

Cassandra shouted back. "The guitar player arrived and is in the kitchen looking for you."

Miss Fairchild waved her hand. "Thank you, but he must wait until this situation is under control."

Cassandra made her way to her bedroom and closed the door, muffling the hallway noise. She found sanctuary in the sparsely deco-rated purple room with two twin beds, a dresser, a wall mirror, a built-in closet, and two bedside tables. Arabella Dalton always slept in the spare bed across the room when she came to visit. The ladies enjoyed talking late into the night, like pre-teen girls at a slumber party.

Cassandra's colorful luggage and her large travel purse sat next to her dresser. She unpacked the clothes, stored the suitcase, and tidied the room. She fluffed the lime-green throw pillows on the beds. The soft, matching, cream-colored quilts, with lime-green vines and purple grapes, coordinated everything in the room. She kicked off her black driving flats into the shoe bin in the closet, pulled out a pair of silver heels decorated with rhinestones, and set them on the floor. After a peek in the mirror, she opened the door.

The passageway had quieted. She made a quick, barefoot trip to the bathroom across the hall, washed and dried her face, and returned. Flopping on her bed, she sighed and closed her eyes. *I'll change and put on makeup in a little while. It's going to be a late night.* Her body had almost settled comfortably into the quilt.

The papers.

Cassandra opened her eyes and saw the paperwork on the dresser. She got up, grabbed the stack, and read aloud. "List of suppliers." She flipped through the pile. "From the law office of . . ." Pages ruffled again in her hands. "In violation of . . ." *I don't care about this now.*

She shoved the paper burden into the top drawer.

Chapter Four

Cassandra approached the top of the staircase during the final tolling of nine from the grandfather clock. Live classical piano and guitar music floated through the air. She draped her raspberry scarf around her shoulders and descended halfway to the landing. This was her favorite view, a bird's-eye perspective of the elegant manor. She paused and took a breath in, searching for familiar faces. Down in the great hall, past the glittering Christmas tree, a few guests arrived for the start of the party. When she reached the first floor, underbutler Nathan opened one side of the double doors. Frosty air and Miss Ruby Lightfoot, with her over-size camera bag, rushed into the hall.

"Miss Lightfoot." Cassandra smiled. "It's so good to see you. How are you?"

"Late, Miss Haywood. Hello!" She smiled and removed her coat, handing it to the butler. Ruby brushed the snowflakes off the top of her short, sassy hair. "I don't know what happened to the time."

"The party just started." Cassandra pointed to the closet under the stairs. "You may put your camera bag in there so you can have access to it during the party."

"Brilliant idea." Miss Lightfoot removed her camera from the bag and positioned the strap around her neck. When she tucked away the equipment sack, she took a deep breath and grinned. "Time to get to work."

She held the camera up to her eye with one hand and braced the long lens with the other. Ruby scanned the room. *Click.*

Cassandra, picking up a crystal glass of sparkling cider from the tray of a passing butler, became the first photo of the evening.

The photographer looked at the screen on the back of the camera and revealed the shot to Cassandra. Fairy lights from the Christmas tree created a twinkling, golden background. "Beautiful." She fixed something on the body of the camera. "Flora texted me earlier. Lady Lemington wants me to take natural pictures of everyone. No formal, posh photos, thank goodness. I'd rather catch people casual. It makes for a better story."

"Story?" Cassandra tasted her bubbly drink.

"Photos tell a story. I put the best shots into a soft-cover book for clients. The images are then enjoyed and don't sit in an envelope unseen for years. Events like this are lively and fun. My other job is that of a crime scene photographer." She grinned. "I don't make books for those assignments."

"I suppose not." Cassandra frowned.

"I'd better dash. If Lady Lemington looks at the time stamps on the photos again, she'll know I arrived late. Flora said Lady L. might want to talk before I started. Glad I know my way around the place. Blast! I need to get shots of the food tables before the guests descend. Ta!" The photographer rushed to the dining room.

Cassandra strolled into the parlor. The high ceiling's ornate, white cornices and butter-colored walls supplemented the many traditional portraits of vintage relations. Several Victorian-style sofas and walnut settees were scattered throughout the enormous room. The decadent, upholstered, dark wood furniture made for comfortable seating no matter where one sat. Fabric from the assorted antique pieces complemented one another like elegant garments of a stylish wardrobe. Heirloom mahogany chairs bordered the room, adding an exquisite art gallery frame to the space. Although not the only source of light, tall, golden, burning beeswax candles contributed to the ambiance. Cassandra sighed at the elegance of the party atmosphere.

At the far end of the room, Poppy Fletcher's holiday repertoire filled the air from the black grand piano. The instrument, highly polished and its top raised, was the focal point of the other end of the parlor. Miss Fletcher, in a forest-green concert gown, played loud enough to be heard and enjoyed, but quiet enough for conversations. Owen Savage bent over his guitar case, searching for something.

"Miss Cassandra Haywood!" exclaimed a deep voice behind her. Recognizing the source of the salutation, she straightened her spine and braced for a verbal assault. Cassandra turned, carefully choosing her words. "Greetings, Baron Rupert Von Pickle. I didn't realize you were joining us this evening."

"Lovely to see you, my dear." Von Pickle circled his finger around in Cassandra's direction. "What do you call this look with the muddle of scarves? Homeless chic? It really isn't working for you, sweetheart. It's always a pleasure to receive an invitation and sample how I would never throw a party." The thirty-nine-year-old entrepreneur, with styled, short, wavy, auburn hair and a custom-made, Italian, dark-blue suit, gazed around the room. He sported handcrafted, leather shoes and a stylish watch, each costing more than Cassandra earned in six months.

"If it's too disagreeable, you're welcome to leave." She plastered a smile on her face. "I'm sure Aunt Lily would understand."

"Where's the old bird, anyway? Has she descended from her perch? Is she still dressing in homage to Queen Victoria, the later years?" He smirked at his own cleverness.

Cassandra scanned the room. *Not enough people have arrived.*

No hope of politely disengaging yet. "She has not. She takes great pleasure in entering with a flair."

Von Pickle stroked his expensive lapel. "Still sponging off your aunt? I would think a woman in her late twenties would rather live anywhere than in this fossilized place. Those renovations must cost loads. It's a shame Lemington Cheese hasn't gone international like my company."

Mr. Fartworthy materialized beside Cassandra. Carrying a silver tray filled with mini seafood quiches, he held the platter between the duo. "Hors d'oeuvres?"

"Yes, thank you, Mr. Fartworthy." She removed her choice and a napkin. Grateful for the momentary distraction, Cassandra sampled a bite. "Delicious."

"And you, sir?" Fartworthy directed the serving dish to Von Pickle.

"Get that out of my sight! They're probably ice cold."

"I can assure you, sir, these recently came out of the oven." Fartworthy remained expressionless.

Von Pickle sneered. "Not acceptable for a gala. Too French. Move on. Attempting to have a conversation here."

Fartworthy addressed Cassandra. "Would you care for another, ma'am?"

The rude guest pushed against the silver tray. "No, she wouldn't. Off with you."

Fartworthy held the platter firm, took a step back, and departed.

"Hired help are the worst." He huffed. "I can't find competent servants these days. High turnover rate at my estate. No matter. I can pay starting salary over and over." Von Pickle adjusted his diamond cuff links.

The flaky, buttery crust and creamy, lobster filling danced in Cassandra's mouth and gave her a delicious reason to remain silent. Her chewing slowed.

He puffed out his chest and continued. "Did you hear? My company achieved international status with sales projected in the millions. I can barely keep up with the demand since our selections are enormously popular in so many countries. My cheese is too great to be confined to good old Britannia, like Lemington or Rosewood. Profits are soaring. Official name change to Somerdale *International* Cheese Company."

Cassandra dusted off her fingertips from the mini quiche. "It must have been expensive to alter everything for your business." She took a sip from her glass.

"Very. Updated website, new logo, new packaging for our products, and new signage outside my headquarters. All of it displays our new status. What does it matter when so much money is flowing? You probably don't know what that's like." The braggart laughed, low and deep. "You're stuck at your aunt's company. Is it because you don't possess any marketable skills or because she took pity on you after your failed attempt at business school?"

Cassandra gagged on the liquid. *How did he know?* Only a handful of people on the planet knew the horrible truth of her greatest failure. She coughed and her heart raced.

"Well? Which is it?" Von Pickle's mouth puckered as if he sucked a lemon.

Cassandra swallowed hard and placed her glass and napkin on a dark wood side table. "I need to do something of importance. Pardon me." She strode away. *Not a lie. Self-preservation is imperative.* With her eyes focused on the floor, Cassandra rounded the corner to the dining room and plowed into a woman in a black-and-pink dress. "So sorry! Beg your pardon," she apologized.

It was her best friend, Arabella Dalton. "Cassie! What's the matter?"

"It's you. That . . . um . . . b-b-baron," Cassandra stammered. "Von Pickle. He knows. I can't believe it." Her hands covered her cheeks, continuing her escape.

"Knows what?" Arabella followed.

Cassandra moved through the dining room and dropped her hands from her face. "About business school," she whispered. "How did he find out? He's such a viper. Why does my aunt invite slime to her parties?"

"What?"

"Of all people to be privy to my private information!" Cassandra retreated and paced in the far corner. She took her raspberry scarf off her shoulders and twisted it in her hand. "Did Aunt Lily tell him? Did a servant say something? Unbelievable. Did he hire someone to dig up dirt on my aunt and found information about me? I'm so embarrassed."

"Don't be. Bad form for him to bring it up tonight. Everyone fails at something. I guess no one has secrets anymore with the Internet. What else did he say? Why would he care about your schooling?"

"Bella, we're talking about Von Pickle. He collects data to destroy people like my mother collects Royal Family commemorative teacups. He criticized everything and bragged about his newly international *stupid* cheese company."

"International? When did that happen?" Arabella crossed her arms.

"Recently. I hadn't heard before tonight and don't care." Cassandra placed her scarf on the table. "Maybe his concentration will be overseas and that will leave the domestic market to Lemington Cheese. Or, even better, his business spreads too thin and collapses under its own fantastic weight."

"You mean like his awful cheese spread?"

The close friends chuckled.

"Exactly." Cassandra sighed. "He might be right, though. I don't have the business skills of calculated cruelty. If that's what you need to survive, it's not for me."

"You don't mean that. You have more talent for product design and people skills than Von Pickle will ever enjoy. That's more important. Enough about 'Pickle-head.' We *will* enjoy ourselves tonight!" Arabella gave a sideways hug to Cassandra. "The night is young. One rotten apple—or pickle, in this case—shouldn't spoil the bushel. Keep a stiff upper lip and Bob's your uncle."

"Are you done with the clichés?"

She let go. "I have a few more in my pocket, if you need." Arabella picked up the discarded raspberry accessory and handed it to her friend. "You're fine."

Cassandra ran her hand over the thinly woven scarf. "I have to be, Bella. Von Pickle can't see me distressed."

"No, he can't. It will drive him mad to think it doesn't bother you." Arabella pointed to the fascinator on her own head. "Well? What do you think? Ta-dah!" Attached to the all-black headpiece, black, net veiling shielded one of her eyes. Raven-like feathers mixed with narrow loops of tight, black tulle and matching satin ribbon, tilted from the top of her head toward her left ear. "From my latest collection of designs."

"The new prototype." Cassandra nodded. "Nice. It coordinates perfectly with your outfit. I like the stiff feathers and the shiny texture of the ribbons. The loops of tulle. The style is good, but I would simplify that. Maybe three or five loops instead of seven."

"Thanks, Cass. I love how I can count on your honesty. You always tell me how it is and not a blanket 'it looks great' and move on." Arabella tugged on the veil. "Thoughts on this part?"

"When I wear fascinators, I don't like things blocking my vision, but it looks darling on you."

"Thank you for the feedback. I'll see if it annoys me tonight."

Lady Gwendolyn Bilford, a woman of exceptional means, joined the ladies. "Greetings, Miss Haywood. Miss Dalton, might I have a word with you privately about a business matter? Is this a convenient time?"

"Absolutely." Arabella placed a hand on Cassandra's arm. "Pardon me, luv. We'll talk later." Before Cassandra could respond, Arabella and Lady Bilford moved across the dining room, conversing.

Cassandra watched her friend for a few moments. *That was sudden.* She shrugged and moved over to the sea of delectable provisions. She draped her raspberry scarf around her back and arms again and sampled a bleu cheese. The creamy texture and sharp, tangy taste filled Cassandra's mouth. She closed her eyes and sighed. "Scrumptious. We know cheese." She took another glass of sparkling cider from a passing butler and glanced around at the guests milling about the room. *Oh good. More people have arrived.*

Mimi and Hamish York entered the dining room.

"Do you need to sit down, my darling?" Hamish pointed to a seat near the wall.

Mimi leaned on his muscular arm. "No, I don't. Thank you. Stop fussing, dearest. I'm not a china doll." With a twinkle in her eye, she patted his supporting limb. "Holding on to you is all I need."

Married for two years, Mimi and Hamish still acted like honeymooners. Single people who spent time in their presence aspired to find a partner to share that kind of love. Married couples sometimes harbored a combination of jealousy and sadness for the lack of the Yorks' magic in their own marriage.

The Yorks were co-owners of Rosewood Cheese, another rival company, and Hamish held the title of CEO. The blond, blue-eyed, rugged man frequented his private gym and his beloved rigorous outdoor activities. He often refused invitations for coffee or dinner with infatuated females. Hamish had found his soul mate in Mimi three years ago. When the couple met, they were well matched in physicality and temperament.

Mimi's strong, athletic figure and energy had once equaled that of three women. In the last year, Mrs. York became beleaguered with mysterious health issues and transformed before everyone's eyes. She looked the same in stature, but her ailments left her weak, perpetually pale, and unable to keep up with her husband's outdoor adventures. Despite her health challenges, Mimi retained a positive attitude.

Cassandra made her way to the happy couple, and the three exchanged pleasantries and small talk.

Hamish liked to focus on business. "Miss Haywood, how is Lemington Cheese doing?"

Although Cassandra enjoyed conversing with the Yorks about most topics, she tried to avoid revealing too much about her aunt's company with a competitor. "The lawsuit forced Aunt Lily to restructure and reinvent. It has been a few years of anxiety, but business is better than ever." Cassandra tapped the top of her glass. "I heard Somerdale went international. Any plans for Rosewood to do the same?"

"Not a chance." Hamish rocked back on his heels. "Rosewood prides itself on producing top quality, soft, French-style cheese. We'll stick with artisan products, stay domestic, and make the best cheese in England. No offense." He flashed a handsome smile. "I also heard Von Pickle went international. It would be like him to swallow markets whole. He peddles products that shouldn't be labeled 'cheese' in any country."

Cassandra frowned. "Be advised, his fangs are out and sharp this evening. Avoid him, if possible."

Mimi chuckled. "That makes two to dodge. Since my husband returned home so relaxed from his trip, he wants to steer clear of Lady

Lemington tonight. She stresses him." Mimi patted his arm again and smiled. "Why did we come here tonight, dearest?"

"It's *the* event of the holiday season, darling." Hamish surveyed the room. "Would you like something to drink, my love?"

"Yes, dear. Whatever is available without alcohol," said Mimi.

Cassandra shook a finger. "No worries there. Aunt Lily doesn't serve the champagne until we're closer to midnight. The bubbly drinks are all alcohol-free for now."

"Perfect. I'll have one of those, please." Mimi let go of Hamish and he left the ladies.

"Where did he go on his trip?" Cassandra took another sip from her glass. She watched Hamish converse with Fartworthy across the room. Hamish pulled a small, plastic bag of cheese pieces out of his pocket to show the head butler. *Even for an owner of a cheese company, that's odd.* She turned to Mimi. "Was he gone long?"

"Switzerland, for cheese buying and a series of conferences. A two-month jaunt, including a silent retreat for the first week. I couldn't talk to him or text. It was a little strange, but I managed to keep myself busy. A 'world detox' for him. It worked. He's been so tense lately with the business. I swear he aged before my eyes. He said he'd come back tranquil and a whole new Hamish. His prediction came true. See how lovely he looks?"

The ladies couldn't hear the conversation across the room but could see Fartworthy shake his head several times. Cassandra squinted. *What's he saying to Mr. Fartworthy?* Hamish stuffed the cheese back into his trouser pocket, took two crystal glasses off the head butler's tray, and headed back.

When Hamish returned, Mimi accepted the drink and the stability of his arm. "I told Cassandra about your trip and how wonderfully relaxed and handsome you look." Hamish stood taller. She continued. "The downside of attending the conferences is the non-stop talking about varieties and processing."

"Hazard of owning a cheese company, my darling." Hamish took a sip.

"True, but you must admit it's been excessive over the last month. I don't mind. I think it's endearing." She turned to Cassandra. "We're usually talking about food. He's so adorable the way he obsesses over the latest, bleeding-edge research on the healthiest way to eat. It keeps our personal chef busy."

"Is this the result of your health issues?"

Mimi smiled. "No. Even while we were dating, he was enthusiastic about food. We've done every combination, elimination, exotic meal, and novel ways to prepare the familiar. Right now, Hamish is eating twelve tiny meals a day. We used to eat the same things, but I can't follow that program. The last thing we did together . . . was that the American porridge? Yes, the fermented oatmeal."

Cassandra cringed. "Fermented oatmeal? Never heard of that. How is it different from regular porridge?"

Hamish explained, "Leave the oatmeal soaking in apple cider vinegar on the counter for twenty-four hours. The enzymes break down the part of the oatmeal our bodies cannot digest. Heat for a few minutes, and it's ready to consume when you get back from a morning run. It's a perfect breakfast."

Cassandra grimaced. "That sounds revolting."

"It is," said Mimi, sipping her beverage.

Hamish gestured in a circle with his glass. "It's delicious once you get used to the taste."

"Not really, dearest." Mimi grinned. "The paste I ate in primary school tasted better."

"But this oatmeal is all natural and good for you."

"My love, arsenic is all natural, too, but you won't catch me eating that." Mimi laughed with Cassandra.

"Fair enough." Hamish smiled, drank, and glanced at his reflection in a nearby mirror.

Cassandra ran a finger around the lip of her glass. "How are you feeling, Mrs. York?"

Mimi shrugged. "The migraine pain is tolerable today, and we discovered that the source of my troubles is heart related. I manage my issues with prescriptions, and after trial and error, figured out the correct dose. It isn't a cure, but it's better. Thank you for asking."

"I'm glad to hear that. I hope you enjoy this evening." Cassandra lifted her glass.

"I will, Miss Haywood, as long as I can keep my stress levels down. Too much tension requires more medication, and I'm not myself afterward."

At that moment, Lady Lemington glided into the dining room like a queen attending her coronation celebration. Her purple-feathered headpiece waved like the winner of a beauty pageant. She spotted the Yorks and headed in their direction. Mr. York locked eyes with the lady of the manor. A gasp escaped his lips.

"Helloooo, Mimi! Helloooo, Hamish! So glad you could join us!" she crooned. The enthusiastic greeting startled the other guests, and the room grew silent. With an air kiss near each of Mimi's cheeks, Lady Lemington continued. "So lovely to have you here tonight. How are you, my dear? You're looking pale again."

Cassandra cringed.

Miss Lightfoot slipped out of the shadows of the dining room and snapped photos.

"I am as expected." Mimi's pallid face flushed. "The manor is breathtaking tonight."

"Thank you. I'm looking forward to a new year and a fresh start." Lady Lemington turned to Hamish. "Speaking of *new* things, you look wonderful. You cannot even *see* the scars. They did a brilliant job!" She looked at both sides of Hamish's face.

He chuckled and stammered, "Nice t-t-to see you, t-t-too, Lady Lemington. I'm starved. Eating twelve tiny meals a day, and, oh look! Time to eat again." He peeked at his Swiss watch. As his wife continued to lean on him, Hamish attempted to shift them toward the food.

Mimi didn't move. "What are you talking about? What scars?"

"Knife wounds around his ears and temple, Mrs. York." Lady Lemington pointed to Hamish's face.

"It's nothing. Let's get our food, darling." Hamish turned to the table.

"The face lift scars." Lady Lemington smirked.

"My husband didn't have a face lift."

"He was in Switzerland for two months for the surgical procedure and recovery." Lady Lemington smiled. "This is a surprise, Mrs. York?"

Mimi retorted, "He was in Switzerland for a cheese-buying trip, conferences, and to meet CEOs of other cheese companies."

Hamish shifted in his spot.

"Oh no, my dear! Not true. I'm scheduled to go to Switzerland *next* month for those conferences. He had an operation. Ask him."

"Aunt Lily, stop. Please," Cassandra pleaded.

"Hush, now." Lady Lemington waved her hand. "How would I know he didn't tell this news to his wife? Highly irregular."

Mimi's eyes searched her husband's face. "Tell me what she said is utterly untrue."

Mr. York remained silent, an unusual circumstance for the confident and talkative CEO.

"Hamish?" Mimi's voice cracked. "Clear this up."

He took in a deep breath. "She's correct, my darling. I went to Switzerland for a face lift and recovery." Hamish looked at the floor like a young schoolboy caught in a lie. "I wanted to look better for you," he whispered.

In a nanosecond, the honeymoon ended.

Mimi released his arm as if it were a scorching surface and moved away. "You lied to me. You know how deceit has wounded me before, and you still chose to do this. Why?" The pitch of her voice rose, and her face grew scarlet.

Hamish's eyes grew wide with alarm. "Darling, don't excite yourself. Remember your heart."

"I can't look at you." Mimi took a step back. "I need fresh air." She walked out of the dining room.

Hamish turned to Lady Lemington and pointed. "You're a nasty piece of work! You aren't happy unless everyone around you is miserable," he growled, and followed his wife at a near run.

"I'm not the one who kept such a secret." Lady Lemington clasped her hands together.

Cassandra huffed. "Were you aware that Mrs. York didn't know?"

"That's why I told her. She needed that information."

"Mrs. York has a newly diagnosed heart condition." Cassandra whispered, "It wasn't your place to reveal Mr. York's secret. Why would you divulge it tonight? At a party? How could you be so cold?"

"I have my reasons. Do *not* glare, my dear. Too juvenile."

Chapter Five

Cassandra strode out of the dining room through the main hall and into the parlor again. *Why does Aunt Lily act this way?* She peered into the massive room. *I don't wish to be around her, and I don't want another verbal thrashing from Von Pickle. Where is he?* She spotted the egotistical man leaning on the piano across the room, circling his arm in a sweeping gesture. *No doubt he's telling Miss Fletcher how to play or how much money he spent on his piano.*

Relieved the braggart was on the other side of the room, Cassandra wandered over to her favorite sofa. The butter-yellow upholstery, covered in neatly embroidered vines, was soft and comforting. Her right hand settled on the curved, walnut armrest, a familiar anchor. Cassandra sighed. *I've had enough of uncomfortable conversations.* Her sparkling silver heels, though darling, were murder on her feet. She peered down. *These were a mistake.* When she looked up, a visitor approached.

"Miss Haywood, happy to see you."

"Mr. Spooner. Good evening."

Alexander Spooner, a young, local pharmacist with short, dirty-blond hair and dark-chocolate eyes, moved to the sofa. "Please call me Alexander. My dad was Mr. Spooner, and he's long gone."

"Welcome, Alexander. I'm sorry to hear about your father. Was he a pharmacist, too?"

"No." He smiled, and his eyes danced. "He was a farmer, but that didn't work out. Dad was a lovely person but was complete rubbish at running a business." Alexander gestured around the room with his crystal, flute glass. "This place looks amazing. So elegant." He looked at her. "I feel like I'm towering over you. May I sit?"

"Please do." Cassandra repositioned herself on the sofa to face the young man, who sat at the opposite end. Is this your first party visit?"

"Yes. I usually arrived in the evening, but it never looked like this. This is smashing. I'm sorry I missed the summer garden party. I'm shocked I received an invitation this time. How's your aunt? It's been many months since she needed anything from the store."

"She's recovered and hasn't complained. Hard to believe it has been eight months since she threw out her back. She invites everyone she does business with to her parties. I'm pleased you're here."

"This is so sophisticated. I feel out of my element tonight." Alexander brushed the sleeve of his dark-gray, thin-pinstripe suit jacket. He wore a deep-royal-blue shirt and a black suit vest. He tugged on the knot of his blue-and-black tie.

Cassandra flattened the raspberry scarf around her shoulders. "You look nice this evening. Have you seen anyone else you know?"

"Thank you for the compliment. I said 'hello' to Lady Lemington in the main hall." He released his tie. "I know the guitar player. Mr. and Mrs. York, I saw them when I arrived." He looked around. "I've spent plenty of time with Mr. Fartworthy and Miss Fairchild. Are they around? Does that count?"

Cassandra chuckled. "That does. You will see Mr. Fartworthy, but he'll be working. Miss Fairchild usually remains downstairs in the kitchen during parties. Do you know Mr. Chamberlain?"

"The jeweler?"

"Yes."

"By sight, mostly. His shop isn't too far from us."

"He was invited and should be here. At least you'll have people to converse with."

Alexander looked at his feet. "Good . . . good. Um . . . Cassandra, do . . . do you have a date for this evening?" He exhaled as if extinguishing candles on a birthday cake.

"No, I don't." She smiled. *Oh no.*

"Would you be interested in spending time with me for New Year's? Like a date-ish thing?"

She fidgeted with the edge of the raspberry scarf she wore as a shawl. "Thank you for the offer, Alexander. You're a charming fellow." Cassandra held her breath for a moment. "I'm not looking for exclusive companionship tonight. I enjoy your company but think of you more like a cousin. So sorry to disappoint."

Alexander remained silent, swirling the drink in his hands.

"Well, then," she said, staring at her crossed ankles.

"My apologies. I dislike being alone." Alexander swirled the glass again, gazing into the liquid. "It's tough out there, and it's New Year's Eve. Loneliness makes it worse."

Cassandra's guilt rose.

"So many pretty ladies here tonight. I already asked the piano player, and she's busy working. The photographer isn't interested because apparently she's involved with some chap."

Cassandra scrunched her nose. "She's old enough to be your aunt."

"I know. I thought, maybe. Do you know of anybody who's unattached?" He took a gulp of his drink.

Guilt gone. How to help him? Ah. "Miss Arabella Dalton is single."

Alexander perked up. "Who's she?"

She pointed. "Wearing the dress with the black top, pink

bottom. Across the room, near the piano. See her?"

"Yes, great! Thanks for the tip. Well, I'll see you around. Happy New Year."

"Same to you." She waved. *Bella's going to kill me.*

Noise coming from the windows to Cassandra's right caught her attention. The rapid fire of ice pellets hitting the eight-foot tall windowpanes sounded like a drum mustering soldiers.

From her comfortable seat, Cassandra turned and spied Robin Turner, wearing a festive, solid-red, silk dress with a green, gossamer scarf draped around her neck.

Mrs. Turner did show up. I was hoping she would miss tonight. Aunt Lily can't stand her. Roland is agreeable and amusing away from the controlling mouth and eagle eyes of his mother.

Robin's adult son, Roland, handed her a small plate of food. As Lady Lemington's right-hand man at the company, Roland spent plenty of time with Cassandra at the manor discussing business affairs with their mutual aunt. The non-cousins had a few laughs together in the past. Cassandra pitied the gentleman. His mother left tension in her wake, and her son frequently got swept up in the current.

Now, Roland, tall and slender in his well-fitting, charcoal-gray suit, followed his mother around as her demur shadow.

Should I say hello? Robin's face twisted, she pointed, and her natural curls bobbed. A few speckles of gray peeked out from her short, black, curly hair. Cassandra grimaced. *She looks annoyed. I'll stay here and avoid eye contact.*

From Cassandra's end of the parlor, Lady Lemington drifted in, conversing with Lady Gwendolyn Bilford. Lady Bilford dripped of old money. Her dark hair piled high on her head was topped with a tiny tiara. She wore a black-and-red, beaded dress, and two wide, diamond bracelets jingled on her wrist. In a past century, one would have expected her to have a set of spectacles on a stick.

Lady Lemington ran her fingertips on the diamond, flower brooch fastening her shawl. "And after my Richard died unexpectedly, I took over the reins of the family company. We went through a rough patch. Fortunately, the difficult time is over."

"And your business is in the black?" The rich woman waved her hand around.

"Fully recovered and flourishing. It's miraculous how well it has turned around." Lady Lemington raised her glass.

"Your family helped with the upturn?" asked Lady Bilford.

The lady in black pointed to Cassandra, sitting on the sofa. "My niece and my nephew, Roland, are working for me. Yes, they assisted." Cassandra smiled at the women.

Lady Bilford tipped her head to Cassandra. "Rumor has it that Roland will be CEO one day."

Lady Lemington laughed. "He'll never hold that position. Lovely nephew, hard worker, but he's not leadership material."

At the mention of Roland's name, the Turners focused their attention on the conversation. Roland stormed over to his aunt, his bright-blue eyes flashing. "I've been working for you for years. You own my sweat and blood. I've given you all my time. I have no life, and as a result, I thought I would eventually be in charge!"

"No dear, you won't be CEO of my company as long as I'm alive." Lady Lemington pulled the velvet shawl closer around her shoulders.

The young man clenched his teeth. "When did you decide this?"

"Quite some time ago." The lady of the manor crossed her arms and held her glass near her face.

The walls of the parlor resonated with a slamming of a plate on a nearby side table. A livid Robin Turner charged at Lady Lemington. "You evil woman! My brother should have never married you. I knew it was a mistake from the beginning. He's turning over in his grave with what you've done to my father's company."

"You mean saved it, no thanks to you." Lady Lemington sneered.

"Roland is the rightful heir."

"It's a business, not a monarchy, dearest sister-in-law."

Cassandra bolted to the battling ladies, rushing past Ruby Lightfoot. "Mrs. Turner, perhaps we can table this discussion for another time?" Roland mouthed a "thank you" to Cassandra when she arrived to help tame the lionesses.

"No, I shall not be silent on this topic."

"Mother, I'm sorry I said anything. Please, please contain yourself," Roland pleaded. "You're making a scene."

"Contain myself?" Robin growled. "Don't reprimand your mother. I don't care what others think. She has mistreated you long enough."

"Please, Mrs. Turner. Would you like to talk about this in private?" asked Cassandra.

Robin whirled to face the young woman. "You have no say in this conversation. Keep your nose out of *our* family company. I trust you haven't poisoned your aunt's mind with thoughts of becoming CEO?"

Before Cassandra could assure the distraught woman she had no desire to be head of the company, Lady Lemington spoke. "Get used to the idea, Robin. In a few years, after I'm ready to retire or if I should die, Cassandra will be in charge."

"What?" Cassandra, Robin, and Roland spoke in unison.

Robin snarled, "This . . . this . . . child? This flaky girl who always loses her things is going to run my father's company?"

"First, she's twenty-nine, only two years younger than your precious son. Second, she's a woman, not a girl. And third, it's my company, not your father's. It hasn't been since Richard assumed control. And why did your younger brother take over? Oh yes, they kicked you out for impropriety."

Cassandra and Roland watched, slack-jawed, as the two older women verbally clawed at each other.

Robin crossed her arms. "I'll do whatever it takes to stop your arrangement."

"Go ahead and try." Lady Lemington smirked. "You attempted to beat me in court before and lost. Badly."

"Roland has earned the right to lead, and you're thwarting his way. As his mother, I know what's best."

"I understand." She moved closer to Robin. They stood less than a foot apart. The sparring ladies locked eyes, and Lady Lemington placed a hand on her hip. With the other, she pointed her crystal glass at Robin. "You want Roland as CEO because you know he's an ineffective leader, and you would be the one pulling the puppet strings, ultimately controlling the company. Nice master plan, but it's *never* going to happen."

Robin's face twisted in disgust. She grabbed her son's arm and together they stormed off. A victorious smile radiated across Lady Lemington's face, and she sauntered in the opposite direction, heading out of the parlor.

The aftermath left Cassandra in shock and staring at Lady Bilford and the photographer. "Miss Lightfoot, you should avoid taking photos when there is a disagreement."

"I have specific orders from her." Ruby pointed after the woman. "Follow and take shots no matter what. If people are arguing with Lady L. I need to be there."

Cassandra stared in disbelief at her aunt, who paused at the doorway to talk to someone. "That's bizarre. She's planning these confrontations?"

"I know, right? A bit of a wonky assignment." Ruby wiped a cloth on the front of her lens. "I need the paycheck, so whatever she wants." She pocketed the cloth. "Got to go. She's on the move again." She followed Lady Lemington through the parlor to the doorway.

"I'm so sorry, Lady Bilford," said Cassandra. "Please forgive my aunt's—and everyone's—behavior."

Lady Bilford caressed her diamond bracelets. "Amusing when it isn't your own family."

Cassandra fake-smiled. "My deepest apologies. Pardon me." She walked through the parlor to pursue her aunt. Cassandra's uncomfortable silver shoes dug grooves into the sides of her feet and prevented any hurried steps. She acknowledged people as she passed by. With several more nods and pleasantries to others, she caught up with the woman. "Please wait a moment, Aunt Lily."

"Yes? I have people to see." Lady Lemington looked over her shoulder.

"What's going on?" The ladies stopped in the great hall under the golden glow of the Christmas tree. Cassandra touched her aunt's arm. "Are you upsetting the guests on purpose? First, you go after Mr. and Mrs. York, and then you target the Turners? This is supposed to be a pleasant evening." She twisted the ends of the ivory scarf that held back her hair.

"Stirring the pot, my dear. Sometimes one must go on the offensive." Lady Lemington fluffed the purple feathers in her headpiece. "If you always play defense, you'll never get ahead."

"You're not making sense. This isn't conduct suitable for a lady in your position. Please reconsider a truce for the rest of the night."

"I know what I'm doing." She waved off Ruby Lightfoot. The photographer spun and left.

Cassandra leaned closer to her aunt. "Making me CEO? I don't have the capacity to do the job properly. Roland can have the position. He wants it."

Her aunt smiled. "No, he doesn't, my dear. Roland needs to grow a backbone first. He doesn't have the instincts needed to run my company. You have the innovation, the skills, and the intuition. Don't argue with me. I'm an excellent judge of character."

Cassandra whispered, "Did you tell Von Pickle about my issues with business school?"

"No." She stood taller. "Why would I reveal anything to that scaly creature?"

"He told me tonight that he knows. He'll tell everyone, and you don't need that kind of company scandal."

Lady Lemington's jaw clenched. "Don't worry about the baron. His life will never be the same after tonight."

"How?"

"Just trust me."

For the first time, Cassandra savored the promise of her aunt's improper behavior.

Chapter Six

Sleet and ice continued to pelt the windows, and the wind howled through the poorly insulated window frames. Cassandra looked at the glass panes that shimmered with a fresh, frozen layer. "Have all the guests arrived?"

"I believe so. It sounds like the forecast was wrong." Lady Lemington placed her empty crystal glass on a passing butler's tray. "Have you seen Mr. Birch? Did he return?"

"I don't know. I wanted to talk to him."

Her aunt fluffed her hair, and the purple fascinator shifted. "What about?"

"An idea I have for something outside." Cassandra breathed in deeply.

"I need to speak with him, too."

"If he's on the staff, why would you invite him to the party?"

"I've been wondering that myself." Lady Lemington looked up the grand staircase and then at Cassandra. "Come to think of it, he asked to be here."

Before Cassandra could ask anything more, Frederick Chamberlain, the local jeweler, appeared in the dining room doorway. The handsome man wore a crisp, black suit and a white shirt paired with a red-and-black, diamond-patterned tie. He caught Cassandra's attention, and his green eyes shone. "Lady Lemington and Miss Haywood! Happy New Year. I'm so glad I found you. Thank you for inviting me." He extended his hand to both ladies.

"Mr. Chamberlain, I'm pleased you're here." Cassandra smiled, returning the handshake.

The young man glanced at the enormous Christmas tree. He looked at Cassandra. "Everything is gorgeous." He cleared his throat. "The selection of cheeses you have on the buffet is impressive. All Lemington products?"

Cassandra tucked the knot of her ivory scarf on her head behind her ear. "Yes, they are."

"Did you like the earrings your aunt picked out for you for Christmas?" The jeweler ran his hand through his lustrous, ebony hair.

The gold, Victorian-style, drop earrings with the pearl centers were Cassandra's favorite Christmas present. She laughed. "They're perfect." Her hand found the earring and caressed it with her fingertips. "I deduce she purchased them from your lovely store."

"Yes, she did. I have to say, they look dazzling on you. Much better than in our display case."

Cassandra's cheeks warmed at the compliment. "Thank you, sir. You're too kind."

He turned to the older woman. "And how's the new watch working for you, ma'am?"

Lady Lemington held out her wrist to admire her new accessory. "Excellent, Mr. Chamberlain. Thank you for your assistance with both selections."

Cassandra stared at her aunt's new, silver wristwatch with diamonds encircling the black face. "That's stunning. I didn't notice that before."

"Part of the new line we carried this fall." Frederick pointed to the timepiece. "All hand-crafted, exquisite, but extremely delicate. Be careful not to drop the watch. If you do, though, I can repair it."

"Good to know," said Lady Lemington.

Jack Birch, the head gardener, approached. He wore a tweed suit that coordinated in hue to his brown-and-gray hair and matching, trimmed goatee and mustache. He held two full crystal flute glasses. His dark eyebrows pressed downward.

Cassandra smiled at the late-middle-aged gentleman. "Good evening, Mr. Birch. Nice to see you. The flower arrangements you crafted are exquisite. On the way here, I had an idea about the trees in the driveway."

"Not now. Not tonight," snapped the gardener.

The cantankerous answer surprised Cassandra. *He usually reserves some pleasantries for me. He's extra irritable.*

"Lady Lemington, you look . . . well . . . put together." Mr. Birch handed her a glass of sparkling cider. "Thank you for inviting me to the party. Your headpiece is . . . purple and . . . full of feathers." He downed a gulp from his glass.

Or distracted. Is he trying to woo my aunt? No. Can't be.

"Thank you." Lady Lemington narrowed her eyes. "I looked for you before the party. They said you went somewhere. When did you get back?"

"A while ago. I had some errands to do in town." The man in brown took another sip. "There's a matter of utmost importance I wish to discuss with you tonight. Alone. It must be alone."

"I need to have a conversation with you, too." Lady Lemington smiled. "Shall we go to the veranda?"

Mr. Birch shook his head. "I wouldn't recommend going outside. There's a thick coating of ice on the paths and lawns all around the manor. The roads are quite treacherous."

Lady Lemington rolled her eyes. "The forecast said light snow tonight. With the road coated, the drive down our hill could be dangerous. Will the ice fall all night?"

The gardener ignored her question. "How about the sunroom? With no heat in there, it should be free from guests, but nothing to slip on. Shall we?" He offered his arm in a gentlemanlike manner.

Lady Lemington took a step toward Mr. Birch when Fartworthy appeared and interrupted.

The head butler leaned in close to the lady of the manor. "Pardon me, ma'am. There's something that needs your immediate attention."

"About the weather?" Lady Lemington gestured to the ice-covered, tall windows over the main doors.

"No, ma'am. A situation *in* the manor."

"In regard to what or whom?" she asked.

"Mr. Savage." Fartworthy then whispered to Lady Lemington. Her face grew stern. Cassandra couldn't hear the details.

"Fartworthy, are you sure?" asked Lady Lemington.

"Quite certain, ma'am."

She turned to the gardener. "I regret our conversation must be postponed, Mr. Birch." She pointed at the head butler. "Fartworthy, check road conditions and the weather. Mr. Birch informs me the ice buildup is hazardous. Find out how serious it is."

Birch glared at Fartworthy.

Cassandra's eyes shifted from one man to the other. *The dislike is mutual. How did I never notice this before?*

"Yes, ma'am. Would you like me to deal with Savage?" Fartworthy offered.

"No, I'll rectify the matter. Check the weather." She turned to the others. "Please excuse me."

Cassandra, Mr. Chamberlain, and Mr. Birch watched as she walked into the parlor. The gardener left for the dining room without a word.

"I want to know what's going on," whispered Cassandra.

Frederick smiled wide. "I second that. Let's follow your aunt."

The musicians played a lively rendition of "God Rest Ye Merry Gentlemen" as Lady Lemington strode across the large room. The lady in black waited until the song finished and the musicians received due applause. The delay allowed Cassandra and Frederick to sidestep other guests, catch up, and come close to hear the conversation.

"Mr. Savage, a word," demanded Lady Lemington.

Smiling from the accolades, the guitar player looked up and noticed who addressed him. His face fell in seconds. "Yes, ma'am?"

Lady Lemington pointed. "Open your case."

Owen shifted in his spot as his guitar swayed. "Why would I be needin' to?"

"You know the reason. Do it." Her purple-feathered headpiece waved.

"I need this job, ma'am. Me mum is in poor 'ealth, and I'm 'er support. Mum's medications are what's killin' us. Please understand," Owen pleaded.

"Open it." She repeated her demand without emotion.

Owen bent down, unlocked the latches, slowly raised the lid, stood, and hung his head. Cassandra peered into the long, black case. Inside contained several items, including a small, stuffed, white paper bag with the local pharmacy logo, a butter knife, a candlestick, a length of rope, a wrench, and a package of Hello Kitty erasers.

Lady Lemington called over her shoulder. "Fartworthy!"

"He's in trouble," Frederick whispered to Cassandra.

"I agree," Cassandra murmured in reply.

Lady Lemington turned to Poppy Fletcher. "Play something."

Miss Fletcher took a deep breath and a moment. The forlorn notes of Chopin's "Raindrop Prelude" began and dripped from her fingertips. The non-holiday piece reflected the change of mood in the room.

"Mr. Savage, your employment is hereby terminated. Do not apply for another opportunity to perform here ever again. I cannot tolerate thievery."

"I'm so sorry, ma'am but it ain't my fault. I got an issue. I pinch stuff. They tellin' me I got kleptomania. I can't 'elp meself. They say stress makes it worse."

Lady Lemington picked up the candlestick. "This is from the upstairs hall. You were found on the second floor. You were sneaking around to steal from me?"

"No, ma'am. I luv to explore 'em fancy places. Yours is the fanciest from all them 'ouses I been workin'. I never meant no 'arm."

She picked up the erasers. "I don't own these."

"No, I nicked them at the store when I picked up Mum's pills earlier. She can't walk too good anymore. The medication in the bag is paid for. I do the liftin' thing all the time, everywhere. It's an awful cross. Please forgive me," Mr. Savage's twenty-year-old, freckled face begged.

I hope Aunt Lily goes easy on him. Cassandra held her breath. *I don't think she will.*

Lady Lemington fluffed her headpiece. "You need to find yourself another line of work or another area. Rest assured none of my acquaintances will ever hire you again because I'll let them know you're a thief. Fartworthy!"

He appeared. "Right here, ma'am."

"Escort Mr. Savage downstairs to the kitchen. Call the constable and find another butler to stay with him at all times until they come."

Owen cried, "Police? I never meant no one no 'arm!"

"I'll decide later whether or not to press charges. If I do, they'll arrest you. I want them to make sure you don't leave the premises with any of my property."

Fartworthy removed the rest of the contraband from the case. Owen packed up his guitar, his eyes brimming with tears.

Mr. Birch stepped up next to Cassandra. "Hey! He was outside before. That's my good wrench and rope from the hothouse. Stupid kid." He grabbed his items from Fartworthy and stormed off. The head butler led the dejected musician out of the parlor.

While everyone stared after the departing kleptomaniac, someone slid into place beside Lady Lemington. A deep voice hissed in her ear, loud enough for Cassandra to take notice.

"Did dear, departed Richard realize the horrific blunder he made by putting you in charge of his supposedly glorious manor and his precious company? You're a dreadful judge of character. Is it because you're a woman, or do you lack vision due to your blinding middle age?"

"Baron, lovely to see you. Hearing you is a different story." She turned to face him. "Handsome to behold, a toxin to heed."

Cassandra turned and stiffened at the sight of the braggart. *Not again.*

"Lady Lemington." Von Pickle gallantly picked up and kissed the back of her hand. "Charming, as always."

"Likewise, I'm sure." Lady Lemington smiled and took a sip of her beverage.

He pointed to her glass. "Are you sure you want to drink anything? I thought liquid would melt you. You're certainly dressed for the part. Speaking of which, how is the head flying monkey? I see Fartworthy is still cleaning up after your disasters." The baron adjusted his diamond cuff links.

"Efficient and steadfast as ever. That means an employee who does the job well and stays around for more than six months." Lady Lemington laughed. "I recognize you need an explanation, since your employees frequently leave you in droves. Your reputation as an abysmal employer precedes you, sir."

Cassandra stifled a laugh.

Von Pickle sneered. "I, at least, discharge people one at a time or they leave on their own. Firing your entire household staff at once is your definition of loyalty? You managed to cause the regional unemployment rate to skyrocket. Sounds like the pot calling the kettle black. How appropriate."

Lady Lemington grinned. "Baron, you dress in a lovely, handcrafted suit and an expensive pair of shoes. Yet, when you open your mouth, one is instantly reminded of your lower-class heritage and intelligence. Sounds like trying to make a silk purse out of a sow's ear."

He paused a moment to take a sip from his glass. Von Pickle reloaded and retaliated. "Speaking of sows, are you and your sister-in-law squealing at each other again in court? Quite a bit of mudslinging the last time. Did she leave you to rule the pigpen, I mean, the company, all by yourself?"

"Mrs. Turner and I came to a suitable agreement and have no plans to repeat our days in court. Thank you for asking. By the way, I heard your company went international. Congratulations. That's impressive. You needed to go abroad. The people of England know better than to consume your subpar cheese. Who are you peddling your chemical-laden products to? They must not have access to food."

Von Pickle responded without a smile this time. "A number of countries. Our profits are soaring, unlike your measly company." Regaining his verbal footing, he struck back. "Tell me, you're not seriously thinking of making that shadow man Turner your successor?"

"No, Cassandra will take the helm when the time comes."

The baron guffawed. "That's even better! Fantastic. When you're dead and gone, the company will collapse under her. I'll scrape up the remainder of the rubble and win. Kudos on your choice."

Cassandra winced. *Don't react. Stay out of the fray. Aunt Lily is handling him with the skills of a snake charmer.*

The piano music stopped.

No longer smiling, Lady Lemington paused and ran a finger along the rim of her glass. "Actually, I would love to speak to you alone." She blinked at him with a tilted head.

"Absolutely, my dear. Shall we take a turn around the parlor?" he asked.

"Let us go over to the far corner."

"I'm intrigued. You aren't going to tempt me with a poison apple?" He put a finger on his lips.

"Not at all," Lady Lemington said through a wide smile.

Von Pickle offered his arm and Lady Lemington accepted. The pair strolled through the parlor.

Cassandra's mouth dropped. "What is she up to?"

Frederick looked at Cassandra. "Most extraordinary."

Arabella Dalton appeared at Cassandra's elbow and playfully slapped her friend's arm.

"Ow! What was that for?" Cassandra rubbed the spot.

"For sending that boy over to ask me out. I'm not that desperate." Arabella grinned and adjusted her black-feathered headpiece.

Cassandra smiled. "You turned Mr. Spooner down, too? Poor gentleman. You mentioned you needed a partner for New Year's Eve."

"I like a date who can grow decent whiskers." Arabella's eyes followed where Cassandra and Frederick focused. "What is going on over there? I thought she hated the odious man."

"I'm as shocked as you are. The two of them traded insults like a tennis match with grenades," said Cassandra.

Frederick blew out a breath. "I have never seen anything like it. Gruesomely entertaining."

"What is she telling him?" asked Arabella.

Cassandra shrugged. "No idea."

The trio observed the sparring partners across the room. Lady

Lemington talked adamantly and smiled. The baron showed no reaction as the couple stopped near the edge of the room. She leaned in and whispered into his ear. His face flushed.

He slammed his fist on a nearby side table and shouted, "You can't do that!"

"Watch me!" A mischievous grin spread across Lady Lemington's countenance.

The reptilian man stormed out of the parlor.

Cassandra crossed the room at a quick pace with Frederick and Arabella close behind. "Aunt Lily! What did you say?"

Her aunt smirked. "I told you I would take care of things. Remember that paperwork in your room?"

Before she could explain further, Fartworthy returned to Lady Lemington's side.

"Excuse me, ma'am. The police cannot come to get Savage tonight. The roads up the hill are much too hazardous. They advise all your guests should spend the night."

Cassandra looked at her friends. "Oh my."

Chapter Seven

Cassandra volunteered to inform Flora Fairchild and Rose Forest about the change in plans. The visitors would find out from Lady Lemington.

"Miss Fairchild, I have some news," Cassandra called into the kitchen as she descended to the ground floor.

"If it's about the fireworks at the party, I've already heard. It sounds more interesting than minding the kitchen," replied Flora.

Cassandra entered the archway. The flurry of activity that ruled a few hours ago had died down. Two staff members arranged the cuisine from the warming trays onto silver platters. Butlers ferried the food upstairs. Others scrubbed counters and equipment in the last stages of cleanup. The smell of pungent pine cleaner hung in the air and mixed with the lingering aroma of grilled beef, a hint of garlic, and baked pastry dough. Despite people milling about completing their assignments, peace dominated the atmosphere.

Owen sat on a chair against the far wall, tapping his feet and twirling his keys. Butler John stood near the musician with his eyes glued to his mobile phone screen.

Poppy Fletcher and Ruby Lightfoot chatted with Miss Fairchild and Mrs. Forest. The four ladies drank tea while sitting on stools around a high, stainless-steel island. They greeted Cassandra.

Poppy sipped her beverage. "I had to get away. I couldn't concentrate on my music after Owen got fired."

"Made for some interesting photos," said Ruby as she raised her teacup.

"I imagine. If I didn't need the job, I wouldn't work here anymore." Poppy stretched out her fingers. "No offense to you lovely ladies. I enjoy visiting. The galas used to be so much fun. Last summer's garden party became unbearable. This event looks like it's going in the same direction."

"True," said the photographer. "I took my break after Lady Lemington sacked Owen."

Flora pointed to the stove. "Fancy a cuppa, Miss Haywood? The kettle's hot since I made tea for us and your aunt."

"Yes, that would be lovely." Cassandra spotted a full cup on the counter. "I'll have that one, if you don't mind."

"That's your aunt's nightly brew. I'll make you a fresh cup." Flora headed to the tea kettle.

"Thank you. Come to think of it, I've barely eaten tonight," replied Cassandra.

Mrs. Forest stood and moved to the warming trays. "Let me get you some food."

"You're both sweet, but you won't have time. The police can not come to get Mr. Savage due to icy weather. They advise guests should stay the night."

Owen perked up and stood. "No police? Maybe me luck 'as gone and changed. Maybe Lady L. will let me go."

Flora pointed at the young man. "You're short a shingle. There's little chance for that. Sit." Flora turned to Cassandra. "Everyone? You must be joking."

"I wish I were." Cassandra shrugged.

"Oh, no," replied Poppy.

"We have to stay, too?" asked Ruby.

"I'm afraid so," said Cassandra to the stunned gaggle of women.

Rose took her teacup to the sink. "Bang goes that break. The breakfast self-serve station in the dining room is already planned, but we'll need more food." She pulled out a pen and small notepad from her apron pocket and scribbled. "Luncheon. If the roads are still bad, people will be here late. Platters of meat. Relish trays." Mrs. Forest snapped her fingers. "We need homemade bread with that."

"Absolutely, Rose." Flora tucked a loose hair into her bun and smoothed the sides. "This certainly changes things." She downed the rest of her tea like a whiskey shot and walked across the kitchen to retrieve her clipboard hanging on the wall. She flipped through its stack of papers. "Not having the guest quarters available on the third floor will make things cramped. I have a list of everyone who was invited."

"Not everyone came, did they?" asked Ruby.

Flora secured the pile, and the metal clip on the board snapped. "I'll confirm with Mr. Fartworthy when he returns. He knows everyone, and his memory is impeccable."

Miss Fletcher turned to the clock and gulped her remaining tea. "I need to be back upstairs. They should have music." She stared at the head cook, who took out some flour from the pantry. "You're going to start baking? Isn't it late for that?"

Rose pulled out other ingredients. "I'll make the mixing mess now and clean up. The dough will rise overnight in the fridge, and all we have to do is bake it in the morning." She signaled to two kitchen staff members who hustled over. "We need lots of dough." She pointed. "You do the rye, you do the regular rolls, and I'll get the rest."

"Yes, chef," the duo replied in unison.

"Don't worry, Miss Haywood. We'll have plenty to feed the hoard." Rose strode across the large room. "I'll make more of those new scones for breakfast." She tugged open the silver double doors of one of the many refrigerators and filled her arms with supplies.

Miss Fairchild pulled out a room map and spread it out on the counter. "Wait, Poppy." The ladies in the cluster moved closer to stare at the paper. Flora pointed. "Mr. Fartworthy, Mr. Birch, and I are the only staff members with separate rooms in this hallway with Lady Lemington's bedroom. The rest of the staff are around the corner and down this hall. Poppy and Ruby, you should sleep in my room. It will be easier that way."

"That makes sense," said the piano player.

Ruby tapped the counter. "Whatever you need." She gestured to the clipboard with the list. "You need to fit that, here? You got four hallways of bedrooms. How do you plan to do that?"

The four women gazed at the map. Mrs. Forest and her kitchen noises across the room punctuated the silence.

Cassandra looked up. "Anyone walking in would think we were trying to retake Sword Beach." They laughed.

"Military strategy is what's required—and maybe a crowbar to cram everyone in. Miss Dalton will stay with you, Miss Haywood, as we discussed." Flora ran her hand across the map to smooth it. "Older guests should have single rooms. Mrs. Turner's room is made up since she always stays." She pointed. "All the staff and younger people can double up. This large room can be for the Yorks, although it's near the master bedroom and Lady Lemington." Flora wrote on the room map in pencil.

Poppy massaged her fingers. "I must return upstairs. Please don't put Mr. Spooner near us. He asked me out, and I turned him down."

"He asked me, too." Ruby smiled.

Cassandra grinned. "Same here and Bella said no. Poor man. Did we all reject him?"

"There's an unattractive quality to desperation." Ruby finished the dregs of her tea.

"You ladies *all* broke his heart? Send him down to me. He liked to hang out in here when he used to visit." Flora made more notes on the map.

"We didn't break his heart." Poppy winced. "He's nice, but not for any of us. I need to dash. Ta! Thanks for the tea, Flora. Bye, Rose." She headed to the white stairway.

Flora gave a quick wave. "You're welcome. I'll put Mr. Spooner all the way down the hall. We'll chat later."

"I should go, too." Ruby tucked her stylish, short hair behind one ear. "I'm sure I missed some important fight. Needed that cuppa. Thanks." She grabbed her heavy camera off the counter and left.

Flora gathered up the soiled teacups. "I must think where the rest of the guests should sleep. Mr. Fartworthy can have someone in his room. I'll speak to him later. I'm thinking he needs to child-mind that one." She gestured with her chin to Owen, who smirked.

"Sounds reasonable." Cassandra shrugged. "I should return upstairs to help keep the peace."

"I thought you wanted some tea and food?"

"I'll eat eventually."

"It's no trouble."

"No, I'm fine. There are still plenty of nibbles upstairs. Thank you."

"Come down again if you need to escape." Flora resumed working on her map. The noise in the kitchen escalated as Mrs. Forest bustled, mixers whirled, and the staff launched into their newly assigned tasks.

Cassandra walked down the short hallway and slowly climbed the white stairway. Her shoes pinched her feet, and each step became more painful than the last. On her sore ascension, Alexander Spooner bounded down the wooden, white painted, creaky steps, two at a time.

"Miss Haywood, your friend wasn't interested. Are there still some kitchen maids around?"

She suppressed a giggle and placed her hand on his arm. "Alexander, you don't need a date. Just enjoy the evening as it is. Sometimes when we try too hard, it drives people away."

Alexander looked at Cassandra's hand. "I'm coming across too needy?"

"A bit."

"I knew it. You're alone, too. Doesn't it bother you tonight?" He ran his hand down the white, metal handrail. "Don't you wish there was someone by your side to share private jokes and conversation? At least you have people here at the manor to talk to at night. I go home to an empty flat. It's ever so lonely."

Cassandra took her hand off his arm. "Yes, sometimes. It'll change when we least expect it. That's what I'm hoping. You can't plan everything."

"You're right." He sighed. "I'll hang around the kitchen with Miss Fairchild. It's getting uptight at the party anyway. Thank you, Cassandra. I promise to relax."

She smiled. "Good. It's more attractive to ladies when you're sure of yourself."

"Really? Cool. Are you free—"

"Alexander!"

"I'm absolutely kidding! See you later." He smiled over his shoulder, winked, and continued to thump down the staircase.

Shaking her head and grinning, Cassandra resumed her climb up the creaky steps. Moments later, she was back in the dining room, surveying the company. Von Pickle swaggered across the room. Mimi York held on to Hamish's arm but looked miserable, and Hamish showed off his bag of cheese to Lady Bilford. Robin Turner lurked near the table, sampling a cheese cube and a cracker while talking to Arabella. Others in the crowded space engaged in lively conversation or were eating.

Where's my aunt?

Cassandra moved to the great hall. She spied several people wearing party hats and holding colorful horns. She gazed at the dark wood grandfather clock.

Approaching midnight. Maybe I can leave this party soon and get these shoes off. Did she go upstairs? She wouldn't leave. Should I check on her?

Fartworthy appeared, carrying a woven basket of horns and hats. "Miss Haywood, care for something?"

"Where is my aunt?"

"She's in the sunroom, ma'am."

"Thank you." With her mind eased about her aunt's where-abouts, Cassandra took a purple horn from the festive basket. "Mr. Fartworthy, earlier, I noticed Mr. York asked you about the bag of cheese he's carrying in his pocket. What was he saying?"

He rearranged several paper horns in the container. "He inquired if I wanted to try his superior, soft, French cheese."

Cassandra chuckled. "He did? It's always a competition between companies, isn't it?"

"It appears so. When I replied 'no thank you,' he said if I ever have the need to seek employment elsewhere, he would be interested in hiring me." He smirked.

Her merriment ceased. "He wants to steal you from us?"

"Yes, ma'am. No worries. I won't be leaving this manor anytime soon. If you'll excuse me, duty calls." Fartworthy gave a short bow.

"Yes, of course. Thank you." Cassandra watched him turn on his heel and proceed to the dining room. *Interested in hiring him?*

Unbelievable. Invite guests to a party and they stab you in the back.

She walked into the parlor, shaking her head. Holiday music drifted through the air from the opposite end of the room. Many guests were festooned with the evening's celebration paraphernalia.

Directly across from the parlor's arched entrance, four sets of French doors led to a sunroom. In warmer months, the white doors, with multiple panes of glass, were opened, and the parlor took on a grander scale. Unfortunately, the sunroom's outer windows, installed several generations prior, allowed frigid air to seep into that room. During the winter, it was impractical to keep the space open for gatherings.

Cassandra approached and peered through the closed French doors that were temperature and soundproof. In the unheated room, her aunt wrapped her black, velvet shawl tightly around herself. Mr. Birch shared the chilly space.

Cassandra glanced to her right and saw Ruby Lightfoot crouching down, pointing her camera into one of the small, glass panes.

Mr. Birch pulled a small, black box from his tweed pocket and awkwardly dropped to one knee. He flipped the lid of the jeweler's box open to reveal an enormous, diamond engagement ring.

Oh. My. Goodness.

Frederick Chamberlain appeared next to Cassandra, looking into the sunroom, giggling. "He did it! He bought the ring from me shortly before we closed shop today. Three carats, silver setting, 1920s retro design. Extremely fashionable and on trend. He said he bought it for a friend. He lied! Wow."

How could a gardener afford such a diamond? Cassandra stared at the couple in the sunroom. *This plan explains his earlier distraction.*

Lady Lemington mouthed "no" and shook her head.

A real 'no,' or an 'I can't believe this, I'm so happy' shake of the head? What is she saying? Blast these energy-efficient doors!

Lady Lemington continued to talk while the gentleman's face tumbled into a scowl. Jack Birch stood up hastily and still held out the ring. Suddenly, he snapped the box shut, jammed the small package into his trouser pocket, and stormed toward the French doors.

Those observing the failed marriage proposal quickly turned away. Mr. Birch flung open one of the doors with a bang, rattling the panes. Startled, everyone in the room looked at the source of the noise.

Frederick, not keen on reading body language, asked the gardener, "How did it go, Mr. Birch?"

He halted to face Mr. Chamberlain. "Terrible. She turned me down flat. Even worse, she fired me!" The tempest of a man strode out of the parlor.

Frederick looked at Cassandra with his mouth agape.

Cassandra cringed. "Happy New Year?"

Chapter Eight

"Fartworthy!" called Lady Lemington, reentering the warm parlor. She moved to the center of the room with Cassandra and Frederick following. "Where is that man?"

Cassandra touched her aunt's sleeve. "I saw Mr. Fartworthy distributing horns and hats in the hall. What happened? Did Mr. Birch honestly ask you to marry him?"

"I'm not sure anything he does is honest." Lady Lemington smoothed her velvet shawl over her upper arms. "Yes, he did propose. Insufferable."

"He's in love with you!"

"My dear niece, not everything is so apparent." The purple feathers in her headpiece swayed.

Fartworthy materialized. "Ma'am?"

Lady Lemington waved her hand. "Mr. Birch no longer has a position here. Start inquiries for a new head gardener in the morning."

Fartworthy drew an audible breath and whispered loud enough for Cassandra to hear. "I don't know what he has done. Perhaps it would be better to sleep on the idea. This is a mistake."

Lady Lemington pointed a finger in his face. "Never question me on my decisions. I own this manor and know what's best. Do as you're told."

He spoke uncharacteristically quickly. "Ma'am, I ask you to reconsider. Finding a quality head gardener who can handle the hothouse, the cut flower orders, the seed business, and the groundskeeping crew on short notice would be impossible. Firing a second person at the party might not be good for your reputation."

"I'm surprised, Fartworthy." Lady Lemington huffed. "You know how little I care what people think. How dare you question my authority on any matter."

An icy stare passed between employer and employee.

Fartworthy regained his composure. "My deepest apologies, ma'am. I only thought it best to advise you about my concerns. As you wish." After a quick half-bow, Fartworthy strode away.

Frederick looked at the ground. "I'm . . . going to go get something . . . to eat. Please excuse me." He hurried off.

"Aunt Lily, you're making this party uncomfortable for everyone."

Lady Lemington smirked, removed another bubbly drink off a passing butler's tray, and downed half the glass. When she came up for air, she grinned. "Time for some more fun."

Cassandra followed her aunt across the room. She spied Mimi and Hamish entering the parlor. "No, leave them be. Please."

Mrs. York's face soured as they approached.

"Mimi, you're not ready to ring in the New Year." Lady Lemington pointed to her own drink. "Where is your champagne?"

"I can't drink with my medication." Mimi leaned on Hamish's arm.

Lady Lemington took a sip. "Half a glass of bubbly shouldn't make a difference."

"No, ma'am." Mimi opened her small, sparkling evening bag and pulled out a prescription bottle. "These little ones are potent with dangerous side effects a mile long. If you don't need them for your heart, a small dose could kill a person. Mixing these with alcohol is risky. I can't take a chance and make myself more ill by having a drink tonight." She popped the pills back into her little bag and snapped it shut.

"It's a shame you're so sick. I remember a short time ago how much I was concerned Hamish wouldn't be able to keep up with you." Lady Lemington sighed.

Mimi's smile crept up the sides of her mouth, but her eyes were sad. "We were well matched."

Hamish urged, "Mimi, let's go to the hall and get a perfect spot for midnight."

The lady of the manor laughed. "You have plenty of time to get set. Anyway, when you get older, one cannot be as good as in the past."

"Dearest, to the hall. Please." Hamish tugged on Mimi's arm. His lips formed a thin, tight line and a vein puffed up on his neck.

What's wrong with Hamish? Cassandra's eyes darted between the couple.

Mimi remained rooted to her spot. "Yes, yes, the face lift. You spilled that news earlier."

"Aunt Lily, we should let our guests find a place for the count-down."

"We're mere steps from where everyone needs to be. No, Mimi." Lady Lemington stepped closer. "I'm referring to his age."

The ailing woman chuckled. "I don't understand your meaning, ma'am."

"Excuse us, Lady Lemington. We need to move on." Hamish pulled on his wife's limb.

Mimi clenched her teeth. "Leave me be." Defeated, Hamish released her arm. She faltered for a moment, causing a knee-jerk reaction from her husband to catch her. She shoved his hands away. "Are you going to tell me Hamish is not thirty-seven? That he lied about his age, too?"

"You're a smart one after all." Lady Lemington smiled.

Hamish dropped his head.

Observing her husband's reaction, Mimi crossed her arms. "I'm right? Don't tell me he's in his early forties?"

"Fifty-five."

"What?" The word dropped from Mimi's mouth scarcely above a whisper. She shot a look to her husband. "What?" she repeated, louder.

Lady Lemington continued. "Confession time, Hamish. She has the right to know. Trust and honesty. That's what relationships are based on." She turned to Mimi. "You see, my dear, he's closer to my age."

Mimi stared with contempt at her husband, who cowered.

Cassandra's mouth remained open. *It must be true.*

Flora Fairchild approached, holding a full teacup with a saucer. "Ma'am. Your evening tea."

"Fairchild, that is the routine, but use your brain. It's a party, and this," she said, lifting the bubbly drink, "is what I will have. Put that on my bedside table for later."

"Yes, ma'am." Miss Fairchild stopped for an instant when her eyes caught Hamish. She diverted her gaze to the floor and walked away.

"Fifty-five? As in retirement age?" Mimi covered her mouth with her hand.

"Retirement is sixty-five with our twenty-first century health advancements," replied Hamish.

"Don't get into semantics with me. You told me you were thirty-four when we met three years ago." Mimi held her forehead. "The face lift was necessary to continue the charade, to keep your poor, sickly wife in the dark."

"No." Hamish stuffed his fingers through his blond hair. "When we first met, I lied because I never thought you would talk to me if you knew my real age. It was a vain and brainless thing to do." He released his head. "You bewitched me from the beginning.

Our relationship and my love for you exploded before I could confess. I've kept this terrible secret because I didn't want to ruin everything. You're the love of my life. It was a foolish mistake I bitterly regret."

"I can't believe you. To be married to an old man and a phony! It's a fate worse than death. How shall I go on?"

A small, unnatural cry of anguish escaped Hamish's lips.

Mimi turned to Lady Lemington. "I despise you for telling me this and ruining my joy."

Lady Lemington played with the stem of her glass. "True happiness cannot be based on deceit. You'll thank me later."

"No. This was twisted entertainment in your sick mind." Mimi stormed away with Hamish following.

Cassandra, disgusted with her aunt for the third time in one evening, stood silent.

Fartworthy and the other butlers glided between clusters of guests throughout the parlor, making the announcement, "Please go to the great hall for the countdown." The visitors made their way into the grand space with the buzz of anticipation like a crowd in a theater lobby before a show.

Cassandra joined the throng, anxious to remove herself from her aunt's side. *I've had enough of these shoes, my aunt, and this party.* She situated herself near the base of the stairway.

The photographer took position halfway up the staircase on the landing. She clicked away, unnoticed by everyone—except Cassandra.

As the stoic grandfather clock's hands inched toward midnight, more partygoers assembled and mounting excitement filled the room. The guests' fancy attire contrasted with the jewel-tone, metallic, paper hats. The words "Happy New Year!" imprinted in silver glitter made the silly effect complete. Paper horns in the hands of adults proved some were little children at heart. The butlers swarmed around the revelry, equipping everyone with a crystal flute of champagne. Some people moved onto the lower steps to gain some space.

Lady Lemington entered the great hall and made her way up the enormous, curved staircase to the landing. Deliberately perched higher above her guests, she held a noisemaker in her hand. The purple feathers in her headpiece fluttered as she looked around the room with delight.

Cassandra surveyed the room and fidgeted with the paper horn in her hand.

Mimi York leaned on the end of the scrolled, oak banister rather than her husband's arm. Cassandra could hear Hamish pleading. "Darling, dearest, please look at me. We need to talk. Forgive me, please." She didn't respond. He glared at Lady Lemington.

Poor Hamish, poor Mimi.

Robin and Roland Turner positioned themselves before the grandfather clock across the room. Robin glowered at the early hornblowers and turned to give eye daggers to the lady of the manor. Roland stood with his hands clasped behind his back. A silly, royal-blue hat rested on his head, held on by the thin elastic that stretched under his chin.

Roland seems unnaturally calm and relaxed. Odd, considering the company he keeps. Robin could make a bomb specialist jittery. Cassandra avoided eye contact with the mother and son.

Von Pickle remained obnoxious, repeatedly tooting his golden horn before midnight. The repugnant businessman flicked his hand around. "Get on with it! It's midnight somewhere in the world, probably where they serve my cheese. Grab your drinkies, and let's go!"

Cassandra studied Von Pickle's face. In the few moments he decided to be quiet, his expression looked like that of an angry, dirty, five-year-old who had been told it was bath time, and he couldn't go out to play.

Flora Fairchild stood inside the wide dining room doorway with the kitchen staff. She looked around with something midsize and rectangular secured under one arm.

What does Flora have? Cassandra squinted. *Who is she looking for?*

Eliza, the housemaid, stood timidly, tucked in the corner on that side of the room. Lady Lemington allowed the help to participate in the yearly tradition of ringing in the New Year, but they didn't mingle with the guests. As soon as the clock struck midnight, the staff had a few minutes to enjoy the merriment. After that, they would need to retreat to their usual stations, mostly out of sight.

Balancing his silver tray of bubbly drinks overhead, Fartworthy scanned the crowd and set to rights anyone who didn't possess the proper celebratory beverage. His butler crew lined the large, arched doorway to the parlor, along with Sean Johnson and the other valets. Sean waved at Cassandra. She returned the greeting.

The din grew in the great hall. The clamor came from all directions, like various birds singing to one another near a woodland creek on an early summer morning.

Alexander Spooner, Frederick Chamberlain, and Arabella Dalton clustered in the middle of the room, laughing.

Cassandra smiled. *At least Alexander found people to chuckle with this evening. What is Bella doing with those two? I don't want to talk to Mr. Spooner. Mr. Chamberlain? That's a different story.*

Additional members of the assembly milled around, looking for the perfect spot to bid the old year farewell.

The piano player in the parlor teased a jazz version of "Silent Night" from the keys. The slow-moving, jarring chords sounded too somber for the festivities. *Poppy, wrong choice for this moment.*

Jack Birch made his way through the crowd to stand beside Cassandra. He glanced at his mobile, pocketed the device, and spoke close to her ear. "Enjoying yourself this evening, Miss Haywood?"

Cassandra, pleased Mr. Birch found his pleasant side again, tapped his arm. "It has been an interesting evening. Are you all right? Did I see what I thought I saw?"

Despondent, he looked up at Lady Lemington. "You mean my failed attempt at happiness. Yes, you did. Maybe it's too late for this old gardener. I guess the flowers I left in her bedroom every night for the last year meant nothing. Do you think you could talk to her for me and get my job back? If she won't accept my hand, the work will have to do. I don't want to leave."

"You're not old. Stop that talk." She smiled. "I'll see what I can do. We'd miss you terribly if you left."

The left side of his mouth inched upward. "You might, but the others wouldn't care. Thank you, Miss Haywood."

Lady Lemington marched down the steps to her niece. "Cassandra, do *not* talk to him. He's no longer employed here. The only reason he's still on the property is the weather. Birch, as soon as the roads are clear, I want you to vacate the premises. I'll have your things sent to wherever you need them."

"Maybe you'll reconsider this in the morning." Mr. Birch took a step closer. "I'm sorry if I made our relationship difficult. Please allow me to stay on as your gardener."

"No. Gone for good. Don't ask again. This conversation is over." She returned to the landing.

With renewed fury, he stormed up the steps past Lady Lemington and Miss Lightfoot. When he got to the second floor, he disappeared.

Cassandra stared disbelievingly at her aunt. *How could she?*

At Fartworthy's command, the butlers shouted in unison. "Ten . . . nine . . . eight . . ."

Cassandra refocused on the multitude to force herself to enjoy the moment. Some guests joined in the countdown while others started blowing their horns. The piano fell silent.

"Seven . . . six . . ."

Ruby Lightfoot snapped photos of the crowd below.

"Five . . . four . . ."

Fartworthy signaled to Flora.

"Three . . . two . . ."

Lady Lemington looked down at her guests, smiling.

"One! Happy New Year!"

The noise from the celebratory group grew thunderous.

Horns and cheers echoed.

Pop! Pop! Pop! reverberated through the air.

Lady Lemington opened her mouth, clasping her chest in surprise.

Bits of shiny, metallic paper flew from confetti poppers aimed over the crowd by the kitchen staff, housemaids, butlers, and valets on either side of the room. Additional servants threw paper streamers that merged with the sparkling, descending pieces.

Lady Lemington, thrilled with the dazzling, dramatic, theatrical effect, shouted above the crowd. "Happy New Year! Happy New Year!"

The clinking of glasses, exchanges of well-wishes, and the mingling of people continued. The strains of "Auld Lang Syne" drifted into the hall. The notes gradually rose to a crescendo as the crowd joined the piano with the well-worn lyrics. Soon, almost everyone raised their voices with a song heard once a year. The crowd crooned, and some swayed as they sang.

Cassandra blew her purple horn and gazed around at the merrymaking. Mimi held the sides of her head with her fingertips. Hamish crossed his arms, and his festive hat, hung by the thin elastic, bobbed from his wrist. He rocked back and forth on his heels in time with the music.

Flora threaded her way through the crowd with determination. The head housekeeper made her way to Hamish. Cassandra, curious over the intensity of her friend's search, moved closer to hear over the singing.

Flora spoke loudly. "Mr. March? I can't believe it's you! I'm so, so sorry to bother you. I have a moment before I must retreat downstairs."

"I don't know what you mean, miss." Hamish held up his hand.

More people in the crowd muddled through the words of the song everyone thinks they know, but don't.

Mimi, holding her left temple, shouted over the singing to Flora. "Excuse me? Mr. March? No, this is Mr. York, my husband."

"He's Mr. March! Would you please sign this?" Flora retrieved the rectangular papers from under her arm.

"Mr. *who*?" Mimi cupped her ear.

"Mr. March from the calendar of Parisian male models of the 1980s." Flora held up a calendar and flipped the pages to the month of March. In full-color glory appeared Hamish York in a black tuxedo with a silver vest and a faraway, smoldering look. "I'm usually not this bold, but this is one of my few prized possessions from my years spent in Paris. Would you please do me the honor of signing my favorite page?" begged Flora.

"For Auld Lang Syne . . . for Auld. . . ." The group continued the song.

Mimi uttered in disbelief, "You were a model in Paris? In the '80s? Enough revelations for one night. I definitely need more pills." She shook her evening bag in Hamish's face, grasped the oak banister, and hurried up the stairs.

Hamish started after Mimi, but Cassandra touched his arm. "She needs some space."

"She'll never trust me again. My life has blown up before my eyes tonight. No amount of waiting will change that." Hamish chased after his wife. Flora retreated to her place in the doorway without the signature she craved. Cassandra followed the Yorks.

Mimi stopped in front of Lady Lemington on the stairs. "Where am I staying tonight? This floor?" She pointed over her shoulder to where the curved staircase led.

The lady of the manor raised her voice over the commotion. "Yes, dear Mimi, but it's much too early to think about retiring. The celebration just started. I have no idea which room you have been assigned. Talk to Fairchild."

"Who's Fairchild?" Mimi yelled back.

"The woman you just spoke with." Lady Lemington pointed to Flora with her glass.

"The one with the ridiculous calendar?" asked Mimi.

"Precisely."

"Never mind. I need to get away from the noise." Mimi resumed her climb up the stairs.

"Wait, Mimi!" Hamish pleaded.

She faced him. "Don't follow me. I want to be alone. I don't know you anymore." Mimi ascended the remaining steps. Hamish looked back at Cassandra with a frown. The man froze as the celebration continued below. Suddenly, he ran up the stairs after his wife.

The last of the gold, glitter confetti floated down.

As the holiday song ended, so did the singing. The rest of the revel-making continued. Cassandra surveyed the crowd from her aunt's vantage point. Lady Lemington smiled at her. Cassandra couldn't return the pleasantry.

Lady Lemington offered her glass. "Don't be so grim, my dear. Happy New Year."

The niece clinked her glass in return out of habit, not joy. "You destroyed their relationship." She drank her beverage.

"Clarified it, you mean."

"You think that was kind?"

Lady Lemington smirked. "Who ever claimed I was kind? You're too innocent to understand."

Cassandra, from the landing, smiled at Arabella, who tucked back her headpiece veil and returned the greeting from across the room. She leaned into her aunt's ear. "You need to stop treating others so harshly."

Lady Lemington faced her niece. "Perception is everything. People may be delightful to your face but then plot against you. And sometimes, what seems to be cruel is helpful in the end. Someday, you'll understand."

"I doubt it." Cassandra stomped down the steps to rejoin the crowd. *I refuse to let my aunt ruin the rest of my night.*

She made her way to Alexander, Frederick, and Arabella. "Happy New Year!" Cassandra greeted the trio with a forced smile.

"Happy New Year!" they replied in unison.

"To happy people!" Alexander held his beverage up. They returned the toast and clinked glasses together. The quartet drank to seal the salutation. The crowd's clamor started to die down as most moved into the other rooms.

Arabella asked, "What were you and your aunt talking about up there?"

"Nothing of consequence. Usual business." Cassandra looked over her shoulder. Her aunt remained at the sentinel position.

Bella pressed. "Come on, out with it! She fired the gardener after he proposed to her? Mr. Chamberlain told us."

"Yes, she did, but it's minutes into the new year. I don't wish to discuss this unpleasantness. My aunt has her reasons."

"But to get sacked after a proposal? That's harsh even for her."

"Enough, Bella. What were you laughing about?"

Alexander leaned in. "I saw the room map downstairs. I thought I would let Mr. Chamberlain know we will be roommates tonight. I figured we better get to know one another besides the 'Hello, chap' we've done in the past. Funny, when you talk to people, you find more in common than you might think. Turns out, we both enjoy listening to American Country and Western music."

Frederick added, "And we like to play a variety of card games."

"Especially poker and sometimes other games. Except solitaire. Frederick doesn't mind that one. I can't stand it. But we're night owls who—"

"I asked him if he snored," said Frederick with a grin.

"And I said, how should I know? I live alone. I guess you'll find out tonight!" said Alexander.

Arabella chuckled. "And that made us laugh hard, for some reason. It isn't that humorous in the retelling. Maybe we need more champagne. Where's a butler when you need one?" She looked at the staircase and sighed. "Cassandra, your scarf." She pointed with her empty champagne glass to the banister.

"I don't even remember removing it."

Arabella turned to the gentlemen. "She would leave her head on the side table if it wasn't attached, and yet, she's the most brilliant businesswoman I know." She pushed back the veiling on her headpiece.

Cassandra mouthed *Stop* to Arabella.

Frederick tipped an imaginary hat in Cassandra's direction. "Beauty and brains."

Arabella flashed a grin.

"I'll be right back." Cassandra's face warmed.

As she turned around, she heard Alexander say, "Full marks for that! You *must* teach me how to talk to the ladies." Cassandra stifled a snicker, threading her way through the crowd.

After she retrieved her raspberry accessory and took a step to make her way back, Robin Turner grabbed Cassandra's arm. "I don't know what you have done to influence Lily, but you'll reverse this. Roland shall become CEO, and that's final!"

"Remove your hand from me this instant!" Cassandra squirmed under the middle-aged woman's grasp. "My aunt's decision isn't mine to make. I have no desire to be in charge."

Robin let go. "Keep it that way."

"Mrs. Turner, you have no say in the matter."

"When your aunt is no longer at the helm, I'll fight you in court," snarled Robin.

"Is that always your answer? The change is years away. Enjoy your evening. I'm not discussing this further." Cassandra sidestepped around the angry woman.

Robin lunged for Cassandra again.

"Enough." Roland stopped his mother's swipe midair. "Leave her be. It's not her fault our aunt is difficult. We don't need to do this tonight, Mother. Everyone knows Lady Lemington can't live forever, and we'll figure it out then."

Cassandra drew a deep breath. *Bite tongue. Bite tongue.* "Happy New Year, Mr. Turner. Mrs. Turner."

"The same to you, Miss Haywood," said the young man.

Lady Lemington descended the stairs. "Dearest sister-in-law, coming to blows on my account?"

"You misused my son."

"Perhaps. Perhaps not. My choice is set in stone. I own and control all, and you don't. Live with it."

"Money-grubbing wench!" Robin roared.

"Low-class insults with a medieval flare? You *are* stuck in the past." Lady Lemington finished her champagne. "Not conquering my kingdom. *Ever.*"

Robin wagged her finger. "This isn't over."

"Please. Sheath your verbal and finger swords. You never could let anything go. There's no dragon to slay here," sneered Lady Lemington.

"Don't be so sure." Robin stormed up the staircase with Roland following.

Cassandra, without a word, turned to leave.

"Cassandra," Lady Lemington beckoned.

The niece stopped but didn't face her aunt.

Lady Lemington moved closer. "I'll explain everything later, my dear. Please trust me."

"It's difficult when every nasty thing people ever said about you turns out to be true. I can't think highly of you right now." Cassandra strode off to rejoin the cluster of twenty-somethings and try to rescue some joy from the night.

Chapter Nine

Strange sounds infiltrated Cassandra's dream. *Ta-ta-ta-ta-ta-ta.* Rap. Rap. *Ta-ta-ta-ta-ta.* Rap. Rap.

An icy, skeletal hand reached out of the darkness and grabbed Cassandra's arm.

"Ahhh!" She woke up with a start.

Mr. Fartworthy's cold fingertips proved to be the source of the gaunt hand in her dream. "So sorry to frighten you, Miss Haywood. I knocked, but you didn't answer. I needed to wake you. It's a matter of utmost importance." He stood straight.

His voice woke Arabella, who squinted at the time on her mobile phone. "Little early to talk over menus, don't you think, Fartworthy?" She rubbed her face and ran a hand through her hair.

"Yes, ma'am, it is." His eyebrow furrowed. "There's been an accident. Please dress quickly and come with me. I'll wait outside."

At the mention of the word "accident," Cassandra bolted upright in bed and Arabella put down her phone. "Tell me, please," Cassandra pleaded.

"I'm not permitted to say, Miss Haywood."

Cassandra whispered, "Mr. Fartworthy?"

He took a deep breath. "It's your aunt."

Cassandra stood, and her long, white, cotton nightgown straightened. "What's happened?"

"Please, Miss Haywood, get dressed. I'll wait in the hall." He turned to leave.

"Is my aunt going to hospital? Is that a helicopter I hear?"

He faced the ladies. "Yes, it's a helicopter. The roads are too icy and dangerous to come up the hill by car. The snowplows are having difficulty maneuvering at all." He breathed deeply. "No, ma'am. I'm sorry. It's too late for hospital."

Arabella sprung out of bed. "She's dead?"

Fartworthy looked at the floor. "Yes, ma'am. May God rest her soul."

Cassandra's knees gave out and she sat on her bed. "Dead? No. That's not possible." The room swirled.

Mr. Fartworthy knelt on one knee and took Cassandra's hand in his. The shock of his frosty fingers centered Cassandra. Gently and quietly, he continued. "I found her early this morning and called the constable. I waited to wake you until the last possible moment. Detective Chief Inspector Carter and her team have arrived. She told me I wasn't to reveal Lady Lemington died. You must get dressed."

Cassandra squeezed his hand. "Are you sure she's gone?" She searched Fartworthy's face for the truth.

"Yes, ma'am. Confirmed a few minutes ago." His lips formed a hard line.

Cassandra's hand went to her mouth, and she looked at Arabella in disbelief.

"Cass, I'm so sorry." Arabella crossed the room to put her arm around her friend.

Fartworthy whispered. "They wish to question everyone who stayed overnight. Miss Fairchild and I wanted to be the ones to awaken the guests. However, the detectives said they must do it. I requested to wake you. It was allowed since you're her niece. There's an escort outside your door. Please hurry. I know you don't like to spill your emotions to strangers. I thought if you heard it from me, you could have a few moments to pull yourself together. Remember, I told you there has been an accident, nothing further." Fartworthy regained his emotional aloofness, released Cassandra's hand, and stood. In a louder voice, he continued. "Everyone is requested to dress in the clothes they wore last night. Meet me in the hallway, ma'am." Fartworthy left the room.

Arabella and Cassandra changed in silence.

Cassandra's thoughts bounced around like a hard rubber ball in a cement room. *This isn't happening. No. I'm going to go see Aunt Lily, and everything will be fine. Mr. Fartworthy is mistaken. I can't recall the last thing I said to her. Oh no. I do remember.*

When the two friends opened the bedroom door, reality hit them like a bucket of frigid water. The hallway teemed with law enforcement personnel, and the steady hum of hushed voices hung in the air. Officials with neon-yellow vests escorted guests amid flashes from an unseen camera, and lines of yellow crime scene tape wound in different directions. The lavatory down the hall and Lady Lemington's bedroom contained clusters of grim-looking people near the doorways.

"This way. We can't use the main steps right now." A constable wearing the garish overvest walked next to Cassandra. Fartworthy accompanied Arabella. They moved away from the bustle and down the hallway, made a left, and walked down another long corridor of rooms with more guests and staff to the servant staircase.

Cassandra glided through the downstairs in a surreal blur. The glow of the early winter light filtered into the parlor. The staff working into the wee morning hours had cleaned up any evidence of a party. No whiff of stale champagne, celebration paraphernalia, or leftover food remained. Instead, the mixed tang of Earl Grey tea and orange-scented floor cleaner permeated the air. The official business of the detectives further altered everything.

Detective Chief Inspector Carter, in her mid-forties, her auburn hair in a just-below-shoulder-length bob, led the investigation. Smartly dressed in a black pant suit and crisp, white blouse, she crossed the room with another detective. She extended her hand. "Miss Haywood?"

"Yes, that's me." Cassandra returned the handshake. She mindlessly shook the hand of the second person.

"I'm Detective Chief Inspector Carter. This is Detective Sergeant Jenkins. Please sit." Carter joined Cassandra on the butter-yellow sofa. "Thank you for coming downstairs. What have you've been told?" Jenkins remained standing, ready to take notes.

"There has been an accident. Can you please tell me what is going on?" Cassandra's voice drifted out like a whiff of smoke. "It's so early in the morning."

"Informed of anything else, Miss Haywood?" asked Carter.

Cassandra thought for an instant. *I can't get Mr. Fartworthy in trouble.* "I needed to get dressed in last night's clothing and come down immediately to see you."

The investigator blew out a long breath and leaned forward. "I'm so sorry to be the one to tell you. Lady Lily Lemington has died. One of the members of the household staff found your aunt deceased this morning. Our deepest condolences for your loss."

Cassandra closed her eyes to hold back the torrent itching to pour out. "No, it can't be. You must be mistaken," she whispered. Hearing the news for a second time didn't make it easier, but it helped to keep the tears at bay. She'd do anything to avoid weeping in front of anyone, especially strangers. She opened her eyes. "What happened?"

"I was hoping you would have some information," replied Carter.

"I don't know anything. Was she in her bedroom?" Cassandra grasped the ends of her ivory headband scarf.

"Ma'am, I'll pose the questions. Protocol." Carter removed a notepad and pen from a pocket of her suit jacket.

"Of course." Cassandra scanned the room. Other detectives quietly interviewed guests in separate sections of the large parlor. Several constables in uniform stood around the room. "You have to query everyone?"

"Yes. Usually, if we have a situation in a home, we remove the people from the premises. Questioning takes place elsewhere. Ice from the storm last night made the roads impossible to use. We arrived by helicopter this morning. Our department doesn't have the budget to fly all guests and household staff to another location. Too much petrol required." Carter tugged on her jacket. "We'll make do. The second floor has been closed off until we have what we require. Interviews will happen on this floor."

"Interviews?"

"We need to know if anyone has information to assist us. When was the last time you saw your aunt?"

"At the party last night. Well, this morning, technically."

Carter didn't take her eyes off Cassandra. "Did you have any interactions with her?"

"Loads."

The DCI raised her eyebrows.

Cassandra sat silent. *My aunt made me angry for most of the night.*

"Ma'am?"

Cassandra twisted the ivory scarf's long tails. "I spent a good part of the evening with her."

Carter crinkled the notepad. "Can you describe her mood? Did she have any disagreements with anyone last night? Does she have any enemies you know of?"

Cassandra burst out laughing. Horrified, she quickly composed herself. "She has many."

"Moods, disagreements, or enemies?"

"All of the above," answered Cassandra.

The DCI breathed out. "All right. Let's start with the disagreements. With whom did Lady Lemington argue?"

Cassandra bit her lip. *In what order?* "It was more like tense moments. Mimi and Hamish York would fall under that. She argued with Robin and Roland Turner. She fired the guitar player, verbally sparred with Baron Von Pickle, saying something that angered him, and turned down a marriage proposal from Mr. Birch, subsequently firing him. She disagreed with Mr. Fartworthy and again with the Yorks, and then again with Mrs. Turner."

DS Jenkins scribbled furiously. Carter added to her notepad.

"My aunt is normally argumentative, but she amped it up last night. She said she had reasons for the confrontations but didn't reveal them to me. I begged her to leave the guests alone. Do you think one of them knows something? Can you please tell me what happened to Aunt Lily?"

"Give me a moment, and I'll share with you what we know so far. Why did you beg?"

"She made everyone uncomfortable. A New Year's Eve gala is supposed to be lovely and fun. She seemed to have a list of people she wanted to upset last night."

"Did she upset you?" Carter signaled to another detective to come forward.

"Yes." Cassandra twisted a scarf tail. "She didn't stop stirring the pot."

DCI Carter stood. "Can you recollect the last time you spoke to your aunt?" She pulled over a wooden armchair directly before Cassandra.

DC Greenfield approached. "You wanted me, Chief?"

"Go summon the photographer. She's probably still upstairs." She fixed her jacket and sat. "Sorry, Miss Haywood. When did you speak to her?"

Cassandra looked toward the high archway leading to the hall. "We rung in the new year in there. Something happened with Mimi and Hamish, and I joined my aunt on the staircase. Everyone—guests and staff—participated when we had the countdown. I talked to her and went to my friend. I proceeded back to the stairs because I left my scarf on the handrail." She ran her hand down the lilac scarf around her neck. "Mrs. Turner started an argument with me. My aunt came down the steps and spoke to her sister-in-law. I walked away from Aunt Lily. After that, I saw her across the room a few more times, but we didn't speak for the rest of the evening."

"Mrs. Turner is Lady Lemington's sister-in-law?" asked Carter.

"Yes, Uncle Richard's sister. He died several years ago and left the manor and Lemington Cheese Company to his wife, my aunt," replied Cassandra.

"When did you retire upstairs? Were you alone?"

"I don't know when we went upstairs. Late. After one or two, maybe? Miss Dalton and I chatted with Mr. Spooner and Mr. Chamberlain for some time. When we decided to leave the party, the gentlemen invited us to their room to play cards. I was exhausted and my feet hurt. Arabella and I both said 'no thanks' and retired to my room. We spoke for a bit and went to sleep. What does this have to do with my aunt?"

"We need to know the location of everyone." Carter ran a hand through her auburn hair. "Is this the exact outfit you had on last night?"

"Yes. No. Well, it is, but I'm missing a raspberry-colored scarf I wore as a shawl."

"You're wearing two scarves already." Carter moved her hand around in a tight circle.

"I like my accessories."

Carter pointed. "Miss Haywood, is that the only thing missing? Is this the precise outfit you wore last night?"

Cassandra shifted her feet in the backless sandals. "These are different shoes. The ones I wore last night gave me blisters."

"Where are those shoes?"

Ruby Lightfoot arrived. She gave Cassandra a small smile. "Yes, Detective Chief Inspector?"

Carter asked, "Did you finish upstairs?"

"All complete." Miss Lightfoot removed the card from her camera. "I can't get back to the department to put these on the server. Any suggestions?"

"Pardon me for a moment, Miss Haywood." Carter stood. "Download those to the department laptop, please. It's secure and with the detectives in the next room. I'll add the photos to the server when we get back. Miss Lightfoot, you were the photographer on call for last night and the photographer for the party? How did that happen?"

"I do parties on the side." Ruby Lightfoot put her equipment away in her camera bag. "Can't wait for the department wages to pay my regular bills. This isn't London. The schedule is all wonky, too. I'm on, I'm off with no rhyme or reason." She snapped a clip together. "Besides, the last four times I was on call, nothing happened. Certainly not going to stay at home and miss an opportunity for a fat paycheck for a few hours' work. Plus, New Year's Eve? Not sitting in my flat alone. I had my mobile on me."

"I wouldn't have sat at home, either," admitted Carter. "You gave your statement before you started today?"

"Of course. Do you want the photos from the party?"

"We need written permission, and then, yes." The head detective gave a thumbs-up.

Ruby handed Carter several papers. "I know that. The slip is in there. Lady Lemington hired me."

"Next of kin, then." Turning to Cassandra, Carter asked, "Any objections, Miss Haywood?"

"For looking at last night's photos?" Cassandra looked around. "It's not my decision to make."

"Miss Haywood?" Ruby shrugged. "You're the closest relative, correct?"

"Along with Roland Turner, I guess. Yes. Yes, go ahead." Cassandra let go of the scarf tails hanging from her neck.

Carter jostled a sheet out of the paper stack, handing it to Cassandra with her pen. "Sign this waiver." Carter glanced at the photographer. "Mr. Turner needs to be asked, too. Wait until I have his permission before you do anything with the party photos. Get started on the others." The DCI turned to Cassandra. "Where are the shoes you wore?"

Ruby said, "I'm so sorry about your aunt, Miss Haywood."

Cassandra handed back the paper. "Thank you." Miss Lightfoot nodded and left.

"Miss Haywood? The shoes?" Carter's voice skated on the line of impatience.

"In my room, in my closet, I think. Silver pumps. I can't put them back on. The backs of my heels are raw. Look." She removed the Birkenstock slide sandals she wore, exposing the large Band-Aids on the backs and sides of both feet. Blood had seeped and dried through the bandages.

"Ouch," said DS Jenkins.

"No need, Miss Haywood." Carter continued. "Do you recall if Lady Lemington had been drinking last night?"

"It was New Year's Eve. She probably had sparkling cider for most of the evening, with champagne near midnight," answered Cassandra.

"Probably sparkling cider? The drink looks almost identical to champagne. How do you know it wasn't all alcohol?"

"At parties, my aunt offers sparkling cider for most of the evening, and near midnight, the champagne is served. Too many guests over the years made fools of themselves well before the clock struck twelve. My uncle Richard started it years ago."

"Interesting," replied Carter.

"I gave you what you want. Please, what happened to my aunt?"

The detective sat on the sofa again, turning back pages in her notepad. "She was found in the second-floor lavatory. It looks like she may have tripped. She had a head wound consistent with such an event." Carter touched her head. "She could've had too much to drink. After looking at the scene, I'm leaning toward an unfortunate mishap."

"If you think that she fell, why all this?" Cassandra asked, pointing around the room.

"We must treat every case as a non-accident scene. Much easier if we decide to investigate the case further. My colleagues don't always agree, but I'm in charge and have been for the last eleven years. We do it my way." Detective Chief Inspector Carter signaled to Greenfield again. "I'm deeply sorry for your loss, Miss Haywood. I may have additional questions for you later. Please go with Greenfield to the library. Don't converse with any other guests or household staff until we have gathered their statements." Carter stood.

"I can't talk to anyone? I must sit there alone?" Cassandra rose from the sofa.

"Until I have their statements. I'm terribly sorry this is the way it must be until we can sort this out. Please follow Trainee Detective Constable Greenfield. He'll stay with you."

Greenfield held up his index finger. "Excuse me, Chief. Respectfully, I finished the Trainee Investigator Program several weeks ago."

"Sorry, Greenfield. You're correct. Not calling you 'T/DC' will take me a few weeks." Carter gave the new DC a warm smile. To Cassandra she said, "Please follow Detective Constable Greenfield."

Another constable whispered something to Jenkins, and the DS came over to Carter. "Mr. Turner, the nephew, is ready for an interview across the room. He gave verbal permission for the party photos."

Carter pointed to the new detective. "Tell Miss Lightfoot, and we need to get that in writing." She turned to Cassandra. "We're finished for the time being, Miss Haywood. We'll talk later." The DCI strode across the room to Roland.

"If you please, miss." Greenfield gestured to the doorway.

Cassandra walked across the parlor in a semi-trance. *It must have been an accident. Aunt Lily can be insensitive, but no one would want to kill her.*

Hamish York, Owen Savage, Robin Turner, Mimi York, Alexander Spooner, and Baron Von Pickle were separated and in some phase of questioning in different sections of the room.

Our friends and family? None of them would take a life . . . would they?

Chapter Ten

Cassandra followed DC Greenfield to the dining room. Law enforcement transformed this room in similar fashion to the parlor. Detectives questioning guests and staff talked in quiet, serious voices. The low murmur of multiple conversations prevented Cassandra from deciphering any single exchange.

Greenfield said, "We'll find out what happened to your aunt. I assure you."

"Thank you. This doesn't seem real." Cassandra twisted her ivory scarf tails.

"I can imagine."

They walked past the sideboard buffet. A self-service breakfast of tarts and scones, with several ceramic containers filled with marmalade, honey, or Marmite, had been laid out the night before. An oversize, crystal bowl held various pieces of whole, fresh fruit. Two large, sterling silver carafes dominated the long tabletop, one labeled 'coffee' and the other 'hot water.' A fine selection of teas stood on end in a shallow, walnut box. An impressive number of matching bone china teacups and saucers stood like a brigade of soldiers on parade.

Greenfield paused by the sideboard. "Would you like something to drink or eat, Miss Haywood?"

"No, thank you. I want to go to the library."

"Understood." He resumed his pace. "You know, the DCI is brilliant at what she does. She'll find out what happened. I've seen her many times invade the personal space of an accused person, and they always crack like a nut under her scrutiny."

"Really?"

"She has a gift to peer into the soul of those she questions. Fantastic to witness. People at the department call her a 'force of nature.' Some call her 'Hurricane Carter.' Not to her face, of course." Greenfield smiled.

The corner of Cassandra's mouth rose. "If she's so good at reading people, she probably knows what they call her."

"True. She's the most meticulous detective I know. On another case many years ago, a gentleman took a fall down a flight of stairs that looked like an accident." Greenfield leaned toward her and spoke softly. "Turned out to be foul play, and sloppy handling of evidence by some of her colleagues allowed a conviction to slip away. Carter blamed herself. She couldn't put the guilty party behind bars. Since then, she treats every investigation as a crime scene until proven otherwise."

"Shouldn't every case be handled that way?"

"They normally are. She takes it to the extreme, usually when others will wrap things up." Greenfield opened the heavy, oak door to the library.

Inside, the smell of antique furniture mixed with aged paper. The room contained several well-worn, saddle-brown, leather armchairs scattered about with small, circular, dark wood tables nearby. Tall, built-in bookshelves covered three walls. The extensive collection of tomes, most with leather bindings and pages with foxing around the edges, contributed to the unique scent. Cassandra adored this cocoon-like refuge.

Heavy, green, velvet curtains lined and covered the far wall from floor to ceiling. Normally, the drapery would have been opened by the housemaids long before this hour of the morning. Cassandra flicked on a small, brass lamp near the doorway. The jade fabric drew light into the folds and suffocated the glow.

Pointing to the drapes as she walked to the other side of the room, Cassandra asked, "May I open these?"

"That would brighten things up. Let me help." The new detective constable strode over to the opposite end from Cassandra. He pulled back a set of drapes on one window, and Cassandra did the same on her end. "Much brighter. Blast! These are heavy." He proceeded to his second window.

"They're quite a handful." She moved over and opened another set on her side. "The maids must take them outside several times a year to beat them to remove dust, like they used to have to do with the carpets. No hoovering these. No dry cleaner, not even in London, would touch them. A person can get lost in the folds."

Greenfield looked around. "This room is two or three times the size of my entire flat!"

"I love this library." She walked over to the third window with Greenfield. "We can each grab a side."

Working together, they opened the largest of the five sets of drapery. Cassandra looked out the window. Thick ice encrusted the long panes of glass. Outlines and colors muddled together, a clear view of the outside impossible to observe. She stared at the translucent layer in a daze for some time. "How long will this take, Detective?"

"They still have quite a bit to do since gathering statements from everyone present takes hours. No stone unturned. Processing upstairs should be completed soon."

"Processing?" Her eyes followed the labyrinth of frost lines. The blurry world through ice hypnotized the sorrowful woman.

"Photos, gathering evidence, sketching the scene, lifting

fingerprints. We have two rooms to do—maybe more—if the DCI believes we should be looking elsewhere after the interviews are completed."

"Two rooms?"

"The lavatory and her bedroom."

Cassandra spun around. Her face pinched tight in grief. "I'm trying to make sense of this. Can you please tell me any additional details besides she died in the water closet?"

"Sure." The detective retrieved his notepad from his pocket. "Female, approximately fifty to fifty-five years old, found in the second-floor lavatory. The body discovered by Archibald Fartworthy at 5:03 a.m., 1 January. Body facedown near the sink, left arm slightly overhead, right hand near the victim's right shoulder. A liquid substance, reddish brown in color, surrounded under the head and upper torso area. Preliminary findings—liquid believed to be blood. Color indicates it has been out of the body for several hours. Time of death approximately between two to three a.m. A deep gash across the forehead. The watch worn by the victim, not working. Stopped at two thirty-five. Coroner stated. . . ." Greenfield looked up from his notes.

Her hands covered her mouth in revulsion. "No, stop, please. I'm so sorry I asked." She shut her eyes tight. *Reddish-brown liquid. Aunt Lily. Facedown. I'm going to be sick. Breathe.* Her hands trembled uncontrollably.

Greenfield shoved the notepad in his pocket and rushed across the room. "Miss Haywood, I'm so sorry. I shouldn't have read all of that to you. I wasn't thinking. Please forgive me. Don't tell the DCI."

Cassandra held the sides of her head and sunk into the comfort of an old, leather friend. *Pull yourself together. Breathe.*

The library door flung open and slammed against a bookshelf. Baron Von Pickle burst into the room. "I can't possibly be held here! I have a business to run. Don't you know I'm an important man?"

Ignore him. Cassandra closed her eyes, trying to slow her racing heart and control her shallow breathing.

DS Jenkins stepped behind the human squall. "Carter wants him in here. I'll bring anyone whom we're finished with."

Greenfield scrunched his nose. "There's plenty of room, but don't you think the niece deserves her privacy?"

"Sorry, Carter's orders." Jenkins tilted his head in Von Pickle's direction. "Yes—that. Good luck." He shut the door.

Von Pickle stormed around like a caged, predatory animal. "I need to know exactly when I can leave this relic of a house. I have an international cheese company that needs attending. You can't hold me here against my will."

"It's a national holiday, sir." Greenfield pointed to an armchair. "Won't you sit down, Mr. Von Pickle?"

"It's Baron Von Pickle to you, 'Bobbie.' It most certainly isn't a holiday in some of the countries I deal with."

Temper tantrum from a grown man. Unbelievable. Cassandra sighed. "It's a general holiday everywhere. Let the detectives do their job."

The serpent spun around to face the young woman. "I didn't see you sitting there. Did your aunt clock her head because she got sloshed, or was it plain, old clumsiness? I overheard what happened. A stupid mistake made by a dead woman is ruining my day."

Cassandra stood quickly, but no words escaped her stunned lips.

"Yes?" Von Pickle glared in anticipation. "Are you going to say something, or just stand there catching flies with your frog mouth? You know what I say is true. It's ridiculous."

"You're a cold-blooded monster." Cassandra walked back to the window, far away from the fuming man.

Greenfield stepped between the baron and Cassandra. "Sir,

I don't know if you realize the woman who passed away was Miss Haywood's aunt."

"I know. So?" taunted Von Pickle.

The new detective raised his voice. "A little decorum, then, and respect for the dead."

"Decorum? Are you in a BBC historic film? Where are your top hat and tails? Your concern should be to get me out of this place." He adjusted his cuff links and flopped down in an armchair, his legs spread far apart. A long, tormented sigh escaped his lips.

Greenfield crossed the room and whispered, "Are you all right, Miss Haywood? I'm sure he's actually sorry, probably a bit stressed being here."

She stared at the daylight coming through the ice-covered windows. She replied in a quiet voice, "No, he's always a jer—, difficult. He's always difficult. He likes to get everyone's monkey up." She looked at Greenfield. "Von Pickle and my aunt got into an exchange of insults last night. She despises him."

"Anything you can tell us might be helpful." Greenfield took out his notepad and pen.

Cassandra, barely audible said, "She took him aside and told him something. He got angry and shouted, 'You can't do that!' Do you think he could have hurt her?"

"Entirely possible."

They both turned to the seated man across the room. Von Pickle sat, sprawled out like an octopus, and picked at the skin on the side of his thumbnail with his teeth.

The library door opened once again.

Chapter Eleven

Jenkins held the door open for Robin Turner. "Please wait in here, ma'am." She hesitated but then walked into the reading sanctuary as he motioned to the new detective constable. "Greenfield?"

Greenfield crossed the room. "Yes, sir?"

"Carter is moving along at a jolly pace, and there should be several others arriving in the next few minutes. Maybe we'll finish soon." The older detective smirked.

Greenfield pointed to the door. "Can we allow them to get breakfast from the dining room and bring it back in here?"

"Wait until you've heard from Carter. Better yet, I'll ask her. Everything all right?"

Greenfield shrugged. "Interesting. Any leads?"

"Still looks like we're wasting everyone's time. *Again.* It keeps Carter happy, I suppose. It's holiday pay rate, so I'm not blubbing. I should go." Jenkins stepped out and closed the door.

In the library, Robin tapped Miss Haywood on the shoulder. "Sorry about your aunt."

Cassandra, intent on the detectives' conversation and surprised by Mrs. Turner's cordiality, could only muster, "Hmm?"

"I said, I'm sorry about your aunt. I know you cared about

her." Robin's downturned mouth and deep-purple circles under her eyes aged her from the night before. She stared at the hardwood floor.

"Thank you, Mrs. Turner. It's quite a shock." While she talked, Cassandra studied Lady Lemington's rival. *Did she sleep at all last night?* "Did you find your room satisfactory?"

"I'm glad to have a regular room." Robin shrugged. "No complaints. The decor could use an update and the mattress needs replacing. The closet reeked of cedar, and I don't care for the scent. The light bulb in the reading lamp next to the bed is exceedingly dim. One can't read comfortably with that wattage. I ended up taking off the lampshade to see. I didn't sleep well. It was the cheese I ate at the party. Indigestion. Yes, no complaints. Thank you for asking."

"Oh. Glad to hear. What were you reading?"

Robin's head jerked up. "That's none of your business. It's not important." She played with one of the jade, velvet curtain edges.

"Sorry, didn't mean to pry." Cassandra studied the room for inspiration for the stalling conversation. *Think of something. What do we have in common?* "I enjoy reading at night, too. I've a large collection of choices next to my bed. What different books do you like to read?"

"I don't do different. Just one. Bring it with me everywhere." Robin's fingers flicked the curtain.

"A Bible?" asked Cassandra.

"No," snapped Robin.

Dead silence hung in the air like a thick, London fog.

From across the room, a low voice sneered. "You two are pathetic. You can't even make small talk, let alone cheese." The baron sat up. "So, speaking of dairy products, what's going to happen with the Lemington Company? Who needs to be buried next?"

Greenfield scoffed. "Sir, your choice of words is inappropriate."

"Go guard the door like a good little public servant and mind your business." Von Pickle stood and swaggered over to the women.

"I remember. Lady Lemington told me last night of her 'after I pop off plan.' Miss Haywood would be in charge. Ding-dong, the witch is dead, and you've stolen the ruby slippers. Congratulations. This will be easy."

Robin shoved the jade curtain aside. "Don't you dare destroy my father's business! Cassandra said last night she doesn't want to be in charge. My son, Roland, will be CEO."

Fartworthy crossed the room. "Official arrangements are set for Miss Haywood to take over." He moved to stand by Cassandra's side.

Von Pickle startled and sized him up from head to toe. "Where did you come from? I swear you materialize out of thin air, Fartworthy. Are you a hologram or a ghost?"

"A little of both, sir. I did use the door." The head butler turned to Cassandra. "How are you holding up, Miss Haywood?"

"As well as can be expected, thank you. Are the transfer documents among the paperwork you told me were left in my room last night? I gave them a fleeting look, but I didn't read them. One was from a law office." Cassandra coiled the ends of her ivory scarf around her fingers.

"Maybe it's best we discuss this at another time, Miss Haywood," said Fartworthy.

Von Pickle guffawed. "So, it's true then. The great Lemington Cheese Company will be run by someone who flunked business school! My day has improved tremendously."

Robin huffed. "You failed? And Lily still wanted you in charge? We could never agree on anything. This proves she was off her nut. No, Roland is the better candidate, and it remains in my family. That's the most important thing."

Fartworthy straightened his square-rimmed glasses. "Not quite, ma'am. After your brother suffered his heart attack, before his death he made Lady Lemington promise to keep the company running—no matter what. She took the vow seriously. He never said to keep it in his family."

The baron frowned. "This doesn't make any sense. You're a butler. Why do you know so much about Lemington Cheese, and why do you care? Don't you just set the table and fill the glasses around here?"

"The job of head butler is more involved than the handling of food and drink, sir. We're a trusted member of the staff. That confidence can include business affairs, as it does in this case. It's unusual, but it was her way of doing things."

Cassandra studied Fartworthy. *He knows something more. I need to get him alone.*

The library door opened once again. Mimi York leaned on Detective Sergeant Jenkins' arm. "I assure you, ma'am, we'll locate it. Can't have gone too far. Purses don't have legs."

Mimi's brow furrowed. "You don't understand. I don't care about the bag. It's my medication inside. Why would someone take an evening bag, and how did they get it out of my room?"

"You're assuming someone stole it, Mrs. York. Maybe you left it somewhere during the party? Please have a seat." Jenkins gestured to an armchair.

"That's simply not possible. I cannot go more than a few hours without my prescription. I know I took my pills last night. I'm always careful to keep track of my medications. No, someone took it." Mimi eased into a leather chair. "I find it highly suspicious."

Jenkins called to his colleague. "Greenfield, Carter said that they can leave for tea and breakfast, one or two at a time. It's on the sideboard in the dining room. She wants you to stand in the doorway and observe."

"Understood, sir."

"A few more people will be coming. I'll leave you to it." Jenkins left.

The remaining detective clicked his pen and walked over to Mimi. "Ma'am? You lost an evening bag? Your name?"

"I already went through this." She sighed. "Yes, I did. Mrs. Mimi York. My heart medication, digitalis, is in the bag. I desperately need to take it soon."

Greenfield wrote a note on his pad. "Ms. York, I heard DS Jenkins telling you—"

"It's Mrs. York."

"My apologies, *Mrs.* York. I agree with the DS that it's probably close by. We'll find it in short order. Please try to recall the last time you remember holding the purse. Can you tell me what the bag looks like?"

"I brought it into my room when I retired for the night." Mimi held her left temple. "It's a black bag with black-and-charcoal gray beadwork, and it has a silver clasp."

"Which room were you in when you last took the medication?" Greenfield scribbled on his pad.

Von Pickle chuckled. "Mimi, sweetheart, misplaced an evening bag? Have you been hanging around Miss Haywood? I do hope her unfortunate habit isn't contagious."

Cassandra glared. *He must be more observant than I give him credit for.*

Mimi's chair faced away from Von Pickle. "Not left somewhere. Stolen."

Cassandra went to the sickly woman. "Mimi, how are you feeling?"

"I'm so sorry about your aunt." Mimi grasped her hand. "You don't know how worried I've been about you. This is an awful way to start the new year. I'm utterly beside myself. We also have a purse thief in our midst, too."

"What did the detectives tell you?" asked Cassandra.

"They said not to worry, and it'll turn up soon. Carter won't suffer the consequences of missing a dose. Did you see my evening bag?"

Cassandra released Mimi's hand. "I remember your purse dangling from your wrist right before you went up to the second floor."

"I knew I had it then!" Mimi made a fist. "The DCI is convinced I'm mistaken. Dearest, I knew you could assist me." She stood and grabbed Cassandra around the neck in a tight hug.

She patted the woman's back in a light embrace. "I need to breathe, Mimi."

Mimi released her hold. "So sorry. Last night proved to be horrendous, and this morning, the nightmare continues."

Baron Von Pickle jeered. "Emotion, Mimi. Keep it in check. Hamish might be convinced you're rational, but not me. I'm smarter than him." He swaggered across the room to the ladies.

"This might be hard to believe, Rupert, but I don't care what you think." Mimi waved off the baron like an annoying fly. "If I wanted your opinion, I would check my temperature to make sure I wasn't feverish and out of my mind."

"What's this? The demure, candy-sickening sweet Mrs. York has a forked tongue? Does Hamish know this, or does your marriage flourish on deceit? I heard about his face lift. Ha. He lambastes my cheese as fake, and all the while, he has a fake *face*." The baron snickered.

Mimi faced the arrogant man. "My medication is missing, and I feel ill. I'm not wasting precious breath bantering with a reptile like you. Pardon me." She crossed the room to the windows.

"I know it's easier for you to give up, like your husband, right?" declared Von Pickle, pointing a finger in Mimi's direction.

Cassandra stepped in front of Von Pickle. "Enough."

The baron redirected his venom. "Protector of the weak and

innocent, Miss Haywood? Fancy yourself a hero, perhaps? I watched you last night, always smoothing over your aunt's indiscretions. Is that how you crawled your way to the top of the company? Most people earn leadership by knowing the business."

"Here, here," said Robin.

Von Pickle sprawled out into a leather chair again. "Thank you. You see, I'm not the only one who knows you don't deserve the position, Miss Haywood. Sometimes a challenge is preferred, but I'll take this to start the new year off right."

Greenfield interrupted, pointing to the doorway. "Miss Haywood, why don't you go out to the dining room to pour yourself a cup of tea and perhaps take some breakfast? When you return with your food, I can let one or two more do the same."

"Thank you, Detective Constable. Capital idea." Cassandra thought for a moment. "May Mr. Fartworthy come with me? I want to make sure the buffet is set properly. If it's not, he can quickly rectify the situation." Cassandra twisted one end of her lilac scarf from around her neck.

Greenfield smiled. "That would be fine."

Fartworthy's long legs enabled him to reach the entrance first. He opened the door and held it. When Cassandra met up with him, she raised one side of her mouth, unseen by the company in the library.

He touched the side of his glasses and whispered, "I suspect this is about something besides breakfast, Miss Haywood?"

"Yes," Cassandra muttered and smirked. *Sometimes I wonder if Mr. Fartworthy is a mind reader.*

Chapter Twelve

Cassandra and Mr. Fartworthy walked silently into the noisy dining room. The grand space still housed detectives and guests in interviews.

When they were out of earshot of Greenfield, or anyone else, Cassandra inquired, "Was my aunt alive when you found her? Any chance she could've been saved?"

He didn't make eye contact. "No, ma'am. She'd been deceased several hours. There's nothing you or I could've done."

The pair headed to the sideboard buffet against the wall, halfway across the room. Words tumbled out of Cassandra's mouth like a waterfall. "Someone must know what happened. There are so many people the detectives still need to speak with. Is there enough food on the buffet for everyone? Greenfield told me everything when they were examining her body."

"Everything?" Fartworthy's eyes grew wide.

"Yes, blood and all. I don't think I can take breakfast. I'm also glad to be out of the library and away from Von Pickle." Cassandra tugged on the lilac scarf around her neck.

"I'm terribly sorry. Detectives aren't supposed to do that to the family. They always bungle things. Why would Greenfield tell you that?"

"It's my fault. I pressured him for more facts, and he's a brand-new detective. I overheard him mention his new status during the end of my interview."

"Excellent job remembering information. It's imperative to pay close attention to any conversations going on around you today." When they approached the sideboard buffet, Fartworthy gently commanded, "Miss Haywood, don't turn around. DC Greenfield is watching us closely. Keep your back to the library door."

"Whatever for?"

"Don't look at me. Study the table, open things up, and gesture like you're giving orders."

Cassandra followed his instructions. "Why are you talking like your mouth is wired shut?" She pointed to the scones and examined the contents of the marmalade container.

"If Greenfield has been trained properly, he should be well-versed in reading lips, and I *don't* want him to read mine. If you keep your back to him, he can't see your mouth. Observe. No one else in this room is paying any attention to us. They have too many people to question."

"What are you saying?" Cassandra noted Fartworthy made a correct assessment.

His hands deftly straightened a renegade corner of the starched, white, linen tablecloth. "I overheard the DCI suspects some haven't been 100 percent honest in their statements. Additionally, I read her lips when I waited to be questioned. She has a suspect in Lady Lemington's death in mind, and this may not have been an accident. She's concluded there's more to this story than a simple fall."

Cassandra's knees turned to gelatin, and she steadied herself with her hands resting on the sideboard. "Who does she think knows something more?" Her weight on the tabletop caused the teacups to jingle together.

"Steady, ma'am. You'll be all right." Keeping his eyes on her, he shifted some of the brigade of teacups and matching saucers. "Move items on the table. Point to the carafes and look inside. I don't know. She didn't reveal that information. Carter is the only one, as far as I can tell, who believes events leading to your aunt's demise aren't what they seem. Her subordinates are only appeasing her. DS Jenkins, who is close to retirement, seems to have a problem answering to a younger, superior detective and believes an in-depth inquiry will be a complete waste of time. He mentioned the last bit out of Carter's earshot. On the other hand, I fear the DCI might be correct. I'm privy to many secrets contained within these walls. We owe it to Lady Lemington to find out what happened."

"And then tell the investigation team?" Cassandra shifted the silver tray of fruit tarts.

"No, ma'am. Please refrain from updating them with any information until you talk to me."

Cassandra's hands froze on the tray. "Don't we want to help them discover the facts?"

"When detectives get an idea in their cranium about the sequence of events at a scene, they sometimes get stuck in the rut of those impressions. I . . . well, we . . . can root out the truth. Sloppy investigation methods rarely yield that."

"You act as if you know them." Cassandra resumed rearranging tarts.

"Not this group personally." Fartworthy set aside several soiled teacups. "I know the mentality and methods of a pack of detectives. They also don't take kindly to others doing their job. No, it's best for us to observe and gather whatever we can. If we come to the same conclusion, then we know we did right by your aunt. Did you notice anything else when you were in the parlor?"

"The DCI remarked there are interviews taking place in the kitchen, too. Have you been there yet to see or hear anything?" She straightened a line of teaspoons with slow precision.

"Not since the detectives arrived and I retrieved you from your room." He continued to organize the teacups into perfect lines. "The team has everyone under close watch before they take their statements. After the interviews, the detectives, except for Carter, will be more relaxed about conversations and movements. Maybe I can get downstairs to assess the situation later."

Cassandra flipped up the lid of a hot water carafe and peered inside. "Do you know something more?"

"About her death, no." He finished fine-tuning the placement of the teacups. "Alas, I do have something to tell you. A secret I must disclose. You must trust me."

Cassandra snapped the lid shut and stared at him.

"Miss Haywood, please keep your attention on the table. It's imperative." He paused and smoothed the tablecloth again. "I'm not just a butler."

She arranged the tea bags in the shallow, wooden box that resided in front of the carafes. "What are you?" she whispered.

Fartworthy lifted the lid of the Marmite jar. "I'm a private investigator, ma'am, hired by your aunt for several jobs. The most recent assignment included trying to discover the leak of information that gave other cheese companies an advantage."

"You're an amazing head butler. How—"

"How can I fake this job? I'm not a fraud. I'm a butler *and* a PI. It's an extremely specific skill set." He rearranged the remaining scones on the platter to form an artistic pyramid. "Please close your mouth, Miss Haywood. Someone will surely notice."

"You're the 'source' Aunt Lily talked about when we discussed how she got information?" Cassandra rearranged the same three tea-bags in the box.

"Correct. My deepest apologies you didn't know sooner. Lady Lemington didn't want to burden you with my secret." Fartworthy moved a tray of tarts. "You asked your aunt last night why she argued with or angered the guests. She did it deliberately, and I participated in the plan."

"I don't understand." She ran her fingertips across the table-cloth.

"Let me explain. Your aunt instigated those incidents, and I circled and served those guests. The offended partygoers griped and complained about Lady Lemington in the aftermath. When people are angry or upset, they let their guard down. Information spills forth easily." Fartworthy poured the hot water into a cup. "No one notices the butler."

Cassandra stared at the torrid water tumbling into the cup. "Did it work? Did you find out anything last night?"

Mr. Fartworthy handed her the drink. "Many discussions. Numerous pieces of undisclosed imprudence revealed. The source of the leak, unfortunately, never emerged. Your aunt was sorely disappointed."

Cassandra tore open a peach tea packet and slowly plunged the bag repeatedly into the cup. "It was on purpose."

"All calculated, Miss Haywood. We believed we were close to uncovering the identity of the mole. Regrettably, it was not to be."

"A wasted effort, and she ruined the party for many. And me." Cassandra picked up the delicate, bone china teacup and blew across the surface of the steaming beverage.

"Don't be too harsh. Information gathered is always valuable. Sometimes things need to be discovered out of order." Fartworthy removed the expended wrapper from the tea bag and swept it into the rubbish container that resided on the floor beside the table. "Please don't fault your aunt for her extreme behavior last night. With the company turned around and currently profitable, she desired to protect it from predators. I agree her methods could be construed as callous." He opened the lid to the honeypot.

Cassandra scooped a teaspoon of white sugar into her fruity, dark-amber drink and slowly stirred. "Her actions last night aggravated me. How was I to know that would be the last time I would ever see her?" Her breath hitched. "We argued. No, rather, I was . . . thorny and obstinate. The guilt I carry over my words of irritation to her all night is—" Cassandra looked up, her voiced jagged. "And now she's gone, just like that, and I can't talk to her. It feels like someone has their bootheel pressing on my upper chest. The pressure is so incessant, there are moments I can't catch my breath." She took a tentative sip of hot tea. "To try to talk civilly and say I'm fine makes the weight far worse and almost unbearable." The rising lump in her throat fought to be unleashed.

Fartworthy stopped shifting a silver tray on the table and spoke normally for the first time since they left the library. He stared at Cassandra. "Grief, ma'am. What you describe is your body experiencing profound anguish. Please ease up on yourself. Adding guilt over your natural reactions from last night won't help you. Eventually, you'll get used to carrying that disbelief of your sudden loss around with you. One day, that bootheel feeling will disappear. It won't mean you miss her any less or your intense sorrow doesn't exist anymore. It becomes your new normal."

Cassandra shut her eyes for a moment. She then looked up at Fartworthy with a tear teetering on her lower eyelid. "How can you be so . . . so sure?" Her voice cracked.

"Trust me. I've been there. I know." Fartworthy gave a small, sympathetic smile.

A deep voice behind them spoke. "You know what?"

Cassandra and Fartworthy turned away from the sideboard. Detective Sergeant Jenkins stopped near the food. He was escorting

Jack Birch and Alexander Spooner. Jenkins repeated, "Do you know anything more about the investigation?"

Fartworthy responded, "I know we need to refresh some things on the table. There are many to feed this morning."

"Yes." Cassandra whisked the renegade tear away with a flick of her hand. She took the verbal cue from the head butler. "The carafes for the coffee and hot water for tea are nearly empty. They need to be refilled soon before people get sore from missing their morning beverages. My aunt would be appalled if we let the tea and food run out." She smiled.

Jenkins cleared his throat. "Oh yes, of course. I'm sure your aunt would be proud. It's a nice spread." He scanned the fare.

Mr. Birch spoke, not looking at Cassandra. "It's a terrible shock to wake up to such news. I'm sorry for your loss, Miss Haywood. Changes everything, doesn't it?"

"It does, and it doesn't. You're still employed for the time being, sir." Cassandra stared at the head gardener. *How can I even make that statement?*

Mr. Birch raised his eyes to meet Cassandra's. "Are you sure?"

"Nothing will be altered until everything is sorted." She took a sip of her tea.

Alexander clasped his hands together. "Quite a day, Miss Haywood."

Cassandra swallowed. "Certainly unforeseen, Mr. Spooner."

"The ice storm undoubtedly changed things up. I never expected to slumber in this lovely manor. Thank you for your hospitality." He gestured to the sideboard. "Wow. This is amazing."

"We prepared breakfast for overnight guests, but not for the law enforcement team here this morning." Cassandra peeked at Fartworthy. *I have an idea.* "Sergeant? I know we're supposed to remain in the library, but may Mr. Fartworthy go to the kitchen to refill the hot water and replenish the scones? Enough food and beverage for all is wanting."

Jenkins lifted the lid to one of the carafes and peered inside. He did the same to the second and the third containers. "Deprive the English populace of their morning tea and pastry? Never. Feel free, Fartworthy. I fancy another cuppa myself."

"Thank you, sir. Miss Haywood? Is there anything else you see that needs attention?" asked the head butler.

"The marmalade and sugar both need a refill. There are also soiled teacups around the room. You might need to make several trips." Cassandra inhaled deeply.

"Yes, ma'am," replied Fartworthy with a small grin, glancing at the others and then at Cassandra. He collected the used teacups near the sideboard and put them on an empty silver tray.

"Whatever it takes." Jenkins, still looking at the table, reached for a plate and a baked breakfast treat. He tasted the pastry. "These scones are delicious. Is there cheese inside?"

"Yes, there is—Stilton. Bit of a bite to wake one up. There are also plain ones on the left." Cassandra took a sip of her tea. "Glad you like it."

Alexander moved to the buffet. "Bleu cheese in a scone? May I? I love mold. Whole reason I got into pharmaceutical work." He grabbed the cheese-filled selection before Jenkins gave him permission. Mr. Spooner took a giant bite, closed his eyes, and sighed. "Oh, my," he said with a mouthful of cheese and pastry. "These are exquisite. Is this Lemington Cheese?" A few small crumbs of beige scone popped out onto his cobalt shirt and his undone tie.

Cassandra grimaced. "Thank you, Mr. Spooner. It is. This is one of our new ways to sell cheese. We've come up with innovative recipes and have them on our revamped company website. Each cheese package has a QR code that leads you to recipes containing the type that was purchased. This way, customers can experiment with new flavors with suggestions right at their fingertips. Having the cheese and new recipes at the party, and for overnight guests, seemed to be a good idea for promotion."

"Your ideas, Miss Haywood?" Alexander took another large piece into his mouth.

"To have them at the party or the QR code link? Yes, to both. It's a brand-new initiative we launched in November. I can't take credit for the scone recipe. Mrs. Forest is the genius behind that masterpiece." Cassandra sipped her tea.

Jenkins removed an apple from the fruit bowl, tossed it playfully into the air, and caught the red orb in the other hand. "You gentlemen make your breakfast selections before we go to the library." Glancing at Alexander, still chomping on his scone with pastry remnants cascading down his shirt, the sergeant frowned. "Sir, why don't you fetch a plate?"

"Good idea." Alexander selected a dish, several more scones, a banana, and a tart.

"Mr. Birch? Going to have anything?" Jenkins polished the piece of fruit on his shirt.

"Not hungry," replied the gruff head gardener.

Jenkins turned to Cassandra. "I'll take you back, too. Do you need anything else?"

Answers. A shoulder to weep on. My aunt alive and well. The swarm of detectives out of the manor immediately. Peace. Cassandra smiled. "I'm fine." She rubbed the base of her neck in a futile attempt to disperse the enormous heaviness pressing down.

Chapter Thirteen

DS Jenkins escorted Cassandra, Alexander, and Jack to the library. The quartet met Owen coming from the opposite direction with another detective.

DC Baker, a young, redheaded woman, addressed Jenkins. "Sergeant, DCI Carter is looking for you. She requires your immediate presence."

"Righto. Is this gentleman to go in here?" Jenkins opened the library door.

"Yes, sir." Turning to Owen, Baker pointed to the room. "Here you go. I don't think you'll have to wait long."

"Thank you kindly, ma'am. Been waitin' an age in the other room." Owen tipped his head to Cassandra. She smiled at the musician.

"Greenfield?" Jenkins called into the open doorway. "Baker, wait a moment."

"Yes, sir?" came the voice and footsteps belonging to the DC in the library.

"How many people do you currently have in there?" asked Jenkins.

Greenfield appeared at the entrance. "I have three people in here, sir."

"Fine. DC Baker will escort those who've been there awhile to get breakfast. Miss Haywood and these two gents have already been. The butler chap is tending to refills and will return in short order." Jenkins turned to Baker. "After they select their food, you need to get them right back. By the way, the scones are phenomenal. You must try them. Excuse me. Got to dash." He took a bite of his scarlet apple before walking to the parlor.

"Right, then." Turning, Greenfield called into the room, "All who have been in here, please come to the doorway. You can get your breakfast." He looked at Cassandra. "How's your tea?"

"Fine, thank you."

"Everything all right for the food?" pressed Greenfield.

"Replenishing some items is necessary. Thank you." She smiled. *And to send Mr. Fartworthy to eavesdrop downstairs.*

Jack Birch and Cassandra slid by Greenfield into the library. As they walked in, Robin, Mimi, and Von Pickle queued up to leave.

Robin and Mimi said nothing to the incoming group. Von Pickle looked at Mr. Birch's empty hands and Cassandra's cup of tea. He sneered. "I do hope there's more than tea and air being served."

Cassandra rolled her eyes. "You'll be satisfied." She stared over her shoulder at him.

"Huh," he muttered. "I doubt that." Von Pickle watched Alexander's crumb-coated mouth and stuffed plate as the two men passed each other. Alexander, oblivious of Von Pickle's disdain, had his attention on the departing redheaded female detective.

"Please step in, sir." Greenfield motioned to Alexander.

"Of course," replied the young man.

Cassandra spoke to Greenfield as he shut the door behind those who had left. "Glad to be rid of some, I imagine?"

Greenfield gave a side nod and a smile.

Jack Birch made a beeline to the white-and-red flower

arrangement on a small table situated on the room's far side. He rearranged some blossoms in the tall, Waterford crystal vase.

Cassandra walked over to the gardener. "The hothouse flowers are gorgeous. You coax such magnificent blooms in the dead of winter. How do you succeed year after year?"

Mr. Birch pinched a slightly dry leaf off a stem. "Gobs of planning, first-rate manure, and a bit of luck." He shifted a white rose to the front of the botanical array. "She liked the ones I grew, especially the white. They were her beloved," he murmured as he caressed the rose petal between his thumb and forefinger.

"White flowers were her favorite?" asked Cassandra.

Jack tilted his head as he looked at her. "You didn't know that?"

"No," whispered Cassandra, staring at the flowers. "I never inquired or noticed."

"She adored white roses, magnolias, freesia, and, of course, her namesake, the lily. Didn't you detect a disproportionate number of flowers devoid of color in the hothouse and growing on the grounds in the spring? I'm always on the lookout for white varieties. I added seasonal colors, but her favorite was always present." Mr. Birch smiled. "The bouquets I brought to her bedroom every evening were mostly shades of white. I'm going to miss making those up." He sniffed.

Cassandra took a step closer. "Did you truly love my aunt?"

Jack's voice cracked. "It doesn't matter now, does it?" He cleared his throat. "Excuse me, Miss Haywood." He wiped near his left eye with the back of his hand and walked away.

I've never seen him this emotional, poor man. She placed her empty teacup and saucer on the flower table. *He did love her. I'm sure of it. I'm not the only one who will miss Aunt Lily.* Cassandra breathed in deeply. *Lily. White flowers.* She untied the lilac scarf from around her neck and played with the fabric. *I never knew that.*

Owen walked over, his mouth open in amazement. "I never seen this many books outside a public library in me life! In your own 'ome? Must be thousands."

"A few." Cassandra unwound and rewound the scarf, around her hand as if it were an Egyptian mummy. *I don't want to make small talk. Be kind, Cassandra. Let others speak.*

Owen continued. "Me mum would luv to be 'ere. She reads loads of 'em novels since she don't get around too good. I'm not much of a novel buff meself. I read some so I can talk to Mum about 'em. Too emotional and unrealistic, and the writers of 'em things are *completely* daft. Music is me love. It moves faster."

"Music is emotional, too." Cassandra grinned.

"Not in the same way, ma'am," responded Owen. He dragged his fingers along the shelf and stopped at a small, ceramic figurine of a peacock sitting on a branch. He ran his middle finger down and over the garish, painted tail feathers. "Music fills life with color, not cryin'." He took the petite fowl statuette off the shelf and turned it over. "Hmm. 'Occupied Japan'," he read. "That's interestin'. Mum likes 'em collectibles."

"Reading can fill life with color, too." Cassandra scanned the shelves. "There are more than novels in here. We have many books on music. Actually, those are right here." She pointed at a section behind the flower table.

"Well, that's more like it." Owen put the statuette back on the shelf and moved over to read the book spines aloud. *"Life of Beethoven, Chopin and His Homeland* . . . ah . . . Bach. You got 'em masters. What a collection, Miss 'aywood."

Cassandra draped her lavender scarf over her arm. "I've been here for years and not made a significant dent in what I wish to read from this library. I hope you find something to capture your attention, Mr. Savage."

"Thank you kindly, ma'am. I'll be busy for 'ours."

She left the musician to explore the books and walked across the room. *I want to be alone for five minutes.*

The door opened again as Flora Fairchild rushed into the library. She spied Cassandra and hastened to her. "Miss Haywood." The head housekeeper's eyes and nose were swollen a dark pink. "What a sorry mess this is. What ever shall we do?" She flung her arms around Cassandra, who returned the intense embrace.

"Wait and see what the detectives come up with." Cassandra pulled away and held Flora at arm's length. "Are you all right?"

"No." Flora sniffed and dabbed her eyes with a lace-edged handkerchief gripped tight in her hand. "This is so unreal. It can't be true, but I saw her and I still refuse to believe it."

"You saw her?" whispered Cassandra.

Nodding, Flora blew her nose into the vintage cloth. "Mr. Fartworthy woke me and gave me the news. I insisted on going to see her in the lavatory before we called the constables. He warned me not to look, but I wouldn't take no for an answer. I should've listened. I can't get the image out of my mind." She shut her eyes. "Death follows me."

"What are you talking about?" Cassandra put her hand on the sobbing woman's back. Cassandra fought a lump in her throat. *Hold it together.*

Through her tears, Flora continued. "I watched two friends die and caused the death of another. Now this." Miss Fairchild looked at the ceiling. "I'm paying for my sins."

Greenfield called from across the room, "Ma'am? Is there something you should tell me about this case? Do you have any information at all?"

In an instant, Miss Fairchild ceased weeping, and her stare could have iced running water. "I did *not* kill her, if that is what you're implying, sir. She was my employer, and she gave me a chance at a new life when others would not. I'll forever be grateful to her." She turned to Cassandra. "Please tell me. Am I still employed?"

"Yes, of course you are." Cassandra guided Flora to a leather chair. "Why don't you sit down." *Please stop crying. I can't hold back my tears if you keep at it.*

The sniffling woman shook her head. "I'm too worked up to sit. I can't believe anyone would think I would have something to do with her death."

The detective continued. "I'm asking if you have anything that could help solve this case. I didn't mean to imply you were responsible for the passing of Lady Lemington. My apologies."

Flora blew her nose again and shut her eyes. The door opened and Hamish entered.

Greenfield greeted the newcomer. "Sir, please come in. You'll be in here until the DCI is satisfied with everyone's interviews."

Hamish glanced at his Swiss watch. "How long is this going to take?" The two men then continued their discussion quietly.

Flora looked up and gasped. "Oh, my giddy aunt! He's here, and I look like a half-sucked mango. Hide me!" She ducked behind Cassandra like a shy child scooting behind her mother.

"Miss Fairchild, what's gotten into you?" Cassandra spun around to face the suddenly bashful housekeeper.

The head housekeeper's eyes filled with panic. "I made a fool out of myself last night asking him for an autograph. He's a celebrity. I'm mortified."

"Miss Haywood!" Hamish called as he crossed the room. Cassandra turned around to face the gentleman at the sound of her name.

Flora gripped the back of her employer's cream-colored blouse. "No! He's heading this way!"

Cassandra hissed. "Hush. You'll be fine. You're acting ridiculous." She smiled at the fast-approaching man.

"How are you faring?" Hamish extended his hands to take up Cassandra's. "My deepest condolences, my dear. This is all dreadful business."

"Indeed it is, sir." Cassandra struggled to remain unruffled. The woman behind her continued to use her as a human shield.

Hamish peered around and grinned. "Cheers. I remember you from last night."

Flora reluctantly stepped out and curtsied. She wiped her eyes, dusted off the front of her apron, and flattened the sides of her tight, blonde bun. "Mr. York," she said, not lifting her gaze from the floor.

Hamish placed a hand on his chest. "Miss, I must apologize for my behavior last night. I was terribly rude to ignore your reasonable request. I was a bit stressed. I don't know what I was thinking. Are you and I good this morning?"

A nervous laugh escaped Flora's lips as she looked at the man. "A-a-absolutely." She shifted in her spot, clutching her handkerchief. "It wasn't a problem to ask for an autograph, then?"

Hamish flashed his wide, perfect smile. "Not at all. If you still want me to sign, I'll be happy to oblige." The sides of his eyes crinkled.

A shy grin spread across the head housekeeper's forty-five-year-old face. "Thank you. It's an honor to meet you, sir."

"I know the calendars were a special edition in Paris for a short time a few years ago. A bit of a retro '80s thing. Were you visiting or living there at the time?" Hamish took a step closer to Flora, and his voice dropped an octave. "I love Paris and everything about my adopted city. *Such* amazing cheese everywhere. My home away from home."

Flora's smile vaporized.

Sensing her friend's discomfort, Cassandra intervened. "You really were a model?"

Hamish's blue eyes twinkled. "Yes, an embarrassing yet profitable time in my life. I've kept it secret for so long and, surprisingly, when revealed last night, it came as an enormous relief." He smiled at Flora. "Thank you for that."

"Why would you keep it confidential?" Cassandra gave a sidelong look at the housekeeper who stared, dumbstruck, at Hamish.

"Do you think anyone in the business world would take me seriously knowing I was a former model?" He smirked. "I did enjoy my time in that profession, but there's a limited shelf life. When the contracts dried up, I took my money and love of Parisian cheese back to England and created Rosewood Cheese Company, makers of fine, artisan French cheeses. Ha! I sound like a press release."

The library door clicked open, alerting everyone. Jenkins stuck his head in. "Carter wants to see Mr. York again about the medication. Is he still here?"

DC Greenfield called across the room, "Mr. York, you're wanted. It has to do with your wife's pills."

Hamish gave another thousand-watt smile. "Excuse me, ladies." Without waiting for a response, he left the room.

Flora found her voice. "My goodness!" She held her arms together. "I can't believe he's so nice! I can't believe I'm acting like a schoolgirl. My hands are still shaking. Look." She held out her hands, which moved like branches in a stiff breeze.

Cassandra chuckled. "I've never seen you like this. You're a fan."

"Paris doesn't have such glowing memories for me as it does for Mr. March . . . I mean, Mr. York." Flora looked at the floor, sadness spreading like a tsunami. She whispered, "Miss Haywood, I need to talk to you about my past without the DC listening. It's vital they don't know."

Cassandra moved closer. "Does it have anything to do with Paris?"

Flora nodded.

Jenkins stuck his head into the doorway again. "Greenfield, come here, please, and Carter wants Mr. Birch to clarify something."

Greenfield and Birch stepped out of the room.

Flora whispered, "Perfect. I can tell you now. I have much to share, but I'm afraid you'll never view me the same way again."

"What is it? You can tell me anything." Cassandra touched Flora's elbow. "My high regard for you won't change."

Flora took a deep breath. "I left England years ago in haste for an immature reason. The move to Paris seemed like a good idea at the time. The friends who traveled with me seemed trustworthy. Unfortunately, the druggie chums they eventually made while we were in France ultimately became my druggie mates. Mind-altering substances became a new way to escape from myself. I started off light. It took the edge off, and I didn't hate myself for a few hours a day."

"Oh, my. Go on."

"It was a pleasant feeling my brain hadn't known for years." Flora wiped her eyes with her handkerchief. "The hard stuff crept in slowly, and I don't know when it became a problem. I thought I could handle it and stop anytime. I was so, so wrong. I lost a great deal of weight, and my hair even fell out. I was miserable."

"How and when did you come back to England?"

"It became progressively harder to support my monstrous habit. I made some bad decisions. After ignoring signs to quit, I was forced to do so in a most painful way. When I became clean, a non-drug-taking friend convinced me to return to my home country. I arrived, searching for work, and was told they were hiring people here at the manor. Lady Lemington had recently fired the whole staff."

"Did she know your history?" asked Cassandra.

"Yes, *everything*. I figured being clean required me to be up front and honest. A scary place to be since I spent many years hiding what I was—a drug addict. She hired me first, maybe Mr. Birch was, I believe. I don't know. That time is a bit fuzzy for me. Anyway, she suggested I become the head housekeeper to take some control in my life. Also, I'd be too busy for drug use. When she hired the rest of the staff, Lady Lemington implied I'd been here for some time. I had their respect since no one knew my past. She was right. This job is what I needed to turn my life around."

"You always pleased her with your hard work, and she told me on several occasions." Cassandra put her hand on her own forehead. "My aunt was more compassionate than I gave her credit for."

"Lady Lemington saved me from myself. She was a stern taskmaster, but I learned to work under those conditions. I'm safe, have built a new life here, and am starting to like myself again. Running this household has given me a real purpose. Her death is dredging up emotions I had shoved away with my endless to-do lists. I'm terrified."

"You're safe here." Cassandra moved closer. "No one will hurt you."

"There are constables and detectives everywhere, and I'm a nervous wreck. I don't want them to find out about my past. If they discover I was arrested twice for petty drug possession and several times for shoplifting, they'll be after me. I only did that to pay for my drug habit. I haven't done anything of the sort since."

A voice from behind the housekeeper spoke. "I'm so sorry you went through that, Miss Fairchild."

Flora spun around. "You listened? How much did you hear?"

"I heard it all," replied Alexander in a soft voice. "Please forgive my eavesdropping. I know illegal drugs are a one-way ticket to misery. I'm so happy you're released from its demonic grasp."

Cassandra turned to Mr. Spooner and scolded. "Why on earth were you listening to our conversation? You can't tell anyone what you heard."

"I know. I'm sorry. I promise I won't." Alexander wrung his hands and moved closer. He continued to speak quietly. "You see, I heard a little of what you were saying, and I kept listening. I have a personal connection with addiction." Alexander shuffled his feet side to side. "My older brother died of a drug overdose." He looked at Flora. "I'm glad you didn't end up like him. We were the best of mates and did everything together when I wasn't at school. He was my only sibling and he wanted to stop, but couldn't." He whispered, "Not even for me."

Flora and Cassandra exchanged sympathetic glances. Flora took a step toward the young man. "I'm so sorry, Alexander. Was this recent?"

"A few years ago, but I still can't believe he's gone."

"And you work in the drug industry," added Cassandra.

"That's different. I help people become healthy. Look at Lady Lemington. When she hurt her back, she was miserable. After she had the prescription to help her, she improved. Street drugs destroy people and their families. I want no part of that." Alexander hung his head.

"Oh, Alexander," said Cassandra.

Flora gave him an all-encompassing, sisterly hug. Cassandra watched the young man melt into her friend's arms. *He looks as if he hasn't been hugged in a long time. Poor boy.*

When the extended, atypical, English embrace ended, he pulled away and smiled at Flora. "Thank you for that. It has been ages since anyone has hugged me."

Called it.

Greenfield opened the door and announced, "May I have your attention, ladies and gentlemen? DCI Carter would like to see everyone in the parlor."

Without a word, Flora touched the young man's shoulders to guide him, and they walked to the doorway. Cassandra noticed Owen engrossed in a book titled, *The History of Polka Music*. "Mr. Savage?"

"Hmm?" The guitar player looked up.

"They want us to leave here." Cassandra motioned for him to follow. "You can look at that book later."

"Jolly good. Fascinatin' stuff, ma'am." Owen snapped the leather-bound tome shut and slid it back into place on the shelf, next to the ceramic peacock.

Cassandra turned around and walked to the front of the room. Owen jogged up next to her. "Mum really wants me 'ome. She takes many kinds of pills and needs to be reminded when to 'ave 'em. Even when I call, she forgets."

"Oh?"

"It's a tricky business, but I've been 'elpin' with that for years. Some meds you can't take with food, some you 'ave with a bite of somethin', and she can never keep it straight. When she takes too much at one time, it causes loads of problems. Where are we goin'?"

"They want us in the parlor. Perhaps they're wrapping up their investigation, and you could go home soon. Why don't you catch up with the others?" urged Cassandra.

The long-legged musician nodded and sprinted out of the room.

Cassandra took her time leaving the library. Through the open door, she could see Greenfield pointing Owen to the group. *I hope they have figured out what happened. I'm weary of revelations, discussions, and secrets.*

She tightened the ivory scarf knot under her ear and strode out to join the others.

Chapter Fourteen

The crowd from the library stood like a gaggle of tourists waiting for a tour guide at a museum. Hamish York rejoined the group.

"Mr. York? Why are you still here?" asked Cassandra. "I thought you were looking for your wife's medication."

The left corner of his mouth rose. "She didn't want my assistance. The DCI was unhappy with her team's lack of progress on the search and accompanied Mimi. They decided to explore downstairs, where we never even set foot last night. Maybe a fresh set of eyes will discover the blasted purse."

Cassandra held the tails of the ivory head scarf. "I told your wife I remember it being on her wrist when she went upstairs for the evening. I hope that helps her find it in short order."

"Perhaps." Hamish turned to the group. "Did any of you see a small, beaded purse sometime last night or today? Mrs. York's medication is in there, and it's imperative to have it returned."

"Was it a big, leather one?" asked Owen. "Me mum has 'em purses that look like suitcases. Well, she used to, when she would go out."

"No, it's an evening purse. Silly little thing one could stick in a pocket. It can only hold a bottle of pills, a tissue, a few coins, and her lipstick. Seems like a waste of time to carry." Hamish fluffed the front of his hair.

Members of the group shook their heads and remained silent.

Owen chuckled. "Glad I'm not a lady to remember all 'em things they lug. I keep me wallet in me back pocket. All I need is the guitar case, and I don't go anywhere without that."

Baron Rupert Von Pickle and Robin Turner stood with full plates of food.

Von Pickle chomped on a tart. "We're moving to a new location? Good. I have things to do."

Cassandra's eyes narrowed. "You've said that." *I'm done being nice.*

"Well, it's true. I don't have time for standing around, all boo-hoo. Someone has died. Figure it out, bag the body, and get on with it." Von Pickle took a drink from his tea, making a loud, slurping noise. A gasp from some caused him to look up. "What?"

Hamish glanced at Cassandra. "You're being overly cruel, Rupert. Even for you."

"Zip it, York. Don't act like you're not thinking the same. I'm man enough to say it out loud." The baron blew across his hot tea.

"A true man is never abusive," replied Hamish.

"A true man is never a liar," sneered Von Pickle. "Liars are cowardly, like you. Shall the wizard pin a medal on you? Want to be King of the Forest?"

Greenfield held up a hand. "Enough, gentlemen. It has been a long morning for everyone. We're wrapping up the first round of questioning, and on behalf of the department, I'd like to thank all of you for your patience."

"First round?" asked Jack Birch. "Aren't you chaps almost done?"

"That depends, sir. Sorting out last night's timeline of events will reveal one of two things. If it was indeed an accident, you may leave when road conditions improve." Greenfield paused. "If that isn't the case, more questioning will be necessary, and the DCI will determine who must be retained and who can leave."

"We could be here longer if she suspects we know something?" asked Robin Turner. "Not everyone would stay?"

"Exactly. Prepare yourselves for that possibility." DC Greenfield spread his hands wide.

DC Baker came in and motioned. "Please come this way."

As they passed the female detective, Alexander smiled. "Hello there, and Happy New Year. Did you have a pleasant evening last night? Perhaps we could go get a coffee when all of this is done?"

"Sir, we're conducting an investigation." Baker circled her finger around in the air.

"I know," replied the clueless man.

The redheaded detective pointed to the next room. "Sir, please follow the others. I had a nice evening, thank you. It would be inappropriate for me to do anything with you at this time."

"Yes. Brilliant. I understand. So, when all this wraps up, are you interested in coffee or perhaps a cup of tea? There is a lovely cafe in the village, not far from where I work. You're pretty."

Baker scrunched her nose. "Thank you for the compliment, but I'll be busy for the next few months."

"Doing what?" asked Alexander.

Cassandra and Flora exchanged a glance.

Flora touched his shoulder. "Alexander, the lady is telling you she's not interested."

Alexander whispered back, "Really?"

DC Baker mouthed a silent "thank you" to Flora and turned and walked into the next room.

"Yes," Flora instructed the oblivious, young man. "When a

woman tells you her life is hectic for the next few months without offering an explanation, she's trying to let you down gently."

"That's interesting. Nearly all the ladies I meet are busy." Alexander walked ahead.

Flora and Cassandra shook their heads and smiled as they entered the parlor.

When she observed the continued law enforcement presence, Cassandra's brief mirth ended. Another group of guests, finished with questioning, were waiting. Frederick Chamberlain, standing in that cluster, caught Cassandra's eye the moment she walked to the middle of the room.

The young man strode over, unease spread across his face. "Miss Haywood, are you all right? I'm so sorry about your aunt. She had such excellent taste in jewelry." He cringed. "Beg your pardon. That came out all wrong. I don't know what to say." They moved away from the rest of the pack.

"Thank you for your concern, Mr. Chamberlain. You're correct. She has lovely taste and always raves about your establishment." Cassandra unconsciously reached up and touched her aunt's Christmas present of the gold, pearl-drop earrings. "I'm not ready to believe she's gone." Cassandra looked down for a moment.

Frederick moved closer and whispered, "Miss Haywood . . . Cassandra. Is there something I can do? Anything at all?"

Cassandra swallowed hard, the ever-present lump in her throat growing larger by the moment. "I want to know the truth about what happened and hope the detectives will be more forthcoming in short order. All this mystery is driving me bonkers. Did you hear any information?"

"They questioned me about our conversation in the great hall last night. I mentioned we discussed her recent purchases." Frederick shifted in his spot. "The DCI had me look at the watch since she was wearing it when . . . she passed. It was broken."

"How?"

"I could tell the watch was hit once, on one side. Do you want me to continue? Isn't it too painful?" asked the jeweler.

"Please go on."

"The force that struck the timepiece could be from either hitting the floor when she fell." Frederick slipped into silence.

"Or?"

"Or she . . . um." The young man's green eyes focused on Cassandra.

"Or she what?" whispered Cassandra, moving closer to him. "Please, Frederick. I need to hear what you know."

He paused. "She might have blocked a blow."

"Someone may have hit her?"

"It's possible. It's one of two explanations."

"Struck her with what? Their hand or an object?" Cassandra gripped her scarf tail.

"I can't tell that. Maybe the detectives will figure that out. If she fell, the damage suggests she didn't catch herself and went down on her arm, flat. She could have passed out. A wristwatch of this fragility can yield similar results either way with the impact shattering the internal mechanisms. The glass face of the piece is undamaged. I'm sorry I don't know more."

Cassandra shut her eyes. "Aunt Lily, what transpired last night?" She opened her eyes. "The more I find out, the more questions I have."

Frederick reached over and tenderly held Cassandra's hand. "I'll help you any way I can."

His touch relaxed her throat, and the impending tears melted away for the moment. "Thank you. You can tell all that information from looking at a piece of jewelry? You're quite talented in your profession, sir." Cassandra gave his hand a gentle squeeze.

Frederick beamed. "Broken watches always tell a story." He tilted his head. "I wish this one didn't affect you. Maybe the detectives can clear out of here soon to leave you in peace." His eyes fixed on hers.

"It has been a day of constant questions, and I want to be left alone." She sighed.

"You wouldn't . . . always want to be alone, Cassandra, would you?" Frederick caressed the back of her hand.

Cassandra's quick, quiet gasp betrayed her feelings.

Before she answered with words, DCI Carter strode into the parlor with Mimi and Arabella. "What is going on in here?" demanded the head detective. Everyone looked to see who asked the question. Cassandra's and Carter's eyes locked. Cassandra released Frederick's hand as he stepped back.

Carter continued. "Greenfield, Baker. We separated individuals for a reason." She spoke to the two women beside her. "I'm sorry our search hasn't found your missing purse and pills, Mrs. York. They must be here somewhere. Thank you for volunteering to assist, Miss Dalton. You may return to the group now."

"You're welcome." Arabella rejoined the group, which didn't contain Cassandra.

"I need my heart medication—soon." Mimi sank into a nearby chair.

"I understand and will do the best I can to find it." Carter took several strides to the center of the room. "Mr. Chamberlain, I left you with Jenkins and not with the group from the library. Where is he?"

"I believe he stepped out for a moment to the dining room," replied Frederick.

"Please return to the other side next to Miss Dalton," Carter commanded.

Frederick complied, looking back at Cassandra for a moment.

"Greenfield, move the library crowd over here." DCI Carter motioned to Baker. "Bring the others over there." Carter pointed to two spots around sets of sofas.

Why is she focused on me? Cassandra dropped her gaze, moving with the others like a flock of sheep through a pasture. *Why did Arabella volunteer to search for anything? That's not like her.* She caught Bella's eye from across the room.

Arabella mouthed, "Are you all right?"

Cassandra shrugged her shoulders. *Carter is still looking at me. Maybe she has something to tell me.*

Jack, Alexander, Flora, Owen, Hamish, Robin, Von Pickle, and Cassandra were in Greenfield's group. Frederick, Mimi, and Arabella joined the piano player, Poppy, in the other cluster with DC Baker in charge. The photographer, Ruby Lightfoot, also present in the room, stood with them.

Jenkins, eating a cheese scone, sauntered back into the parlor with Roland Turner from the dining room. Carter's eyes fixed on her older subordinate. "You were supposed to be in here. Where were you?"

"Mr. Turner wandered off, and I found him entering the dining room. I thought perhaps he was heading to the breakfast buffet," replied the DS.

"Was he?" asked the DCI.

"No, ma'am."

"Mr. Turner, you were instructed to remain in the parlor." Carter pointed. "What were you doing?"

"I was looking for Mother. There she is." Roland walked to the group led by Greenfield. "Mother, how are you?" He held out his hands to reach for Robin. She stepped forward.

Before any words could escape her mouth, Carter interrupted. "Please remain with the group you were separated into on that side of the room, and no excessive talking with one another at this time."

Roland turned to the DCI. "I have not been allowed to see her all morning. This is stressful. I'm concerned about her well-being. She's easily stressed."

Carter exhaled. "I understand that, sir. This is an unusual circumstance for all, but you're impeding the investigation. Please follow my instructions to the letter. If you fail to comply, I'll detain you longer or possibly take you to town when the roads are free of ice. Do I make myself abundantly clear?"

"Yes, ma'am, crystal." He shoved his hands into his trouser pockets.

"Join Jenkins' group." She pointed to the people on her right.

Roland assumed his familiar, browbeaten posture as he retreated.

Robin growled, "How dare you threaten my son with detainment! All he did was pose a question." She called to her son. "I'm well, my boy. Good of you to ask. I could've slept better, though. This is most unpleasant."

Carter's hands went to her hips. "Ma'am, you may not talk to one another at this time. Don't undermine my authority or I'll be forced to act."

Robin, conceding defeat, took a step back into the folds of her tribe.

Carter looked around the parlor. "Jenkins, where is the head butler fellow? Fartworthy? Is that his name, and do you know where he is?"

"Yes, ma'am, his name is Fartworthy." The detective, near retirement age, snickered. "I let him go to the kitchen."

"Sergeant." Carter took a sharp, inward breath. "Did he have an escort?"

"No, he didn't."

The DCI set her chin. "Why?"

Jenkins crossed his arms. "Hot water for tea and the bleu cheese scones needed to be replaced on the breakfast buffet. I used my professional judgement."

"That wasn't your call to make. Protocol. Follow it." Carter cleared her throat. "Ladies and gentlemen, please listen up, and thank you for your patience and understanding. I know this has been a long morning for everyone."

Von Pickle spoke loud enough for only his group to hear. "That's the understatement of the year. Get on with it."

"Hush. You're being rude again," whispered Cassandra, looking over her shoulder.

"Miss Haywood, do you have anything to add?" Carter stared at Cassandra like a school librarian who caught someone talking in a loud voice.

Von Pickle shielded his mouth, snickered, and muttered, "Not the teacher's pet, I see."

The man is revolting. "No, ma'am. Sorry to interrupt. Please continue."

"Thank you." Carter resumed addressing the others. "The first round of questioning is complete. Unfortunately, the roads are still impassable at this time."

A murmur of discontent spread around the room.

"Yes, yes I know," continued the DCI. "We've been told within the next several hours the temperature will rise a few degrees. Our team will monitor the situation. It's a possibility we may need to keep some of you here overnight for a second time if we don't move this investigation along. Interruptions, disappearances, arguments, or anything of the sort will delay us and your potential release. Are there any questions at this time?"

Jack Birch spoke up from the back of the group. "What's the next step, ma'am?"

"Excellent question. We would like to speak to a few of you for a second time. We need to clarify some aspects. It's a complicated business to sort." Carter made a sweeping motion with her hands. "Anyone else?"

Mimi raised a finger. "If you haven't solved this today, will you still keep everyone overnight? I thought you would've figured this out by now."

Carter's smile dripped of condescension. "Mrs. York, this isn't a show on the telly that gets solved in an hour or a quick detective novel you finish reading at two in the morning. Police procedure and protocol in real life is much slower. We may not have the full answer, but we'll have our evidence to work with later. Thank you for your patience."

"And then you'll let us go home?" added Poppy.

"We'll detain people longer only if we cannot determine with clarity what people know. I need to repeat this speech to those in the kitchen and the smaller group wrapping up interviews in the dining room. Greenfield, please escort your group upstairs to their bedrooms to pack up anything they own and remain there until further notice." Carter pointed across the room. "Baker, have your group stay in the parlor. Mrs. York, don't go upstairs. We need to expand our search for your pills."

"We have to remain locked in our room for what, hours?" asked Robin. "That is entirely unreasonable."

Carter sighed. "Please go up to your room for the time being."

Von Pickle huffed. "How come that group doesn't get kicked upstairs?"

"Sir, I'll run this investigation. Our detectives still need to speak to some of them, and I want some of you to get some rest." Carter called out, "Miss Haywood? May I see you for a moment?"

"Absolutely."

Carter pointed to the great hall. "Shall we go in there for some privacy? I want to bring you up to speed."

Cassandra nodded. *Finally. Answers.*

Chapter Fifteen

They crossed the parlor with Cassandra synchronizing her gait with the DCI's quick steps. "Do you have new information about my aunt?"

Carter removed a notepad from her suit jacket pocket. "I know this is tedious to have my detective team in your home for so long, but we're doing everything we can to ensure your family will have closure."

"Thank you. I understand you're doing your job. I just want to be left alone."

"Perfectly understandable."

The two women entered the empty great hall. The giant Christmas tree, sparkling and dazzling the night before, appeared gaudy in the gray light of day.

The DCI spoke in a hushed voice. "I'm sorry to have been tough on you in the parlor. Crowd control. If people think I'm a pushover, no one listens." She clasped her hands together before her. "We've finished upstairs, removed your aunt's body from the manor, and flew her to the morgue. We've gathered some evidence. This phase is complete, and members of our team have restored the rooms."

"Restored?" Cassandra wrapped her fingers with an end of her ivory scarf.

The detective paused. "To clarify, this phase deals with the removal of blood and fluids from where your aunt's body was discovered."

Cassandra's stomach flew to the floor, and her knees turned to putty. She grasped the oak banister for support.

"Easy there." Carter steadied the young lady by the elbow. "Come. Sit." The detective guided the woozy woman to the stairway. "Did you get breakfast?"

Cassandra sat on the second step from the bottom. The edge of her floral, tiered skirt spread and covered her feet. She looked at the white, oak floor. "I had tea. My stomach couldn't handle anything else." Covering her eyes with her hands, she rested both elbows on her thighs.

The DCI sat next to her. "I have to ask. Were you ill last night or this morning? It was New Year's Eve. Quite understandable if you didn't feel well before any of this. Did you drink alcohol at the party?"

"No, not at all. I was perfectly well last night." Cassandra cradled her face.

"Do you normally have issues with anxiety? Panic attacks?"

"Nothing of the sort."

"We have statements from the guests. They're still working through the staff. I saw you speaking to Mr. Chamberlain. Are you two a couple?"

Cassandra's head popped up, and warmth spread in an instant to her cheeks. "No! He's . . . a nice chap. I enjoy talking to him. He asked how I was doing, that's all. No, not a couple."

Carter smiled. "No worries. I'm curious if you had a connection beyond friendship with him, Miss Haywood."

Cassandra explained, "No, no. We're, well, friends."

"But there's a definite interest there. Hmm?" pressed Carter.

Cassandra said nothing but gave a slight nod and grin.

The DCI laughed. "It's my job to notice things. Your body language gave you away. Anyway, is there anything else you remember about last night? Did you visit your aunt after the party?"

"Miss Dalton and I were in my room. I went down the hall to the bathroom at some point, and I saw Mrs. Turner leave my aunt's room. She stormed past me. I asked her if she wanted anything, and she told me she needed a new sister-in-law. Could she have done something?"

The head detective flipped the pages in her notepad. "You never know. Anything else?"

"I don't remember."

"You're sure?"

"Fairly certain." Cassandra twisted her ivory scarf tail.

Carter stood and offered her hand to help Cassandra. "Are you fine to stand?"

"I think so. Thank you." She took the detective's help and rose. "I could never stomach blood. I'll stick to finance and marketing." Cassandra brushed off the back of her skirt.

"What do you do for a living, Miss Haywood?"

"I work for my aunt at Lemington Cheese. Marketing, distribution, suggestions for new products, that sort of thing. Although, last night she said several times I would be CEO when she retired or died. I never thought it would be this soon."

"Upon her death, you would become the head of the whole company?"

"Yes, there's paperwork I need to sign. Mrs. Turner was furious about that decision."

Carter scribbled something. "She wanted to be in control?"

"No, Mrs. Turner wants her son, Roland, in charge. Aunt Lily told me he doesn't have the backbone for business. She said I did."

Cassandra reached into a pocket from deep in the folds of her skirt to retrieve a tissue.

"This was part of the discussion at the party?"

"Yes, Aunt Lily and Mrs. Turner argued about this point last night." Cassandra unfolded the packet, dabbed her nose, and returned the tissue to her pocket.

"Did your aunt say anything more to you about this?"

"No." Cassandra took in a deep breath and looked up. "My aunt has confidence that I can handle the job and run this manor."

Carter furrowed her brow. "You inherit this place, too? Jolly good deal for someone so young. What's your age, Miss Haywood?"

"Twenty-nine, but I feel much older today. The weight of this bears heavily, and I truly hope I can rise to my aunt's expectations."

"You seem like a confident woman who can handle anything. Is there anyone who would wish to hurt your aunt?"

"She angered people, but I can't imagine anyone wanting to kill her." Cassandra twisted the scarf tail into a cloth sausage.

The DCI stepped closer and whispered, "The smallest details can crack a case wide open. It could be information relating to where someone was when the victim died, or past business dealings that went sour. Greed drives some to do the unthinkable. Inheritance fights are common. Sometimes, a family connection is the reason, or a betrayal. Could be revenge or something the victim recently learned and was silenced. When we have the puzzle pieces, facts get linked, create the whole picture, and the solution becomes obvious. Other times, it's a random, freak accident."

"It can't be easy doing your job."

"No, but helping people like yourself, Miss Haywood, is the reason I do what I do." The DCI exhaled a long breath. "I must dash to give my speech to the kitchen staff and guests in the dining room. I need you to return to the parlor and stay there for the time being. We'll find out what happened."

"Thank you, Detective Chief Inspector. May I ask a favor?"

"Anything."

Cassandra pointed to the heavy, antique, exterior double doors. "May I step outside for a breath of fresh air? I'm stifled in here."

"Yes, then go straight away to the parlor. I'll let DC Baker know where you are. Please don't stay outside too long. It's icy cold out, and you wouldn't want to catch something." Carter smiled.

"Thank you. I'll be quick about it." Cassandra headed to the doors. She turned and saw the DCI speedwalking. *She is the perfect person to help. I'm ever so grateful.*

Cassandra reached the entrance and tugged on a scrolled, metal handle, pulling it with effort. A frigid blast of air erased her sluggishness and cleared the cobwebs from her mind. The wind iced her bare legs. She instinctively grasped her upper arms in a self-hug as she stepped over the threshold. Several layers of ice coated the ground beneath her feet.

"Oh, my," she said to no one. Her sandals slipped. *They weren't exaggerating. This is treacherous.*

She tiptoed carefully onto the slick surface and pulled the heavy door almost shut. She continued to shuffle, testing each spot for traction.

The large trees lining the driveway wore hats of dark-gray clouds. She groaned. *I hope everyone has left by the time that squall gets here.* Cassandra shivered, her thin blouse and long skirt doing nothing to impede the wind gusts' sharp daggers. She shut her eyes for an instant and breathed deeply.

I can do this. She looked down. *This is a sheet of ice. If you flop, there will be nasty bruising. Get away for a moment to turn into an ice lolly? And my toes are frozen. Brilliant.*

The twin dwarf pine trees at the top of the stone steps sparkled in shimmering, icy tombs while the large, red bows tied around the white, marble pots drooped with frosted weight.

Someone should take a photo of these. Looks like a Christmas postcard of peace and tranquility. Nothing of the sort.

Tires crunching on the gravel woke her from her reverie. Headlights belonging to a constable car cut through the frosty air as it came up the driveway.

Cars can get up here?

At that moment, near one of the frozen evergreen guards, something orange on the ground caught Cassandra's eye.

What is that? Cassandra made her way closer to the object. *A bottle of pills!* She half-walked, half-slid to the item and picked it up. She read the bottle label aloud. "Mimi York. Aha!"

Forgetting about safety, she turned to run back into the manor. A moment later, she skidded, and her left knee hit the stone landing. Her hands smacked the ground, and the bottle of pills flew, gliding across the ice. She took a moment to recover—her knee and hands getting colder by the second—resting on the large, frost-covered, flat rocks. *That wasn't smart.* She stood and brushed herself off.

With renewed caution, she made her way forward, picked up Mimi's meds, and headed inside. She shoved the heavy door open, and her feet hit the highly polished wood floor. She hollered, "I found them!" and ran into Detective Constable Baker. The two women collided with such force that it knocked the detective down on her behind.

"Oof! Whoa, there, miss!"

"My deepest apologies. I found them!" cried Cassandra.

"Found what?" asked the seated detective.

"Mrs. York's medication! The bottle was on the ice right outside the door." She helped the detective up, took off her sandals, grabbed them, and sprinted into the parlor. "Mimi!"

Mimi, on the opposite side of the space, hurried to meet her. "What?"

Cassandra's feet slapped the hardwood floor as she ran. She held up the orange pill bottle. "I found them!"

When they met up, Mimi clasped her hands around the bottle and let out a shrill cry. "Dearest! Thank you!" She threw her arms around Cassandra's neck. "You've saved my life. Literally." DC Baker caught up to Cassandra.

Carter appeared next to the three women. "You found the meds? Where?"

"Outside, next to the potted evergreen. Right on the ground!" Cassandra grinned.

"In plain sight? Lucky you happened to go out there." The DCI looked at Baker.

"I know!" Cassandra's faced beamed. "I looked on the ground and there they were." She let the sandals drop and slid her feet into them.

The DCI held her hand out. "May I see the pill bottle please?" Carter turned to a constable standing nearby. "Fetch Mrs. York a glass of water so she can take her much-needed medication. Be quick about it." She opened the bottle and held it out to Mimi. "Does it look like the same amount you had before you lost it? Can you count these to make sure all are there?"

Mimi investigated the little, orange bottle. "I don't count them. I take them several times a day. It looks to be about the same, I guess." Mimi turned to grasp Cassandra's hand. "I'm eternally grateful, my dear."

The constable hurried back with a glass of water for Mrs. York.

Mimi poured out the correct dosage and swallowed the pills with the water.

The DCI pointed across the room. "Please go have a seat, Mrs. York. I'm sure your heart is having a hard time with all the excitement. Why don't you leave the pill bottle with me since it might be evidence?"

"I'm terribly sorry, but I'm not letting these out of my sight." She clutched the bottle to her chest. "Please send someone to tell my husband my medication has been located. It worried him."

"I'll send someone upstairs to relay the news. You remain here." Carter pointed to Cassandra. "Please stay with Mrs. York for a few minutes, if you don't mind."

"I'll be happy to."

The head detective gave a thumbs-up. "I need to get cracking to get to the other groups. Baker? A word."

Mimi and Cassandra walked over to Cassandra's favorite sofa.

"Why don't you sit here for the time being? Is your medication working?"

Mimi sat, closed her eyes, and breathed out. "The anxiety is going away. I can relax."

"I'm glad I could help." Cassandra moved in front of the large floral arrangement on a small table near the sofa. The red-and-white natural display provided a sweet and earthy aroma. Drawn by the intoxicating smell and exquisite beauty, she stared at the botanicals for some time. Her racing heartbeat from the excitement calmed.

After a few minutes, Mimi chuckled. "You're positively transfixed, Miss Haywood."

Cassandra continued to gaze at the elegant beauties. "I am." She reached out and touched one of the white rose petals. "These are always here, and yet, I never noticed."

"Doesn't the gardener make these arrangements for every party? Don't tell me they're fake?" asked Mimi.

"They're real and all from the hothouse." Cassandra moved her concentration to a different white bloom. She caressed the small, bell-shaped flowers. "Always here, but you stop seeing and appreciating them. It's been ages since I've paid attention to their lovely fragrance." Cassandra added in a whisper, "She likes white flowers."

Mimi looked around the room. "Who likes them?"

"Liked." She bit her lip. "Aunt Lily liked white flowers, and I wasn't observant enough. Mr. Birch told me earlier. Her name should have been a clue."

"My dear, we don't know everything about the people we live with and love." Mimi ran a finger over the wedding band on her hand.

"I have no idea what these are called." Cassandra touched the small petal again.

"The trumpet-shaped one is foxglove."

"I didn't know you were familiar with flowers. Do you garden?"

"No." Mimi sighed. "*Digitalis purpurea* is its scientific name, from the Latin for finger—digitus—referring to its shape like a top of a finger of a glove."

Cassandra turned around. "Digitalis? Isn't that the name of your medication I found?"

"Yes." Mimi tapped her pill bottle. "I'll be forever thankful to you and that magical flower." She blinked slowly and took a deep breath. "The active ingredient in my prescription is from the same botanical source. Did you know that for two hundred years, they would make tea from it to treat heart patients? It wasn't an exact science. Sometimes it worked, and sometimes not. Here is the most interesting part. The plant only makes the heart medication compound when it grows in full sunlight."

"You seem to know quite a bit about this humble, little bloom."

"W-w-well I . . . well," stammered Mimi. "Anything I put into my body I research. Isn't it interesting that bringing it out into the light made all the difference?" She cleared her throat.

"That's true for many things," said Cassandra. She moved away from the table and sat on the other end of the sofa. *A few other guests and several detectives remain. When will this end?*

A shuddering gasp caught her attention. Cassandra turned to her companion on the sofa. Mimi's eyes fluttered closed, her head tilted back, and her chest rose and fell rapidly with shallow, uneven breaths. Alarmed, Cassandra said, "Mimi? Are you all right?"

The woman didn't respond.

Cassandra jumped up and waved a detective over. She kneeled before the seated lady, patted her knee rapidly, and shouted, "Mimi? Mimi!"

Chapter Sixteen

Cassandra's panic rose at Mimi's continued silence. She leaned in close. "Mimi!"

In a quiet voice with her eyes still shut, Mimi uttered, "I'll be fine. I took my dose late. Sometimes I faint for a moment. No worries."

DC Baker and a constable hurried over. "Mrs. York?"

Mimi's eyelids fluttered while she lifted her head. "This intrigue is positively exhausting." She smiled weakly at the trio of concerned faces.

Cassandra, still kneeling, blew out a breath. "Do we need to take you to hospital?"

Mimi waved her hand. "Unnecessary. Sometimes my brain takes a mini holiday." She chuckled. "If you take me in, they'll run the same tests, with the same results, and admonish me about missing a dose of my medication ever again. Quite maddening."

"Would you like to retreat upstairs?" DC Baker offered her hand. "Carter gave the clearance for you, Mrs. York. Why don't we accompany you to your room?"

"Thank you, I appreciate your concern." Mimi took the detective's hand, rose, and moved away a few steps. She waved the pair off. "You're not needed. I can make it alone."

Baker said, "We're supposed to escort everyone."

Cassandra stood. "Someone should be with you."

"After one of those events, I don't want company. I'm fine, just embarrassed. You detectives do what you must down here." Mimi patted the DC's arm. "No one needs to babysit me." Without another word, Mimi left the room.

Cassandra stared, bewildered, as her adrenaline dissipated and sweat formed on her body.

Arabella crossed the space. "What's the excitement?"

"Mimi fainted, needs to rest, and doesn't want company." Cassandra's attention remained focused on the doorway. She wiped the back of her neck.

"It would be best for her to go to her room and be quiet." Arabella addressed the DC. "May I be with my grieving friend? How about we retire to our room upstairs? Out of everyone here, don't you think she needs a little rest? This is so stressful."

Baker looked at the others across the room. "I'll ask the DCI. Stay here for the time being. Let me get clearance. We still have some interviews to finish up." The detective and constable retreated to the opposite side of the room.

"Nicely done, Arabella," Cassandra spoke in a hushed voice. "How long did they talk to you?"

"Forever. Loads of questions that didn't make sense." Arabella moved an ivory scarf tail over Cassandra's shoulder. "Why do they care about my personal life for an accident? Never mind about me. How do you feel?"

"Surreal. At least the DCI understands and wants to sort this out. I'm pleased how she's handled everything so far."

"Handled? They're treating us like criminals, and we didn't do anything. Wish to sit?"

"Yes." The women sat on Cassandra's favorite sofa.

"You've been blind, Cassie. I volunteered to search for the medication so I could find out what Carter knows. Blasted business. Out of all, Carter is the most tight-lipped. She said nothing."

"Bella, they're doing their best." Cassandra pointed to her friend's head. "We're supposed to wear what we had on last night. You forgot your fascinator."

Arabella rolled her eyes. "And why must we comply with that direction? Bits of looped tulle and ribbons won't make a difference in figuring out what happened. You're not wearing the same shoes."

"I told Carter that. You're right. It doesn't matter." Cassandra sighed. "Aunt Lily probably had an accident. Unless . . . why else would they keep everyone after they questioned them?"

Arabella leaned into her friend. "Cassie, there's a possibility someone wanted to hurt her based on how she acted last night."

A shiver crawled up her spine and Cassandra stood. She twisted her ivory scarf again. "That's not a reason to kill her. We've all had disagreements." *Where's my lilac scarf?* She paced in a circle, glancing at the floor.

"A person in their proper mind would not, but Lady Lemington was in rare form and someone could have cracked."

"I'm sick with the idea."

"Sorry, dearest. Did Carter give you any information?"

"Aunt Lily hit her head on the lavatory sink when she fell. Mr. Fartworthy found her, and he called the detectives." Cassandra pushed her fingertips into her temples. "I want everyone out so I can process this."

"You said last night Lady Lemington wanted you to be in charge when she is gone. Are you going to do it?"

"I don't know. There's so much. I'll have Mrs. Turner breathing down my neck as soon as the detectives leave. There are staff problems and other obnoxious individuals. I don't want to think about the lot."

Arabella got up and put her arm around her chum's shoulders. "I'm here to listen. You do well when you talk it out. You look like you're on the brink."

The sudden closeness and the touch of her friend unleashed the torrent of teardrops dammed up. Cassandra turned into Arabella's arms and wept. A long, quiet cry escaped, and she did nothing to stem it. Pent up, the flood of emotion flowed out in a river of grief.

Arabella rocked her companion side to side. "There, there. We'll figure this out." Her hand made circles on Cassandra's back. "It's all right. It will be all right."

A minute later, Cassandra's sobs melted into discreet gasps. "I'm so sorry," she whispered, her fingers pressing into the plush, black velvet on the back of her friend's dress.

"Why ever are you sorry? Friends do this. I signed up for this part, too, and not just the fancy party invitation. Blub all you need. I'm here." Arabella took a deep breath. "You want to sit again?"

Cassandra shook her head, her gasps morphing into silent weeping.

"You know what I saw when you left with Carter? Von Pickle lost his mind when they insisted he retreat to his room for a few minutes. The man exploded."

Her friend sniffled.

"He ranted, like he always does, about his international blah blah business. He looked purple in the face. A purple Pickle!"

Cassandra chuckled in her friend's arms. She pulled away. "You know how to make me laugh, Bella."

"Part of my job." Arabella smoothed Cassandra's hair. "Feeling tolerable?"

"Yes, thank you. I needed that." Cassandra stepped back, removed a tissue from her skirt pocket, and dabbed around her eyes and nose. "That's certainly humiliating."

"Crying or being human? Please. If people expressed their emotions more unabashedly, there would be far fewer health issues."

"Careful, Bella. One might think you're turning into an American. We can't have that happen."

The friends exchanged smiles. Cassandra glanced around. "Where's Mr. Chamberlain?"

"You would take notice of his absence. DS Jenkins sent him upstairs. Ugh. Don't look. Roland approaches."

"Really? I don't want him to see me this way. I look like a frumpy monkey." Cassandra wiped under her eyes again.

"Please, not a frumpy monkey. The rest of you is perfectly fine. Well, your eyes are red and swollen and your mascara has run. Demonic badger perhaps?" Arabella smirked.

Cassandra rolled her eyes. "Nice way to make me feel better."

"Anytime, luv." Under her breath, Arabella said while grinning, "Here he is."

Roland drew near to the ladies. "Miss Dalton. Miss Haywood, I saw you crying. Are you all right?"

So embarrassing. "I'm fine, Mr. Turner. Thank you for asking." *Of course I'm not all right.* Cassandra returned the tissue to her pocket. *Why did he have to be in here? I'm sure he'll tell his mother.*

Roland pointed. "Have you been like this all morning?"

"No." Cassandra sniffed.

"I haven't seen you since the dreadful party." Roland looked around. "Big change from the gathering. Who's mobile is on the sofa?"

"That would be mine." Arabella reached down to retrieve her device. "Blast these shallow pockets." She stowed the phone in the confines of her outfit.

The young man continued to scan the space. "Have you talked to Mother? Was she agitated?"

Cassandra answered, "We chatted while we were in the library together. She's fine."

"I must converse with her. Speak to the head detective to get me permission to do so," commanded Roland.

"She has no influence on the detectives," jeered Arabella. "You're an adult. You needn't be at mummy's side all the time."

"Bella," Cassandra admonished in a harsh whisper. She turned to Roland. "What she means is I have no say with law enforcement."

"Are you going to run our aunt's company or not?" snarled Roland.

"Maybe," replied Cassandra.

"I can't work for you." Roland crossed his arms.

Cassandra pulled back her head. "Pardon?"

"You heard me. Mistreated by our aunt, I endured too much for years. I cannot bear being manipulated by someone else. Give me my termination notice and let me go today. What's the point of working there if I'll never run the company?" Roland clasped his hands.

"Where is this coming from? We're friends, Roland, and I would never try to control you. You're more than welcome to stay with the company if you wish. If you want to leave, I understand."

Roland didn't hide his scorn. "You wish for me to remain to help run things since I actually know what to do. I get it, but I have no interest in being someone's puppet again. To work as hard as I did and for what purpose? I'll remain if I'm in charge of my own destiny and not stuffed into a trunk somewhere."

Arabella leaned in. "Can you make that decision without talking to your master, I mean, mother?"

Roland's electric-blue eyes pierced Cassandra. "It's a good thing this happened. I mean, it's an amazing opportunity to make a change. Mother was correct last night when she said things cannot stay status quo forever. Certain events can utterly transform the course of someone's life. She doesn't always go about things the proper way, but I usually fix that for her." He moved closer to Cassandra. "This is a new day. Aunt Lily and the company needed to break from one another."

Cassandra searched his face. "How can you see anything good about this situation?"

A nervous laugh escaped his lips. "This shall be a turning point for cheese production, for you, and for me. She held us back at Lemington Cheese with her old-fashioned ideas. We're the generation that will follow dreams. Everything is changing now."

Arabella chuckled. "With your mother pulling your strings, Roland? I don't think you'll be any different, despite what you say."

"You don't know me!" Roland shouted, clenching his fists. "No one does. I have grand ideas, a fantastic imagination, and its high time people listened to me!"

Arabella and Cassandra stared, shocked into silence.

Red-faced, Roland looked at the floor. "My apologies. That was uncalled for. The stress of being me is sometimes too great. I beg your pardon." With shoulders and head slumped, he walked away from the ladies. DC Baker met him in the parlor's middle. The two spoke for a moment before the pair strode out of the room together.

Cassandra turned to her friend. "What on earth? Have you ever seen him lash out like that?"

"Never. The man has stifled anger issues." Arabella blew out a breath. "Then again, his mother could make a saint swear and drink for days. One day he'll snap, and woe to anyone who's around and gets caught up in that psychological tornado."

DS Jenkins approached. "The DCI gave permission for you to go upstairs. We'll come get you when we're ready."

"Aren't you going to escort us?" asked Arabella.

The DS smirked and shook his head. "No, I think you can find your way."

The friends walked out of the parlor to the great hall.

When they reached the stairs, Arabella sighed. "I'll dash up and pop into the shower."

"The detective said to retire to our room."

"No, he said to 'go upstairs.' The shower is upstairs. I want to freshen up."

"They'll know you weren't in the bedroom."

"Simple, I won't wash my hair. I'm desperate for hot water on my shoulders." Arabella stretched her arms. "A long shower is calling my name."

"You want to raid my closet and get a change of clothing?"

"No, I'll put this back on. No sense annoying the DCI at this point. You require a little alone time, and this will be perfect. I'll catch up with you later, luv." Before Cassandra could answer, Arabella planted a kiss on her friend's forehead, sprinted up the curved staircase, and disappeared.

That was odd. Why would she want a shower now?

Cassandra grasped the oak handrail. The heaviness in her chest contributed to her slow ascension up the steps. She paused at the landing midway and turned around to view the grand space. The large windows above the heavy, oak doors let in gray light and illuminated the area in muted colors. *Who would have known everything would change by morning? Happy New Year.* She continued her climb to reach the top.

Muffled voices behind multiple closed doors accompanied her walk down the empty hallway. *Please don't come out. I thought a constable would be up here.*

Cassandra entered her silent, tidy room and sighed. The door shut with a click. *This day has been unreal. I don't even remember making my bed or Bella making hers.* She kicked off her sandals and flopped on top of the purple-and-green quilt. Staring at the ceiling, her mind skidded and crashed. *I'm glad I found Mimi's medication. She can relax. Can I? I'm in charge of the company. Is that even a good idea?*

She popped off the bed and paced around the furniture, twisting her ivory scarf. *Why would Roland say any of that? Does he want in or out? Did his mother hurt Aunt Lily? I'm lucky to have Bella by my side through all of this. And then there's Frederick.* Her heart bounced. *He showed concern about me. Huh.* She shut her eyes for a moment. *Aunt Lily. Her favorite flowers were white, and she hired Flora, knowing she had been a drug addict. Secrets from everyone. Mr. Fartworthy? A private investigator? Do I know anyone?*

Cassandra touched her neck. *Where is my lilac scarf? In the parlor. No. Where? The library. I can't recall having it after that. It must be in there. I still don't know where my raspberry one is from last night.*

I should get my lilac one. She looked under her bed for her sandals and slipped them on, careful to avoid hitting her Band-Aid-covered blisters. She moved over to the mirror hanging over her dresser. *Ugh.* She grabbed a makeup remover pad from a jar. Cassandra dragged the cooling, disposable cloth under her eyes a few times and sighed. *That's better. More human, less badger.* She straightened her blouse and skirt and moved the knot under her ear on the remaining scarf. *I'll go back to the library. What is the worst the detectives will do? This is my home, and I own it.*

She exhaled. *I guess.*

Chapter Seventeen

Cassandra slipped out of her room to the maroon-carpeted passage. Quiet voices seeped through closed doors, overlapping the sound of shower water hitting tile. She walked past the three doors until she made a left turn to the next hallway. She slipped off her sandals and, in a tiptoe sprint, raced down the empty corridor to the back exit. *Glad we have these servant entrances.*

She opened the squeaky, dark-cherry door and slipped on her shoes. She seldom used the winding, narrow, semi-dark staircase from the second floor. This stairwell extended from the third floor all the way to the kitchen in the basement. The horizontal, brown-painted, tongue-and-groove covered walls, the linoleum from the start of the twentieth century, and trapped kitchen smells from countless meals gave the stairwell a distinct, antique pong. When she arrived on the landing for the first floor, Cassandra opened the door and peeked down the long corridor. *No one. I don't want to get caught sneaking around like a defiant teenager. Get my scarf and head back.*

At the dining room's far end, a few detectives were engaged in conversation. With the stealth of a cat seeking to pounce, she moved down the narrow hallway to the library. Cassandra opened the oak entry, slipped inside the room, and closed the door behind her. *Where could that scarf be?*

She glided through the room, peering around the leather furniture. *There you are!* By the table with the flower arrangement and her used teacup, the lilac scarf lay on the floor like a pile of dirty laundry. She bent down. *Right near my teacup and . . . where's my saucer?*

Voices clamored outside the door.

No! She scanned the room. *The curtains. That could work.* She darted to the far end of the room and hid between the heavy, jade fabric and ice-covered window. The commotion came closer. *Don't be the detectives, don't be the detectives.*

The door swung open, hitting the bookshelf behind it with a bang. Cassandra's heart skipped a beat as her adrenaline surged.

Footsteps entered the room. "In here, Jenkins."

That's the DCI. This is bad.

Carter continued. "Greenfield, Penwarden, all of you. Let's go. Did you tell Henslowe where we are? I thought they finished in the dining room. I need his interview report."

"Yes, I did, ma'am. He'll be here in a minute," replied Greenfield.

DS Jenkins' heavy footsteps thumped on the wooden floor coming into the room. "This is a waste of everyone's time. It was an accident. She fell."

Carter grunted. "I think it's foolish to be so dismissive of any facts, Jenkins. Rushing through this case isn't going to pull your retirement date closer."

"Do we always need to pay for the mistake you made years ago when you let the Hoffman case slip away?" The door closed with a weighty thud. "Our department endures this *every* single time, and it always proves pointless."

Cassandra stifled her breath, holding the lilac scarf bunched up over her mouth. *Don't breathe heavily.*

The door creaked open. Another voice chimed in. "I'm here."

Carter spoke. "Henslowe, come in. We're discussing our next move." The door closed. "Sergeant Jenkins, humor me. Go over the facts, and let's hammer this out. Who would you say had the most to gain by Lady Lemington's death?"

"Fine. I'll play this for a few minutes." Jenkins sighed. "It's a holiday, you know. Some of us have a life."

Carter sneered. "As did Lady Lemington, and we owe it to her to discover the truth." Her tone changed. "There are family members and friends missing her, and their closure comes first. We get to go home and have a life, as you said in your callous comment. For the people who knew her, their lives will never be the same. Remember that. All of you."

A respectful silence engulfed the room.

I like her. She's looking out for the greater good. Chilly here between the drapes and these windows. These aren't energy efficient at all. She attempted to peer through the glass pane. The thick ice had retreated some from the white, wooden framing. The entire middle remained sheathed in frozen water. *Still can't see outside, but it must be warmer since I can make out some shapes and colors.*

Someone sighed. "You're right. My apologies, Chief," said Jenkins.

The new detective chimed in. "How did our victim's head hit the sink is what you're asking?"

"We'll determine that, Greenfield," replied the DCI, "but first, we need to focus on motive. Who do we keep here for more questioning and who do we release, either back to their jobs at the manor or to leave the estate?"

"Are the roads still a mess with ice? Quite a chore to get here this morning by helicopter," remarked DC Penwarden.

"I told the guests the road conditions still prevented departure. That isn't true," said Carter. "The streets are manageable off this hill and they can leave. However, there's more foul weather expected later today. Some people need a little extra pressure to reveal information. The threat of having to stay another night might make their answers more forthcoming. No one wants to stay longer than necessary."

She lied to us? The constable car I saw coming up the drive. Of course.

Carter continued. "Take out your notepad, Greenfield. Start two lists. One is for who we shall retain to question further, and the other is for the people we will release. Let's start with your interviews, Penwarden."

Notepad pages flipped and crinkled and a throat cleared.

Cassandra shifted in her spot, minding not to move the curtains. She hugged herself. *Blast. It's cold here. Wrong spot to hide.*

DC Penwarden spoke up. "Right, then. I haven't seen most of you all morning, so here's what I know from the kitchen staff. No one, save two, had any extensive contact with Lady Lemington last night or yesterday. They were all in the great hall for ringing in the new year and saw their employer but didn't talk to her. The head cook, Mrs. Rose Forest, spoke to Lady Lemington the morning of the party to review menu plans for the gala. My recommendation is to release the kitchen and household staff. Mrs. Forest told us she had luncheon to get on with, and her staff needed to get back to work. She told me we 'wrecked her timetable.' Nothing unordinary with anyone as far as I could see. The only exception? The head housekeeper, Miss Flora Fairchild. Carter heard the end of that discussion when she came downstairs. Thoughts about her, ma'am? I have notes."

"I went to the kitchen when I was looking for the missing medication with Mrs. York and Miss Dalton. If you haven't heard, we found the pills outside. More on that later. Yes, I saw her. Fairchild is hiding something. She could be hiding a petty offense since she wouldn't look me in the eyes. She looked like a scared rabbit. Maybe she knows a key piece of information. Would you keep her, Penwarden?"

In a gruff voice, DC Penwarden replied, "Eh. I agree about the eye contact, and she clutched her handkerchief tight. Fairchild has definite anxiety, although when talking about running the household, she seemed confident and relaxed. Quite a puzzle, that one. I believe we should question her further, Chief."

Flora was right. They suspect her.

"Agreed. Move on. Head butler, Fartworthy."

"I didn't have him," replied Penwarden. "I had the rest of the butler staff. No one suspicious in that group."

"Wasn't he in this room with you, Greenfield?" asked Carter.

"Yes, for a brief time."

"What did you observe while he remained in here?"

Greenfield spoke. "Nothing out of the ordinary. When I let Miss Haywood and Fartworthy go to the breakfast buffet, she had her back to me the entire time. They both fussed with the food. I couldn't tell what the butler was saying for most of the conversation, since he didn't open his mouth more than a sliver when talking. Later, Miss Haywood seemed quite troubled."

"Stands to reason. Her aunt died," quipped Jenkins.

Carter commanded, "Continue."

"At one point, he spoke with a regular mouth movement so I could catch what he said." Greenfield cleared his throat. "Fartworthy consoled her." His notepad rustled. "I have some of what he uttered. Here goes. 'What you describe is your body experiencing profound anguish. Please ease up on yourself. Adding guilt over your natural reactions from last night will not help you. Eventually, you'll get used to carrying that heaviness, that disbelief of your sudden loss around with you. One day, that bootheel feeling will disappear.' Afterward, Mrs. Turner asked me a question. Next thing I knew, Miss Haywood returned here without Fartworthy."

Cassandra's hand covered her mouth. *He was reading Mr. Fartworthy's lips!*

"Romantic entanglement or former relationship between Haywood and Fartworthy? Your take, Henslowe?" asked Carter. "He was on your list."

What? No! Never!

"I interviewed him in the dining room before he was in here," said Henslowe. "He found the body and informed us the bathroom door was unlocked at the time. Fartworthy's manner and answers to my questions indicate he's more like a protective, older brother to Miss Haywood."

That's a suitable description.

"And Jenkins sent him unsupervised to the kitchen. Did you see what he did when he was down by you, Penwarden?"

"No. Interviewing the others captured my attention. I couldn't tell you how long he remained. He dealt with the food and hovered over by the sink for a while. He came down several times. I know that."

"Did he talk to anyone in the kitchen?"

"Not that I can recall," said Penwarden.

"Monitor him. Butlers see and hear much." Carter cleared her throat. "He could be a resource or a suspect. His idea to check and replace the food on the buffet?"

Greenfield answered, "No, it was Miss Haywood's plan."

I need to talk to Mr. Fartworthy to see what he discovered.

"Hmm . . . interesting." Footsteps paced the floor once

again, paper crinkled, and Carter spoke. "Next on the household staff. The head gardener."

"Jack Birch asked Lady L. to marry him, she said no, and fired him to boot. Loss of love and job. Could be two impressive motives there," said Jenkins.

"Cut the cheek, Sergeant," admonished Carter. "Yes, those are two reasons. He has a revolving door of groundskeepers under his direction. Is he horrible to work for, or is there something else? It might be the former since his grumpiness seems to be epic, according to others. I believe more questioning of him is necessary. Who else?"

What? Mr. Birch is heartbroken, that's all. How can they suspect him? Cassandra's hands held the scarf and sides of her face.

"What about Ruby Lightfoot, the party and crime scene photographer?"

"Well," said Carter, "I worked with Miss Lightfoot for years. Nothing in her demeanor has changed. Her story checks out. Ruby's helpful photos are now on our server. We have a documented photo timeline of the party."

"Timeline?" asked Greenfield.

"Time stamps on the photos place the guests at certain times," replied Carter. "Miss Lightfoot informed us Lady Lemington wanted her near when she interacted with people. Intriguing character study of the victim."

Cold, but desperate to avoid detection, Cassandra moved her arms at a snail's pace and wrapped the lilac scarf around her freezing neck.

"You're sure the photographer isn't suspect?" asked Greenfield.

"Unlikely, but she should remain since she hovered around our victim most of the time at the gala. Her point of view might help place a puzzle piece. I need to review those photos again. I only took a quick glance. Some stories from the others aren't correct or complete."

"Faulty memory or outright lying?" Cassandra couldn't tell who asked the question.

"Our brains are a tricky thing. We give people the benefit of the doubt, but sometimes it's a bold-faced lie. It's human nature to avoid trouble or get involved. Who's next?" The head detective scoffed. "Here we go. Baron Von Pickle."

Greenfield chimed in, "Von Pickle is a pompous a—"

"Greenfield!" interjected Carter.

"Come on. He is." Jenkins snickered. "Chief, you wanted to drop-kick him into the nearest well after his interview."

"Indeed. Someone's obnoxious and loud behavior doesn't automatically make him a suspect or subject to arrest." Carter laughed. "If that were true, half my family would be in the clink."

"Doesn't help his case, though."

"No. Is there a reason to detain him?" asked Carter.

"To tick him off?" said Jenkins.

"Not good enough." Carter chuckled again.

"Beg your pardon, Chief." Greenfield spoke. "His comments to Miss Haywood about her aunt were cruel, and he makes a dreadful fuss out of everything. When I talked to Miss Haywood in here, she reported the baron argued with Lady Lemington. Afterward, her aunt told him something and he became furious."

"Sounds like a potential motive, but remember the source of that information. He could have hurt her. Keep him," said Carter. "Let's move along. Group people together. We've got to get back out there."

Jenkins rustled papers. "The nephew and his mother squabbled with the victim at the party. Mrs. Turner wants her son to head the company."

"One or both in cahoots, perhaps. Several witnesses stated Mrs. Turner argued with Lady L. several times. Miss Haywood told me she saw Roland's mother storm out of her aunt's bedroom. Mrs. Turner has a temper several of us witnessed during her interview in the parlor. She's a tigress when protecting her son. Then again, Mr. Turner, with the revelation of the CEO position going to Miss Haywood, may have been pushed to his breaking point. Or it was his mother's idea, but he physically did it. Possible. Both mother and son on the keep list. Go on. Who else, Jenkins?"

"The Yorks. Lady Lemington revealed several secrets about Hamish York at the party. The information exposed upset both husband and wife. Based on the interview with the photographer, Mr. York, at some point, called Lady Lemington a 'nasty piece of work' and declared she 'wasn't happy unless everyone around her was miserable.' Mrs. York's medication went missing. Could that have been used? Someone could have slipped it into a drink, and it's for heart problems, right?"

"I believe so. Yes, the pills. The missing medication is a puzzle. Where was it all morning? Retain the couple. Something doesn't make sense with them."

Jenkins continued. "Mr. Chamberlain and Mr. Spooner are both merchants in town. They worked with the victim during this year, and this was their first time at an event here for each." Pacing footsteps crossed the room.

The DCI chimed in. "Mr. Chamberlain's knowledge about the watch was enlightening. You didn't hear, Penwarden and Henslowe. The jeweler said the victim either went down without catching herself or blocked a blow. The hit was severe enough for internal injuries on the watch to stop it from functioning, and yet, the clock face was left unbroken. Did someone come up behind her and slam her head into the marble sink, or did she pass out, hitting her head that way?"

Jenkins huffed. "She could've fought someone. There was definite anger directed toward Lady Lemington last night. Did someone snap?"

Cassandra grasped the scarf ends to her mouth, and her stomach dropped to her toes.

"That was a serious gash on the victim's head. Quite deep and long, clear across her forehead. Before we turned the body over, we thought there could be another wound with all that blood covering the floor. Wasn't the case. There were no other bruises on the body, so a fight seems less likely." Carter exhaled. "Remember, Fartworthy said the lavatory door was unlocked when he found her. She could've gone in there for a moment for a tissue or something. When you do that, no one locks the door."

"And someone snuck up behind her. If she were leaning over to wash her face, it would be easy to attack without detection," said Greenfield. "Boom . . . hits into the sink."

"And she's on the floor immediately. It would explain the watch damage."

"Precisely. A head split like that could cause the killer to panic, flee, and forget to lock the door."

Another moment of silence, as Cassandra fought to keep the contents of her stomach inside.

Carter clapped her hands once. "We can get back to that, but we need to finish who we're letting go. Good ideas, everyone. Keep mulling it over. The lists. Mr. Spooner had a goal for the party. He wanted a date, and most of the single females reported they interacted with him. The two young gentlemen roomed together. Chamberlain mentioned playing cards for hours after they retired upstairs. When pressed for further information, their stories didn't match. I want to talk to them again."

"Do you think they saw or heard something?"

"Possible, Greenfield. Or were they up to something illegal or otherwise? Add them to the keep list. Is that it for you, Jenkins?"

"I covered everyone."

"Next up, Henslowe. What do you have?" asked Carter.

"Poppy Fletcher, the piano player, was livid the guitar player got fired during a set. She stayed with Lightfoot and Fairchild. The women are friends."

"Those who were employed at the party might give a useful perspective. They were here to work and could think with a clear head." Footsteps paced the room. Carter continued. "Let's hold on to the piano player."

Henslowe added, "A few more on my list. Lady Bilford. Nothing. She was a friend of Lady Lemington. Old money. I don't think she had motive. She smells like my grandmother's parlor—heavy on the rosewater, cedar, chamomile tea, with a touch of camphor."

"Greenfield, add Bilford to the release list."

"Next, Arabella Dalton. Best mate to Miss Haywood. She made her way around the party networking for her profitable hair accessory business. She knows everyone, asks an extraordinary amount of questions, and has an impressive memory." Henslowe cleared his throat.

"Hold her. She's the niece's best friend and may remember something," Carter commanded.

What are they doing? Bella?

"I have a list of the other guests from the dining room, but no one stands out." Henslowe flipped pages in his notepad. "Barnaby Winchester, Victoria Barrett, Charles Sharp, Olivia Evans, and Chloe Davies all clear. Nothing extraordinary. I cleared all the valets. Nothing from them."

"Seems to be it," Jenkins remarked.

"I have another suspect," stated Carter.

"Who?" asked DC Greenfield.

"Miss Haywood."

Cassandra muffled a slight gasp into the scarf while remaining in her velvet hiding spot. Every hair on her body stood at attention.

Greenfield spoke. "I spent some time with her in this library. Miss Haywood is trying to process all of this and speaks of her aunt in the present tense. I don't think she's capable of murder. She's sweet."

"She wouldn't slam her aunt's head into the sink," answered Carter. "When I had her alone, I posed the guts question to her. The woman went white and almost hit the ground. No, that wouldn't be the way she would have done it. She could've hired someone to do the actual deed, or she was part of a plot with another."

Carter played me! Cassandra's shoulders trembled.

"Really?" asked Jenkins.

"Who here stands to gain the most from Lady Lemington's death? Miss Haywood. She told me she inherits the manor and becomes CEO of Lemington Cheese Company upon her aunt's demise. Perfect motive."

Cassandra shivered to the core.

Carter continued. "A scarf found on the floor in the victim's bedroom is Miss Haywood's. It's bagged as evidence. Twice when asked, she neglected to mention she was in there yesterday. In the photos at the start of the party, she's wearing that raspberry scarf."

That's where I left it! Evidence? How could I have forgotten I was in there? I went to see her before I retired for the night. She wasn't even in her room.

"Why retain everyone else if you're so convinced of Miss Haywood's guilt?" questioned DS Jenkins.

"I could be wrong. There are people here who might still be the guilty party. That's why we'll continue to question the others. Shake every tree. As I said earlier, perhaps someone had a hand in Miss Haywood's scheme. We want to rule out other possibilities or accomplices." The DCI cleared her throat.

"Or that Miss Haywood is the key suspect," responded another detective.

"Pleasant people commit crimes all the time. One mustn't let that impede the facts. Miss Haywood went outside for a moment to clear her mind and just found Mrs. York's medication?" remarked Carter. "It doesn't ring true."

"They found the pills?" asked Henslowe.

"Yes. Outside, supposedly on the front steps."

"She didn't have a purse when she was in the library or the parlor. Where would she have kept it hidden?" asked Greenfield.

"When I had her alone in the great hall, she removed a tissue from a pocket in her skirt and the pill bottle is small enough. The thing everyone is searching for, the object Mrs. York is desperate to find, is where she took a two-minute break to get a bit of air? Come on. What do you think her game is?"

"Do you believe she poisoned her aunt with the medication?" asked DC Penwarden. "Someone else could have stolen the pills and used them."

Despite the cold, Cassandra began sweating. She gripped her upper arms in a self-hug in a desperate attempt to keep from screaming.

"Possible. However, Miss Haywood had motive and was angry at her aunt all night. She had opportunity. I know how to read body language, and you've seen me assess people with precision. She was hiding something the initial time I questioned her. Miss Haywood knew her aunt died. Who would have that knowledge?

The killer or, at the very least, an accomplice."

"Someone could've told her."

"Greenfield, they woke Miss Haywood up and escorted her right to my questioning. Those are the facts," replied Carter.

Mr. Fartworthy told me. She shut her eyes and pressed her hands to her mouth again. *I want to wake up from this nightmare. I'm the number one suspect!*

Chapter Eighteen

Cassandra's body shuddered, threatening to betray her in the hiding space. Fear of detection and the newfound weight of suspicion sent ice running through every vein.

Greenfield piped up. "Hold on. What about Owen Savage?"

"Who's he?" asked Penwarden.

"The guitar player," replied Jenkins. "Lady Lemington fired him at the party. He 'borrowed' a few items from the manor and stashed them in his instrument case. She talked about having him arrested. He stated he's the only one working in his household."

"Angry enough to do something rash?" asked Greenfield.

A notepad rustled and Jenkins spoke again. "Mr. Savage told us he suffers from kleptomania and was apologetic about his condition. He's pushing to go home soon because he handles his mother's medication. His younger sister is at their house, but according to him, he's the only one that knows his mother's daily schedule for her many expensive pills. He also monitors her symptoms and has been doing this for years."

"His paycheck is vital, he got fired, and he's worried about his mum. Not a pleasant combination for rational thought. I would like to question him again since Lady Lemington threatened him last night," said Carter. "A serious discussion with Mr. Savage about where this might lead and provide him with mental health numbers is necessary. Greenfield, I'm putting you on that after I interview him again."

"Yes, ma'am," replied the new detective.

"That covers it. Let's move." Carter clapped her hands twice. "Penwarden and Henslowe. You take the list of those we're releasing. Snatch a few constables and give them the official word, and make sure you're quiet about the entire matter. Baron Von Pickle and Mrs. Turner will scream foul play if they realize we allowed others to leave. Assemble the release group downstairs in the kitchen. The staff we won't retain may go back to their regular duties. Arrange for the guests to return to their cars. If someone needs a ride, organize car service. Jenkins and I shall talk to those we wish to interview again. I think we should leave them separated in their rooms for the time being. We don't want to alert them to anything out of the ordinary. Chat with them, and they'll relax and reveal more."

Jenkins replied, "And you're the master of that."

"Yes, I am. Cheers you recognize the ways of 'Hurricane Carter.'"

The remaining detectives gasped and chuckled.

"You honestly thought I didn't know what I'm called behind my back?" She laughed. "Get a move on." The DCI clapped her hands again, like someone trying to scatter chickens out of a coop. The door clicked open, and multiple footsteps left the room.

Greenfield piped up, "What should I be doing, ma'am?"

"Come with me and Jenkins. There will be people griping. I'll send you to soothe egos. You might have to fetch tea, or we can find a moment for you to chat with Mr. Savage about his problem."

Please leave. Cassandra held her upper arms, the cold piercing her clothing. *This is worse than outside.*

Footsteps retreated, a door closed, and then . . . silence.

Cassandra remained hidden. She waited a minute and then peeked around the curtain. The library contained no other living being. Cassandra stepped out from the chilly holding cell.

She alternated between blowing into her hands and swinging her arms across her body. *If I'm in charge of the manor, we need to get insulated windows. What am I going to do? Suspect?* She crossed the room. *Mr. Fartworthy and Flora were correct. Carter won't see me as innocent unless I can prove another guilty, or it was an accident.* She stopped almost at the door. *I'm in charge of this manor and the company.* She looked around. *I'm in charge. I can do this.* She squared her shoulders. *I must.*

Cassandra pressed her ear to the entrance.

She strained to make out a sound. Hearing no noise, she took a deep breath. Like molasses dripping off a spoon, she cracked open the door, slipped out of the room, and made her way down the hallway to the servant stairwell. Once through the exit, she sprinted up the small, winding flight of stairs in hopes of getting to her bedroom before the detectives ascended the main steps in the great hall.

As she rounded one of the many stairway corners, she plowed into someone. "Oof," cried Cassandra, bouncing off another.

This time, it was Frederick.

"Cassandra!" exclaimed the jeweler. "What are you doing running up the stairs?" He backed up a step, his face red.

"I was about to ask you the same. Except . . . coming down, I mean." Cassandra panted and retreated several steps with an equally warm complexion. "I had to get my scarf I left. See. Found it." She lifted the lilac scarf tails. "Where were you going?"

"I'm heading to the kitchen for a drink of something. Water perhaps? The air is awfully dry up there. Should I go to the dining room?"

"The detectives want to see us soon. We should go back upstairs," said Cassandra, pointing in the direction she faced. *I can't tell him anything I heard. Could he have harmed my aunt? Everyone is a suspect.*

"They want to get us out of their hair. They'll let us go soon. I'm sure going to the kitchen is fine. See you in a few." Frederick sprinted down the stairs before Cassandra could respond.

Watching him descend, she squinted. *Odd.* Cassandra climbed the steps to the second-floor landing. Again, she slipped off her sandals, picked them up, and stealthily ran down the corridor.

At the corner, she slipped on her shoes and peeked around. Cassandra could hear muffled talking, and yet the hallway remained empty. *Still no one around. Good.* In the bathroom her friend occupied, the sound of water continued to rain down. *Bella, that's an extraordinarily long shower.* She made her way to her room and opened the entrance. She gasped.

Beds unmade. The closet doors flung wide. Drawers pulled out at various angles, and her clothing scattered on the floor. Her mouth fell open. She stepped in and shut the door behind her with a soft click. *What happened? Someone robbed me?*

Frost crawled up her spine. Cassandra held her forehead with her hand, tiptoeing around the fabric debris. *My purse is still here.* She opened the handbag, and her wallet remained tucked inside. *My laptop is on the desk. What would someone want from me? I own nothing of significant value. If a thief sought to steal something, there are so many other expensive items here at the manor.* She closed her desk drawer, picked up a stapled group of papers off the floor, and tossed it on the desktop. *That's the list of suppliers.*

She whirled around. *The papers. The papers to sign so I run the company!* She leapt over the pile of clothes to her dresser, yanked the crooked top drawer open, and drew in a quick breath.

"No! Where are they?" she spoke aloud, rummaging through her selection of legwear with no paperwork in sight. Rolls of navy, charcoal, and black tights bounced around in the confined space like potatoes in a wheelbarrow. She shoved the drawer's contents to one side and then the other. Nothing.

I need the detectives. She marched to the exit, and her hand touched the doorknob. She stopped. *What am I doing? They told us to be in our rooms. They expected me to be in here. How would I explain this? I wasn't in here because I was hiding behind a curtain listening to you discuss the case?* Cassandra collapsed on the edge of her bed. *This day is getting worse. I decide I want to be in charge, and then this. Hang on. Other paperwork was in that batch. Was there something else in those documents to incriminate a person who would hurt my aunt? I never even looked at the whole stack. Blast my laziness.* Cassandra picked up several pieces of clothing on the floor by her feet.

Arabella walked in. Her mouth resembled a fish gasping for air. "What did you do?"

"This wasn't me. I came into this disaster. Shut the door."

Arabella entered, surveying the room. "Did a detective do this while the others were questioning us downstairs this morning? That's got to be illegal."

"No, the room was tidy when I came in after parting with you." Cassandra surveyed her friend. "You took a long time."

Bella undid the messy bun on top of her head. "You know how the old pipes work. It takes forever for the water to get to the perfect temperature." She ran her fingers through her dry hair. "The point right before skin blisters is optimum. I feel loads better." Arabella walked around the room. "Did your aunt forget to give Christmas bonuses to the household staff?"

"Not funny, Bella."

"Sorry, luv. Trying to make sense of this. Anything stolen?"

She peered inside her purse. "My wallet is here."

"Mine, too. Laptop, jewelry, nothing of that sort is gone. Someone rummaged through my things for papers. That's what is missing."

Arabella faced her friend. "What papers?"

Cassandra moved over to her desk, careful not to step on her scattered possessions. "Paperwork I shoved into the top drawer last night before the party." She picked up the remaining stapled group from the desk. "There was a stack with these. Part of it was the legal documents for me to sign to become CEO of the company."

"Wait. Someone did this while you were in here?"

"No. I realized I forgot my lilac scarf in the library and left to get it. While there, the detectives arrived. I panicked and dodged behind the curtains."

"Cassie!" snickered Arabella. "You were hiding like a child?"

"Ridiculous, I know. They didn't discover me. Anyway, I heard them discussing the case, and they were making lists of who to keep and who to release. You're on the keep list, and Carter believes I had something to do with Aunt Lily's death!"

"What? That makes no sense."

"The DCI tried to convince the other detectives of my guilt."

"Why would she think you would do such a thing?" Arabella pulled the quilt up on her bed and sat. "You wouldn't hurt a fly."

Cassandra sat on the edge of her bed and faced Arabella. "She seems to have these reasons I could explain away."

Arabella waved her hands in the air. "We're all suspects if we're still here. They can't do anything to you without proof. We know you didn't harm her. You loved your aunt."

"I did, and I'd never hurt her." Cassandra wrinkled the papers in her hands.

"I know." Arabella patted her friend's knee. "Back to what you mentioned. What's missing?"

"Several things. First, the legal documents giving me control of the company upon my aunt's retirement or death. Mr. Fartworthy hinted they were in there."

"That's huge. Are you going to at least consider the position? Please, Cassandra, think it over," pleaded Arabella.

"Relax, Bella. My aunt told me we were tea bags and stronger when we got ourselves into hot water. I'm definitely in cuppa territory." Cassandra took a deep breath. "I can handle the job, and I've decided to do it."

Arabella squealed with delight, jumped up, and hugged her friend. "I know you can! This is amazing!"

"Okay, okay, thank you," remarked Cassandra, pulling away from the excited embrace. "I can't do this until I have the missing paperwork. That's why I must find it. Who would take it? Who knew it was in my room?"

Arabella sat on the bed. "Roland could've removed it."

"Maybe, but no one knew about it, and I don't believe anyone at the party did, either. Maybe someone overheard my aunt." Cassandra stood up and paced in her small room. "There are other missing documents of importance to keep the company running and safe. I barely saw them." She picked up a few more pieces of clothing off the floor and placed them on her bed.

"How do you know they are critical if you never read them?"

"Aunt Lily told me about them last night. She alluded to them being vital in taking down Von Pickle. She said they spelled everything out, and it would be easy with that proof. I don't see anything here." Cassandra rolled the papers in her hand. "Remember at the party, she got into it with him and he yelled? I'm guessing it has something to do with that."

Arabella stood and walked over to her friend. "You want to tangle with him as you're taking over the business? He's a ruthless serpent. He'll bury you. You *need* that paperwork."

"Maybe he took it! The missing documents would put the company leadership in turmoil long enough for him to fix whatever she had on him. Maybe Von Pickle killed Aunt Lily because of the information."

"Cassie, you're pulling at straws. Are you certain you even had it in here?"

"Yes, I'm certain. When I came home, Mr. Fartworthy told me about it." She paced, and her fingers twisted the ivory scarf ends. "I retreated to my room to rest and change for the party. I had no interest in looking at anything for work. I shoved the stack in the top drawer and never peeked at the papers after that."

"What's that in your hand?" asked Arabella.

"I'm positive this batch was with the others." She pointed to the top of the page. "I remember this as the top sheet. After the legal troubles, Aunt Lily needed our suppliers to be almost perfect. We wouldn't survive another lawsuit. In a desperate move, she reviewed the dairies we had and dismissed any that could be problematic. I wasn't part of those decisions when it happened. These are all the dairies released. She needed me to look at these. Why? Could I defeat Von Pickle with this list? Maybe the paperwork to sign is the only thing missing." Cassandra read from the paper in her hands. "Rafferty Acres, Wells and Nicholas Farm, Miller's Landing. I don't understand why she wanted me to read this. Nothing of Somerdale is on here." She ran her finger down the list.

"Maybe to be familiar with the farms so they didn't weasel their way back?"

"Possibly." Cassandra pointed to the paper. "This one, Brie-Z Dairy, fun name, loads of marketing potential. Cited several times for not dealing properly with an overabundance of manure. That could be a problem leading to many health issues. A lawsuit to a supplier could mean they might include Lemington Cheese, and we're back in court."

"Manure? That's literally and figuratively sickening. I'm glad my business had nothing to do with mucking about in anything."

Continuing to read aloud, Cassandra scanned the paperwork. "Anna's Lamb and Cheese Paradise, Wormhill Farm. Wormhill? That's a revolting name for a dairy. I hope they don't make Casu Marzu cheese."

"I'm not well-versed in cheese names. Which is that?" asked Arabella.

Cassandra spoke in a monotone. "Made in Italy, illegal, nauseating." She didn't look up while she scrutinized the writing.

"Why is it illegal?"

"I see. Wormhill was a regular, legal dairy, made Stilton. Here's why we canceled." Cassandra read from the paper. "Tested positive for listeria on four occasions. We gave the owner and his family three warnings, and they didn't follow the protocol for listeria elimination. Dairy closed." She looked up at Arabella. "That would make sense to end our contract. If you don't adhere to the specific removal procedure, that bacterium comes back and can be deadly."

"Cassie! What is Casu Marzu cheese? You didn't finish explaining."

"The Sardinians in Italy have made this cheese for hundreds of years with their sheep's milk. They cut a small hole in a cheese wheel and leave it outside." Cassandra's eyebrow arched. "Flies land and lay their eggs. When the larvae hatch and eat, their excrement breaks down the cheese, producing a creamy texture, beloved by some. 'Larvae-driven fermentation' is the correct term for the process, otherwise known as maggot cheese."

"You must be joking." Arabella's mouth twisted in revulsion.

"Utterly true. Gets worse. Dead maggots signify the cheese

has gone bad, so many individuals consume it with the live larva intact. When eating it, shut your eyes. The sight of crawling cheese isn't the problem. The critters can jump as high as six inches, and you don't want to get poked in the eye with a maggot. It's a delicacy that people will pay black market prices for." Cassandra grinned.

"Gross, Cassie. You won't catch me eating that. Cheese people are all bonkers."

"I don't eat it, I only know about it."

Raised voices pierced the door.

"What on earth?" Cassandra strode to the room's entrance to open it.

In the long, maroon-carpeted hallway, like two cowboys in the American Old West, stood Hamish York and Baron Von Pickle, facing off in a verbal showdown.

"Von Pickle, you're spouting off sarcastic nonsense as usual," barked Hamish. "You have nothing real to say—the same as your cheese products."

The baron's disdain dripped from his mouth. "You think you're so clever. You don't scare me, Frenchy. Go off to your cave and ripen like all the other overpriced, aged products you sell. I heard you match. You know . . . pungent and skin all wrinkly."

Cassandra and Arabella stepped onto the carpeted battle zone. They joined Robin, Owen, Roland, Alexander, Flora, and Poppy as witnesses. Mimi stood in her room's doorway, holding the molding for support.

"This doesn't look good," remarked Cassandra.

"What got them all fired up?" whispered Arabella, sliding along the wall.

While the men continued shouting at one another, Cassandra spied Frederick slipping around the corner from the other hallway. The duo in the room's middle captivated everyone's attention so no one else seemed to observe the jeweler's action. *What's Frederick up to?* Cassandra smiled when she caught his eye.

He returned a quick grin. Frederick stayed near to the wall and made his way past three bedroom doors until he stood by Cassandra's side. "What's going on?" he muttered.

Cassandra shrugged her shoulders. "We came out of my room to this."

Arabella leaned over to Cassandra. "Maybe the tension of staying here caused them to snap. I know I feel like an overstretched rubber band."

Cassandra shook her head. "No, look at them. This is something else."

Motion next to the men caught Cassandra's notice. She watched Alexander slide past the skirmish and move down the hall to them. In a quiet voice, the young man, new to their cluster, uttered, "Are they going to come to blows? Should we call the detectives?"

"They should have been here already," remarked Cassandra in an equally hushed tone.

"How do you know?" asked Frederick.

"I overheard them," said Cassandra as she glanced at the young men. *Don't ask anything else about that, please.* Frederick stared at her.

The argument grew louder.

"Always snark from you." Hamish, in his light-blue dress shirt unbuttoned at the collar, rolled up his other sleeve to match the first as he walked closer to Von Pickle. "Ignorant in so many things. I'm not French. I promote and sell amazing French cheeses. Yes, some are pungent and beautiful. Thank you for the compliment. So different from you! Your uncouth behavior left a bad taste in everyone's mouth since you stepped in the front door last night. Again, like your cheap, unappetizing cheese. Tell me, how is it possible you're allowed to sell counterfeit creations next to real food?"

"Counterfeit? You should talk!" growled Von Pickle. "Can't make true Roquefort so you created that artisan fake, 'The Rogue Fort cheese.' I'm surprised the INAO hasn't shut you down for that violation, York."

Frederick leaned over to Cassandra. "What's he talking about Roquefort?"

Without taking her eyes off the conflict, she responded, "Only bleu cheese ripened in the limestone caves under the village of Roquefort-sur-Soulzon in France can legally be labeled that name. The cheese must also be made from raw sheep's milk from that area. After the wine industry had the Protected Designation of Origin, the cheese trade did the same. They allow products from a specific region to have the name. Roquefort was the first cheese to gain that safeguard in 1925. Mr. York's company, Rosewood Cheese, has been making a knock-off for years that pushes that regulation. We all wonder how he gets away with it."

"Who or what is the INAO Von Pickle is talking about?" asked Arabella.

"The French government body responsible for the labeling. Financial ruin is a possibility if you tangle with them," answered Cassandra.

Alexander hooked his thumbs in his trouser pockets. "This cheese business is serious."

"You don't know the half of it." Cassandra fixed the lilac scarf around her neck.

Hamish raised his voice. "My cheese is perfectly legal, thank you."

Von Pickle snickered. "I have to thank you for the excellent night's sleep. I laughed myself to dreamland last night after I heard about your real age and the lies you told to keep it from your wife. Fifty-five? Mimi made *such* a good choice. She's sick *and* blind."

Arabella laughed, covering her mouth with her hand.

"What could be so funny, Bella?" Cassandra glared.

With a wide grin, Arabella asked, "Am I the only one who finds this argument amusing since a ham and a pickle are fighting over cheese?"

Cassandra rolled her eyes. "You're nutters."

Hamish ran a hand through his blond hair. "Somerdale Company *used* to be one we aspired to imitate. You had a Havarti that smashed the competition for decades. The company existed for over a hundred and fifty years with four generations of your family running the place."

The baron crossed his arms. "Yes, four generations. And your point?"

Hamish flashed his handsome smile. "I'm wondering how such a prestigious company tumbled from award-winning products across categories of cheeses to marketing sludge." He sauntered closer to his rival. "I know. This started with your father. He made the first poor decision of where to take the business to keep it alive. When you took over the helm, your choices created a quality free fall. Here you're slamming me for artisan French cheese, but wasn't that the kind of cheese your great-grandfather sold off his farm to start Somerdale?"

"I don't need a history lesson about my family. Stick to your own story." Von Pickle slapped his own forehead. "Aha! That must be a lie, too. You started Rosewood twenty-five years ago, not your father! You've been fabricating your history for years." Von Pickle's thunderous laughter bounced off the close walls.

Hamish's grin vaporized. "That's not important. My company might have embellished its history to lend credibility. It didn't matter. From the beginning, our sales skyrocketed for our quality products."

"Quality soaked in lies. Sounds closer to feta than French." Von Pickle sneered.

From the doorway, Mimi called out, "Rupert, enough."

The baron glanced over Hamish's shoulder. "You stay out of this." He locked eyes with Hamish, who halted his forward movement. "I'm right, aren't I? My father wasn't fighting for survival against your father—it was against you. This revelation is too perfect. So many things make sense."

Mimi hissed. "I will not be silent."

"We've all known it for a long time, sweetheart," said Von Pickle with a smirk. "Somerdale International will bury you in sales this year with our expanded markets and our innovation."

Hamish's hands flew up. "You believe chemical-laden, insipid, homogenized pond scum manufactured in one of your labs—sorry, cheese processing facilities—is superior? How is that better than methods that have been around thousands of years, delighting generations around the globe?"

Von Pickle's mouth formed a thin line as a brief silence engulfed the hallway. He glowered at Hamish's arms. "Are you going to have plastic surgery on your elbows next? You know they're showing your actual age."

Hamish stared at his exposed lower arms. "What?"

"You can tell a woman's real age by her hands and a man's age by his elbows. I guess you missed that memo. So did your wife, old man."

Cassandra exchanged a glance with Arabella. "He hits low."

"I'm getting to you." Von Pickle continued. "I can see the blue veins popping out in your neck. They match your products. You're as ridiculous as Mimi. I'm glad you ran and our business deal fell through. I can't imagine going through such a venture with an epic liar."

Hamish huffed. "I didn't run. Working with you would have been the worst decision we could've made for our company. Mimi cautioned me when she found out you were behind the deal."

The baron turned to face her, and his neck and cheeks burned red. "You made him renege? That partnership had nothing to do with you. Have you any idea the kind of chaos you've caused for me by Rosewood withdrawing from our agreement? I made different business decisions because of your selfishness. You let a golden opportunity slip through your fingers. Again."

"Yes, I know." Mimi walked closer to the sparring men. "And as a married couple, it involves me. I work at our company, too, designing all the labels for our cheeses, and I'm responsible for marketing. If we formed a partnership with you, we would lose power over our own product." She stood by her husband's side. "I warned him of your controlling, ruthless behavior. People don't change on a fundamental level. Even if it's been sixteen years."

Hamish pointed to his wife. "I trust her instincts."

Von Pickle laughed. "Her instincts of sniffing out the truth? That seems broken. Deciding? She passed on an amazing life years ago."

"Rupert, we were dating for two months when you asked me to marry you. It was too soon," said Mimi.

"When I want something, I don't waste time. Glad you said no." The baron adjusted his cuff links and looked at the audience.

Mimi crossed her arms over her chest. "Like I said, controlling and unchanging."

"You knew each other years ago?" asked Cassandra from down the hall.

"Rupert and I were at university together." Mimi sighed. "I read English and art and he read business. We dated for a short time."

"How hilarious is it you weren't interested in marrying someone older than you by two years?" sneered Von Pickle. "What else was it? 'I can't marry a businessman who deals with cheese.' I think those were your exact words. Look where you are now, *darling*."

Mimi shouted, "You didn't take no for an answer!" Her voice dropped in volume. "I was trying to be nice and let you down gently. Your father always pushed you to finish, and he made it clear you were joining him to run the family company. I knew it would be easier for you to walk away with something non-negotiable than to say my true feelings."

"Which were?" Von Pickle smirked as he glanced at Cassandra and Arabella.

Mimi sighed at the arguing men. "I couldn't trust you."

The baron remained silent, and his attention returned to his former girlfriend. Hamish's head dropped to his chest, and his hands slid to his sides.

DCI Carter, DS Jenkins, DC Greenfield, and Mr. Birch entered the hallway from the main staircase.

Carter's face twisted. "What's everyone doing out of their rooms?"

Chapter Nineteen

Silence greeted the newcomers.

The head detective strode to the middle of the hallway. "Can anyone tell me exactly what is going on here?"

Owen spoke. "These gentlemen 'ad 'em issues with cheese, money, and a girl. Besides the cheese, it's what me and me mates argue about all the time. They're just usin' 'em fancy words is all. We all came out 'ere because they were louder than squealin' pigs on slaughter day. We was all watchin' 'em go at it with words. No one threw a punch, but if I be a gamblin' man, like me uncle, I'd 've sworn someone was goin' to 'it the carpet soon. This 'ere gentleman, with 'is sleeves rolled up, turned a tail out of a deal and 'as somethin' wrong with 'is elbows. The other gentleman makes bad cheese and used to love *is* wife. And the lady is married to 'im, used to date 'im, and doesn't like either of 'em right now."

"Thank you, Mr. Savage, for the complete and colorful summary. I appreciate it." Carter approached Von Pickle and the Yorks. "This discussion is over. Move away from each other." She surveyed the crowd. "Where are the constables that were supposed to be up here? Where is the butler, Fartworthy?"

Flora Fairchild clung to her handkerchief. "Maybe he's still in the kitchen and didn't get the message to be here."

"We informed him," responded Carter as she walked down the passageway. "Since we're all here, we might as well use our time wisely." She put her hands on her hips. "All of you stand by the doorway of the room you slept in. I'm trying to form a visual of where people stayed last night."

The group moved like molasses.

Cassandra turned to Frederick and Alexander. "You better go before you get in trouble."

Frederick smiled. "I feel like I'm in primary school, lining up for morning exercises again."

She grinned at him. "Go on. If we listen, maybe this will be over soon." The young men obeyed.

DS Jenkins spoke from the opposite end of the hall from Cassandra's room. "Thank you for your cooperation."

The head detective turned to Greenfield. "Look downstairs for Fartworthy and tell him we require his presence on the second floor. Let him know I sent for him. And find out which constables were supposed to be in this hallway."

"Yes, ma'am." Greenfield sprinted to the main staircase.

Carter touched Cassandra's arm. "How are you doing?"

"Swimmingly." *I'm not falling for your tricks.* "This is my room." Cassandra pointed over her shoulder.

"Great, thank you." The DCI tilted her head and moved down the hall. "This will clear things up for my team. We appreciate your assistance."

Cassandra whispered to Arabella, "Why would she switch from separation to this? What's she thinking?"

"You got me," replied her friend. "You don't have to solve all the pieces of the puzzle."

Cassandra played with her ivory scarf tails. "Carter is keeping us up here so we don't see the other guests and staff released."

"Way to go, Sherlock." Arabella examined her nails and yawned. "Hopefully, this doesn't take too long. This isn't how I planned to spend today."

"No one planned for this, Bella."

Arabella grimaced. "Sorry, luv. That was callous of me. Yes, of course. No one planned for the day to be like this." She gave her friend a side hug.

The left side of Cassandra's mouth rose. Observing Carter direct the others, Cassandra became lost in her thoughts. *Is this everyone Greenfield had on the keep list? Roland in the single room. The Yorks in the largest guest room. My aunt's bedroom. After the main staircase, there's Mrs. Turner in the second largest guest room. Ruby and Poppy stayed together in Flora's.* Her attention jumped to her side of the hallway. *Mr. Birch in the bedroom next to my room on one side, and Owen next door in Mr. Fartworthy's. Von Pickle after that loo in the third largest guest room. Frederick shared the smaller room with Alexander across the hall from my aunt's. Mr. Fartworthy is the only person missing from the list. Wait. Ruby isn't here. They're keeping her, but as a colleague. She was in Flora's room, across from me. I remember hearing laughter last night.*

Mr. Birch walked down the hall toward the ladies. After he passed them, he leaned against the molding on his bedroom door with his arms crossed on his chest.

Cassandra moved away from Arabella and closer to the gardener. "Are you all right, Mr. Birch?"

He whispered to her. "Why is this necessary? I have things to take care of and so do you. They should allow us to grieve in peace."

"Were you interviewing downstairs all this time?" asked Cassandra.

"No, that was earlier. I thought they were finished with me, and I left. I needed to get more heaters hooked up in the hothouse.

It's too cold out there. Some of the heirloom seed plants could die. The head detective and those other two found me and gave a reprimand to stay with the group. For what purpose? It was a horrible accident, and we must live with the consequences. She fell, plain and simple."

Cassandra turned to the cantankerous man. "They think someone might have hurt her."

He uncrossed his arms and stood away from the doorframe. "What?" His face fell. He murmured, "You can't be serious. Who would harm Lily? I mean, Lady Lemington?"

"They don't know." Cassandra untied her lilac fabric. "It's a precaution, and it sounds like they'll be here for some time."

He took a step closer to the young woman. "For how long? Who do they suspect?"

She wrapped her hand in the scarf while she investigated Mr. Birch's face. *I shouldn't confide in anyone, but I know him. He would be fine.* "It seems they're questioning all of us. Her bedroom is right down the hall. Maybe one of us saw something last night." When she finished with the scarf, Cassandra's hand resembled a lavender beehive.

He held her gaze with squinted eyes, like a parent looking through to a child's soul. She blinked and looked away. He blew air from his mouth like the former smoker he was. "After your aunt repeated that my services were no longer needed, I went to my room and fell asleep, trying to plan my future."

"Did you see anything when you came upstairs yesterday evening?" asked Cassandra.

Mr. Birch's thumb and index fingers smoothed his mustache and his brown-and-speckled-gray goatee. "No. What about you?"

"We were downstairs for another hour or so after midnight. Arabella and I saw nothing when we retired."

Mr. Birch leaned back onto the molding again, crossing his legs at the ankles. He resembled a cowboy in an old, American western. He cocked his head to the side. "Are you in charge of the manor for sure?"

"I am."

"You have authority. You can convince the detectives they must leave. We don't need them here anymore. They should at least stick to the main house. No use for them to be poking around the hothouse or the grounds, making a mess of things. And where *is* Fartworthy? I think he's up to something. He has been acting strange for days."

"Has he?" Cassandra studied his face.

"That butler makes a nuisance of himself. I don't need him telling me how to run my crew. I'm capable of having a groundskeeping team complete their tasks without the help of the almighty Fartworthy. His prowling around my plants is uncalled for. You should reconsider whether to retain him in your employment."

"Mr. Birch, I have no desire to change his employment status—or yours—until we have the situation of my aunt's death sorted."

"I don't think anyone hurt her. This is a complete waste of time if you ask me."

That's the grumpy man I know. Cassandra leaned closer. "They're being cautious. I wish for them to leave, too, but if someone murdered Aunt Lily, the suspect is right here in our midst and they might lose their chance to catch them."

Carter, from the other end of the hall, spoke up. "Miss Haywood? Please pay attention here. No other conversations. The excess noise is distracting. Thank you."

Cassandra stood straight. "My apologies." She unwrapped her hand and tied the scarf around her neck.

Birch smirked. "She has the real power today."

The head detective pointed at different people. "We'll establish when each of you went to your rooms last night and what you saw. Thank you again for your cooperation." She removed a notepad from her interior jacket pocket and flipped pages. "We already spoke to Mr. Birch about his retreat upstairs moments before midnight. Next, Mrs. York. You remarked earlier you left the New Year's celebration immediately after midnight. You spoke to Lady Lemington on the main steps beforehand, correct?"

Mimi leaned against the wall and nodded. "I came upstairs and went to the lavatory across the hall. I thought about returning to the party but decided to go to my bedroom. The evening's events proved exhausting. I ended up going to sleep."

"How did you know which was your assigned bedroom?" asked the DCI.

"My husband received a small card with our name and our room number on it. Some butler handed the card to Hamish before midnight."

"Mr. York? You stated you followed your wife to your room, but she wasn't there right away."

"Yes, I found her minutes later. She told you where she went." Hamish shrugged. "We chatted for a short time, and we determined it was best for her to have complete quiet. I went back downstairs to the party for another half hour. When I returned, she was fast asleep."

Carter squinted. "Determined, or she asked you to leave since you argued over revelations from the evening?"

Hamish turned to the gilded, oval mirror hanging on the wall beside him. Running his fingers through the front of his blond hair, he chuckled at his reflection. "Correct. There appear to be no more secrets in this place." He smiled at the head detective.

"Can't be too sure about that, Mr. York." Carter walked away from the couple. "Mrs. Robin Turner, please repeat what you told us earlier about what happened past midnight with you and Lady Lemington."

Robin sighed. "What was the point of interviews downstairs if you planned to do this here?"

Jenkins raised a finger. "I'm sorry for the inconvenience, Mrs. Turner. The DCI is looking for clarity. Maybe a guest or staff member can add something to our understanding. Can you recall what happened? We sincerely appreciate your cooperation."

Robin rolled her eyes. "I talked with Lily and Miss Haywood at the bottom of the main stairs, came up here, and changed into bed clothes. I spent the rest of the night in my room. Alone. Reading."

"Talked with or argued?" asked Carter.

"Fine. Argued, I suppose. Lily was obstinate about my son not becoming CEO. I know this decision is an absolute mistake. Miss Haywood is too young and incapable of running my father's company."

Cassandra bristled at the insult. *Age doesn't determine talent. Why is Carter questioning us in this way?*

The head detective tugged on her jacket lapel. "My team and I are here to discover what occurred last night. The fate of Lemington Cheese Company is not mine to determine. That's for the business and a gaggle of lawyers to iron out. Back to what you said before, what were you reading?"

"That doesn't matter," replied Robin.

"Everything matters. You never answered me during our first interview, and I let it slide. I'll ask you again, respectfully, what were you reading?"

Robin's hands flapped around in the air. "I don't see what this has to do with your investigation. It's something I bring with me everywhere to help me relax at night. Nothing new."

The DCI moved closer to Mrs. Turner. "If staying overnight

was unexpected for everyone, how was it you had a change of clothes to sleep in and your favorite book with you?"

Robin sighed. "Lily always had the option to stay after a party. I grew up here, and then they denied me ownership of this house. Do you think I would pass up an opportunity, even for one night? Like an old coat, it's comforting here, although I must endure my sister-in-law."

"Fair enough. So, you're stating you planned to stay until morning before the weather made it necessary for everyone to remain?" remarked Jenkins.

"Yes. I'm always in this room, between the main staircase and the lavatory." Robin pointed.

Carter asked, "How many lavatories are in this hallway?"

Cassandra raised her fingers. "Three. This one across the hall from me and next to Mrs. Turner, the one at the top of the stairs that had the caution tape across the doorway, and one at the far end."

"I see." Carter tapped her pen on her notepad. "We would like to move this along, Mrs. Turner. One last time. What did you read last night before going to bed?"

"Calvin and Hobbes."

"Pardon?" The head detective's eyebrows arched.

Robin puffed herself up to her full, but still short, height. "You heard me. Calvin and Hobbes."

The others in the hallway looked at one another.

Arabella's hand went to her mouth, suppressing a giggle.

Cassandra whispered, "Bella, no."

Carter grabbed the back of her neck and sighed. "That book is an interesting choice for nighttime reading. You take it everywhere?"

"Yes, I do." Robin coughed. "It's the one thing to calm my mind before I sleep. When my only child, Roland, was a little boy, he used to go on many imaginary adventures. He carried with him a stuffed rainbow penguin named Skittles. The two of them went everywhere together. Calvin reminds me of the innocent time in my son's life."

"That's reasonable, Mrs. Turner. Books are old friends, and falling asleep can be tricky in a strange bed. Thank you for your honesty." Carter tapped her notepad. "Your son, Roland Turner. He's next. Where are you, Mr. Turner?"

Roland, at the hallway's far end, walked to the detectives and his mother. "Here. I'm not sure anything I have to say would be of any help."

"What happened after midnight with you?" asked DS Jenkins.

Roland cleared his throat. "After Mother climbed the main steps to this hallway, I followed. I asked if she needed anything, and she told me we should take care of this problem. I'm sorry, Mother."

"Sorry for what? We did nothing wrong." Robin's short, black curls bounced.

The DS pressed. "What did she mean by that?"

"Not a clue." Roland shuffled his feet.

DCI Carter asked, "Mrs. Turner, why did you tell your son that?"

"Roland needs to be in charge of the cheese company, and Lily needed to be convinced otherwise," answered Robin. "That's all."

"What did you do after, Mr. Turner?"

"My head pounded, so I returned to my room and went to sleep." Roland shook his head. "I didn't see or hear anything else."

"Mrs. Turner, what did you do after you conversed with your son?" Carter asked, pointing at the woman.

"Went to my room and stayed there, like I told you before," answered Robin.

"Did you go anywhere else?" asked Carter.

"I went to see Lily in her bedroom when she came upstairs."

The Detective Chief Inspector tapped her pen on her notepad. "You were in her room?"

"Yes, briefly. She refused to discuss Roland's future at the business. I left her alive and well."

"So, you bid her a cheery good night and happily removed yourself from her room?"

"Anything but."

"You were angry with her." Carter moved closer.

"Yes."

"How angry?"

Robin raised her voice. "We were shouting at one another, and she demanded I leave."

Mimi crossed her arms. "Then it was you I heard yelling next door as I was trying to sleep. That was obnoxious."

Robin glowered at Mimi and then spoke to Carter. "You don't understand. She used him for years, having him believe he would take over the company. She had no plans to give my son what he wanted. It's unfair and an abuse of power."

Roland stepped forward. "Mother, I don't wish to be in charge. That's your dream, not mine."

"No, you do. You don't realize what you want. Listen to your mother."

"I know precisely what I want today and what I want to do with the rest of my life. Dealing with cheese is not on that list. Aunt Lily made a correct assessment." Roland stuffed his hands deep into his trouser pockets and studied the carpeted floor.

Robin took several steps closer. "It's our wish for you to run the company. You always said that."

"You're not listening, Mother. I realized today I can be free from this job I so utterly despise. I did it only for you. You used me for your own gain."

"I have no idea what you are talking about." Robin backed up two steps.

Roland stood a little taller and took a deep breath. "You know exactly what I mean." He turned to Cassandra. "Remember last night at the party when our aunt mentioned Mother getting kicked out for impropriety and Uncle Richard stepping into her place?"

"Yes," answered Cassandra. "Do you know more about this?"

Roland nodded and continued. "When she was in her twenties, Mother was her father's right-hand person. She operated for years in the inner circle of upper management, with Grandfather training her to take over Lemington Cheese. All the while, tens of thousands of pounds disappeared under her watch. When Grandfather discovered the embezzled funds, he had two choices."

Robin waved her hands around, trying to erase her smokey past. "We don't air dirty laundry in front of everyone. Honestly, Roland. You pick such a topic to discuss."

He spun around to face his mother. "You stole money from your own family! How honest is that?"

"Roland! Enough!" Robin walked away.

Carter spoke. "Wait a moment, Mrs. Turner. I want to hear the rest of this story. Come back here."

"What's there to say?" Robin halted and wrung her hands.

"Much, and I'll tell you," said Roland. "Grandfather could have had her arrested, pressed charges, and she would've gone to prison for a long time. He had solid proof. Not wanting to send his only daughter to jail and create a family scandal for the company, he chose another option. He quietly booted her out of the business, made her repay every single shilling, and the next time the board met, he added an addendum to the corporation bylaws."

"No more!" shouted Robin.

"No more secrets! I'm tired of hiding the truth at the expense of my life." Roland walked toward the DCI. "The addition to the bylaws, which I didn't discover until the lawsuit against Lady Lemington, included my mother's exclusion from any positions of authority within the company. Forever."

Cassandra's mouth fell open. "Is that the sudden information that had you drop the lawsuit? This? Aunt Lily said you settled. You didn't settle."

"Correct." Roland faced Cassandra. "Mother had no choice with the absence of a legal leg to stand on. Grandfather made her permanent expulsion ironclad and binding. He forgave her transgressions but never trusted her again."

"Your mother used you to slip back into the company?" Cassandra twisted the ivory and lilac scarf tails around her fingers.

"Precisely." Roland addressed Cassandra yet looked at his mother, his intense, blue eyes brimming with a storm of sadness and resentment. "I arrived at the office of Lemington Cheese Company every day to do my aunt's bidding and her rival's. I forwarded the list of things to do and the problems to Mother at the start of the day. During work hours, she would text me." Roland stared at his shuffling feet. "She sent instructions on what I should do."

Cassandra glared in disgust. "You knew this and acted as her puppet?"

Roland looked up in surprise and laughed. "You could say that. Yes, I was, but no longer."

"This isn't funny, Roland," Cassandra scolded.

"Not in the least." He moved away from his mother. "I have another dream I wish to pursue, and it has nothing to do with cheese."

"No, Roland. We know what—"

"Mother!" Roland raised his voice and stormed back toward her. "What part of 'no' do you not understand? I hate my job in the corporate world. I loathe wearing suits. Quarterly numbers, marketing, all of it makes me numb. I despise every topic. This isn't my love, it's yours. My secret hope, my desire, is to . . . um . . . is to go . . . to go. . . ." Roland covered his face with his hands.

"Out of town? Out of the country?" Robin shouted. "Is to go where?"

"The LSP," he blurted.

The people in the hall remained silent.

Robin commanded, in a harsh whisper, "What on earth is the LSP?"

"London School of Puppetry."

Roland pulled out of his trouser pocket a hand puppet resembling his face. He slid his palm inside the plaything and held it up for all to see. The felt-and-fabric Roland trembled like a leaf in a strong wind.

"Are you joking, my dear boy?"

"No, Mother. Never been more serious in all my life. 'The London School of Puppetry is the only school of higher education in the UK devoted to tailored specialist courses for puppeteers.' That's from their website, which I visit daily. I wish to enroll immediately since the new semester starts the first week of February." The man stared at the carpet.

Cassandra stepped forward and reached out to Roland's puppet. She cradled the cloth encasement in her hands. "You stitched this yourself?" Her thumbs ran across the fine, embroidered face.

"Yes, I made it some time ago." Roland lowered his arm. "Cassandra, I don't want to be a part of Lemington Cheese Company anymore. You can have it. In case you're wondering, I *never* leaked any information to rivals. I don't know why I became brave today. This is the thing I want to do with my life."

"It's the new year and a fresh start." Cassandra smiled.

"You don't think it's silly?" He slipped his hand out of his fabric friend. "They have courses in shadow work, marionette building, rod puppetry, therapeutic use of puppets, and so much more. Graduates of the program use their knowledge all around the world, creating exciting shows and innovative ways to use puppets. Mesmerizing stuff." His bright-blue eyes danced.

"It's something unique, and I see it makes your heart sing." Cassandra touched his arm.

"Interesting way of putting it. It does." Roland beamed. "Nothing about cheese fits the bill. Not even fine-aged, sharp cheddar can do that for me."

Robin recovered from the shock. "I don't care about singing hearts. You have an obligation to your family to run the cheese company!" Her short frame moved to stand toe-to-toe with her tall son.

Roland, with sad eyes, smiled down at her. "Mother, I'm saying no to you." He spoke in a quiet voice. "No more hiding. Just because I'm your child doesn't mean your desires are my reality. Your definition of success has colored my world for years. I thank you for all you've done for me, but now, I must lead my life. I'm sorry if this will embarrass or hurt you." He shook the hand puppet in front of him. "This. *This* is my future. I hope you can see past your rage one day and appreciate who *I* am."

"Some two-bit player in a traveling puppet show with little money, no prestige, no way to advance, and doomed to be surrounded by other freaks?" sneered Robin.

Roland's bottom lip quivered for a moment. "Maybe." His voice cracked. "Something else could develop, but even if my life turns out as you say, I'll be much happier than as your personal puppet. You won't change my mind." Roland crammed the felt creation into his trouser pocket, walked to his room, and shut the door.

Everyone stood in shocked silence.

After a few seconds, Robin turned to the onlookers. "This isn't over." The angry woman stormed off to her room, and the bang of the wooden door reverberated in the long space.

Chapter Twenty

Carter exhaled. "Let them be." She flipped the pages of her notepad. "Miss Haywood and Miss Dalton?"

"Yes?" the ladies answered in unison.

"You left the party simultaneously, correct?"

Arabella replied, "Yes. Mr. Chamberlain and Mr. Spooner retired upstairs at the same time."

"That's true," added Alexander from the other end of the hall. "We spent the last hours at the party together."

Frederick stood next to the pharmacist. "We invited the ladies to play cards with us, but they declined. We played until three, or was it later? It was early in the morning."

"What were you playing?" asked the head detective.

"Cards," the gentlemen replied as one.

"Yes, you said that. What card game?" Carter demanded.

"Poker." Alexander's eyes darted to Frederick.

"Yes, poker." Frederick cleared his throat.

Carter pressed, "And?"

"Different poker games. We mixed things up all night." Frederick tugged on his ear.

Alexander shuffled his feet. "Five-Card Draw, Softball, Follow the Queen, and Texas Hold 'Em."

The DCI moved closer to the young men. "Did you do anything else?"

The men looked at one another.

Down the hall, Cassandra leaned into her friend. "What are they hiding?"

"Hiding?" Arabella's brow furrowed. "They're answering her questions, Cassie."

"No, something is up." Cassandra crossed her arms.

"Gentlemen, we've had a long day." Carter sliced the air with her hand. "Cut the nonsense. What games—cards or otherwise—were played when you stayed in that room?"

"Gin Rummy," said Frederick.

"Blackjack," answered Alexander at the same moment.

"Which is it?"

"Both," replied Frederick.

"Neither." Alexander turned to the other young man. "She's onto us. We might as well tell."

Frederick stared at the maroon carpet.

The Detective Chief Inspector drew a deep breath. "The truth would be refreshing."

Frederick wiped his forehead with the back of his hand. "We started playing poker for hours. We talked the whole time. I've seen him for years in the village. We've always been cordial, but we never had an in-depth conversation until last night. Ever meet someone and the two of you click instantly? Well, that's what happened. We didn't stop, and it was as if we were old friends. It doesn't happen too often. When it does, it's delightful."

"That's nice, but you're not answering the question." Carter's eyes remained locked on the young men.

Alexander smiled. "It's true we talked for hours. In that time, we discovered several things we have in common. Turns out we both enjoy John Wayne movies, green, pickled tomatoes, Key lime pie, and . . . and . . . blast." He chuckled.

"Not too many people would admit this," added Frederick.

Alexander looked at Cassandra. "So embarrassing. Do we have to confess in front of everyone?"

The DCI frowned. "What were you doing?"

"It's simple. We were playing Old Maid," answered Alexander with a boyish grin.

Frederick shut his eyes tight and winced. "We're both obsessed with the game. That's how we lost track of time." He opened his eyes and turned to his friend. "It was hours, wasn't it?"

"Absolutely," said Alexander. "A bit of silliness, really."

Carter sighed. "Did you notice anything or hear anything else besides the shuffling of cards?"

"There was a loud argument and a door slamming soon after we started." Alexander pointed across the hall. "The noise came from there."

"This bedroom?" The head detective gestured over her shoulder to Lady Lemington's room. "Did you see who argued?"

"Yes," answered Frederick. "I watched Mrs. Turner storm down the hall to Miss Haywood. The ladies talked for a moment."

"Did you talk to Mrs. Turner, Miss Haywood, or Lady Lemington?"

"No, I didn't," replied the jeweler.

Carter looked at Alexander. "Where were you when this went on?"

"I was dealing the cards at our table. He informed me of what happened. Later, we discussed the nasty-sounding fight and decided I would check on Lady Lemington."

"How was she?"

Alexander shrugged. "Fine. When I peeked my head into her

doorway, she was sitting on her bed, drinking her tea. She told me she was exhausted. I asked her if she needed anything and she said no, so I went back to our card game."

"What time was that?" Carter pressed her lips together.

"I don't know." Alexander looked up. "Two?"

DCI turned to Frederick. "Mr. Chamberlain, where were you and what did you see?"

Frederick answered, "I stayed in here. Our door was open, and I saw him lean in."

"Did you go into her bedroom, Mr. Spooner?"

Alexander shook his head. "No, I stood in the doorway."

Carter flipped through her pages. "Thank you, gentlemen. Anything else?"

"No, ma'am," the card-playing duo answered together.

Cassandra watched Flora turn her back to the detectives and look at the mobile phone she had stashed in her apron pocket. The head housekeeper peered up at Cassandra.

Does Miss Fairchild wish to talk?

Carter read from her notepad. "Owen Savage? After Lady Lemington terminated your employment, you were downstairs in the kitchen for the remainder of the evening, correct?"

"Yes, ma'am," replied Owen.

Miss Fairchild moved closer to Cassandra. They stepped away from Arabella.

Flora shielded her mouth with the handkerchief and whispered, "Mr. Fartworthy is waiting for you in the servant stairwell, near the first floor. He wishes to speak to you at once and hopes you can slip away without the DCI noticing."

Cassandra's eyes grew wide. "Where has he been? Does he know Carter is looking for him?" The head detective continued to question Owen.

"Mr. Fartworthy loves this cloak-and-dagger stuff. Have you ever seen the bookshelf in his room? All thrillers and PI novels. Will you meet him?" Flora slipped her handkerchief into her apron pocket.

Cassandra chuckled. *Of course he reads those books. I can't mention to Flora he's an actual PI.* "Tell him yes. How will I slip out and avoid Carter's watchful eye?" Cassandra twisted the end of her ivory scarf.

"I'm sure an opportunity will arise. I'll help." Her fingers flew on her device. "There. Done. Don't mention this to anyone. Someone might betray him." Flora glanced down the hall.

"Thanks." Cassandra moved back to her friend.

Arabella wrinkled her nose. "What was that?"

Cassandra shrugged. "Staff concerns. No worries."

Carter continued talking to Owen. "And after you visited the lavatory, where did you go?"

"Me and me guitar case left the loo and stepped next door to Fartworthy's room."

"Who escorted you?" pressed the DCI.

"Butler John or Butler Nathan. They took turns watchin' me last night. I can't tell which one I followed upstairs. They 'ave the same face," replied Owen.

"They're twins, as it happens. Were you alone then?" Carter ran her fingers through her shoulder-length, auburn hair.

"No, a butler stayed with me until Fartworthy came. 'e didn't come in for a good long time. I was dozin' by the time that 'appened. 'e told the other butler to leave when 'e got 'ere."

"Then you stated earlier you were with Fartworthy until morning light. To repeat, you came upstairs with your guitar case and went right into this lavatory where Lady Lemington was found this morning." Carter paused. "So, the only time you were alone after you were fired was when you were in the lavatory?"

Owen laughed. "I should 'ope so! Wouldn't want an audience when I'm doin' me business!"

Multiple chuckles filled the air.

Greenfield returned. "Chief? Mrs. Forest wanted me to inform you they have prepared luncheon and it's currently available in the dining room. The two constables assigned to this hallway were getting coffee downstairs." He raised an eyebrow. "They're with Penwarden now because he needed assistance. Everything else is set, as instructed."

Carter shook her head. "Thank you." She addressed the group. "Everyone should get something to eat. We'll take this downstairs. Please stay together, and we'll wrap this up soon."

Flora Fairchild, standing before Robin's doorway, raised her hand. "Pardon me, Detectives. Should we retrieve the Turners out of their rooms?"

"Yes," replied DS Jenkins.

"Mrs. Turner?" Flora knocked on the older woman's door. "Mrs. Turner, there's luncheon set up downstairs. Will you join us? Mrs. Turner?"

Robin cracked open the door. "Yes, I shall. Thank you for informing me." She smiled at the head housekeeper. "You look familiar. Forgive me, my memory isn't the best."

"I'm just a servant ma'am, and you're welcome. This way." Flora pointed to the main staircase.

Robin stepped out. "Will there be cheese?"

Flora nodded. "The talented Mrs. Forest always ensures several kinds are on the menu."

"As it should be." Robin fluffed her curly, black hair and walked down the hall.

At the other end, Mimi knocked on Roland's door. "Mr. Turner? Mr. Turner?" She listened. "Detectives, he said he isn't coming out. Can you persuade him?"

Carter pointed. "Greenfield, take the group to the dining room." The DCI and DS Jenkins arrived at Roland's bedroom. "Mr. Turner?" She rapped on the door.

Flora's robin's egg-blue eyes caught Cassandra's attention. The housekeeper whispered to Poppy. "You mentioned Mr. Turner talked to you for some time last night while you were playing. Could you convince him to come out? He must be hungry, and a friendly voice might persuade him to open the door. They aren't having any luck."

"Flora, that poor man. You're right. I'll go see what I can do." Poppy strode to the growing cluster outside the young man's door. The others flocked to the main staircase.

Arabella turned to Cassandra. "I'll hit the loo before we have luncheon." She pointed to the small room closest to them. "This one, not the one that had the yellow tape on it. See you downstairs." She stepped into the lavatory across the hall and shut the door.

The head housekeeper watched the others and whispered to Cassandra, "Go. Meet him. Shoo." Without waiting for an answer, Miss Fairchild moved toward the group from the almost empty end of the space. "The dining room is this way." She spread her arms wide, guiding the remaining guests to the main stairs like a farmer corralling cows.

Cassandra moved down the hall. Before she reached the corner, she peered back for a moment. No one noticed her. She made her way down the new corridor, slipped through the servant doorway, and down the winding steps. After a few turns, she spied Fartworthy.

"So glad I found you!" she declared.

He put his finger to his lips. "Shh. We don't want to draw attention to ourselves."

She returned to a quiet voice. "I'm learning. Remember, I'm new to these covert methods of yours."

Fartworthy peered up the stairwell. "Did you discover something of importance?"

"Did I ever!" Cassandra then relayed the information she had overheard when she hid behind the library curtains.

"Bravo for your detective efforts, Miss Haywood. I'm impressed! You might have the makings of a good PI."

Cassandra beamed. "There's more." She filled him in on how Carter believed Cassandra to be her number-one suspect.

"She's basing her summation on her supposed talent of reading people. It'll come out in the wash. I wouldn't worry."

"She's out for me. In addition, someone broke into my room."

"Can't make an arrest without proof." Fartworthy smiled. "What? No one broke in."

"Someone did. I came back from the library, and my tidy, little room was in disarray."

"That's different."

Cassandra smirked. "That's what I said. My valuables were still in place, but they stole the papers."

"No, they didn't."

"I put them in my top drawer, and they're gone."

He looked up the passageway. "You mean this lot?" Deftly, he opened his suit jacket to reveal a packet of folded paperwork in the interior pocket. "I thought you might need these later."

"How did—"

"Premonition." He handed her the papers. "One must always stay many steps ahead to survive. Didn't I ever tell you that a good head butler can predict the future?" His green eyes twinkled.

Cassandra rolled her eyes and rifled through the stack. "You trashed my room?"

"No, the person or people who wanted these did that. When I left you to go to the kitchen, I went upstairs to retrieve the paperwork.

While we were in the library with the others, you revealed information about their existence. I surmised it would be wise to extract them for safekeeping. The place was in order because I made the beds. Habit."

"I knew I didn't make my bed, but I don't remember saying too much in the library. Brilliant of you, Mr. Fartworthy. This is getting so confusing." She scanned the paperwork. "There are more than the company transferal things here. I have nowhere to keep these."

"I'll take them. They're safe in my pocket from whomever redecorated your room."

"Right. Who can we trust here? No one is who they seem. Mr. Turner told us he wants to be a puppeteer and has no interest in running the company. And Mr. Spooner and Mr. Chamberlain were playing a child's card game into the early morning hours because it's a ridiculous obsession for both."

"A puppeteer? Mr. Turner? I wouldn't have guessed that."

She handed the papers to Fartworthy. "I need to study these later."

The head butler stuffed the stack into his jacket's breast pocket. "Stress can bring out the best and worst in anyone. You saw that at the party." The papers crinkled into submission. "You can trust me."

"I know I can. About the party, help me understand. Aunt Lily attacked the Yorks with such vengeance last night. Hamish's secrets affected his wife. Why did my aunt care?"

Fartworthy rubbed his forehead with the back of his thumb and squinted. "Ah . . . that. Lady Lemington had received information that connected the Yorks and Von Pickle."

"Mrs. York's and Von Pickle's association at university and of the failed attempt of their two cheese companies joining on a business venture." Cassandra flipped an end of her lilac neck scarf over her shoulder.

Fartworthy's mouth dropped. "Where did you hear that, Miss Haywood? She told me she wasn't going to tell you."

"Mr. York and Von Pickle got into a verbal altercation in the upstairs hall. Everyone knows now." She crossed her arms and smirked. "Aunt Lily randomly found out or you told her."

"There are very few secrets left in this house today." He tugged on his jacket. "Yes, it was I who discovered the connection. After some digging, I also told her about the facelift and Mr. York's age. We were convinced they were the leak of information. The maddening thing was, how did it relate? There was a missing link. We went with the plan of her aggravating guests and my listening. It amounted to nothing. I still believe there's a correlation."

Cassandra shook her head. "No, Mimi wouldn't do that to us, but she's hiding something, I'm certain of that. I'll talk to her and unearth the truth."

The head butler nodded. "That would be good. I've uncovered something myself. I overheard two detectives in the kitchen talking about waiting for the preliminary toxicology report."

"What does that mean?"

"During routine death investigations, they run toxicology tests on the body for alcohol, drugs, or perhaps, poison."

Cassandra held on to the tongue-and-groove wall.

"The autopsy report will take weeks to get back, even if they rush. They can run a preliminary on objects to see if certain substances were anywhere near the victim. Was it something she touched or ate or drank? It could rule out certain theories."

"I'm not following what you're saying."

"My best guess, since they're exploring that route, is something she consumed could be the culprit. I'm not sure about that since they washed the dishes. To get information back quickly, the test would have to be for specific substances. She had a glass in her hand for most of the night. Did someone hand her the cause of her own death? Did she consume a food that had something on or in it? I never found out what objects they're testing. It's difficult to recall all her interactions last night." Fartworthy glanced down the staircase.

"The photos from the party would show us!" exclaimed Cassandra.

"By Jove, I forgot about Miss Lightfoot's photos. Yes, that'll do nicely and possibly catch something missed."

"How do we get to view them?"

"An opportunity will present itself." Fartworthy smoothed the paperwork in his pocket and straightened his jacket.

Cassandra held up a finger. "That reminds me. I almost forgot." She poked him in the shoulder. "You were correct."

"About what?"

"Greenfield tried to read our lips when we were in the dining room at the breakfast buffet."

A triumphant smile crossed the butler's lips. "How do you know?"

"He told Carter when I was hiding, but you must have forgotten at some point. Your counseling and kind advice about grief . . . he had it all. I heard him read every word from his notepad."

Fartworthy's face fell. "I must have dropped my guard."

"You did. He repeated exactly what you said. I couldn't believe it."

"Neither can I," whispered Fartworthy. "This changes everything."

"I know. I shall be cautious around Carter and Greenfield. I talked to her alone in the great hall. Her kindness felt genuine, but she was interrogating me. She thinks I'm the murderer, or a key player. I had nothing to do with my aunt's death." Cassandra twisted her lilac scarf. "Mr. Fartworthy, you must believe I'm telling the truth."

"I know you didn't kill her. You don't have to convince me. I'm in your corner. Always. You can count on that."

Fartworthy and Cassandra descended several steps in silence. He asked, "Did they mention their next move?"

"The staff not under suspicion or believed to have information are being sent back to work."

"I know. I saw."

"You did? They have a list of who they will continue to question. You're on it. So is Flora."

He stopped in his tracks. "Flora? They suspect her?"

I can't tell him about her past. "They upset Miss Fairchild. The detectives read into everyone's actions. The DCI feels she might know something."

"She doesn't. She wasn't at the party for more than a few minutes. Why would they detain her? Anyone else from the household staff?"

"No, just you two. Wait. Mr. Birch is on the list."

"That makes sense."

Cassandra pursed her lips. "If you don't like someone, it doesn't mean you get to suspect them of murder."

"I have my reasons for distrusting him."

"Are you going to tell me?"

The head butler smiled. "Not now. It's between me and him. I promise I'll inform you later. Go."

"What about you? Carter is looking for you."

"I saw Mrs. Forest downstairs. Food is being served. I'll go to the kitchen and to the dining room with trays to finish setting it up. Easily explained." He gave her a warm smile. "Don't worry."

"I can't help it. If worrying were an Olympic sport, I would be a multi-gold medalist."

He chuckled as they reached the landing. "Try to remain as levelheaded as you've been. You're an intelligent woman. Between the two of us, we'll figure out the truth about what happened to your aunt."

From somewhere upstairs, the antique, tongue-and-groove stairway creaked. The pair froze and collectively held their breath.

Fartworthy gave a nod. "Go."

Cassandra agreed. She cracked open the door to the first floor, and Fartworthy descended to the kitchen.

She slid out of the stairwell. *If anyone asks, I took the servant staircase. At least that is the truth.* She made her way down the hallway to the dining area and peered into the room. Several people had their backs to her, picking out their food at the enormous buffet table. Greenfield and Owen, engaged in a conversation across the space, didn't see her. Cassandra moved to the buffet and picked up a plate.

Carter and Jenkins walked into the room with Roland and Poppy from the great hall.

Cassandra turned to the food, breathing a sigh of relief.

Chapter Twenty-One

Mimi turned around. "Cassandra, there you are! I wondered where you'd slipped off to. I was worried."

"Took my time." As she leaned into the table, Cassandra held the delicate, china dinner plate like a shield over her still racing heart. "What wonderful selections did Mrs. Forest prepare for us this afternoon?" She peered around the room. *I think I'm in the clear.*

"That woman is an absolute genius in the kitchen. Look at these incredible dishes. I overheard that she had her staff back for only a short time." Using a pair of long tongs, Mimi selected three Greek black olives and a slice of Stilton.

"This is impressive. She had little warning last night there would be many overnight guests." Cassandra surveyed the large table covered in starched, intricate, white lace.

Silver tray after silver tray dotted the table's expanse. Various large, circular platters became works of art under talented hands using cherry tomatoes, hardy winter greens, and the symmetrical placement of sliced meats. The cheese boards contained exotic and popular selections. Fresh bunches of plump, red grapes added a still-life impression to the Lemington products. Some aged dairy choices permeated the air with their pungent aroma. Relish trays containing several kinds of olives, pickled beets, garlic, dill pickles, and tangy, green tomatoes glistened under the overhead lighting. Multiple trays piled with carrot sticks, slices of red and yellow peppers, broccoli bunches, and crisp cucumber slices added many colors to the table. Baskets of homemade croissants, sourdough rolls, baguettes, and rustic rye slices, all warm from the oven, heated the air above them. The intoxicating scent from the hot bread caused many to close their eyes, breathe deeply, and sigh.

Cassandra was no exception.

She opened her eyes, drunk on the smell no scented candle could truly replicate. "Ah . . . fresh bread. This must be one of the few fragrances that's universally appreciated." She used silver tongs to select a croissant.

Mimi chuckled. "You're correct. How did Mrs. Forest have time to make bread? I don't bake or cook, so I don't understand. From what I've heard about baking, it seems like this would be impossible on such short notice."

"When I went to the kitchen during the party to tell them everyone needed to stay, Mrs. Forest immediately began mixing up the dough. It rose in the fridge overnight. Today, she formed the loaves and put them in the ovens." Cassandra added some ham to her plate. "The actual baking takes no time at all."

"She must be a planner to do something this impressive." Mimi selected a slice of rye bread. "I admire those who can plan every little detail beforehand and pull it off with ease."

"I'm glad she did. Freshly baked, warm bread is a soothing hug."

Mimi touched Cassandra's arm. "This is strenuous for me. I can't imagine how you're feeling."

"The reality hasn't sunk in."

"That might be a good thing, at least until you have time to be alone." Mimi turned to the table and scanned a meat tray. "Carter is not following protocol with her questioning. The weather made the whole situation so different than standard practice. I guess she's doing her best. Still, highly irregular how she handled the scenario in the upstairs hall." Mimi used a serving fork to stab a piece of roast beef and drag it to her plate. "If they suspect foul play, you would think they would question us outside of the manor."

Cassandra picked up the cheese tongs and gazed at the cheese boards.

"It feels like they're using the weather as an excuse to hold us here. Why? I studied the road I could see from my room's window. The ice doesn't appear too terrible for us to leave."

"They must have their reasons." Cassandra placed cubes of Havarti on her plate.

"And another thing . . . I have my heart medication returned, but my evening bag is still missing. I'm fairly certain somebody stole it." Mimi added a garlic pickle to her plate.

"I'm sure the detectives haven't forgotten about your purse. They're busy."

Mimi faced Cassandra and whispered, "What if someone took my purse to steal the pills to hurt your aunt? I heard them talking, and no one seems to entertain that idea."

"It's possible. You know, Mimi, maybe they've thought of that and remained careful with their words. It would be unprofessional for the detectives to share the investigation information with us." Cassandra peered over her shoulder toward the DCI. "Have you brought this concern up with Carter? If that idea didn't occur to them, you could help with the inquiry."

"I have other thoughts, too." Mimi took a step closer. "They should check the hothouse, don't you think? There are so many flowers that can be used to make a poison, and Mr. Birch has disappeared several times over the course of the day."

"Who said anything about poison?"

"A theory that popped into my head earlier. What about the others? Lady Lemington *stuffed* this manor with people last night." She leaned into Cassandra and murmured, "If you ask me, they let everyone else go. They're not in the parlor. I peeked in there when we came down the main steps. Where is everyone?" Mimi straightened up. "Why would they keep me and Hamish? If they can be quick about this, we could be home soon. A headache storm is brewing in my head. And the detectives keep looking for Fartworthy. Did you notice? Where is he?"

Cassandra stared at the woman, stunned. "I don't know why the detectives. . . . They're doing their job. Maybe they let everyone go." *How did she figure that out?* Cassandra spied Hamish talking to Flora across the room. "I agree. The upstairs questioning seemed unconventional." *I don't want to answer all her questions.* "What started the argument between your husband and Von Pickle?" She moved the cheese on her plate with her bread.

Mimi put her fingertips on her forehead. "Hamish left our room to use the lavatory. They passed each other in the hallway and, you saw the result. The typical conversation any time we see Rupert, and that man cannot leave a snarky comment tucked hidden in his brain. It must come out. He's proud of his supposed cleverness."

"I had no idea you knew him long ago."

A sad memory flickered across the sickly woman's face. "Oh . . . yes. That."

Cassandra moved closer to Mimi and whispered, "You knew him at university?"

"You want to know how I could have dated him."

A chuckle flew from Cassandra's lips. "Exactly."

Mimi looked up wistfully. "Unafraid and so sure of himself, he stood out. The other young men I knew at that time were dreamers and idealists, with no confidence in themselves. Rupert had been working with his father in the family cheese business for years. Real world experience and knowledge translated into a secure demeanor."

"That would be attractive."

Von Pickle was on his mobile across the room.

Mimi tilted her head, staring at the baron. "It was, and he's handsome in the traditional sense." She looked at Cassandra. "It didn't take me long to realize his deep obsession with making money." She studied her plate of food. "He treated me like a queen when we were a couple. There were moments when the cutting remarks you see now snuck out. He never directed comments at me, so I ignored them."

"What changed your mind?"

"He came up with an idea. The plan involved creating a network for gathering information about other students and using it for monetary gain. Not exactly blackmail but hovering on the line. I asked him not to do it based on moral grounds." Mimi sighed. "He tried to convince me to support the plan by claiming it was legal and the potential it held."

"Seriously? At university?"

"Yes. His justification included trying to dazzle me with what he could buy with the profits. Rupert didn't know or understand me. I thought I made an impact when he told me—no, swore on an imaginary stack of Bibles—he wouldn't proceed and praised my noble insight."

"Really?"

"Turns out, Rupert formed the covert network anyway and created money off the misery of others. I discovered he lied shortly before he asked me to marry him. How could I accept his hand after that, even if I *had* loved him? This event removed the veil from my eyes about his true personality. He never knew I found out. Liars and hoarders of information are reprehensible." Mimi turned her head toward Hamish. "Once someone has shattered your trust, you question everything that comes out of their shrewd lips. In my mind, Rupert couldn't repair the damage."

Hamish and Flora chuckled together across the room. Mimi drew in a sharp breath.

Cassandra placed her hand on Mimi's arm. "Your husband loves you. Everyone can see that. And I'm sorry he deceived you, but he isn't Von Pickle. It sounds like Mr. York had entirely different motives. Don't punish him based on your past."

"Perhaps you're right." Mimi sighed. "Pardon me, I should go." She sailed by the remaining table selections, collected a bundle of utensils, and headed to her husband.

Cassandra watched Mimi rejoin Hamish.

Alexander slid in the buffet line behind Cassandra and tapped her on the shoulder. "Blimey! There is so much food. What do you recommend?"

"Cheese is always a wonderful place to start," said Cassandra to the young man, "and end." She placed several cucumber slices on her plate and looked up for a moment. "That should be on a Lemington Cheese promotional T-shirt."

Alexander chuckled. "That would be funny. Didn't realize how hungry I was until I saw this." He speared four cubes of cheese. "I should listen to a cheese expert."

"I suppose so." Cassandra used a serving fork to place two pickled, green tomato slices on her plate. She held another slice toward Alexander. "Want one of these?"

"No, thanks. Never cared for unnatural looking tomatoes. What's the lady's name who was reading Calvin and Hobbes?"

"Mrs. Turner. Why do you ask?"

Alexander picked up a sourdough roll with his hands and bit the crunchy crust. "She's interesting." Crumbs cascaded down to the tablecloth.

Cassandra grimaced at the young man.

"Quite the temper. What? Did I do something wrong?"

"It's not proper manners to pop food in your face while at the buffet. Besides, you're making a little mess with your bread." Cassandra pointed at the table.

He looked down at the crumbs. "Good to know. Sorry." He placed the cheese on his roll, swallowed, and swept the bread confetti off the table and onto his plate.

Cassandra looked at Frederick at the end of the table. He picked up his utensils and walked away. Hamish and Mimi sat next to one another in silence. He stared forward, as if watching football on the telly, while Mimi studied the crown molding. Greenfield continued to speak with Owen across the room. Carter stood in a group with Roland, Poppy, and Ruby in the doorway to the dining area. DS Jenkins hovered near Robin at the head of the buffet line, engaged in conversation.

"Do you think they're finished with the questioning?"

Alexander followed Cassandra's gaze. "I don't know. My guess is that they're feeding us so we won't be grumpy. You can endure anything if you're well fed." He piled several carrot sticks and broccoli bunches onto his plate. "I don't mind staying if we can eat like this. No one is waiting for me at home."

"No pets?" Cassandra sprinkled salt on her meat choices.

"No. I thought about getting one, though." Alexander scooped out a large spoonful of gourmet, speckled mustard from a dainty, porcelain bowl. "Maybe a dog. Or a fish." The muted, golden condiment made an audible splat as it hit his plate.

"It wouldn't be so lonely if you had a dog. They make lovely companions. You can't pet a fish." She set her plate on the table, picked up a peppercorn grinder, and added the spice to her food. "Would you like some?"

"Yes." Alexander held his plate under the grinder. "Thank you. Do you think anyone else has pets or family to get home to?"

"I don't know. Most who stayed either live here or have their own household staff to take care of things." Cassandra put the grinder down.

"Mr. Savage comes into the pharmacy all the time to pick up medications for his mother, who has health issues and doesn't leave the house often. His sister could be with her." He slapped a hand over his mouth for a moment. "I shouldn't have said that. Privacy laws, and all."

"You probably shouldn't. You don't want to get in trouble, but Carter might not be thinking people have others or animals under their watch." She moved to the end of the buffet and tucked her hair behind her ear. "Um . . . does Mr. Chamberlain have any pets . . . or family at home?"

"From my understanding of our conversation last night, there's no one waiting for him." The young man sauntered down the table. "Why do you want to know that?"

"Just curious." She studied the assortment of tableware with sudden, fierce intensity.

Alexander took a white, cloth napkin and utensil bundle and smirked. "Aha! You like him."

"What? He's an interesting person. We enjoy talking with one another." Cassandra selected a wrapped cluster of sterling silver utensils. "Have you finished picking out your food?"

"You're not answering."

"Precisely." She turned away. Frederick stood right behind her with his full plate. "Miss Haywood, may I sit with you?"

"Oh! Yes, absolutely." Cassandra turned to Alexander and stammered, "W-w-would you care to join us?"

"No, you two enjoy. You know what? I'll go ask Mr. Savage

about his mother." Alexander grabbed his partially eaten roll, took another enormous bite, and pivoted. He peered back with an impish grin, crumbs descending like rain as he walked away.

Cassandra squinted. *Did Alexander give him a thumbs-up? Did Frederick hear me?*

Mahogany Chippendale chairs bordered the room and beckoned for occupants. Frederick pointed to an isolated corner. "Is this acceptable?"

"As good as any." Cassandra sat on one of the white, brocade cushions, placed her plate on her lap, and pulled out her fork from the bundle. "Where did you end up finding water?"

He sat and pointed across the room. "Over there. The staff turned the breakfast buffet into a beverage station. When I went downstairs, someone shooed me out and directed me here. Mission successful." He leaned over, his voice dropping to a whisper. "Do you know what's going on here? The commotion in the kitchen was for the luncheon prep, and some others were exiting the manor."

Cassandra halted her forkful of Havarti midair. "You saw them leave?"

"Yes. Two detectives ushered other guests out the rear entrance. Have they mentioned this to you?" Frederick popped a green olive into his mouth.

She took a moment to chew her food. "No one said anything directly. What else did you observe or hear in the kitchen?"

"Nothing. I came up here, got a drink of water, and then went to the second floor." At a snail's pace, he cut a piece of turkey on his plate and didn't look up. "This entire day is bizarre. Are they keeping our group of people longer? I thought I overheard talk of questionable circumstances involving Lady Lemington's death. That must be incorrect."

"They're exploring every option." She looked over at him.

Frederick's eyes met hers. "You can't be serious."

"I am. The DCI wants me to remember everything I can from the party. Unfortunately, details are blending into one incoherent mess in my head." Cassandra tore a piece off her croissant. "I want it sorted. Maybe the pictures will help." She bit into the tasty bread.

"What pictures?"

"Miss Lightfoot's photos from the party. She hovered near my aunt all night. There could be something there. I need to look at them when I'm finished eating."

"Why would you want to view those so soon?" Frederick munched on a crust of rye bread.

"Why not? There may be a clue there. The photographs could trigger a memory of a conversation or situation to help me assist the detectives. It could be the same as when you helped them identify the type of damage Aunt Lily's watch endured. Maybe armed with more information, they solve this. I'm afraid Carter won't allow me to look at them. She appears to dislike me." Cassandra cut and swallowed a small cube of ham.

"How did you conclude the head detective doesn't like you? The DCI is tough but seems to treat everyone the same. Well, besides when she reprimanded us for talking in the parlor." He smiled.

She blushed at the memory of Frederick holding her hand. She hesitated and dabbed her mouth with a cloth napkin. "Trust me, I know." She took a breath. "My aunt hired the photographer, so the photos would be the property of the manor, right?"

"I suppose so. You sure you want to even ask? If she doesn't care for you, this won't help." He pushed crumbles of extra sharp cheddar around on his plate with the back of his fork.

"Still, it might aid the investigation." *Why is he being contrary?*

"Let me help you remember who your aunt argued with at the party without looking at the photos. Who did she talk to first?"

"I don't want to discuss last night further until I have something concrete. Memory is such a tricky thing. There were so many conversations. As I told you, it's a jumble." She put the bite of cheese in her mouth.

They sat in silence, chewing.

When Frederick finished, he exhaled. "I don't think it's prudent for you to look at the photographs so soon. You received the news of your aunt's death today. Give yourself time to absorb it all." The corners of his mouth rose in a Mona Lisa grin.

Cassandra stood. "If you'll excuse me, Mr. Chamberlain, I must view Miss Lightfoot's work from last night. My instincts demand the action, despite your advice." Before he could respond, she turned on her heel and headed toward Carter. The tails of her two scarves flew in the air, synchronized with her strides.

Give myself time? Honestly! Not helpful. I need to figure out what transpired, and those photos could be the key.

Chapter Twenty-Two

Cassandra found Carter chatting with Roland, Poppy, and Ruby. The DCI nodded and said, "And what did—"

"Pardon me," Cassandra interrupted. "May I speak to you in private, Detective Chief Inspector?" She placed her plate of uneaten food on a nearby table.

Carter finished the last sip of coffee in her cup. "Absolutely, Miss Haywood."

The two ladies walked away from the cluster of people and through the doorway.

When they reached the base of the massive Christmas tree in the empty great hall, Cassandra spoke. "I had a thought." Her fingers interlaced the edges of her lilac scarf. "I want to view the photos Miss Lightfoot took. I inherit this place, therefore they're my property." Cassandra stood taller.

"That's not a grand idea."

"Why?"

"It may be too distressing." Carter crossed her arms.

"You asked me if I remembered any more details. I want to give you as much information about my aunt as possible. We spent most of the evening together, but interactions and discussions are blending in my head." Cassandra paused. "I recalled that Miss Lightfoot followed my aunt around for most of the party. I found it odd Aunt Lily wanted her to do so, especially if she argued with anyone. If I can see the photos, maybe they'll trigger something. This seems to be more complicated than you first implied."

The DCI took a step closer. "Do you think that will help jog your memory?"

"Anything is possible." Cassandra released the scarf tails.

Carter grabbed the back of her own neck. "On one condition— we view them together. You tell me what was going on in each photo, and I'll jot down notes on anything you might recall. Sometimes the smallest detail can provide the largest break in a case. Understood?"

"Whatever is most helpful for your investigation." Cassandra smiled. *And necessary for me to clear my name.*

The DCI beckoned another detective forward. DC Baker obliged. "Get the department laptop. Miss Haywood and I will look at last night's photographs."

"Yes, ma'am." Baker left to complete the request.

"Too many curious eyes in the dining area. Why don't we step farther into the parlor?"

Cassandra agreed.

They walked into the large room. Baker joined them a minute later and handed the portable computer to her superior. "Anything else, ma'am?"

"Not at this time and thank you for this." Carter placed the laptop on a side table and pulled two chairs over as Baker returned to the dining room.

Cassandra removed the scarf around her neck and held it in her lap.

The DCI turned the unit toward herself. Her fingers tapped out the password with one hand, shielding the keys with the other. She repositioned the laptop so both women could view the screen. With a double click, an image of a smiling Cassandra reaching for a glass of sparkling cider from a butler's tray popped up on the screen.

Cassandra pointed. "First photo Miss Lightfoot took last night. I came downstairs and she arrived, running in the main doors a few minutes after the party started."

"She showed up late?"

"Yes, and she was concerned. Miss Lightfoot told me someone could check the time stamp to determine when she entered the manor. She mentioned my aunt's direct instructions—come on time and take candid photos all night. Nothing posed."

"Good to know." Carter hit several keys in rapid succession to reveal the time stamp in the upper right corner—9:05 p.m., 31 December. She scrolled through the photographs.

The next ten shots contained views of the massive food table. The photographer then captured guests and staff milling around. In one photo, a raspberry puddle of fabric lay on the large table while Arabella and Cassandra engaged in a discussion.

"There's my scarf. I always leave my accessories behind." Cassandra held up the end of the lilac scarf in her lap. "Terrible habit from childhood. I couldn't recall where I left that one last night."

"Interesting."

"No, I have it back on in the next photo."

Computer keys clicked again, and the first image of Lady Lemington caused Cassandra to draw in a deep breath. The close-up shot featured her aunt's broad smile, engaged laugh lines around her sparkling, brown eyes, and a fluttering, purple fascinator perched atop her head. "This captures the essence of Aunt Lily last night. She walked into the dining room to greet her guests." Cassandra pulled back in her seat and her hand covered her mouth.

Carter placed her palm on Cassandra's arm. "Are you sure you wish to continue?"

I don't know if I can, but I owe it to Aunt Lily. Cassandra closed her eyes for several moments and remained silent to calm her racing heart. The weight of an imaginary bootheel pressing on her chest increased. She opened her eyes. "Let's crack on."

"Right, forward march." The detective studied Cassandra's face. "This is an enchanting photograph. It appears she enjoyed life. Is that a fair assessment? Tell me more about her behavior and interactions last night."

Stop holding your breath. With an audible exhale, Cassandra renewed her mission. "She seemed to have a lovely time at the party. The purple headpiece she's wearing is one from Miss Dalton's company. My aunt purchased many of my friend's creations over the last few years. She loves . . . loved them."

"I see. It's a stunning piece."

"Miss Dalton's little company does well."

Successive snapshots of Mimi showed her leaning on her husband's arm. However, her disposition displayed a drastic progression from adoration and joy to forlorn, stunned devastation. Cassandra recounted the reveal of Hamish York's first lie. "He'd gone to Switzerland for a face lift and recovery—not a cheese conference as his wife believed. My aunt, for reasons of her own, enjoyed disclosing the upsetting information. Look at Aunt Lily here. She hasn't stopped smiling." Several photos scrolled by, and the pair continued in quiet. "This is when Mr. York yelled at my aunt."

Carter flipped through her notepad. "His wife left first?" She added something to the paper.

"Yes." On the next screen, Lady Lemington held a crystal flute and conversed with Lady Bilford. "I didn't see my aunt for a few minutes since I moved into the parlor. When I saw her again, she came into the room and spoke with the Turners."

Scrolling through, the faces on a photograph caused Carter to pause. "This one is interesting . . . Mr. Turner agitated and Mrs. Turner furious."

"Correct. My aunt told Roland he would never be CEO of Lemington Cheese. His mother stormed over and exchanged heated words." The next photo contained Roland, Robin, and Cassandra, all mouths agape at an amused Lady Lemington. "*That* moment. Goodness, I'm a large-mouth bass with frog eyes."

"Explain, please." Carter pointed to the screen.

"She announced I would be in charge of the company when she retired." Cassandra ran her fingers along the edge of the scarf in her lap. "Believe me, it was a shock to everyone. I might have been the most surprised."

"You discovered just last night she wanted you to take over?"

"That's right. Miss Dalton believed, for a long time, that I should press for the position. We've debated this for many months, but I never brought up the matter with my aunt. I didn't consider myself for the role. I thought Roland held more promise for the job."

"But she wanted you instead?" Carter wrote in her notepad.

"Correct."

The ladies scrolled through several more. The image of Lady Lemington placing her empty glass on a butler's tray was followed by a photograph of Frederick during their conversation. Cassandra recalled the compliment of "beauty and brains" she received from him last night. Her cheeks warmed.

Carter clicked the forward key.

The head gardener, Mr. Birch, stood in the next snapshot, handing Lady Lemington a glass of sparkling cider. Cassandra tilted her head. *That's odd. He had two glasses. He clutched the stem of one flute and held it near his chest. Why was he holding the bottom of the base of the other glass, the one he's holding out to my aunt?*

A few photos later, Fartworthy and Mr. Birch scowled at one another. Carter gestured with her hand. "What went on here?"

"Mr. Birch desired to talk to my aunt, and afterward, we found out he intended to propose. Mr. Fartworthy approached her to come with him, and I can see Mr. Birch didn't like the idea."

"Why did Fartworthy need her?"

"I honestly don't recall. About the weather? Can we see the next one?" With a click, the shot showed Owen standing by his open guitar case containing the stolen items. Cassandra pointed at the screen. "Yes, the indiscretion. Mr. Savage lifted several things from here, and my aunt fired him on the spot."

Carter scrutinized the guitar case's contents in the photo. "Hello Kitty erasers and a filled pharmacy bag belong to the manor?"

"No. He said he picked them up at the store before he arrived. The candlesticks were from the second-floor hall." In the following photo, Mr. Birch's face twisted in anger. "He told us Owen stole the length of rope and wrench from the hothouse. Mr. Birch stormed off with the two items right after the discovery." Cassandra crossed her arms. *Owen had medication with him, too? What was in that bag? Why was Owen anywhere near the hothouse?*

The next photograph showed Von Pickle leaning down to kiss Lady Lemington's hand. Carter pointed with two fingers. "I thought this pair verbally sparred."

"They did, and with great malice."

Carter clicked the key forward and then back. Looking in the screen's corner, she pointed to the time stamp. "There's a fifteen-minute gap between photos. Why?"

"There are no photos of the argument between Aunt Lily and Von Pickle, either." Cassandra twisted her scarf. "I remember. Miss

Lightfoot took her break then. She told me she had enough of the disagreements and left when Mr. Savage was fired. That fight directly followed the situation with the stolen items. Afterward, Mr. Fartworthy told us about the icy roads and everyone needed to stay. My aunt and I discussed how to inform guests and staff. That conversation lasted a few minutes. She told the partygoers, and I went downstairs to notify Miss Fairchild and Mrs. Forest. Miss Lightfoot was having a cuppa with Flora Fairchild and Poppy Fletcher in the kitchen. There's your time gap. Ruby had a right to take a break."

"Makes sense. How long were you down there?" The head detective added a note to her pad.

"I don't know. It couldn't have been for more than a few minutes. I came up the white stairway that leads directly to the dining room from the kitchen and passed Mr. Spooner coming down the stairs."

"Why would a guest go to the kitchen during the party?"

"Alexander got rejected many times by the ladies, and upstairs became uncomfortable for him, I suppose. He went to visit a friendly face in Miss Fairchild. He knows some staff members here."

Carter clicked on the next photo. "What room is this? With him on one knee, I gather this is when Mr. Birch proposed to Lady Lemington."

"Yes, taken through a pane of glass in the French doors of the sunroom." Cassandra pointed. "Right over there. My guess is they went in there for privacy. I couldn't find my aunt at first when I came upstairs and was told she was in that unheated space. We don't use it during the winter, so it surprised me to locate her there."

"The sunroom. He proposed. She turned him down and sacked him."

"Correct. He stormed out."

"Did you see Mr. Birch for the rest of the night?" Carter leaned back in her chair and stretched out her back.

Cassandra stared up at the ceiling. "No. Yes, I saw him. Later. Right before midnight in the main hall. I was standing at the bottom of the stairs while we had our horns. Despondent and heartbroken, he wanted to know if I could get his job back. My aunt flew down from where she was standing and told him to get out when the roads cleared in the morning. She didn't want him talking to me. He went upstairs before we rang in the new year."

The DCI gestured toward the screen. "After the proposal, Fartworthy and Lady Lemington appear to be in a serious discussion. He's still doing his job, holding a silver tray, and offering her a drink, but his expression suggests something else."

"He argued about firing Mr. Birch and wanted her to reconsider the decision. I've never seen Mr. Fartworthy question her actions. Surprising, too, since Mr. Fartworthy and Mr. Birch are definitely not mates."

"Not fans of one another? You know this for sure?"

"Yes, I talked with them individually recently, and they both confirmed their mutual disregard." Cassandra put her palms together. "I get along with both. Sometimes members of the staff clash because of their personalities. I suspect that's the case here."

"Duly noted. What's going on in this grouping of photos? Mr. and Mrs. York and Lady Lemington were standing together, visibly tense."

"Aunt Lily renewed her assault on the Yorks." Cassandra sighed.

Carter pointed at the picture where Mimi held up an orange bottle with a small purse hanging from her wrist. "That's the evening bag still missing and the pills you found. Why did Mrs. York take out her medication at the party?"

"My aunt encouraged her to drink the champagne. Mrs. York showed her the reason she abstained."

Hamish tugged on his wife's arm in the next shot. The detective remarked, "He knew your aunt was about to share something he wanted kept secret. Observe his body language in this one. What did she reveal?" She clicked the keys. "It was devastating. Mrs. York no longer holds on to him."

Cassandra closed her eyes for a moment. "That is when Mimi found out Mr. York's true age."

"Fifty-five, correct? He doesn't look like he even left his early forties. Quite the deception. It would explain the shocked expression on many faces. Why was Miss Fairchild present with a teacup?"

"Aunt Lily always had tea around 11:45 before bed—every night without fail—and she drank it at room temperature. Flora brought it to the party. Aunt Lily reprimanded her and told her to put it by her bedside for later."

Cassandra studied the photograph. *After the party, she had a cup of tea upstairs.*

"Is this when Miss Fairchild presented the calendar to Mr. York?" The DCI stared at the head housekeeper's image.

"No, this looks like the moment she recognized him. Flora remains out of sight during parties. Midnight was when the staff, besides the butlers, were to be upstairs, my aunt's command. Even though the Yorks have been here for other events, Miss Fairchild probably hadn't seen him before last night." Cassandra leaned into the screen. "No, she showed him the calendar following the midnight countdown. She must have retrieved it from her room upstairs after she left the tea in Aunt Lily's bedroom."

The guests gathering in the large hall dominated the next several photographs. The grumpy Turners stood under the mahogany grandfather clock. The Yorks clustered by the end of the main banister. Von Pickle's mouth opened in complaint to no one, and Arabella smirked at the man in the same photo. Kitchen staff gathered in the large doorway to the dining area, butlers and valets in the doorway to the parlor. In another shot, Alexander, Frederick, and Arabella laughed together in the middle of the hall, while other guests filled the space to its capacity. The enormous Christmas tree, sparkling in the light, was captured from the photographer's vantage point halfway up the staircase. Guests decorated in party wear, jewel-colored horns, and metallic hats created a kaleidoscope of anticipation.

Cassandra reached out to the image of her aunt on the screen. "She looked forward to this moment. You can see she's thrilled here. I'm glad she got to experience it once more before she died." She pulled back her hand and rubbed the base of her neck.

"You're at the bottom of the staircase. Why?"

"I didn't understand her last night, and well, was embarrassed to be near her. Aunt Lily's unpredictable behavior baffled me. I thought it best to stay away."

"But here she is by your side with Mr. Birch, and then in this one, she's back up the stairs." The DCI pointed at the screen.

"I tried to reason with her to no avail, and then the celebration started."

The following photographs captured the countdown and explosion of color at midnight. Streamers of all hues flew, and sparkling, gold confetti spread like joyful snowflakes from the servants' poppers. Sour expressions graced the faces of a few. Hands and arms waving from the crowd, along with laughing faces and kisses of good luck exchanged, added to the festive photos.

Cassandra pressed her palms over her closed eyes. *Everything changed. I'm no closer to figuring out who would hurt my aunt. Maybe this was an accident.* She sighed and looked at the screen again.

"Do you need to stop viewing these? Perfectly understandable." Carter pulled out her mobile and sent a text. She slipped the device into her suit jacket pocket.

"No, I want to help as much as possible." Cassandra leaned back in her chair and crossed her arms. "Any discoveries of what transpired?" She stared at the color-filled picture.

"We have some theories. Did you hear anyone, at any time, express the desire to harm your aunt?"

"No. She annoyed or argued with many people last night. Her behavior mortified me, but if you are asking, I had nothing to do with her death. Nothing. I can tell you believe this is more than a fall. Your team would have left by this time if it were an accident."

Carter locked eyes with Cassandra, neither party uttering a word.

DC Baker entered the room with a glass of water and broke the silent showdown. "Thirsty, Miss Haywood?"

"Yes, thank you." Cassandra drained half the drink. "Am I correct you've determined that something is not right?"

Baker paused for a moment, turned, and walked out of the room.

Carter smiled at Cassandra. "We're checking all leads and all facts before we wrap up here for the day. We're close to the end of what I may allow you to view. Shall we continue?"

She didn't answer. Cassandra put her drink on the small table. "Here, after midnight, Miss Fairchild showed Mr. York the calendar."

The head detective flipped the page in her notepad. "Yes, I have the details. Anything you'd like to add?"

"My aunt had no part in angering Mimi York that time. Mimi went upstairs to bed right afterward. Hamish followed soon after her. Mrs. York stayed in her room for the rest of the night, and Mr. York returned to the party a short while later. Alone." *Mimi was alone upstairs.*

Carter clicked the forward key, and the next photos confirmed Cassandra's statement about the Yorks' departure. "You and your aunt were engaged in what looks to be a serious discussion at this point." The next photo popped up. "You left her on the stairs. What did you say to one another?"

Cassandra looked down to her lap and whispered, "I berated her for her lack of empathy and decorum. She repeated that perception is everything, and in time, I would see she was correct in all her actions. I'll never hear those reasons, and I don't understand what she meant." She closed her eyes.

"She didn't explain further?"

"No. I descended the steps to join Miss Dalton and stayed with her, Mr. Spooner, and Mr. Chamberlain for the rest of the party."

The detective's finger tapped the key several times. "Here you are again talking with your aunt and Mrs. Turner. Mrs. Turner looks fierce and has a grip on your arm."

Cassandra looked up at the screen. "What? Yes. I left my scarf on the banister, went back to get it, and Mrs. Turner grabbed me. Aunt Lily came to my defense. That was still about her son being denied the CEO position. Yes, I talked with my aunt after Mrs. Turner, and then Mr. Turner stormed up the stairs. Neither returned to the party." *We heard they went to their separate rooms at that time. Before the others were upstairs.*

"Did you notice when anyone else retired for the night?"

"Honestly, no. I chatted with my friend and the two gentlemen for the rest of the evening. I didn't interact with or see my aunt after that, although I went to her bedroom to talk to her before I went to sleep but she didn't return right away. I ended up going back to my room without running into her."

"You didn't mention that before."

"I guess I forgot." Cassandra smiled at the detective. *There's your explanation.*

"So, no more interactions with your aunt?" The photograph on the screen contained the quartet of young people talking and laughing. Lady Lemington was visible in the background, smiling wide. Carter remarked, "She seemed to enjoy observing you having a good time."

"I didn't realize she watched us." Cassandra stared at the image of her amused, deceased aunt. Her voice cracked. "Maybe she wasn't annoyed with me." The lump in her throat rose, threatening her ability to speak. "I loved Aunt Lily. I want to talk to her again and ask her to forgive me." Tears pounded from within, demanding to be released. Cassandra denied the action.

Carter leaned in toward the young woman. "Forgive you for what?"

Cassandra remained stoic and silent, caught in her mind between her grief and her guilt.

Chapter Twenty-Three

The head detective repeated her question. "Forgive you for what?" Before Cassandra could answer, DC Baker ran into the parlor. "Sorry, ma'am. Jenkins sent me to get you. He said your presence is needed in the dining room immediately. We have a situation."

"A situation?" Carter raised an eyebrow.

"Yes, ma'am. He was adamant that you return." The young detective stood at attention.

"Baker, give me a moment." DCI Carter returned her gaze to Cassandra. "Well?"

The young woman ran her fingertips across the scarf in her lap. "For being angry with her. I didn't leave things on a pleasant note before she . . . well, you know. I feel terrible about it." She clenched her jaw. "But I didn't kill Aunt Lily, if that's what you're implying."

"No need to take offense. I simply wanted you to clarify your statement." Carter rose and closed the laptop. "If you think of anything else, Miss Haywood, please let me know." She joined Baker and handed the computer to her subordinate. As the detectives left, Carter added, "Miss Haywood, you need to come along, too."

She followed the investigators.

When they arrived at the doorway, the DCI stopped. "Miss

Haywood, you forgot something. Please meet us in the dining room."

Cassandra turned around and saw her lilac scarf laying curled up like a purple wad of paper on the floor next to her chair. She groaned and retreated to pick up the forgotten item. The detectives proceeded onward.

Standing alone in the room, Cassandra stared at the scarf in her hand. *I let you down, Aunt Lily. What happened? The photographs must contain something. What am I missing?* She held her forehead, looking at the antique portraits that hung on the room's butter-colored walls. *If only these pictures could talk and tell me what happened last night. Carter still thinks I'm guilty. I need to find Mr. Fartworthy.* She drew in a deep breath and strode out of the parlor.

Agitated, loud voices greeted her as she entered the dining room. Von Pickle, Robin, Arabella, and Carter stood in a semicircle near the food table.

Bella barked, "You're a conniving, wicked snake! You did it again!"

Carter held up her hands between Von Pickle and Arabella like a teacher breaking up a schoolyard scuffle. "Calm down, Miss Dalton. I repeat, would someone please clarify what this ruckus is all about?"

Arabella caught sight of Cassandra entering the room. Without an explanation to the detective, she ran to her friend in the doorway. "There you are. You won't believe what happened!" She grabbed her friend's arm and dragged her over to the cluster of people.

"Bella, what's going on?" Cassandra studied her friend's flushed face.

"Picklehead, that's what. He stole your ideas again." Arabella frowned at the businessman. "Go on. Tell her!"

Von Pickle scoffed. "What? Discuss my originality, my brain for business, and how I won the race again? Why the surprise? Just because I got my idea launched first doesn't mean I stole anything."

Confused, Cassandra searched for a clue. The remaining guests at the manor were all in the room and focused on the fray. She turned back to her friend. "Bella? What did he—"

The snarky man cut her off. "Something about a QR initiative you supposedly had first. My Somerdale International rolled out the program in thirty different stores worldwide in October."

"What? What about the QR code?" Cassandra's breath quickened and her cheeks enflamed as she faced Von Pickle.

He laughed. "QR codes on our cheese products linking the consumer to groundbreaking recipes on our company website using the product in their hand. Brilliant, right? It's been a game changer." He adjusted his cuff links.

Robin laughed, eating an olive. "Such a shame."

Cassandra scowled at the middle-aged woman. Turning her attention back to Von Pickle, she said, "That was mine! How did you steal my idea?"

"Your idea? You have an inflated sense of self, sweetheart." Von Pickle took a bite of Stilton on a cracker.

"*Don't* call me 'sweetheart.' You stole another plan from Lemington Cheese. We had that in the works for months. Our launch was in November. Who told you?" Every hair on Cassandra's body stood on end.

Von Pickle's large, brown eyes became wide in mock innocence. "Whatever do you mean? Maybe you're jealous I outmaneuvered you yet again with intelligence and clever marketing."

Arabella turned to Cassandra. "I was chatting with Frederick when I overheard Von Pickle bragging to Mrs. Turner how they had a new initiative. I heard 'QR' and my ears perked up." She faced Carter. "Cassandra has been working on this for some time."

Robin laughed again. "Mismanagement from day one. Lily certainly made the right choice leaving you at the helm. What a wonderful direction you're taking my father's business."

Cassandra squared her shoulders. "Forgive me, Mrs. Turner, but no one asked for your opinion. For someone with your history with the company, I don't think you should speak of mismanagement. You need to stay out of this. Thank you."

Robin bit the roll in her hand.

Von Pickle smirked. "Don't worry, Mrs. Turner. I'm sure Miss Haywood will be out from the position of CEO within the year. My vast cheese empire has many interesting and profitable directions mere mortals would never consider. I'm expanding the company at such a rate, we'll force Lemington Cheese to restructure. Once your son has played around long enough, he'll want to rejoin the real world. Who knows? You might get what you always wanted. Maybe the puppet training will help him so he can finally manipulate live humans in a real job."

Robin threw the rest of the tasty bread at the baron's head and stormed off.

The roll bounced off the obnoxious man's forehead. He roared with laughter. "As for you, Miss Haywood, I'll always be steps ahead in any business innovation. I can read you like a book. Exactly like Lily. I can outmaneuver my competition every time. I beat your aunt, and I'll conquer you."

Cassandra growled inside.

"You beat her aunt?" asked DS Jenkins, moving toward the group.

Von Pickle crossed his arms. "Not literally, you dolt. I didn't kill her. Yes, Lady Lemington's death makes my job easier. I hated the old bird, but I'm too busy with my company to worry about incarceration. Not worth the time away from my empire. So, Miss Haywood, what are you going to do?"

Cassandra widened her stance and tightened her jaw. "My priorities today concern my aunt, but this isn't over. I'll deal with your corporate theft at another time."

"Good. Run away. Right. Savvy business plan. Is that what they taught you in business school? You failed that endeavor. Everyone here knows that, right?" Von Pickle pointed and looked around, smiling. All faces in the dining room focused on Cassandra. "You can't beat me. I *own* this game."

"No, you don't. And I'm not running." Cassandra bristled at the mention of her failure. "My past mistakes don't define my future. I learn from them. I have a lawyer in place and documentation to prove the initiative is mine. You siphon clever ideas off others and then have the audacity to brag about it. You maintain the façade of an ethical businessman, and yet anyone of your acquaintance knows the truth. I'll stop you this time. Legally."

Von Pickle snorted. "What are you going to do? Drop some scarves to distract me?"

Cassandra narrowed her eyes. "There is a smallness of mind and a littleness of character in those who belittle and attack the appearance, mannerisms, and nature of others."

"Getting philosophical, are we? Good gracious, don't quote inspirational memes about rising above adversity and the benefit of discussing ideas rather than gossip. I might lose my lunch. What's next? Butterfly quotes about friendship and happiness?" He smoothed his lapel.

"Stop attacking her," Arabella scolded. "She's been through enough."

Von Pickle turned to Cassandra's friend. "What's your name again? Miss Dalton, is it? What are you, her sidekick? This argument started when you stuck your nose in my conversation. It's entirely your fault since you're the reason she knows. I won yet again."

Arabella bit her lip.

"You know I speak the truth." The baron looked at Cassandra. "Bring legal action. I dare you. The public has seen it on my products first. That's all that matters. They'll think you copied me, no matter what some court says."

Cassandra sneered. "You're a *pirate.*"

"A what?" Von Pickle snorted.

"You heard me. You're. A. Pirate. There have always been those who preferred to steal instead of achieving success through honest, hard work. You don't create or build anything worthwhile on your own." Cassandra stepped closer. "Like the pirates of old, you'll never stop pillaging. Never satisfied. You take pleasure in your theft, then cannonball everyone else. Forever prowling for golden opportunities. The illusion of your superiority is because you've schemed to sink most of your weaker rivals. Those who stand their ground and fight will survive. I'm not going anywhere. Neither is my company."

"I promise that I'll bury you. Somerdale Cheese is larger, international, and superior."

"Anything you've ever built is on a foundation of sand." Cassandra gripped her scarf tight. "Nothing genuine of your own. Your cheese isn't even real. Eventually, you'll fail."

Carter put her hands up. "Enough! It has been a stressful day. I thought if I let you vent a bit you would calm down. Everyone here, take a step away and cool off. Go on. Move away from one another." She gestured to separate ends of the room.

Von Pickle flicked his hand. "You're a detective, not my mother. Go write useless information in your notepad for a case you'll never solve."

"Sir!" the DCI growled, "that is enough out of you."

Cassandra stepped back. "There's no need to turn your venom on the DCI."

Von Pickle brushed a crumb off the sleeve of his suit jacket. "Incompetence. If I ran my company like this inquiry, we would've closed our doors years ago. Instead, we thrive with real leadership."

Cassandra held the end of her scarf but didn't twist the fabric. "Always bragging about your conquests. One day, your actions will catch up with you. Greed will eventually get you." She walked away from the arrogant man.

Von Pickle followed. "You call it greed, I call it ambition, and it has led to my amazing, successful life. You'll never embrace that fact, and therefore, you'll fail. Again."

The DCI strode after them. "Baron Von Pickle, unless you want to spend overnight in a cell for harassment, I suggest you move away from Miss Haywood."

"Try to make that stick," the businessman taunted over his shoulder.

"Unnecessary. All I need to do is steal hours from you. Paperwork can take a long time to process." Carter crossed her arms. "Your choice."

A clatter and shattering of ceramic on the white, oak floor drew the attention of every person in the room. Owen, red-faced and standing, said, "That was me."

Cassandra stared at the smashed object on the ground. "What was that?"

Mr. Birch pointed at Owen. "He stood up quickly when she talked about jail. Something flew out of his pocket and broke. What did you take this time, thief?"

Owen hunched his shoulders. "While I was in the library, I saw this thing."

Cassandra strode over and squatted to inspect the shattered remains. She turned the largest piece over and read, "Made in Occupied Ja . . ." She looked up at the young man. "The peacock! You took the figurine off the bookshelf? Was that in your trouser pocket?"

The kleptomaniac nodded.

Fartworthy appeared behind him. "Empty all your pockets, sir. I warned you about this last night."

Without a word, Owen moved to the food table. From his pockets, he removed a small bunch of grapes, a sterling silver fork, a black, alligator-skin eyeglass case, and a saucer. He hung his head and whispered, "I'm so sorry, Miss 'aywood. I told you I can't 'elp meself."

Cassandra went to the pilfered items on the table. "That's the missing saucer from my teacup I had in the library." She looked up at the tall, young man. "Owen!"

Fartworthy picked up the eyeglass case. "This is mine. Don't remove property from my room."

"I'm awfully sorry." Owen jammed his hands back into his pockets.

Fartworthy placed the eyeglass case into his jacket. "Remember, I told you if you still had things in your possession that were not yours, you needed to return them immediately."

Owen shrugged. "I forgot they's with me. My 'ead can keep 'em notes of dozens of songs, yet I forget what's in me trousers."

Several people snickered.

Carter grabbed the back of her neck. "Mr. Savage? Do you have anything else that you *casually* picked up while enjoying your stay at the manor?"

"No, ma'am. I don't think so. I 'ave no more pockets. They's all empty." The guitar player grinned.

The head detective beckoned DC Greenfield from across the room. "Search him."

"Yes, ma'am," replied the new detective. Owen held his arms out to his side as his shirt and suit jacket were patted down. Greenfield pulled out a flat, silver-glittered snowflake ornament from Mr. Savage's interior jacket pocket. The detective held it up in front of the young man.

"Forgot about that. I got it from the Christmas tree." Owen grimaced and then grinned.

"Obviously." Carter turned to the head butler. "Fartworthy. Speaking of keeping an eye on things, where have you been? We've been looking for you."

Fartworthy replied, "Setting up luncheon, ma'am. We had a bit of a scramble to make sure everything was up to the manor's standard." He knelt and picked up the pieces of the broken peacock.

"I understand. However, we were looking for you long before we gave the kitchen staff clearance to set up the meal." Carter tapped her fingertips together. "I repeat, where were you?"

"Doing my duties, ma'am." He straightened his black, square-framed glasses. "I assisted in rousing the guests and ushering them to your staff downstairs. DC Henslowe interviewed me in this room long before I saw you. Perhaps that's the time you're referring to." Fartworthy placed the damaged collectible in a rubbish container near the beverage station.

"Come back here. I'm not done." The DCI turned to the others in the room. "No one go anywhere."

Fartworthy returned to the spot where the broken peacock lay and inspected the ground. "This looks all cleaned up. Job complete."

Carter sighed. "I wasn't talking about the figurine. There's a time gap in your whereabouts."

Flora Fairchild stepped forward from the other side of the room. "Pardon me, Detective Chief Inspector. Mr. Fartworthy has many duties trying to keep things as normal as possible in this difficult situation."

The DCI moved toward the head housekeeper. "I understand. However, guests and staff were given specific instructions to remain with my team for questioning. Fartworthy ignored direct orders several times." She looked at the head butler. "Where were you?"

Flora moved closer. "He told you he was setting things up."

Carter crossed her arms. "Miss Fairchild, I understand he's your coworker. Do you know where he was all day?"

"He . . . was around." Miss Fairchild turned to Fartworthy. "I was not in his presence for several hours. Your team separated many members of the staff."

"Did you depart at any point to return to your duties today?" Carter sauntered toward Flora.

"I didn't leave, but my job is not as important as his." Flora clasped her hands together.

"You're the head housekeeper. That sounds pretty significant." Carter crossed her arms. "Miss Fairchild? What are you concealing?"

"Why would I hide anything? I don't know where he was this morning." She looked at her colleague and then at the head de-tective.

Carter's stare burrowed into the woman. "Your manner sug-gests otherwise."

Fartworthy stepped closer to Carter. "Miss Fairchild has done nothing wrong. Please leave her be."

The DCI pointed at the head butler and the head housekeeper. "What are you two covering up? Are you romantically involved?"

Fartworthy and Flora answered simultaneously, "No!"

"Good gravy!" Flora removed a handkerchief from her apron pocket. "How could you think such a thing?"

Carter goaded. "You defend each other fairly regularly. Your mannerisms indicate a connection beyond coworkers. Everything suggests an intimate relationship."

"You're mistaken," replied Fartworthy.

"We have worked together for years. He's more like a broth-er." The lace edge of Flora's handkerchief peeked out of her shaking, tight fist.

The head detective moved closer. "Did he help you plan the murder, Miss Fairchild?"

"I would do nothing to harm Lady Lemington!"

"You made her tea." Carter put her hands on her hips. "You brought it to the party. Why?"

Miss Fairchild's face twisted in confusion. "It was her regular time. She had it every night. I thought she wanted it then."

"You had plenty of opportunity to slip something into her brew." Carter pointed at the head housekeeper. "Why did you want her dead?"

"I didn't!" Panic swept across Flora's face.

Fartworthy stepped forward. "Stop. Leave her be!"

"Stay out of this, Fartworthy," scolded Carter. "Miss Fairchild, why not? She was a harsh employer. She ordered you around. You were fed up with how she treated you."

Flora shook her head violently. "No!"

"Lady Lemington made your life miserable!"

"She saved me!" Flora's fists clasped tight.

"She was obnoxious!" The DCI pressed.

"She married my father!" Flora shouted. Her hands flew to her mouth.

A collective gasp escaped from the onlookers.

"What?" asked the DCI.

Flora looked at the floor and whispered. "Richard Lemington was my father. I am Lady Lemington's stepdaughter."

Chapter Twenty-Four

Carter's hand went to her forehead. "Her stepdaughter?"

"Yes." Flora's face contorted.

Cassandra rushed forward to the head housekeeper. "Uncle Richard was your father?"

Tears welled in Robin's eyes as she crossed the room. "My goodness. Violet? I can't believe this." She hugged her long-lost niece. "They said you disappeared decades ago, and Lily told me you died abroad. Is it really you?"

"Yes, it's me, Aunt Robin. I don't go by Violet anymore." Flora's voice cracked. "That girl did die, in a way. You haven't seen me since I was nine years old." She turned to Cassandra. "She and Father had a falling out. I remember the argument involved the cheese company. We didn't see her for over fifteen years before I left."

Robin cupped Flora's chin in her hand. "I always knew you looked familiar. You have your father's eyes." She hugged her again.

Cassandra frowned. "Flora? You said you moved, lived in Paris, and then came back to work here."

Miss Fairchild stepped away from her aunt's embrace. "That's all true, but I left out significant parts. Years of significant parts." She peered at the ceiling. Her breath hitched. Flora's sad, blue eyes locked on Fartworthy's gaze.

The head butler put up his hand to stop her. "You don't have to say anything else. You can tell the detectives in private."

"Thank you, but my identity is out. If I unburden my soul, then it's no longer a secret." Flora shrugged her shoulders. "Maybe then it will cease to have power over me."

"What do you have to confess, Miss Fairchild?" Carter opened her notepad.

The head housekeeper smoothed the side of her blonde, tightly wound bun and turned to Cassandra. "I was a baby when Mother died, and my father was widowed at a young age. It was just the two of us for a long time. Years later, Father found happiness with a newfound love, but I, his only daughter, gave him heartache over it. When Lady Lemington and my father started seeing each other, I was too busy being an arrogant twenty-five-year-old."

"You said you're in your forties, so this was decades ago, correct?" asked Carter.

"Yes. At the time when they started dating, I was so full of pride and angry he found someone only ten years my senior. I refused to get to know her. My younger self was obstinate in everything and knowledgeable in nothing. Everything was a bit of a dog's breakfast in my mind. I even left working at our cheese company because my fury spilled over to my duties there. I got a job working for a greenhouse an hour from the manor. Father was patient and believed I would come around after they got married. Little did he realize the degree of my stubbornness."

Cassandra stepped closer. "So, you left?"

"Without saying goodbye to anyone. Not even Father. He gave me a good upbringing with all his parental love. Aside from the death of Mother, it was an ideal childhood, wonderful teenage and early adult years. I threw it away." Flora paused, shutting her eyes tight for a moment. "I really did have a few roos loose in the top paddock."

No one made a noise in the room.

She breathed in deeply and continued. "Early one morning, while everyone slept, I packed two bags and left them in the boot of my car. In the coming weeks, I planned, emptied my bank account, bought an air ticket, and arranged for a place to stay. Several days later, I left for work, handed in my notice, and disappeared. Running off and not telling him my location for over a decade and a half was a heartless thing to do." Her voice cracked. "I punished the only parent I ever had, and I weep over my younger, foolish self."

Carter narrowed her eyes. "You traveled to Australia?"

"No," answered Cassandra. "When we were in the library, she told me she moved to France."

"No, not France. Not yet." Flora wiped her eye with the hand-kerchief. "Initially, I moved as far away as I could get. She's correct. Detective Chief Inspector, how did you know?"

"Your speech patterns and some sayings are decidedly Australian. Please continue." The DCI wrote something in her notepad.

Cassandra asked, "How long did you live there?"

"Over ten years. Changed my name, got a job, and made friends whom I told a fabricated past. Before social media, it wasn't difficult. Hiding out in the Land Down Under made it easy to disappear."

"Did Uncle Richard ever hear from you?" Cassandra moved closer to the head housekeeper.

Flora shrugged. "Rarely. A note every few months or years. When I wrote, I told him I was fine, not coming back, and gave few details. Nothing to give away my location. I had a new friend who was a flight attendant. I would hand her a letter to mail wherever in the world she went that week. Didn't care where she dumped it, as long as it wasn't Australia."

Hamish walked forward with his arms crossed. "Miss Fairchild, do you know if your father tried to find you?"

"Yes, he did," the head housekeeper replied.

"How long did he search?" Hamish's brow furrowed.

"Years. Lady Lemington later told me his ritual. Like clockwork with each letter, he would hire a private detective and send the investigator to search in the country the letter was postmarked." Flora closed her eyes. "I never imagined he would go to those lengths. He wasted so much money with leads to nowhere." She clutched the handkerchief to her chest.

Ruby spoke. "Flora, why didn't you tell us who you were?"

Poppy, standing next to the photographer, shrugged. "People make regrettable choices at some point in their lives. Decisions you made long ago wouldn't have mattered to us. We like you and enjoy your company."

Flora's mouth smiled, but her eyes remained sad. "Wait, ladies. You haven't heard my whole story. I'm much worse than you imagine. You might change your mind about associating with me."

Ruby crossed her arms. "I doubt that. You're a lovely person."

"Let me continue, or I'll never get this out." Flora paused. "When I was a child, Father always said, 'No matter where you go, there you are.' I'm sure that's a phrase from someone famous. Those words would often haunt me. It took years for me to figure out what that meant. I loathed myself more with each passing year."

"Did you enjoy living on a different continent?" asked Poppy. "Some of it must have been exciting. New adventures and places to see."

"At first, there were moments of fleeting happiness. However, Australia was not the paradise I sought. Life became hard, and I yearned to be closer to home." Flora's bottom lip quivered. "The seasons, all topsy-turvy, got to me. Putting a shrimp on the barbie for Christmas Eve seemed wrong every year, yet my stubborn pride didn't allow me to think of asking forgiveness. I needed a change. I needed to be in the Northern Hemisphere."

Robin coughed. "Where did you go, Violet? I mean, Flora."

"France seemed like a good idea. I had Australian friends going there who appeared trustworthy." She peeked over at Cassandra. "This is what I mentioned earlier. I'm so sorry I didn't include the whole story, Miss Haywood." She turned back to the DCI. "Unfortunately, my acquaintances got involved with narcotics, and so did I." Tears brimmed on her lower lids. "I . . . I became an addict." Flora folded her arms around herself.

Mr. Birch moved forward. "Miss Fairchild? My goodness. You? Did you ever deal in drugs?"

Flora stared at the floor. "No, only a low-life user."

Fartworthy took a step closer to stand by her side. "Don't say that. You've come so far in such a short time. You're no longer that person."

"In my head, I'll always be that person, Archibald." Flora continued to look down.

Von Pickle piped up, "Who is Archibald, and who would name an ankle-biter that?"

Fartworthy turned to the braggart. "That is my first name, sir."

The baron threw his hands up and laughed. "You must be joking! I thought your last name was absurd. Your mother hated having a baby so much she gave you a name from the 1800s? Is that even a first name? That can't be real."

"I assure you, sir, Archibald is indeed a first and a last name." Fartworthy stood taller with his chin jutted out. "Mother was proud of her heritage of Scottish nobility."

Von Pickle adjusted his cuff links. "She could have given you a kilt."

"Rupert isn't exactly on any list of trendy names." Mimi laughed. "Isn't that right, Rupert?"

Von Pickle scowled at his ex-girlfriend.

Carter waved her hands. "Enough. Miss Fairchild, please continue. I gather there's more to your story."

"There is." Flora hugged herself. "Where was I?"

"You're an addict," said the DCI.

"Was. She *was* one," replied Fartworthy in a harsh tone. He turned to his coworker and coaxed, "Go on, Miss Fairchild."

"After the drugs became my life, all I cared about was my next hit. I'm sorry to say, I never thought of home." Flora turned to Cassandra. "All the while, my loving father never stopped looking for me. By the time I went to France, it had been over a decade and a half. I thought he'd given up the search."

DS Jenkins asked, "He didn't stop, did he?" The second-in-command motioned to Carter with a tilt of his head.

"Not at all, Detective. One day, I sent him a letter from Paris. I mailed it myself because I was too high to remember my clever plan of evading discovery. As soon as Father received the letter, he hired another private investigator to find me. This last time, the PI was successful." Flora dabbed her eyes with her lace-edged handkerchief.

"And Fartworthy was the PI." Carter crossed her arms.

Flora looked at Fartworthy. He gave her a slight nod and shrug. "Yes. He found me."

A collective gasp echoed throughout the dining room.

"What?" Jenkins shook his head and remarked, "The butler is *also* a private investigator?"

"Yes, he is. At first, Mr. Fartworthy ascertained I was in Paris but not my exact location. He had intel I had not left the country. Yet, without knowing, I dodged detection by my constant motion. He discovered my illegal activity and relayed this information."

"Your father must have been excited to have a lead after all those years." Cassandra gripped her scarf.

"Yes, but the news of my drug use devastated Father." Flora

twisted the handkerchief in her hand. "He became so stressed and panicked they would find me too late. His health declined. My father knew drugs were a time bomb. The strain was too much. He had a massive heart attack."

Cassandra squeezed her eyes tight, knowing the outcome of her uncle's health challenge.

Mimi's hands went to her mouth. "My goodness!"

"He lingered for two days." Flora bit her lip. "My stepmother never left his side." Her voice cracked. "At one point, he came round and spoke to her. He begged her to continue to look for me, bring me home, and to take care of the family cheese company. She made this deathbed promise, never dreaming that he was dying. In my heart, I know he held on long enough to pass on his final wishes. He died within the hour." Flora buried her face in her hands and wept.

Cassandra wrapped her arms around the tormented woman. Flora accepted the embrace in surrender. People shifted in their spots as the pain-filled, guttural sobs reverberated against the tall manor walls. Cassandra murmured, "Shh. It's all right. It's all right."

Miss Fairchild took a moment and pulled away, wiping bitter tears from her cheeks. Her voice quivered. "It was all my fault, and I can never correct it. I never saw or spoke to Father before his passing. After receiving the news of his death, I spiraled out of control. If Mr. Fartworthy hadn't been there, I wouldn't be alive today. He stayed for weeks, never left my side, made my meals, and listened. I hadn't had a real friend in many years. He convinced me to detox and get off the drugs once and for all. Mr. Fartworthy helped me through that, too. 'It's time to go home,' he said. I realized he was right." She touched Fartworthy's arm. "I will *never* forget what you did for me."

"I couldn't leave you in that condition." Fartworthy smiled. "Remember, you're resilient. You survived. Many people do not. You'll make it through this."

Alexander Spooner stood. "He's right, Miss Fairchild. Remember what I told you in the library? Think of my brother. You're strong to get out of the death grip of substance abuse."

"Thank you, Mr. Spooner." She turned to the young man. "Addiction was something I never saw coming. It rushed in like a dense fog. No . . . more like a black cloak engulfing all my senses, obscuring every good in this world. You don't care about anything except getting more for your habit. No one believes they're an addict until it's too late. Your brother probably didn't, either."

Alexander jammed his hands into his suit jacket pockets. "You're right. He had no idea how his actions would lead to his downfall."

Mr. Birch gestured toward Fartworthy. "You're real lucky he could get you so far away from all that. Quite the hero. What did Lily do?"

"*Lady Lemington* came to Paris. Mr. Fartworthy arranged it. She welcomed me with open arms. She never blamed me—ever. I know it was my fault Father died. I'll never pardon myself. However, I begged for forgiveness and she gave it without question." Flora breathed in deeply.

She continued. "I was the 'Prodigal Daughter,' but I didn't want the fatted calf. I told her I needed to pay for my sins. Would not remain at the manor unless I could be her servant. This way, I could stay hidden from the world, away from dangerous friends, away from the ever-tempting world of drugs, and away from a life of my own. I owed my father that much." She wiped her nose with the handkerchief she still clutched.

"Aunt Lily brought you home." Cassandra stared at the floor.

Flora sighed. "She did everything in her power to convince me to just live here. We could be friends, she said, and not have to refer to her as my stepmother."

Robin smirked. "Your father was stubborn, too. As am I. It's nestled in our DNA." She chuckled. "I still can't believe you're standing here." Her face regained its seriousness. "Did Lily force you to work for her and be a domestic?"

"Aunt Robin, you're not listening. I wouldn't come back unless I was her servant. It was her idea that I become the head housekeeper, so at least I would have some control in my life. Isn't that what we all want? It was precisely what I needed to turn my world around."

DS Jenkins interrupted. "Fartworthy, during your interview, did you mention you were a PI to Henslowe?"

"Didn't think it was relevant." Fartworthy smirked.

"Relevant?" The DS scowled. "Your arrogant—"

"Easy, Jenkins." Carter moved toward the butler. "That's for my team to determine, Fartworthy, not you. We don't need an amateur deciding what's pertinent to solve the case."

"This is exactly why I didn't mention my hobby." Fartworthy's grin evaporated. "Detectives look down upon creatures like me with contempt and scorn. Instead of welcoming a fresh set of eyes not locked on protocol, they try to prove we're obstructing the investigation. Always happens."

Carter put her hands on her hips. "You're right. I have a problem with PIs. You get in the way and distract my team. My job is to solve cases so those who commit crimes receive their punishment. People working outside the framework of procedure can taint valuable evidence that jeopardizes convictions. For what? For you to stoke your ego as you think you show up the professionals? Stick to the missing person cases. You seem to be talented in that niche."

Mr. Birch pointed toward his coworker. "Maybe the butler did it after all."

Fartworthy smirked. "Wouldn't that be such a cliché?"

"A professional PI chap." Birch crossed his arms. "That explains why you lurk about."

"I don't lurk. I'm a butler and keep things running." Fartworthy smiled. "If I happen to see people slacking or taking off to town for no reason, I encourage them to do their job." He looked at Birch. "Thank you for the compliment, and no. Although I would like to be licensed, it's a hobby to help find people. I have a soft spot for that ever since my little brother disappeared forever when we were younger." He blew out a deep breath.

Carter ran a hand through her hair and paused. "I'm sorry about your loss, Fartworthy."

He tugged once on his suit jacket. "It was years ago. As for me, I haven't been working on a missing person case since I found Miss Fairchild. Directing things around here as head butler takes up all my time."

"To clarify, you're not a professional?" asked the DCI.

"Correct," replied Fartworthy.

"I'll talk to you later about that, Fartworthy." Carter turned. "Back to you, Miss Fairchild. Why would Lady Lemington hire a PI to be on her household staff as a butler?"

"Mr. Fartworthy had many years of experience in service. Like he said, the other job is a hobby. She hired Mr. Fartworthy as head butler and me as head housekeeper after she let go of the entire household staff. Well, everyone but Mr. Birch. He was the only one to remain from the old staff, but he was hired long after I left. Lady Lemington wanted the new employees to see us in charge from the start."

Mimi spoke up from across the room. "That's why she did that? I thought it was arbitrary and cruel."

Flora's voice shot out sharp and strong. "Absolutely not. Lady Lemington found better positions for every one of her released employees. In addition, she sought people from far away to replace them. She wanted to guarantee no one had any memory of me as the daughter of her late husband." She searched the room.

Arabella took a bite of cheese. "That makes sense."

Flora continued. "It does in the right context. It's so rare that I go off the grounds. I like the protection of the manor. When I go to the village, it breaks my heart every time. There are always murmurings and rumors about Lady Lemington letting go of her staff. It was years ago, and yet the talk continues. Further grumblings of not hiring anyone local was a sin in the eyes of the self-appointed jury of the village. Gossip is truly the devil's work. Lady Lemington laughed when I told her what I had heard. She ordered me not to say anything and to ignore them. Now you know the real story and can stop sullying her name."

Frederick stepped forward. "You're right. There's always talk about Lady Lemington. When I moved here, and before we met, I believed the rumors. One day, she came into my new jewelry store. I was wary to wait on an individual with her reputation. However, she was pleasant. Over time, she shopped in my store often and always treated me and my employees with respect. We had many delightful conversations. After getting to know her, the two views, rumor against what I saw with my own eyes, didn't match. I found that odd."

"Mr. Chamberlain, some of Aunt Lily's behavior baffled me, too." Cassandra shook her head. "Miss Fairchild, how did she know this plan would work and no one would recognize you? You lived here for the first twenty-five years of your life."

"When I left, I was a sullen, overweight brunette in my twenties. Now, I'm blonde, middle-aged, skinny, and until today, happier. Who could identify me? Besides, who looks at servants? My aunt didn't even remember me." Flora looked over at Robin.

"I'm sorry for that." Mrs. Turner coughed. "Why would Lily tell me you died?"

"It was me. I told her if anyone mentioned my name—ever—she should say I died abroad. Over time, people cease to remember those who leave. I'm forgettable." Flora breathed in deeply.

DS Jenkins clasped his hands together. "Miss Fairchild, is there anything else to add?"

"Lady Lemington and Mr. Fartworthy saved me from myself. I have built a life here and like myself again. Keeping busy running this household has given me a purpose." Turning to the DCI, Flora continued. "Please don't remove me from this manor. I didn't hurt her. I know I did drugs in the past, but I have touched nothing since living here again. Please, believe me."

Carter picked up her head from her note-taking. "I have no cause to remove you from your place of employment unless you had something to do with Lady Lemington's death. Did you?"

"No, I didn't." Miss Fairchild clasped her hands together. "I cared about her. I hope she's at peace and reunited with Father once again. She was devastated when he died. The most upsetting part? Lady Lemington helped me during the worst time of my life, all the while going through the most awful trial of her own. And she perished alone in a water closet." Flora squeezed her eyes shut. "I wasn't there. I wasn't there." Flora sobbed again.

Fartworthy stepped closer and put his arm around her shoulders.

She opened her eyes, tears streaming down her face. "At least Father had Lady Lemington holding his hand when he passed. He could let go of this life knowing his love would look after things. He wasn't alone. For that, I'm grateful." She glanced up at Fartworthy. "And for you."

Suddenly, the ground shuddered and the windows and walls rattled. A deafening noise resembling a rocket take-off and the shattering of glass echoed through the manor.

Everyone's eyes went wide, their mouths opened, and all froze in place.

Von Pickle shouted, "What was that?"

"Did a helicopter crash?" yelled Robin.

Exclamations from many erupted.

Someone's pounding footsteps came running down the hall from the back entrance. "Chief! Chief!" a man's voice shouted. Detective Constable Henslowe burst into the dining area, his entrance commanding attention. "Come! Come quick! The hothouse exploded and is on fire!"

Chapter Twenty-Five

"My plants!" cried Mr. Birch. "No!" He thumped down the long hall. Carter yelled from across the room. "Mr. Birch! Wait! It may not be safe!" She turned to Henslowe. "Fire or explosion first?" Carter jammed her notepad into her pocket. "Where's Penwarden?"

"I don't know which was first, and I don't know where Penwarden is." Henslowe threw his hands up. "I was at the back door when it happened. Debris is everywhere."

DC Henslowe motioned to DS Jenkins, and they sprinted after the gardener.

"What else?" Carter joined the pursuit. Her shouts faded as she dashed away.

For a moment, no one else moved.

Cassandra looked at her best friend. "I need to see what's going on."

"I'm with you." Arabella left her plate on the dining room table. "Let's go."

The formerly paralyzed group's curiosity overcame their fear. Used china plates and teacups clattered as guests deposited them. Cassandra and the others raced after the detectives. They piled through the doorway leading to the servants' entrance, across the landing, and to the outside.

The stench of burning vegetation mixed with chemicals smacked them in the face. The flames, hurried detectives, and patches of ice mixed with shattered glass greeted the new on-lookers. Plant stands, charred chunks from wooden pallets, and half-melted, plastic flowerpot pieces were scattered on the large back lawn like discarded rubbish after an outdoor concert. The flames glowed orange and black, while dark smoke rose high into the air. More people emerging from the manor shouted and cried out as they spilled into the yard.

Shortly after taking in the disaster, Cassandra found herself flanked between Frederick and Alexander.

DC Penwarden shouted over the chaos and sped across the frozen grass to Carter, slipping every few steps. "We just finished our job and it went up. I called it in, and the fire brigade is on its way, along with an ambulance. One constable has lacerations on his hand. No other reported injuries, but we're having an issue with the head gardener." Penwarden pointed across the lawn.

Near the glass building's entrance, Henslowe grabbed Birch's shoulder, blocking him. Several constables in neon-yellow vests as-sisted. Mr. Birch shoved one constable aside and charged forward. Henslowe and the others dove, pulling the gardener back.

Carter shouted to the detectives nearby. "Keep people from going inside the hothouse! I want a perimeter around that burning building." Carter, Jenkins, and Penwarden crossed the lawn to help their colleagues restrain the agitated man. Fartworthy joined them as the head detective reached the confrontation.

The explosion had destroyed most of the hothouse's one-me-ter-square panes, except for a few windows facing the manor. The flames wrapped around the metal girders and extended their tendrils skyward through openings where sections of the glass roof had exist-ed minutes before.

Cassandra's hand grasped her forehead. "No!" She attempted to sprint across the lawn, stumbling in her backless sandals over the debris pieces and ice-coated ground.

Frederick shouted from behind her. "Cassandra!"

"You can't save it!" Arabella added, and she and Alexander joined the pursuit.

The trio of young adults caught up with Cassandra, who had halted midway between the manor and the destroyed hothouse.

Arabella yelled, "What are you doing? You can't save it."

With her throat tight, Cassandra looked up at the gray clouds that tangoed with the black smoke. The bootheel feeling pressing down on her chest intensified. *This isn't happening. Was anyone hurt? Is it all destroyed? At least Aunt Lily didn't see this. She loves her flowers and—* Cassandra gulped. "I can't believe this."

Arabella put her arm around her friend. "It's only a building. Everyone was inside with us, right? Then there should be no injuries. This could have been more tragic. If this happened during the party, you could've had guests out there."

"How can this day be any worse?" Cassandra's hands covered her mouth. She teetered on the brink of hyperventilating. "How could this happen? Did the explosion cause the fire or did the fire cause the explosion?"

"The fire personnel will determine that," said Alexander. "They'll figure out if it was something faulty or arson."

"Arson?" Cassandra looked at Alexander with wide eyes.

"The weather could have caused something." Frederick paced behind the ladies.

Arabella continued to hold her friend in a side hug. "The weather? Since when does ice cause an explosion?"

Frederick ran his hand through his thick, black hair. "Freezing temperatures can short circuit transformers and cause them to pop.

Perhaps not the ice. Maybe some chemicals were left close together and somehow created this."

Across the lawn, the cluster of law enforcement remained unsuccessful in their efforts to calm the gardener. Mr. Birch continued to wave his arms and rant, with his words drowned out by approaching sirens.

Arabella pointed. "Why would he react this way? It's his job not his own business."

Cassandra breathed in deeply. "He spent years researching, cultivating, and perfecting his 'beauties,' as he calls them. He put so much work into the heirloom seeds. He loved that hothouse. As did I."

Frederick shrugged. "I would be frantic if my work went up in flames, too. It's his life."

Alexander chimed in. "All that work gone. When my parents' business went under, it took a toll on them. They never recovered. It's devastating."

From behind them, near the manor, came hollered warnings. Staff and guests were yelling. One voice rose above the others.

"You four idiots!" Von Pickle shouted. "That's not the wizard. The hothouse won't give you any brains for getting closer. It isn't safe!"

The four young people looked at each other.

Arabella glanced over her shoulder at the braggart. "When did he find a conscience?"

Alexander pulled on Arabella's arm and took a step back. "He has a point. He's not a nice man, but he's right. It could still be dangerous."

"We should move back to the house," said Frederick.

"Agreed. I'm not staying out here. This is nutters." Arabella held her arm over her mouth and coughed. "Come on, Cassie. Let the fire brigade handle this. We can't do anything to change it. What's done is done."

Cassandra remained rooted to her spot. "Go back. Leave me. I need to process this."

Arabella scoffed. "Don't be stupid. Let's move."

"I'll be fine, Bella. Go."

"You're so stubborn." Arabella threw up her hands and huffed. "You couldn't pay me a million quid to stay here any longer. We should get out of the way." She jogged back to the manor door with Alexander close behind.

Against advice, Cassandra moved closer to the blaze, her lilac and ivory scarf tails blowing in the icy wind.

"Wait!" Frederick followed her. "The fire brigade is here. They got it. Let's get back inside. It's freezing out here."

She moved forward like the cliché of a moth to a flame. "You're probably right. The manor is far enough away to be out of danger." *I can't believe what I'm seeing. Hold up.* She tilted her head. "What's that hissing?"

"That can't be good." Frederick touched her arm to stop her. "This isn't safe."

A second, smaller explosion shattered the remaining glass walls and sent shards of glass screaming through the air.

Frederick stepped in front of Cassandra, swinging his arms wide around to shield her, his back to the hothouse. He squeezed her to his chest, and she instinctively gripped him around his sides.

For a moment, they remained locked together. Air from the blast rushed past them like a strong ocean breeze but lacked the strength to knock them to the ground. Bits of glass and other splinters of debris clattered about them. Shrieks erupted from the onlookers.

As Cassandra pulled away from his shoulder, their faces were mere centimeters from one another, and his strong arms held her in a protective hug. Breathless, Cassandra surveyed her guardian. The fire's orange glow added to the moment's surrealness.

Frederick's green eyes, wide with concern, searched Cassandra's face. "Are you all right?"

"Yes, I think so. Are you?" Cassandra straightened up, and Frederick slowly released her from his shielding embrace. "What was that?"

"I'm fine." He scanned behind at the dancing flames. "Maybe a propane tank or some fertilizer or gas ignited. Even this far away is not safe. We better move inside the manor in case there are more surprises." He grabbed her hand, and a second later, Frederick paused. "Wait." He placed his hand on the back of his head and gasped. "Ow."

"What is it?" Cassandra's stomach tightened.

He brought his hand around. It dripped crimson. The young man staggered back a step. "Ah . . . it appears that I'm wounded."

"Frederick?" Cassandra's eyes widened. "Let me see." Cassandra sucked in her breath. Frederick's black, silky hair made the investigation difficult. Gently, she touched his thick mane as shards of glass fell to the ground. Her hands had his blood on them. Her stomach plummeted twenty stories. *Pull it together, Cassandra. Can't pass out. He needs you.* "There's glass in your hair. I can't get to your scalp to see where you're cut. The back of your jacket has no marks on it."

Blood ran down the back of his neck, soaking his collar. He looked down as the red, wormlike lines crept down the front of his white shirt. Frederick's knees buckled.

Springing forward, Cassandra steadied him by holding his arm and elbow. "You'll be okay," she said close to his ear, for his benefit and hers. Turning to the cluster of official personnel near the hedge-row who were running in their direction, she shouted, "Detectives! He's injured!"

"Are you hurt?" The jeweler stood straight and blew out a rag-ged breath.

Cassandra looked over her blouse and arms, never letting go of Frederick. "No, doesn't appear so, thanks to you." She returned her gaze to his face.

"Good." He reached up to his injury again. "Ah!" A pained smile crossed his face. "Then it is well worth it."

Penwarden, on the run, yelled at the couple. "Move back! Move back! There might be more explosions. Where are you hurt?" He looked at Cassandra, ushering them to the manor.

"Not me. He's bleeding from his head." Cassandra pointed to Frederick's matted hair and stained shirt.

The detective stopped in his tracks. "Blimey! You got yourself a nasty gash or two." He turned to a constable and shouted, "Is that ambulance here yet?"

At the detective's question, Frederick and Cassandra exchanged a mutual, worried look.

The wail of an approaching ambulance joined the sirens and rotating lights of the fire brigade. Acrid smells of burnt fertilizer and melted plastic mixed with the frigid air. Glass and ice crunched underfoot while the detectives and constables shouted at the other guests to get back. Mr. Birch continued to rant about his loss. Heat from the blaze swirled around, mixing the chaotic soup.

For a moment, none of it mattered. The sights, sounds, and smells of bedlam disappeared for the two young adults.

Cassandra continued to support his arm and hold his one hand as they stumbled closer to the manor. "They'll take good care of you. You'll be fine."

Frederick smiled as he held the back of his head. "I'm hoping. You should get inside. It's not safe out here." They stopped, and his eyes locked on Cassandra's.

Penwarden beckoned to the paramedics. "Here! This man has a head wound."

The two first responders ran over and put down their trauma kits while pulling on light-blue, latex gloves. "Sir, can you tell us what happened?" asked the female paramedic as she slowly moved Frederick's hand from the back of his head and flashed a penlight into his eyes. "Can you stand on your own?" He nodded.

Cassandra answered. "Flying glass from an explosion cut him. How bad is it?" She let go of his arm and stepped back from Frederick.

"Give us a moment, miss." The male paramedic's gloved fingertips turned red when he carefully parted Frederick's hair. More shards fell out and bounced on the dead grass. "Do you remember what happened, sir?" He turned to Cassandra as she tried to speak. "Please. We need him to answer."

Frederick pulled his hand up to his forehead. "Yes, I do. There was a small explosion. My back was to it."

"Can you tell me what day it is, sir?" The female paramedic loosened his tie and unbuttoned his collar, probing around his neck, dusting out any debris and glass.

"New Year's Day." Frederick's face contorted. "All of this has been one day?"

Cassandra exhaled. "Yes, one horrible day."

They continued to examine Frederick's head. "What is your name and where are you, sir?"

He closed his eyes and breathed deeply. "Frederick Chamberlain. Dutch Hill Manor." He swayed again.

DS Jenkins jogged over. "Carter wants everyone moved immediately."

The male paramedic continued his examination on Frederick. "You have several small lacerations on your scalp, sir. I can see one that needs more attention."

His partner peered at the site, too. "Let's get you to the ambulance so you're in a safe area, and we can clean and inspect this injury more closely. We'll have you patched up right quick." She turned to Cassandra. "We have him, miss."

"You should go inside, Cassandra." He held his breath as they continued to examine his head. "Ah." He gritted his teeth. "It's just a flesh wound." Frederick flashed a playful grin.

Cassandra stifled a laugh. "Oh, Frederick."

DS Jenkins pleaded. "Please, Miss Haywood. We're concerned there might be additional explosions. The manor is a safe distance away."

Cassandra reached out, squeezed Frederick's bloody hand, and her gaze didn't leave his face. "Thank you for protecting me."

Frederick smiled. "My pleasure." They let go of one another.

The paramedics flanked him, holding on to his elbows, while Detective Constable Penwarden followed. Cassandra watched them whisk her hero to the ambulance. She uttered a silent prayer for Frederick's well-being.

In an instant, the clamor and odors of the moment came roaring back in full cacophony. Distant sirens of additional rescue personnel played on as background music. The circling lights on top of the fire truck illuminated the scene with flashing reds and blues. Firefighters held on tight to canvas hoses, drowning the flames. Water gushing from the heavy snakes caused clouds of steam and black smoke to rise high into the air from the smoldering remains of the metal-framed hothouse. The stench of melted metal and burning plants combined to envelop everyone in the area.

Away from the destroyed structure, the head gardener had regained his composure and stood with two detectives saying something Cassandra couldn't hear. The fire chief buzzed around in his white helmet, directing his team like they were coming in for a landing.

Cassandra surveyed the side of the manor. *No damage. The windows are intact, and no burn marks from the explosion. This could have been much worse.*

Jenkins huffed. "Come on, miss."

Fartworthy materialized next to her. "Miss Haywood, please come back inside. No one knows what else could happen with that building still on fire."

"Jenkins!" called Carter from across the lawn. "Move that group inside, too." She pointed to remaining kitchen staff on the perimeter.

Jenkins looked at Fartworthy for a moment. "Get her inside, Mr. PI, and then you stay there." He jogged to the staff group.

Fartworthy saluted. "Righto." As soon as the DS was out of earshot, he said, "Go do your job properly and leave me be."

Cassandra leaned closer. "They're not the enemy, Mr. Fartworthy."

"No, but they're so full of themselves they can't see what's right under their feet." The head butler smirked, looking over his shoulder. "Blind fools." He returned his attention to her. "We have a break in the case." He guided her arm, and they moved across the lawn. "Let me pretend to do what he told me."

"Break? Whatever do you mean?" To match his long strides, Cassandra had to take three to four steps for every one of Mr. Fartworthy's.

Flora rushed forward to the duo. "Either of you hurt? I saw that young man was injured."

"We're not wounded, but Mr. Chamberlain went to go get looked at by the professionals. What would cause those explosions?" Cassandra pointed over her shoulder.

"I have a guess, but I'm not certain yet," said Fartworthy.

Cassandra struggled to keep up with Fartworthy's pace. "Flora, how are you after all your secrets spilled out?"

The trio continued on their way, crunching and dodging debris across the lawn. It was no longer slippery since the heat of the fire melted the ice. Flora hugged her black uniform sleeves. "I never realized how my secrets pressed down on my heart. In a strange way, it's a relief."

"I'm glad to hear that. Why did Carter turn on the two of you like that? I thought she still thinks I harmed Aunt Lily." Cassandra blew into her hands. "It's still freezing out here."

"She still believes you're the prime suspect. Carter has new information, and she's assuming Miss Fairchild or I helped you." Fartworthy stopped momentarily to stare at something in the chaos.

"What is it?" asked Flora.

He pulled up to his full height. "Miss Haywood, the DCI pressed Miss Fairchild with the incessant questions, hoping to break her and have her blurt out a connection. She never imagined personal challenges would come to light."

The sirens stopped, but the clamor increased behind them. Additional firefighters jumped off a newly arrived truck. More hoses unwound with shouts of orders. Hissing and spitting like serpents, the flames reluctantly succumbed to the torrent.

"Keep moving, Mr. Fartworthy," urged the head housekeeper over her shoulder. "Why does she think I helped you kill Lady Lemington?"

It was Cassandra's turn to halt. "The photos. Flora, Carter, and I saw a photo of you holding Aunt Lily's teacup at the party. She questioned me about that exchange."

Fartworthy smiled. "I think your PI skills are improving. I overheard from the detectives the teacup found in Lady Lemington's bedroom tested positive for the drug digitalis. She didn't take that heart medication. It would be poison for her."

"What?" said the ladies in unison.

Flora stopped walking and covered her mouth with her hands.

"You said toxicology reports take weeks to finalize," said Cassandra.

"They do. Miss Fairchild, please put your hands down." Fartworthy motioned to the brick building. "Come. We need to keep heading in that direction. Otherwise, those bumblers will return." He continued. "To answer your question, the whole workup examines many elements, so it's time consuming. If the testing is on an object, for one substance, those results can be processed quickly. This seems to be the case here."

Flora's voice cracked. "They think I poisoned her?"

"Not necessarily." Fartworthy touched her arm. "Carter may have thought you were working on behalf of Miss Haywood . . . or someone else."

"My tea killed her?" The head housekeeper's eyes brimmed with tears.

"We know the drug was present in the cup and might have contributed to her death, but you didn't murder her. It is possible whoever put it in there did. Or the medication disoriented her and then someone hurt her in the bathroom." The head butler straightened his glasses. "Who else knew you were serving Lady Lemington her drink as per her nightly ritual?"

Cassandra looked up. "The Yorks were present in the photo when you brought the tea to the party, but I recall she didn't drink it at that moment. You took the cup upstairs, right?"

"Yes, I left it on the bedside table."

"Who was upstairs besides you, Flora? Anyone up there alone might have had the opportunity to add the medication to Aunt Lily's tea."

Carter strode toward them, shouting, "Miss Haywood! Are you injured, too?"

"No, I'm not." Cassandra held out her bloody hands. "This is from Mr. Chamberlain's wound. He went with one of the detectives to the ambulance."

The DCI pointed to Cassandra. "I saw that. No one should have been out here. Keep going to the manor. DCs Greenfield and Baker will be with *all* of you in the library. This isn't a secure area."

"I'm moving them inside." Fartworthy glared at the Detective Chief Inspector. "There's no need to tell me."

"Fartworthy, follow orders. Understood?" Carter huffed.

He set his jaw. "I'm not under your jurisdiction. Think what you want about me personally. However, I have information. You'll want to hear what I have to say."

Why is he going to tell them he knows about the tea? Cassandra glanced at Fartworthy.

Carter sighed. "If I paid attention to your kind, mayhem and the makings of a poorly written show on the telly would be the result. You're not even licensed. I make it a personal rule not to consult with amateur PIs. Actually, any PIs."

"Shortsighted rule," replied the head butler.

The DCI crossed her arms. "I have a death under investigation and a potential arson case to tackle. I have no patience for the hunches and feelings of a pretend detective."

Carter's team continued to shout instructions, ushering guests and staff out of harm's way. Powerful blasts of water from the fire truck hoses surged onto a new section of the destroyed building. A thunderous roar echoed from the waterfall.

Fartworthy hollered over the din. "When an underling might have information to crack a case, an effective leader should check her ego at the door for five minutes to listen! Let me help!"

The head detective and the PI glared at one another.

After a few moments, she growled, "Just. This. Once. What do you have?"

Fartworthy smirked. "I'm honored. Did you notice what was on the ground when we prevented him from going into the hothouse?"

"Debris from the explosion. Flowerpots and pallets and hoses. So?" Carter shook her head.

"The fire was before the explosion. Many partially burnt things were thrown from the building onto the lawn. Second, evidence of multiple burner phone pieces." Fartworthy leaned in closer to Carter. "Birch has many secrets, and that wreckage might be the key I'm . . . w . . . we're looking for."

The DCI's eyes remained locked on Fartworthy.

Part of a supporting beam of the damaged structure collapsed upon itself. The folding metal screeched and clanged like cats fighting in an alleyway lined with rubbish bins. Cassandra covered her ears.

Carter didn't flinch, ignored the noise, and nodded for Fartworthy to go on.

The head butler continued. "It may or may not lead to what caused this, but I'm sure it's relevant. Don't let your pride keep you from seeing these important clues. Birch was out here earlier adding more heaters on extension cords throughout the building. He's fiercely protective of what's inside."

"It's his job. Logically speaking, he would be concerned." The DCI shrugged.

"Yes, fair assessment, but we should search the debris. It could solve your explosion case"—Fartworthy pointed to the house—"or the investigation concerning Lady Lemington."

Carter focused on the hothouse and summoned Baker to them. "Interesting."

"We need to move quickly." The head butler crossed his arms.

"If there is any evidence that he was responsible for the explosion, they'll find it." Carter gestured to the firefighters. "Professionals care about that sort of thing."

Fartworthy stepped closer to the head detective. "Birch will rid the area of items tying him to anything not in his best interest."

"You can't assume he'll do that."

"I know my coworker, Detective. He should not be trusted. Can we at least ask him about the heaters or the phones? If he overreacts, his behavior—"

"Will dictate our next move," Carter and Fartworthy said together.

Carter huffed. "Miss Haywood, Miss Fairchild, please follow DC Baker back to the library. I want everyone who's not fighting the fire or on the investigation team in the manor." DC Baker arrived. "Take them in."

"Yes, ma'am," Baker replied.

"Fartworthy." Carter raised her index finger. "You stay with me. No more disappearing."

"Understood, ma'am." He clasped his hands in front of him. "I'm your servant. For now."

Baker gestured to Flora and Cassandra. "This way, ladies."

Fartworthy added, "Miss Haywood, please listen to Detective Constable Baker. She will take good care of you."

That's different from his usual stance. What is he up to? I'd best play along. "Will do, Mr. Fartworthy."

The three women hurried the short distance, while Fartworthy and Carter headed to Mr. Birch.

The people moving back inside the manor crammed the doorway. Someone near the head of the crowd shouted above the commotion. "Guests to the library. Staff to the kitchen." The two groups diverged as directed, packing the staircase landing. The stench of smoke and gardening chemicals clung to everyone's clothes like marmalade to a scone.

Baker threaded her way through the throng. "Everyone who's going to the library, through this door and this way." She held up her hand like a museum tour guide. "Follow me."

DC Henslowe trailed behind Cassandra and descended the stairs. "Staff, this way. DCI Carter wants everyone to stay calm. Off you go. You may complete your duties inside the manor. Please leave the. . . ." His voice faded as he continued to the lower level.

As she stepped forward, Flora remarked, "I'll talk to you later, Miss Haywood. Let's hope things will clear up soon." With a quick pirouette, the head housekeeper joined the herd making their way down the stairs.

Cassandra put her blood-stained hand up to hold open the hallway door. *Will Frederick be in soon? I hope he'll be all right.* She turned around to see Jenkins remained outside and closed the door. *I should go have a wash before I return to the library. The detectives are outside or up front. Carter isn't here. They won't mind.*

Cassandra slipped away from the group. She found the hidden water closet's door in the hallway's dark wood paneling. Opening the secret entrance, she stepped inside and shut herself in the tiny, charcoal-gray painted room with its gray-and-white, floral wall tiles. With a toilet and sink, there wasn't much space to move. She turned on both faucets and let the cold then lukewarm liquid run over her palms. Blood-tinged water swirled into the tiny, white porcelain sink, mesmerizing Cassandra. *So much blood today. First Aunt Lily and then Frederick.* She rubbed her hands together, and eventually, the red stain disappeared down the drain. The water continued to cascade through her fingers.

Frederick. He saved me from injury. No one has ever done something like that for me. Ever. She closed her eyes, remembering his strong embrace and the security in his arms. Her heart bounced. She looked up into the silver-edged, circle mirror that hung above the sink. Despite her aunt's loss, the stress of suddenly overseeing the company and the manor, being locked in guilt under Carter's suspicion, and the hothouse in ruins, the left side of Cassandra's mouth curled and her eyes gleamed.

Frederick.

The moment flickered past. *He got hurt because of my foolish need to run to the hothouse.* She shut her eyes tight. *Stupid move, Cassandra. How on earth will you run a company when you're so impulsive?*

The water's rising temperature stirred her from her thoughts. She pulled her hands back. Turning the hot faucet off, she splashed cold water onto her face and released a heavy breath.

What a day.

Cassandra dried her face and hands and left the cramped space to join the others. She made her way into her favorite room of the manor to the soundtrack of a shouting Baron Von Pickle, who postured in the face of Detective Constable Greenfield. Baker stood by her colleague's side.

The braggart continued ranting while he ran a hand along a bookshelf, glancing at his fingertips in disgust. "And another thing. How incompetent is your DCI to have a building blow up when the grounds are crawling with her team? On top of that, she had detectives mucking about outside, no direction whatsoever."

Cassandra slipped into the room unnoticed.

DC Greenfield patted the air down, as if subduing an angry panther. "Sir, please calm down. We're doing our best to handle this difficult situation."

"This is your best?" sneered Von Pickle. "What's next, an art heist? Or shall we be robbed at gunpoint? Or perhaps throw in a lovely little assault and battery? That should do nicely."

Mimi sighed from across the room. "Rupert, leave the man alone."

Hamish, Roland, and Poppy nodded in agreement.

"The baron is correct." Robin caressed the edge of a jade, velvet curtain. "We've been detained all day, and a new event will keep us here longer? Utterly ridiculous."

DC Baker walked to Mrs. Turner. "We don't know what the DCI is planning at this point."

"We would like to get on with it." Arabella paced in the back of the room. "I feel like a trapped animal."

DC Baker put her palms together. "This is difficult, ma'am. I apologize for the delay. Please understand we cannot release anyone until we ascertain who might have any information about the hothouse."

Von Pickle adjusted his cuff links. "I don't know anything. There. You've done your job. Let me go."

"We'll wait here until Carter returns." Greenfield smiled at the businessman. "My hands are tied."

"I'm sure someone here can kidnap you and tie your hands if you want." Von Pickle strode over to Cassandra near the door. "You're the new owner of this place and probably want us to leave. Why don't you convince the detectives to release us?"

A true statement. Especially you. "I would like them to wrap up their investigation, but I have no authority. A complete inquiry is the only way they can get answers."

"You're useless." Von Pickle flicked his hand in her direction.

Hamish cleared his throat. "We all wish to leave. There's no need to attack Miss Haywood. Again."

Owen picked up a book from the table behind the sofa. "Me sister wants me 'ome because I know 'ow to care for our mum. We all 'ave 'em places to go." He flipped through the small tome's pages and slipped the book into his pocket.

Von Pickle slumped onto an armrest of a chocolate-brown, leather chair and picked at one of the brass studs. "I want this day to end."

Cassandra crossed her arms. *As if you are the only one. It must be a bad day. I'm agreeing with Von Pickle.* She moved over to the baron and whispered, "Please don't sit on the armrest like that. It's an antique."

Von Pickle rose to stand by the small, round table with a large flower arrangement. "Fine. I'll do it for the antique, not you. I appreciate value." He picked at a petal of a crimson rose in the vase and quietly remarked, "Such a shame about the hothouse. I wonder how badly the property value will plunge."

Cassandra closed her eyes. *Stop talking.*

He continued, unheeding her unspoken desire. "Birch will have nothing to do until you get it rebuilt. He could add those fairy lights to the trees coming up the driveway. It would finally look less gloomy."

"What did you say?" Cassandra tilted her head.

"Your gardener will be bored and can get to those lights you wanted."

She narrowed her eyes. *How did he know that? I didn't tell him. Did Aunt Lily? No, I never had time to mention it to her or Mr. Birch.*

Von Pickle continued to speak in an uncharacteristic, hushed tone, glancing up at the ceiling and around the room. "You definitely need to make some changes around this drafty, old place, but modifications will cost you. Maybe you should cut down on your staff. Let Fartworthy go first. He's a nuisance and hovers too much. You can always find less expensive help. That's my advice, and you should take it. My manor stays in the black because I don't let a little thing like sentiment impede a healthy bottom line."

"What did you say about the lights?" Cassandra twisted the end of her lilac scarf.

"The trees coming up the driveway. Take it as a compliment. It won't happen often. I agree with you that Birch should add some fairy lights." Von Pickle moved to the opposite side of the table.

Cassandra followed him around the furniture. "I didn't tell you about my idea."

Von Pickle adjusted his cuff links. "You must have. Or maybe I overheard it from someone."

Cassandra's spine tingled. She looked over her shoulder. Her best friend was conversing with Alexander at the back of the room. Her eyes snapped back to the braggart, her long hair swinging around. "Did you hear about the idea at the party?"

"I don't recall. I talked to many people about my business. It's hard to keep track." Von Pickle flicked his wrist.

"Well, that's funny since I only told Miss Dalton about the lights."

"Yes, yes of course. I heard it from Bella last night. She must have mentioned it."

"It's *Miss Dalton* to you. *I* call her Bella."

A wide-eyed look flashed across Von Pickle's face. In an instant, the normal glare returned. "You don't own the name. I can call her anything I want. Powerful people can do that, you know. I could give you a nickname, and you would be powerless. How about I call you Scarfy?" he sneered.

"I call her Bella," repeated Cassandra in a low voice. "She told me as her best friend I had that privilege. No one else."

"So what?" Von Pickle turned and walked toward the detectives near the front of the room, his normal, blaring voice returning. "Greenfield, is the hot air in here turned to boiling? Are they trying to cook a confession out of us?"

There must be a mistake. With her breath shallow and rough, she beelined her way to the back of the room to Arabella and Alexander.

Cassandra cleared her throat when she arrived next to the two young adults. The hairs on her neck and arms stood on end.

"Miss Haywood," said Alexander. "Are you all right? You look as though you've seen a ghost."

"Sorry to interrupt." Cassandra grasped her scarf around her neck like a life preserver. "Bella, may I talk to you for a moment?"

Arabella shrugged her shoulders. "What's the matter, luv? Is it about Frederick? How badly did he get hurt?"

"He has cuts on the back of his head and is in the ambulance getting examined. They said he should be fine. I want to talk to you about Von Pickle."

"What did the loudmouth say?" Arabella rolled her eyes.

Cassandra dropped the scarf ends and clasped her own hands together. "At the party last night, did you talk to him?"

"Not that I remember." Arabella played with her ear.

"He just told me you did." Cassandra's pulse quickened.

Arabella pointed her finger. "Yes, I remember. Briefly." She ran her hand through her hair. "We were over by the piano."

"What did you discuss?"

Arabella chuckled to Alexander. "Probably cheese. That's the only topic that comes out of his mouth. And poorly formed insults."

"Was there anything else we talked about yesterday, Bella?"

"Cassie, what's this about?"

"Please try to recall what you said."

Arabella crossed her arms. "We've been here a long time. Why don't you ask the detectives if they can find Carter? You're getting snappish. I think you need a cuppa."

"Did you mention what I said about the fairy lights to him? About me asking Mr. Birch to hang them?"

Arabella grinned. "That. Yes, I talked about that."

"You did?" Cassandra's hands blindly found her scarf again and gripped it tight. "Von Pickle is a snake."

"Loads of people are reptilian in the business world. You need to learn how to charm them so they don't strike. Yes, I told him. We were chatting." Arabella flicked her wrist. "*You* talked to him several times last night."

"Endured insults, you mean. I don't converse with him. Why would you tell him anything I said? You know he'll use it against me."

"It was about lights, Cassie. Nothing more."

Cassandra exhaled as her heart raced. "Why?"

"Why not? The purpose of last night's party was to mingle. I have my business to think of. Networking. It's what people do." Arabella shifted her weight. "Isn't that right, Alexander?" She playfully tapped the young man's shoulder.

The pharmacist stepped away. "I suppose. I don't do that in my line of work." He glanced over at Cassandra. "Maybe I should leave you two alone."

Arabella grabbed his arm. "No, no. Please stay. This isn't a big deal. We have so many more important things to think of. Cassandra has had a rough day." She dropped his arm and touched her friend's and crooned. "You want me to get that tea for you, luv?"

"No, thank you. You're right. There are other things to worry about today." *Maybe I do need that cup of tea. Maybe coffee. Maybe sleep.* She closed her eyes. *I'm unraveling.* The young woman opened her eyes to see Arabella glancing in Von Pickle's direction by the door. Cassandra's stomach dropped. *Did he shrug?* "Did you talk about anything else?"

Arabella waved her hands. "Dear, I talked to so many people last night. I don't have a full transcript of my conversations."

"That's not what I'm asking. You can't trust Von Pickle. We've discussed this many times. You make fun of him. He attempted to ruin my aunt, and he's bragging he'll destroy me, too." Cassandra's scarf squeaked in twisted pain.

"Don't be so overdramatic. We talked and I told him your light idea, which I thought was brilliant."

Cassandra leaned back. "He called you Bella."

She scoffed. "And we call him all sorts of names, like an egotistical cheese windbag. What does that have to do with anything? He probably heard you use my nickname, Cassie. See? I just called you Cassie. It's no big deal."

"You're right. Sorry. It's been an exhausting day. Nothing makes sense." She ran her fingers down the ivory scarf. Cassandra spied Von Pickle chewing the side of his thumbnail, facing them across the room. She stood taller, ice spreading through her veins. *Something is off here.* She whispered, "Are you sure you didn't tell him anything more about me?"

"Really?" Arabella rolled her eyes. "I don't remember. I've been here for other events, you know. We're both regulars on your aunt's guest list."

"You're my best friend, right?"

"Yes, of course." Arabella's mask of indifference remained on her face.

Cassandra spoke slowly. "Have you shared any other information with him?"

"Now you're a DC questioning your guests? Come on. You know me." Arabella folded her arms across her chest.

"What about over the last three years?"

Arabella harrumphed. "What? Why would you accuse me of that? I've been by your side through everything."

Cassandra's voice rose in volume. "You're still not answering my question."

The guests and detectives turned to view the two ladies.

"You must have inhaled some smoke outside." Arabella waved her hand around. "Why all these wild allegations? You're becoming paranoid."

Cassandra clenched her fists. "Arabella!"

Arabella's voice rose in pitch. "Cassie, you need to focus on what the detectives should do and not attack me because you're frustrated."

"Answer the question, my *friend*," Cassandra demanded through gritted teeth.

Arabella sighed. "I suppose I've mentioned some insignificant things over the years."

"Insignificant?" Cassandra's jaw tightened. "Years? Like information from the trial? Business ideas? The QR initiative?"

Arabella held her breath and blinked rapidly.

Cassandra staggered back a step. "No, no, I'm wrong. Tell me I'm wrong, Bella!"

"You're not mistaken."

"How could you?" Cassandra's breath came out shallow and high. "Did he pay you? You're a snitch for hire?"

"No." Arabella sneered. "I have my business and wouldn't stoop to sponge off of someone for a living like you."

"Is that what you really think? You know I worked hard for my aunt. Stop making this about me. You're employed by him?"

"I don't have to answer that." Arabella turned to walk away.

"Yes, you do!" Cassandra grabbed the other woman's arm.

Arabella yanked herself from her friend's grasp. "I don't work for him!"

"You betrayed my trust! For that?" Cassandra shouted, pointing in Von Pickle's direction. "Why? Tell me why!"

"Because he's my husband!" Arabella's hands shot up to cover her mouth.

A collective gasp erupted from the people in the room.

Cassandra's stunned lips failed to form any words.

Chapter Twenty-Six

All was silent. Cassandra squeezed her eyes shut. "What?" she croaked.

"Rupert and I are married." Arabella stretched her neck and her eyebrow arched. "For over two years." She sighed. "Finally, I don't have to hide this from you anymore."

"I . . . I can't look at you," she whispered and hurried away.

Arabella ran after her. "Cassie! I needed to keep this under wraps. You must understand what I had to do, luv. This has been extremely hard on me."

Cassandra's body crackled with everyone's eyes focused on her. She stopped near the doorway. "Excuse me? I'm supposed to be sympathetic, *luv*? Are you completely nutters?"

Alexander stepped up to the arguing women. "Hold on, ladies. Can't you work this out? We had such a lovely time last night. I hate to see you two fighting."

"There is no working this out," barked Cassandra. She attempted to leave, but a detective blocked her escape.

Greenfield waved his hands. "Whoa, Miss Haywood, please. I can't let you out of here. DCI Carter wants all non-law enforcement or fire personnel in the manor."

"Like you said, Carter wanted people in the manor. She never said we had to remain in the library. This is my home. I cannot be with—" She paused with her jaw clenched, shifting her gaze from Arabella to Von Pickle, who stood nearby. Cassandra exhaled sharply. "With such snakes in my pocket."

The baron opened his mouth to speak but emitted an odd, gurgling sound.

Greenfield sighed and moved aside. "At least remain close by, Miss Haywood. Stay in the dining room, please?"

"Agreed and thank you." Cassandra stepped over the threshold and out of the library. She zipped through the dining room. "Luv, indeed. This isn't happening." Cassandra looked over her shoulder at the library door.

Alexander emerged several moments later. He closed the heavy, oak door.

"Wait, Miss Haywood!" shouted the young man behind her. "Greenfield said I could go with you. I don't understand what's going on." He caught up with her.

"I cannot believe this." One hand covered her mouth, and the other rested on her hip. "How could she? How?" Her heart raced. "I need tea. Or coffee. Something."

Alexander continued to follow. "I don't understand what happened in there."

Cassandra stopped mid-stride, facing Alexander. "My best mate betrayed me. What's so difficult to comprehend?"

"She married that obnoxious, pompous man? Isn't that her problem? I mean, she must endure his attitude day and night. Constant put-downs and condescension mixed with a healthy dose of control issues. It's a recipe for a miserable marriage. We should pity her."

Household staff members moved about the main table, clearing it from the luncheon. The steady murmur of voices, coupled with the clanking of dishes and silverware, echoed. The sideboard, which held the breakfast buffet earlier, had transformed into a hot beverage station.

Cassandra resumed her quick clip across the room. "Alexander, sometimes you can be as thick as plum pudding." She stopped at the sideboard, reached for a cup, and knocked over several other porcelain pieces on the table. She snatched one.

Alexander stepped next to her. "Here, let me help. You're in no condition to be touching a pot of boiling water." He took the delicate, bone china teacup from Cassandra, placed it on the table, and held her hands. "Please calm down. I'll fix you something, and you can explain what this means. Maybe I am a bit dense, but I don't see how disliking your best friend's husband is such a problem. Loads of people deal with this kind of situation. You're so agitated. What would you like? Coffee or tea? Cream? Sugar? Whatever you need, I'm here."

Cassandra took a deep breath. "You're right. I'll fumble the whole thing and end up with third-degree burns." She blew a breath out. "Thank you. Coffee, a bit of cream, one sugar, please." Cassandra gently pulled away from him and started to pace. Her scarf tails flew behind her as she reached the end of an imaginary run and spun around.

"Which one has coffee? Never mind. The one with the sign. Found it."

She ignored his inquiry and spoke in a hushed voice. "Why would Arabella marry a man who is more concerned with himself than anything else in this world? And to top it off, why would she keep it from me?" She ran her fingers through her hair. "The secrecy and deceit. Unfathomable."

"Why are you whispering?" asked Alexander.

"The staff members need not know all my heartbreak," replied Cassandra.

"I see. Going back to your question, your reaction might explain why she kept it from you." He poured coffee into the cup. "It could be she wanted to make this choice without your influence. You two seem thick as thieves. Does she usually rely on you to decide things?"

Cassandra threw her hands up. "For business? Yes. Personal? No. Well, I help pick out her clothes for parties since she's absolute rubbish at that. She's a capable woman. I don't hold her hand through everyday life. Whom to marry? I never thought this would be something she'd do without at least mentioning it."

"In matters of the heart, maybe your behavior is too domineering."

"What are you saying? I'm a personality bulldozer? You don't know me at all, Alexander. I've helped her be more decisive. She always asks me about ideas and views for her company. I never forced my opinion on her."

He poured the cream into the delicate cup covered with hand-painted, red roses. "That's not what I'm trying to say. Last night, when the four of us were discussing Von Pickle, I learned how awful he can be. But you've known that for a long time. Maybe she realized you wouldn't approve and wanted to make this monumental decision on her own."

"Stupid decision." Cassandra balled her fists as she continued to pace.

"I'll grant you that." He grimaced. "Please relax. I believe you're ready to punch someone, and since I'm the one talking to you, you're making me nervous." He flashed a wide smile, and his dark-brown eyes danced.

Cassandra looked down at her clenched hands. "I don't hit people. My feeble attempt to hold myself together, I guess." She stretched out her fingers, pressing her palms together as if praying. She took a deep breath and whispered, "It's not that she kept this from me. It's what it means."

Alexander shrugged his shoulders. "What does it mean?"

"The most terrible thing of all." Her voice cracked. "I found the leak."

"What? Like a drippy faucet? Do I need to call a plumber?"

Cassandra rolled her eyes. "Alexander, I'm the information leak! Every time we had a new idea, or product, or even worse, during the lawsuit with Mrs. Turner, Von Pickle was one step ahead of us. Always. Aunt Lily and I couldn't figure out how he knew our next move." She paused her frantic pacing.

"I see. She was Von Pickle's source." Alexander held the cup as he turned. "Wait, you said sugar, right?"

"Exactly. And yes to the sugar, please."

He turned back to the table and reached for the sugar bowl.

Cassandra resumed walking and picked up the ends of her ivory scarf, twisting them into a tight cord. "We knew someone was stealing our information. Was it staff here at the estate or at the company? Was it an outside job? We had the manor and the offices swept for bugging equipment. Nothing. Aunt Lily drove herself mad trying to figure it out. No, the leak sprang from my friendship—my *supposed* friendship—with Arabella. I talked to her, unfiltered and unguarded about everything. She was my best friend. Of course there would be no secrets! She told him everything. The thought of Von Pickle knowing my soul is revolting."

"I understand." Alexander handed her the teacup filled with steaming coffee.

"Thank you." Cassandra inhaled the soothing aroma and raised the cup to take a tentative sip.

"Ah . . . wait on that. It's the temperature of lava."

Cassandra pulled her face back from the cup. "It's not that

hot, and I like my beverages searing. Let's go to the parlor. It's far too noisy to think in here."

"Didn't Greenfield ask you to stay in the dining room? Maybe we should go back." Alexander pointed over his shoulder.

"I don't care. They can drag me back there if need be." Cassandra held her hand up. "I don't want to face Mr. Snarky and Mrs. Backstabbing Mate anytime soon."

"Remember, this was your idea. I don't want trouble with Carter."

"Don't worry, it's on me. I have other things to be concerned about, and Carter doesn't scare me." She motioned to the doorway.

Threading through the cleaning staff, they walked the length of the dining room and continued into the great hall, passing the enormous Christmas tree.

Cassandra paused to look up at the sparkling evergreen. "Nothing is what it seemed. What was real and true?" She turned to Alexander. "Every conversation Bella and I had last night or today or ever takes on an entirely different meaning. My perception of her is forever tainted." She studied the white, oak floor. "Aunt Lily said that *perception is everything*."

"You know where Arabella's loyalty lies. Isn't that a good thing? You can stop Von Pickle from ever getting information again." Alexander shoved a hand into his pocket.

"True. I solved that mystery. Aunt Lily would be pleased. Wait. Did you want something to drink?"

"No, I'm good."

The duo walked to the empty parlor. Alexander's dress shoes echoed on the polished, hardwood floor in the vast space. Cassandra's slip-on, casual sandals made no such noise.

She pointed to her favorite butter-yellow sofa. "Let's sit over there."

As the pair settled on opposite ends of the seat, she took a sip of her coffee. "This is good." She drank more while she wrapped her cold hands around the porcelain. Breathing in deeply and closing her eyes, she enjoyed the liquid's embrace. "I can't comprehend how I missed this. It was right in front of me the whole time."

"Stop flogging yourself. Arabella knew she needed to keep it a secret and you in the dark." Alexander folded his arms. "That's a heavy burden."

Cassandra pointed. "Don't even think of taking her side. She lied to me. Repeatedly. Almost everyone here had secrets. What about Roland and his puppets? And his mother's indiscretions? Mr. Birch is up to something. At the party, I found out about Mr. York and all his lies to his wife. And Mimi has an odd knowledge of random facts, plus she watches everyone like a hawk." She blew out a breath. "You fibbed as well."

"Me? About what?"

"Carter was grilling you upstairs in the hallway in front of us. You and Mr. Chamberlain mentioned several things you had in common, including liking pickled, green tomatoes. Later, in the dining room, when I took a slice of a green tomato and offered you one, you told me no and said they were unappetizing."

Alexander laughed. "I remember. You know how it is. When you make a new friend, you can get caught up in all that you have in common. Sometimes you say things you don't mean."

"Still, a departure from the truth."

He grinned. "Small when compared to everyone else."

"True. What about the news about Miss Fairchild? She's Uncle Richard's daughter *and* a former drug addict?"

"With Miss Fairchild, you understand she wanted to leave her old life behind and be quiet about it. The world of addiction is a nasty place. My brother should have run away from it. He had no idea what he stumbled into."

"How, if you don't mind me asking, did he get involved with all of that? How long ago did he . . . did he . . . well, you know."

"Overdose? It's been several years. How did it start? A few months after our father's passing, Charlie dulled the pain from our loss with anything he could get his hands on. Six months after he took his first illegal hit, my brother died. I always thought there would be time for him to get clean. Miss Fairchild is a success story, Cassandra, not a liar."

The young woman crossed her legs at the ankles. She winced as the large blister under the bandage on her heel pressed on the top of her foot. "You're right, Alexander. I'm so sorry your brother didn't escape." She sighed. "I'm grateful she's here and safe." Cassandra balanced the saucer and cup on her lap. "Logically, her desire to start over makes perfect sense. And to want to serve her stepmother in penance? I understand that. Sort of. However, it's more secrets under this roof. Add Mr. Fartworthy's other occupation! When I found out, that rattled me."

"That he was a PI?"

She nodded. "I learned about it for the first time today. Hired to find Flora was a new revelation in the dining room before the hothouse exploded. I don't know anyone anymore. Nothing seems real."

He smiled. "I'm real."

"Thank you for listening." Cassandra grinned and sipped from her cup.

Alexander shrugged a shoulder. "Just trying to help."

As the pair sat in silence, a large vehicle rumbled upon the gravel driveway outside.

"Sounds like a fire truck leaving, and that would mean the hothouse is no longer burning." Alexander turned his head back to his companion. "Possible good news?"

"Maybe. Maybe more are coming. Doesn't matter. That's a whole other disaster I need to deal with later. It's a building destroyed, not like my trust. I . . . you know what? Whenever I talked to Von Pickle last night, Arabella slipped next to my side and grilled me about our conversation. Every time. And what about that supposed shower today?"

Alexander shook his head. "What shower?"

"I can guarantee she didn't even get wet. I knew it. It was too long, and she didn't smell like soap."

The young man frowned. "Cassandra, what are you talking about?"

"I know what she was doing! Her phone slipped out of the pocket of her dress when we were sitting on this sofa shortly before we went upstairs. I bet you she was sending text messages to Von Pickle to make sure whatever their stupid story was, they would have it straight."

Alexander pointed. "Maybe I should have made you decaf. You're not making any sense, and you're not going to figure out how to deal with them today."

"I suppose you're right. It'll take some time for me not to feel sideswiped by today's revelations." Cassandra ran a single finger along the rim of her teacup.

For several minutes, the conversation ended, slipping into an uncomfortable silence. The faint sound of bustling staff members cleaning up the plates in the dining room drifted into the parlor.

Alexander looked around. "So, I heard the rumor you're newly in charge of the manor and the company. Is that true?"

Cassandra sipped more of her beverage. "Yes, indeed."

"This is such a gorgeous estate. I love the splendor of the place. These portraits on the wall are amazing. There's such family history here." He caressed the armrest of the sofa. "This is quite the inheritance."

"Been in Uncle Richard's family for generations. It's costly to maintain. I have some ideas to make that easier."

"Really?"

She smiled. "I can make it at least pay for itself and not hemorrhage money from the maintenance."

"It's that expensive?"

"The heating and cooling bills are enough to make your eyes pop. I also have some thoughts for the direction I'd like to take Lemington Cheese. Since I've discovered the leak, I can sidestep difficulties my aunt seemed unable to avoid." She breathed in the fragrance of her coffee again.

He continued to run his fingers on the wooden armrest of the sofa. "I . . . I don't think managing the company is for you."

"Jolly good, toffee head. Thanks for the vote of confidence." Cassandra laughed.

"No, I didn't mean to insult you. My deepest apologies." He paused, rubbing his cheek. "Cassandra, you're a selfless, kindhearted soul. That's what makes you so attractive." He smiled. "You're too sweet a person to be in the same circles as these business associates. They're not pleasant."

"Like Von Pickle," said Cassandra between sips. *Did he call me attractive?* With one hand she held the cup, and with the other, adjusted the lilac scarf ends in her lap.

"Yes, Von Pickle. And the others. You must be ruthless to run a company of any decent size. I," he said, grabbing the back of his neck, "enjoy spending time with you, Cassandra, and hope to get to know you better. I would hate for you to become unrecognizable."

"Believe me, my personality won't change. I can run Lemington Cheese. I've been helping my aunt with product development and marketing for a few years."

Alexander ran his hands down his thighs. "This is coming from my heart. I like you and worry what this could do to your health. It will be too much for you. Let someone else be in charge," he begged.

Cassandra stood without a word, moved behind the sofa, and placed the teacup on the three-legged table that held a large flower arrangement in crystal vase. "Why would you say that? You don't know me well enough to make such an assessment."

A nervous laugh escaped his lips. "That I like you?"

She rolled her eyes again. "No, about my ability to run the company."

"Please don't get your knickers in a twist." Alexander smiled. "I've been here enough this last year, an outsider observing things for what they are. It's a tricky thing running a business."

Cassandra started to pace. "It's not just a job for men."

"That's not what I'm saying. Don't be offended. I'm looking out for you." He leaned back and stretched his arm along the top of the sofa, angling in her direction.

He doesn't know me. She wrapped and unwrapped the ends of the lilac scarf around her hand. "Alexander, I have put a great deal of thought into my role as CEO. Yes, it's an immense responsibility, but I'm tougher than I look. Aunt Lily always said that. I never believed her until today."

Alexander softened his voice. "You're a lovely person, but I don't see how you would survive in that position. I'm sorry."

"You don't have to see anything. The thing that matters is I know I can do it. There are great ideas in my head. You know what?" Cassandra waved a dismissive hand. "People come to me for advice on many topics. For years, others have been telling me that I have a natural ability for this. I didn't accept it. I do now."

"Why not stick with the manor upkeep? That sounds like enough for anyone. The business? It's too time consuming and difficult, especially for you."

Cassandra tightened her jaw, turned her back to Alexander, and stared out the long parlor window. *He's spouting off from ignorance. You know you made the right decision. Don't let him change your mind.*

The ice encased on the windowpanes melted throughout the day. Cassandra watched a fire truck move down the driveway, its red lights circling on top piercing the gray weather. *The trucks got up here, so the roads are clear. Alexander can go home.*

He sighed. "Running your own business can be brutal. There are so many decisions, deals to create, and dreadful people you must interact with on a regular basis. It's much harder than it looks." Alexander added, "You don't want to go the way of Wormhill Farm."

"Wormhill Farm?" Cassandra repeated, continuing to stare out from the manor. Her anger dissipated for a moment. *I know that name.*

"My parents' place," he whispered, then cleared his throat. "It went under."

Where did I see that name? She touched the clear glass of the window. The temperature of the pane froze her fingertips.

Alexander continued. "Dad didn't understand the merciless business end of things. We had a small family farm. You're dealing with something infinitely more complex and could lose the whole company if you make one poor decision, especially if someone like Von Pickle is trying to ruin you. You don't want the guilt of bankrupting your aunt's work." He shifted on the sofa, and a squeak erupted in protest from the dark, wooden legs. "Maybe we should go back to the library."

She slowly turned to face him. Her eyes narrowed. *I saw that repulsive name in the paperwork earlier.* "Wormhill Farm used to be one of our suppliers. They were shut down. Remind me, what kind of cheese did you make?"

A nostalgic smile crossed his countenance. "We made the most wonderful Stilton. We did it the traditional way, you know. We never went to the mechanized mixing. Oh no. By hand. The methods of real artisan cheesemakers of yesteryear are the right way. The only way. People always told us they could taste the distinction in our cheese. Hand-mixed Stilton has a beautiful, soft-blond hue. I oversaw mold. Love mold. When we were forced to close, I went to pharmacy school so I could still play with it." Alexander's eyes twinkled. "The smell of a beneficial mold is perfume."

Cassandra walked back near him. "I thought you were introduced to my aunt when you started deliveries from the pharmacy?"

"I never knew her personally beforehand. My dad dealt with the contracts. I was young and away on holiday with my mates when Lemington Cheese stopped dealing with us. Never met her then. It was a long time ago. Back to what I was saying. Why can't you appoint someone else to be in charge? If it all goes wrong, it could destroy you."

"Alexander, why do you say it will ruin me?"

"It's business. There's no room for mistakes. Ever. Ruthless people can take everything, including your health or—your life."

Cassandra moved closer. "When did your father pass away?"

"Dad died within three weeks after we lost the ability to make our exquisite cheese." Alexander's mouth turned down. "The bank took the farm a few months after his passing. We couldn't save our land. The property belonged to my mother's family for generations."

Cassandra's spine tingled. "And then the loss of your brother."

"Yes, then him. Charlie was so wracked with guilt. He didn't listen to the suggestions and didn't persuade our father to clean up our small facility according to the ridiculously long list of standards. He believed he caused Dad's death and the loss of the farm. He buried his pain in narcotics."

Operating a business equals death to him. Aunt Lily dying didn't help his perception. Poor Alexander. Cassandra breathed out. "That's horrible."

His voice cracked. "It was." Alexander stared down at his lap. "My mother, destroyed by the loss of her husband, son, and home, succumbed a month later." He repeatedly massaged his thumb into the palm of his other hand. "I never knew dying of heartbreak was a real thing, but then I watched it happen to Mum." He paused and then whispered, "It almost got me."

His whole family. What a tragedy! "I'm so sorry for your losses, Alexander," replied Cassandra in a quiet voice.

"Me, too. I should stop talking about my family. It leads to deep sorrow." Alexander looked up with his eyes moist. "I'm not trying to tell you how to live because I'm some beastly chauvinist spouting off or that I'm crazier than a bag of ferrets. I care and want the best for you."

She smiled. "I appreciate that."

Alexander hugged himself. "I always try to help everyone. That's how I was raised. You learn that growing up and working hard as a team on a farm. You need each other. You need your tribe. Look out for one another. Sometimes difficult things must be done."

"What do you mean?"

"Well, sometimes a sick cow needs to be put down, especially if contagious. Or a field needs clearing by fire. It could, at first glance, look wrong. In nature, sometimes you must destroy something for the good of the whole."

Destroy something? Cassandra's stomach turned sour. A memory of meeting up with Alexander last night popped into her head. *The white stairway.* An image from Carter's laptop jumped in right behind. *The photo of Flora with the teacup.* "I see." She breathed out. "Alexander?" She twisted her scarf. "Last night during the party, you headed to the kitchen?"

"Yes, to spend time with Miss Fairchild." He wiped his eyes and sniffed. "Miss Fairchild is a lovely lady, and I enjoy talking with her. She took pity on me since I was rejected by every woman I asked out. I don't like being alone. I'm always alone. New Year's Eve without a date is even worse. At least she cared for me, and I got some exquisite apple pie." Alexander smiled. "Mrs. Forest is a genius baker."

"What was going on downstairs at the time?" Cassandra's eyes remained locked on him, her breath shallow. "Was it busy?"

"Like a restaurant kitchen on a Saturday night! I figured it would be quiet down there. I didn't realize at first what happened. Miss Fairchild and I were talking while she bustled around with her lists. After a while, she mentioned something about everyone staying overnight because of the icy weather. Mrs. Forest was busy preparing more food for the next day. The staff were also occupied. I figured I would excuse myself and get back upstairs. I wasn't there long since they didn't need me in the way."

"Aunt Lily and Mr. Fartworthy told the guests the news upstairs. I volunteered to go in the kitchen to inform the staff. They must have missed telling you."

"That makes sense. It changed my plans for the night."

She held her breath. *What plans? Ask. Don't. You're alone. No, there are people still in the dining room. It's Alexander. Always cheery and funny, Alexander.* "Did you notice a teacup on the counter near Miss Fairchild's workstation?"

Alexander laughed. "Dishes in a kitchen? Why would I remember that? I know that after I went upstairs, we rang in the new year. The four of us enjoyed our wonderful time together. The celebration was glorious. I'm so grateful for your friendship, Cassandra. You must recollect I never left your side for the rest of the evening. Well, not until our group retired upstairs."

The young woman forced a smile. "The party was lovely, and I enjoyed your company last night." Her pulse raced. "Did you happen to see my aunt after we parted?"

"Frederick and I heard Mrs. Turner and Lady Lemington get into a dustup, and I was concerned for her safety. I peeked in to check on her and never set foot in her bedroom. Ask Frederick. He saw me the entire time. As a gentleman, I would never investigate a lady's bedroom, but it did sound like a nasty fight. Mrs. Turner has a fiery temper. We worried."

"I recall you telling the DCI when we were upstairs. I don't remember . . . did you say anything to Aunt Lily?" *I must be mistaken.* "How was she?"

"After I inquired about her well-being?" He shrugged. "Um . . . I think I said that she should relax and drink some tea. And then good evening, I guess. She was fine, and I went back to our card game. Frederick will back me up on this." Alexander smirked. "You two seem to get along well. When we were alone, he talked about you practically all night."

He did? No, focus! "That's nice." *Think.* "You must have talked about work and working in the village and—work."

Alexander laughed. "There's more to men than their occupations, Cassandra. But yes, we did discuss business. I now know *all* the intricacies of running a jewelry shop. Goodness, Frederick can talk." Alexander smoothed his pants. "He informed me in detail about the Christmas gift earrings you're wearing. I have been briefed with more information than I ever knew about any piece of jewelry." He tilted his head to see her ears. "They're pretty. Like you."

Cassandra gave a slight grin. "Thank you." *He's a little heavy on the compliments. It's imprudent to stay here alone. The doorway to the hall isn't too far. The staff is still working.* "How and when did you get your job? Why don't we go back outside to see about the status of the fire?"

Alexander stretched out his arms on the back of the sofa again. "Why? It's too cold outside. To answer your question, I got the position after I graduated from pharmacy school. Great luck to get work in the area I was targeting."

"Remind me, when did Aunt Lily meet you?"

"When she hurt her back in February, she used my pharmacy for the first time. Well, not my pharmacy, the one where I work. Someday I hope to own it. I asked my boss if I could take the medication to her myself on the way home, and he agreed."

"Own it? You advised me against running a business. You gave me a heartbreaking reason why. I would think you would shun the idea of entrepreneurship. You're full of contradictions, Alexander."

"W-w-well," he stammered. "I suppose I should take my own advice."

"Yes, you should." An edge slid into her voice. "You came every time she needed medication delivered?" She crossed her arms.

"Indeed. You knew this. It's a service the shop offers." He chuckled.

"You didn't have to. There were always household staff in town, and Aunt Lily was out soon after she strained her back. Did you come to the manor to spy on my aunt?"

The young man stood and whispered. "I can't believe you're asking me this. Here I am, listening to your rants, your concerns, and worries. I'm here trying to help. This accusation is hurtful, Cassandra. I make things better. That's what I do."

"You were angry at Aunt Lily for shutting down your family's farm."

"Come on."

She jabbed a finger in his direction. "And you stole Mimi's pills to put them into Aunt Lily's teacup while you were in the kitchen."

"Enough, Cassandra! You're grasping at nonsense."

"Her medication went missing for too long. You almost killed Mimi, too!"

"I didn't steal Mrs. York's prescription! I had the meds already!"

Cassandra gasped.

Alexander's mouth flopped open. After a moment, a sly smile grew on his face. "I never saw Mrs. York's pills last night. Just like on the farm, there was a remedy to the Lady Lemington situation." He slowly walked toward her.

"What situation?" whispered Cassandra. Sweat instantly formed on the back of her neck.

"She would do this again. And again. And again, to other loving, lovely cheese families." Alexander leaned forward. "No more."

"What are you saying?" Cassandra's breath hitched, and she backed up a step. *This isn't safe.*

"It was necessary."

No words came out of Cassandra's dry throat.

"Like mold slowly growing inside me, my loathing for Lady Lemington grew and festered." Alexander dug his thumb into the palm of his other hand again. "It takes a real genius to come up with such a sophisticated . . . well, operation. That's a good word. Like removing a cancer." He smiled.

Cassandra's stomach sank to the floor.

"I thought it was brilliant. She needed to be stopped before another family would suffer the same fate under her cruelty." He continued to speak quietly and ambled toward Cassandra, blocking a direct line to the close doorway. "I watched what she did, what you did, and the routines of the household staff, including the tea. I waited for the perfect moment. She invited me to her party, and it became a golden opportunity." He stretched his arms out wide. "Magic in the new year! Although, it didn't go according to my plan."

"And all the times you were visiting here, you were planning this? Ingenious. So . . . staying . . . overnight." Cassandra's eyes focused on the young man as she strained her ears. *I don't hear people moving in the dining room anymore. I can't run in these sandals.* She slid over a step to her right.

"Exactly. I'm capable of complimenting women. I get dates easily. At the party, well." He grinned. "Mingle, seem too needy, too awkward, too forward, and then it would lead to repeated rejections. It worked perfectly."

"Oh?" *Pretend that everything is fine.* "You're a good actor. I thought you wanted a date for the evening." *I don't hear anyone out the front door, either.* Cassandra moved slowly two steps to her right, adrenaline racing throughout her body.

"This was part of the design." He countered her move. "I knew Flora would take pity on me. She would let me stay in the kitchen after I told her of my failures. I needed enough time to put my plan into action, and then I would go home. But that backfired in my face after I found out we had to stay. Without a date, I needed an alibi. I glanced at Flora's list. Frederick and I were assigned a room together. He would do."

Every one of her muscles locked. "Frederick helped you?" Cassandra's voice trembled. "He was part of this?"

"That dolt?" His laugh echoed throughout the large space. "He's a nice chap to play cards with, but he couldn't plan something like this. Ha! That's amusing."

"You acted like you were best friends."

Alexander's grin dripped of deception. "No, but easily accomplished. Say you like similar things, and people will adore you and feel a connection."

"Clever. It worked. Frederick enjoyed your company last night." *The doorway across the room is closer to the library and the detectives. Too far. He'll stop me. Stall.* "If you were here so often over this past year, why didn't you do this at another time? Why wait until a party?" Cassandra backed up several steps.

"I thought of that. I originally thought of the summer garden party, but then I became ill and couldn't attend. Hazard of my job. Always around the germ-infested populace. Afterward, I hesitated to implement my plan. She recovered and no more medication deliveries. That was unfortunate. Then, out of nowhere, this invitation showed up. Perfect! With a celebration, I'm a guest in the manor. Plenty of others to suspect." He swaggered forward. "I knew of the routine of her nightly brew."

The sweat from her palms wet the scarf she gripped in her hands.

"The plan was for her to die quietly in bed. It would be peaceful and look like a heart attack. It would be a reasonable assumption. I didn't count on Lady Lemington stumbling out and smacking her head on the sink. You understand why this happened, right?"

"To protect others?" Her voice rose unnaturally at the end of her sentence. *I hope he didn't notice that.*

"Yes." He sighed and smiled. "I'm so glad you realize this was necessary."

Cassandra whispered, "But perhaps Aunt Lily wasn't at fault."

"She destroyed everything I held dear," said the young man. "All we wanted was to live and make our Stilton. The four of us together. We had everything. It was perfect." Alexander stepped closer. His voice dropped an octave. "Now, I'm alone. I'm always alone. I hate alone. I hated her. She needed to die."

The hairs on Cassandra's arms stood on end. "I'm so sorry you're by yourself. Maybe you didn't understand everything since you were away from home when closure occurred." She spoke softly.

"My aunt needed to pull the contract, Alexander. Your father, who I'm sure was a good man, refused to comply with the safety regulations. Listeria is dangerous." Her words wobbled as they rushed out. "You can't have an operational dairy with that bacterium around. You must follow the removal procedure carefully, or it returns with a vengeance."

"No," he said with a voice deep and serene. "It came without notice. We weren't prepared to be shut down."

"She gave multiple warnings that the contract would be terminated." Cassandra slid her feet out of her backless sandals. "I have the paperwork that shows everything." To stop her shaking hands and conceal the sheer terror, she held the scarf tails tight in her fists. "I can show it to you. The information is in my room. I'll go get it."

"Not necessary." Alexander smirked at her bare feet. He moved forward, slowly and deliberately. "Canceling our agreement would have been a blow. We could have recovered. We would have found other buyers. No one in my family should have died." He frowned. "Lady Lemington shut us down in her heartless way."

"Alexander, listen to yourself. You're not talking rationally. She protected the public. If your farm continued and someone got sick—or even died—they would have linked it back to our company and sued you and us for not taking proper precautions. She was paranoid about another lawsuit." *He's clamped his jaw. Something else.* She softened her tone. "Babies, pregnant women, and the elderly are vulnerable to listeria. Aunt Lily did what she had to do."

"And I had to do what was best." His voice was calm and soft. "This is an act for you." He pointed to her hands. "You always twist your scarf when you're stressed. I told you I watched." He grinned. "It was all her fault, and she needed to be stopped before she ruined anyone else." He backed her up to the window. "How can I make you understand? I'm a savior."

"You're far from it. You're a cold-blooded murderer."

Alexander's face tightened, and his eyes narrowed as he stood over her.

She could see past his shoulder to the half-empty cup of coffee. Her insides instantly froze. She stared into his intense, brown eyes. "Did you make me poisoned coffee?"

A dark look materialized, and any virtue in his soul flickered out. His smirking mouth said nothing.

Cassandra's heart pounded in her ears and she growled, "Answer me!"

He clutched her upper arms in a viselike grasp. "You're not running anywhere." His sneer tumbled out like gravel. "Cassandra. You'll tell no one what I did. I'll make sure of it."

Chapter Twenty-Seven

"Let go!" Cassandra shouted.

"Not a chance," he snarled. His hands slid down to her forearms, and she struggled against his harsh grip. "You'll listen to me and come along quietly like the sweet woman you are." As he pulled her close, his fingers pressed deep into her flesh.

She hissed inches from his face. "Perception is everything!" Cassandra screamed, unleashing a verbal cocktail of fear, anger, and pain.

Visibly surprised, Alexander released one hand. His sweaty, left palm slammed into her mouth and nose, and he shoved her body into the cold windowpane. Cassandra's shoulder blade smashed against the framing. He pinned her arm between them while she continued to shriek and attempt to wriggle free.

She failed.

Alexander's jaw clenched near her eyes. "None of that, *Sweetie*. Hush," he commanded, pushing her head back onto the cold glass, his hand muffling her cries and squeezing her nose shut.

She bit down on the side and palm of his hand. Hard.

He yelped and pulled back. It was enough of a space for Cassandra to move her fist and hit the side of Alexander's head. He let go.

She took two steps toward the small table, but he caught her arm. She reached and grasped the flower vase, pushing her fingers into its mouth. Cassandra spun around and heaved the heavy container in her attacker's direction. The water within spilled down the front of her skirt, and flowers tumbled into the space between them. The crystal vessel missed its mark, sailing past him and busting apart harmlessly on the wooden floor.

Alexander laughed and tightened his hold on her wrist.

"No!" she screamed. "Get off!" She pulled forward again to the table, struggling to break free. Cassandra snatched the teacup containing the drink he'd prepared for her. She grunted, repeated her turn, and smashed the cup directly into his face.

This time, she didn't miss.

"Ow!" yelled Alexander. Porcelain shattered as it collided and cracked his nose. The leftover coffee splashed him in the eyes. Shards of the rose cup clattered to the ground. Only the handle remained clutched in her fingers. He grabbed his face and released her hand. "Ow!" he shouted again and dropped to his knees.

Cassandra ran through the parlor. Her bare feet pounded the hardwood floor, putting distance between herself and her aunt's killer.

As she exited the far, high-arched doorway, she glanced behind. Spooner remained on his knees, cupping his face. She dashed into the dining room where nobody remained. She looked at the library door. *Greenfield and the others are in there. Doesn't matter. Spooner isn't chasing you. I've got to get Carter!*

She sprinted down the long corridor to the servants' staircase. Cassandra turned the handle, flew across the landing, and threw her weight against the exterior entry, shoving it open.

The backyard area teemed with unfamiliar people from the fire brigade. Frantic, she ran on the cold, dead grass at a quick clip to the fire chief in the white helmet.

Breathless, she arrived at his side. "Car . . . Car. Carter. Where . . . is Carter?" Fire hoses continued spraying water on the building's burnt-out shell. The rushing water made it difficult to hear. "Spooner did it!"

The fire chief cupped his ear. "What did you say? We got this, ma'am. I don't want anyone else to get harmed. We've already had some injuries today." He put his hand on her shoulder. "There isn't anything to see." He shouted to a firefighter nearby. "Escort her back to the house immediately."

A man in a black helmet pointed to the manor. "Let's go, ma'am."

"No! I need to find DCI Carter! It's imperative." Cassandra forced herself to take a deeper breath to speak up after her sprint. "Where are the detectives? Someone is trying to hurt me!"

"The active flames are out." The chief gestured with his hands. "The building is still smoldering, and we're tending to that. You're not in danger if you stay in the manor." The chief continued to speak louder. "An investigation is underway. Please. It's for your own good."

"You're not listening. I don't care about the fire at this moment." Cassandra demanded, "I need to find Carter or my butler, Mr. Fartworthy!" One of her hands found her hip. "Have you seen them anywhere?"

Another firefighter joined them, holding his black helmet and wiping his sweaty, sooty brow. "He can get your tea in a few minutes, ma'am. It's been busy around here."

His buddy, in a matching helmet, smirked, puffing out his chest. He pointed to her fingers, still clutching the teacup handle. "I'm sure the butler can find another one for you. A blaze is more important than a broken cup, and no tea doesn't mean someone is trying to hurt you."

Cassandra picked up her hand with the handle. "You're cheeky. This has nothing to do with tea." She threw the porcelain piece down into the dead grass and stared at the men. "Spooner did it!"

The chief glared at his subordinates. "Enough." He turned to Cassandra. "My apologies, ma'am. Is that the person that was yelling about?"

"No! Spooner's trying to hurt me because he's responsible for—"

"There was a dustup with some gentleman about the hothouse." The chief looked at one of the other firefighters. "That gardener was the fellow they had so much trouble with when we got here, right?"

"Yes, he kept getting in the way when we were trying to do our job. He ran around the house somewhere," said one firefighter.

Cassandra grunted in frustration. "I'm in danger!"

"Out here, yes. We have it under control, but everyone needs to be inside." The chief removed his white helmet for a moment, scratched his pale, balding head, and replaced the heavy hat. He continued talking loudly over the noise of the water hoses in operation. "There was a ruckus near the left side of the house. They're probably out front by now." He looked down. "You're barefoot! There's debris out here, and you could get cut!"

She looked down at her blister-coated feet turning redder by the moment. "So?" Her heart pounded in her ears. "I need to know right now. Where is Carter or any detectives?"

"None of them are here around back anymore. Only my crew. I like it better that way. Less interference. Ma'am, go before you catch your death out here." The chief shoved the air with his hands.

"Thank you." She sprinted back to the manor. *Get to Greenfield. He'll help me.* Yanking the hefty door open, she stepped inside. She heaved the second door and ran down the dark-paneled hallway, her wet feet smacking the floor. The no-longer adhesive bandages fell off, leaving a trail.

When she reached the library, she flung open the door, and yelled, "Where's Carter?" Cassandra bent over with her hands on her knees, gobbling air into her lungs, searching the room for a detective.

Almost everyone in the library was clustered around the tall windows.

Greenfield, near the entrance, looked at her wet, red, bare feet. "Miss Haywood? Were you outside?" His tone scolded her like a child. "I told you to remain in the manor. I gave you leeway, and you promised. We heard shouting and screaming out there." He crossed his arms. "We heard the commotion and looked. A swarm of people were arguing. Were you involved?"

She stood straight. "Stop! No, I wasn't. The fire chief said there was some problem, but I must find your superior."

"Did you—"

"Spooner did it!" she shouted.

Greenfield blinked hard. "Did what? We saw Mr. Birch hollering with the rest of our team out there."

"No. Alexander Spooner murdered my aunt! Would someone please listen to me!"

His eyes widened. "How do you know this?"

"He told me!"

Gasps erupted from the other people.

Greenfield turned to the windows. "Baker, get over here." He addressed Cassandra. "Tell me again exactly what he said to you, Miss Haywood."

"He confessed and tried to harm me, and I screamed from *inside* the building." Cassandra turned her head toward the voices coming from the parlor. "I hear Mr. Fartworthy. They must have come in the front door and discovered Alexander. He won't hurt me now. I've got to go." She dashed into the large room.

"Wait, Miss Haywood!" Greenfield's voice called after her. "Are you okay? How did you get away? Miss Haywood! Where is he?"

She burst through the open archway into the parlor and skidded to a stop. Across the room, Alexander remained crouched on the floor, holding his face. Carter, Penwarden, Jenkins, and other law enforcement clustered near the bleeding man. Several detectives wore protective blue gloves. Alexander held something white over his nose. Fartworthy and Mr. Birch stood nearby.

Relief flooded over Cassandra, and she raced to the group. They looked in her direction. Carter said something and pointed. Jenkins and Penwarden ran toward her. "I'm so glad I found all of you—"

Before Cassandra realized what was happening, Jenkins whipped her arms together in front and clasped a set of handcuffs onto her wrists. Penwarden arrived at her other side.

"No, wait! Stop!" Cassandra shrieked. "What are you doing? He murdered my aunt!"

Jenkins grabbed her left upper arm and held fast. Penwarden spoke close to her ear, holding her arm tight. "Please calm down, Miss Haywood. We know you assaulted Mr. Spooner with a teacup, and he says it was you who killed Lady Lemington."

"What?" She turned in horror to the detective.

People from the library scrambled into the parlor. Cassandra saw the concerned faces of her acquaintances, her former friend, plus Greenfield and Baker. The crowd's words jumbled in a discordant clamor. They pushed forward and crossed the room.

Jenkins and Penwarden escorted the struggling prisoner, and they guided her to the butter-yellow sofa near Carter and Fartworthy. "Stop! Help!" Cassandra yelled.

The head butler stood a little behind Carter and gave a quick shake of his head.

"I didn't do it!" Cassandra exclaimed. "He confessed to killing my aunt and attacked me."

"Silence from you, Miss Haywood. Sit," demanded Carter.

She pointed a blue-gloved finger at the throng of guests as the noise level rose. "All of you. Quiet."

Alexander remained on his knees, holding his bleeding nose and gasping. "Like I told you, she assaulted me." He sighed, moaned, and rocked back and forth. DC Baker rushed forward from the library mob, pulling on her latex gloves with a loud snap. She reached Alexander and handed him a handful of tissues from her pocket.

The young man threw down the soaked napkin, taking the white cluster with a smile and half-closed eyes. "Thank you so much," he said, his blood seeping through the new, white wad. "Ow. My face hurts. Quite certain she broke my nose. You can't believe anything she says. She's a murderer."

"Liar!" yelled Cassandra. "He killed Aunt Lily."

Alexander coughed and held the bridge between his eyes, squinting at Carter. "She's trying to blame me. Honestly, I never would have guessed such a lovely woman could turn so vicious. She smashed the teacup right in my face, using the cup of coffee I made for her! All I wanted was to be her friend—maybe something more—and she snapped. Crazy cheese lady! I'm so grateful you're here, Detectives." He smiled weakly at the crowd.

DS Jenkins gestured with his hand. "Please get up, Mr. Spooner. Your nose looks odd. I agree it's probably broken."

He rose from his knees and wobbled. Baker, standing nearby, grabbed the crook of his elbow to steady him. He sighed. "Thank you for saving me." Alexander gagged as he viewed blood gathering in the tissues and glanced at the DCI with sad, puppy-dog eyes.

DC Baker patted his arm. "It will be all right, Mr. Spooner. Can you walk?"

"Yes." Alexander coughed again. "Ugh. That tastes awful. Is the ambulance still outside? Could they look at me before it gets worse?" He held the bridge of his nose again and groaned.

"I'm sure the DCI will let you go in a few minutes." Baker smiled at the young man, surveying the damage. She moved his hand down. "You have a few cuts on your face, and your nose is off to the side a bit. You may have two black eyes tomorrow."

Alexander chuckled. "I guess I won't be winning any beauty contests. You have a wonderful smile. Are you—"

Carter cleared her throat. "Mr. Spooner, are you finished? We have some business to attend to. What happened?"

He pointed at Cassandra. "She's an animal."

Cassandra blurted out, "He tried to silence me by covering my mouth and slamming me into the window. I bit him, but I couldn't get away. That's why I threw the vase at him, but I missed. Then I got him with the cup. My aunt shut down his family farm, and he killed her out of revenge. He—"

The pharmacist interrupted. "You're delusional. Yes, they closed the farm, but it was ages ago. You're the one to inherit the company and the manor, not me. You have everything to gain and wanted it all. She told me. Might as well confess, Cassandra. We all know you poisoned your aunt's tea." He turned to Carter. "She's guilty."

The head detective moved closer to the man with the newly crooked nose. "When and how did she do it?" Carter stood right before him and cupped his chin with her gloved hand. She gently moved his head from side to side and grimaced. "You're swelling up. We should get you to that ambulance soon." She looked at Baker. "You have any more tissues for him? We need to clean him up a bit."

DC Baker replied, "I'm sorry, ma'am, I don't."

Hamish spoke. "I have an unused handkerchief. Would it help?"

The head detective reached for the fresh cloth. "Most assuredly, Mr. York. Thank you."

Hamish handed it to her and returned to his wife's side.

Carter gently wiped Alexander's face, staining the handkerchief. "Broken noses can bleed quite a bit. Your hands are covered, too." She took his right hand and continued to sop up the red drips. "It should stop soon." The DCI held the second appendage, repeating the action to his palm and to the back of his hand. "This is better. Not perfect, but better." She refolded the handkerchief and relinquished it to him. "Use this."

Alexander took the stained cloth from her and held it under his nose. "You're so kind. It hurts. You must believe me. She told me she did it." He pocketed the bloody tissues.

"I certainly did not!" shouted Cassandra.

Carter held up a blue-gloved hand. "I want to hear what he has to say, Miss Haywood."

"But—" Cassandra opened her mouth to speak. Fartworthy gave a quick shake of his head. *What is going on? No. I need to talk.* "I have the paperwork to prove his connection with my aunt."

"Quiet, Miss Haywood." The head detective pointed a bloody finger at the young man's face. "Mr. Spooner, how did you come by your current injuries?"

"Cassandra was upset with her best friend. Actually, she was furious." Alexander sniffed and dabbed his nose. "She left the library, and I followed out of concern she would harm herself. I begged Detective Greenfield to let me go with her. Ask him. Cassandra was so distraught, and it hurt me to see her like that. I wanted to help. She was shaking her fists, and I felt threatened, but I didn't leave her side. She requested coffee, and I made some for her. We came in here to sit right on this sofa." He pointed to the furniture piece where Cassandra sat.

She seethed with her teeth clenched. "Did you poison my coffee?"

"You see? So ungrateful." Alexander exhaled. "Why would I

do that? I help." He turned to the detective. "I listened to her complain about her friend's betrayal and everything that had happened today, and how she thought the detectives were taking too long."

DS Jenkins sneered. "You try sorting out the stories with a household of spoiled—"

The DCI interrupted. "Go on, Mr. Spooner."

"Like I was saying, we were talking. She kept going on, and at some point, it popped out what she did to her aunt. I was horrified. When I jumped up to leave and tell someone, she screamed, threw the vase with the flowers, and smashed the teacup into my nose. Look at all this broken crystal and porcelain!" He pointed to the shards on the floor. "She left, I guess. I've been on the floor on my knees until you found me." He cradled his face. "This hurts."

Cassandra's brain whirled as Spooner droned on about his injury and his innocence. *I look more guilty than ever. What would change Carter's mind?* She quietly groaned, shut her eyes, and shifted on the sofa. The wooden furniture legs creaked below her. *The white stairway creaks like that. Staircase to the kitchen. Flora's photo. The teacup.* She gasped, and her eyes flew open. Cassandra cut off whoever was talking. "Last night during the party, I passed him on the stairs on my way up from the kitchen. He was going down." She looked at the detectives and held up her wrists. "Are these necessary?"

"Yes." The head detective turned to Alexander. "Why were you in the kitchen?"

Alexander pouted. "Why are we talking about last night? Aren't you going to take her to the station for assaulting me? Look at this!" He showed the bloody cloth in his hands. "I need to see someone before I bleed out."

Mr. Fartworthy spoke. "There's no danger in that, sir. It looks as though it has stopped for the moment."

"You're not a nurse." Alexander held his face against his forearm, and blood stained his gray suit jacket. "This is agony. May I go?"

Fartworthy clasped his hands behind his back. "I've seen people in worse condition."

"Has she beat up others here whom you needed to patch up? You know nothing. You're a butler. Where's the ambulance? Is it in the back or front of the manor?" Alexander looked at the windows. "I should go."

Carter interjected. "In time, Mr. Spooner. Answer me about the kitchen."

He rolled his eyes. "It was a bad night for getting a date. Maybe it was the weather. Maybe it was the guest list. No lady was interested in spending time with me."

Jenkins huffed. "Difficult night for many blokes. It wasn't just you."

"See?" Alexander dabbed his nose again. "Anyway, I went to the kitchen for company, but they were busy, so I returned upstairs. I wasn't down there for long." He ran his bloody hand through his short, dirty-blond hair. "Ask Miss Fairchild. I talked to her the whole time. After I went upstairs, I was with Miss Haywood and her friends."

Carter jerked her chin up to Spooner. "You got blood in your hair." She pointed to Penwarden. "Go get Miss Fairchild. She should be in the kitchen with the other staff."

Alexander peeked at his stained palm, then at Cassandra, and held his hands together.

Penwarden gave a quick nod. "Right away, ma'am." The detective left.

Cassandra groaned. "It wasn't who went upstairs alone who should be a suspect. It didn't matter who saw the teacup at the party." She turned to the DCI. "When Flora held it in the photo, he had already monkeyed with it. He played her to gain access to the kitchen.

The 'I-can't-get-a-date-let-me-be-here' act was planned out. He spent time at the manor over this last year and knew our routines intimately."

Jenkins put his hand up. "Miss Haywood, we don't have time for riddles."

"This isn't a game!" Cassandra's face warmed in frustration. "The DCI knows what I'm saying. We saw it in the photos. If you test the object, I'm sure you will find what you're looking for. He carried his own supply, and I think he added it to my coffee! Check him! No need to steal anything from anyone." Cassandra tilted her head to the library crowd. "He knew Mrs. York would be here, and it could look like she did it. He lied about everything."

"Why are you doing this?" Alexander pleaded. "I thought we were friends."

Cassandra grunted at the pharmacist and turned to stare at Carter. "His father died after my aunt shut down their dairy. Then their family lost the farm. His brother died six months later from drug abuse, which he got involved with to mask the guilt of losing the land and their father. Alexander's mother died shortly after that. He blames Aunt Lily for all his misery."

The bleeding man's voice cracked. "This takes the biscuit. I'm gutted that you would throw my heartache around to save yourself." He wiped under his eye with the back of his hand. "Cassandra wanted what her aunt possessed and would stop at nothing to get it. She's telling you her plan."

"Liar!" Sweat poured off her brow, and her handcuffed hands trembled in her lap. "He hates being alone. He had motive and opportunity. He gripped my arms, held my mouth, and pinned me against the window. I escaped when I whacked the teacup into his nose. You must believe me." She panted heavily, as though she had just finished a marathon. She whispered through breaths. "That monster killed Aunt Lily, and when I found out, he tried to hurt me, too."

"Nonsense." Alexander clenched his jaw.

Cassandra shouted. "You shoved me against the window!"

"What are you talking about?" He moved closer to her. "You were yelling about what you did. You were screaming in my face!"

Carter interrupted the sparring duo. "Enough." She turned to DS Jenkins. "Cuff him."

"Wait? Why? She's the one who hurt me." Alexander protested and showed the blood-soaked handkerchief to the DCI again. "This is from someone who wants to hide what she did."

"No, sir. You gave yourself away." The head detective smirked. "What you have is a fresh, deep bite mark on your left palm and the side of your hand." She turned to the library crowd. "Miss Lightfoot?"

"Yes?" said the photographer.

"I need you to get a shot of his hand immediately. We can compare that to Miss Haywood's teeth."

"On it. I'll retrieve my camera." Ruby dashed to the hall.

Carter continued. "If someone is yelling in anger, and you're an innocent victim, most people back away. The two semi-circles on your hand are distinct. That kind of injury occurs by a human bite, resulting from going forward and clamping down on someone's face to silence them. That lends credence to Miss Haywood's description of events. I believe her." She turned to Jenkins. "Get him out of the manor after the photo and into a squad car."

Alexander's mouth dropped open, and he shouted at the head detective. "No. No! Don't you see? You can't arrest me! This evil cheese empire destroys families. I needed to prevent it from happening again. I'm a hero! I saved others!"

The crowd gasped.

Cassandra yelled, "No, you didn't! You're a murderer! Did you try to kill me too? Did you poison my coffee?

"No! You didn't do anything wrong." Alexander took several steps closer to Cassandra. "I thought we were friends, and you understood what had to be done. She had to die."

The DCI blocked his way. "Stop talking. You sealed your fate when you took the law into your own hands." Carter patted down his pockets and spoke close to his ear, but loud enough for Cassandra to hear. "I'm sorry for your losses, but no one may seek justice as you did. You should have gone through the court system if you thought you were correct in blaming Lady Lemington. We have all these witnesses who will testify you confessed." She pointed to the dining room. "Detectives, take him in there while we get statements."

DS Jenkins slapped handcuffs on the killer's wrists and issued the *Police Caution*. "I'm arresting you. 'You do not have to say anything, but it may harm your defense if you do not mention when questioned something that you later rely on in court. Anything you do say may be given in evidence.' Come on." He tugged on the accused man's shoulder. "Move."

Alexander Spooner jostled against the two officers escorting him. The man continued his cries of protest while they ushered him from the area.

Cassandra's shoulders slumped in relief, and a sigh escaped her lips. She held up her clasped hands again. "Can you take these off now?"

Carter tapped her pad. "No. I have a few more questions for *you*."

Chapter Twenty-Eight

Carter peeled off, then folded, her blood-stained, blue, plastic gloves. "Miss Haywood, you knew about your aunt's death before I told you. How?" She placed the contaminated protective wear in a clear bag she removed from her pocket.

"Mr. Fartworthy woke me with the news. He thought it should come from a friend, although you directed him not to say anything. I didn't want to get him in trouble."

With an eyebrow raised, the head butler smiled at Carter.

The DCI glared at Fartworthy. "PIs. Always a nuisance." She sealed the glove bag and tucked it away. "Miss Haywood, you showed little emotion over your aunt's death."

"Is that a character flaw? I don't cry in public." Cassandra's gaze fell to her lap. "It isn't proper."

"I see. What about Mrs. York's medication? How did you know where it was?" asked the head detective.

Cassandra huffed. "I told you. I found the pill bottle outside."

A voice across the parlor interrupted, "Ma'am? The purse and 'em pills was in the upstairs loo."

"The lavatory? What?" Mimi sidestepped several people.

Owen nodded and came forward. "Yes, ma'am."

"Where is my purse now?" Mimi squinted. "Why would I leave them there and not remember?"

The Detective Chief Inspector pointed. "Come here. Mrs. York, you were agitated last night. One cannot think properly in that state. Go on, Mr. Savage. Come here, too."

"There was a pretty bag on the shelf when I went to the toilet last night. I wanted somethin' shiny for me mum. I never looked inside it." Owen shrugged as he walked. "Stuffed it in me guitar case in a wink. That's usually 'ow it goes. I take somethin', and it's as if someone else is doin' it. It wasn't til we left the library that Mr. York said the pills were in there. When we were sent upstairs, I found 'em. I lost me 'ead. Before anyone came in, I opened the window and 'eaved the bottle so they were right by the front door."

Carter slowly turned her head to the woman she'd accused.

"I told you they were there." Cassandra smiled.

The DCI wiggled her fingers in the air. "It seemed like a fairy story."

"From your point of view." Cassandra shifted on the sofa. "Not mine."

Mimi tapped Owen on the shoulder. "You have my purse?"

"You're planning on returning my wife's property, correct?" asked Hamish.

Owen smiled. "Oh yes. I will when 'em detectives are done with us."

"Thank you. We'll follow you to your room after." Mimi gestured to the young man. "Hand over the book, please. I saw you in the library."

Owen removed the small hardback from his pocket and handed it to Mrs. York. He looked at the white, oak floor.

Mimi nodded at Cassandra, held the book up, and approached Carter. "I'm not telling you how to do your job, Detective, but

shouldn't you have separated Mr. Spooner and Miss Haywood before interrogating them? That should have been your first move." She
tapped on the leather-covered book in her hand.

Carter crossed her arms. "Yes, that's what we usually do.
However, sometimes suspects give each other away or confirm they
were working together. Sometimes unorthodoxy can work to one's
advantage."

"And the bite marks?" Mimi continued. "That's shaky admis-
sible evidence. Shoddy forensics might have convicted many a criminal, but the courts have been cracking down. I mean, you obtained a
valid confession from the suspect, but Miss Haywood's teeth pattern
won't work as the sole piece of evidence tying Mr. Spooner to the
assault or the murder."

"That's true, Mrs. York. How—"

"And another thing—"

"How do you know so much about police procedures and evidence?" Carter tugged on her suit jacket lapel. "If I were to obtain
a warrant for any computer in your home, would we find anything
linking you to this case?"

Mimi clasped her hands around the book. "That won't be necessary. I had nothing to do with Mr. Spooner's actions. You heard
him."

"I know what transpired. I need to turn over all the rocks to see
what scurries out." Carter pointed. "You're hiding something, Mrs.
York. Lady Lemington revealed devastating personal secrets about
your husband. According to several witnesses, you were furious. You
had a working relationship with Mr. Spooner, as he *is* your pharmacist.
Put those bits of information together, and I'm interested in knowing
if you were involved in any capacity."

"Preposterous." Mimi took in a deep breath.

Carter leaned in, narrowing her eyes.

Mimi looked at Hamish. "I suppose I have a few secrets of my own." She chuckled and sighed. "Can't hold my husband in contempt if I hide something myself."

"What are you concealing?" asked Carter.

Hamish's voice croaked. "Mimi? What is it?" He stepped closer to her. "Is there someone else? Please, I must know."

A smile oozed across Mimi's face. "No, I could never do that. Something more nefarious, I'm afraid."

Hamish took her hand. "We need to be more honest with one another. I'm so sorry for lying to you about my age and the surgery. Should have told you years ago about the modeling. I adore you and would do anything to remain by your side. Whatever you're hiding, sweetheart, I'll be here."

Mimi exhaled. "You should know that I'm . . . I am a published author."

"A what?" asked Hamish.

"I write cozy mysteries."

He squinted. "What in the world is a 'cozy mystery'?"

"A sweet mystery novel that presents puzzles for readers to solve." Mrs. York grinned.

Hamish's mouth hung open.

"I have a pen name and one book out. My second manuscript is with my editor. I should get it back any day now."

Mr. York's hand ran through the front of his blond hair. "I don't . . . when did you write? How have I not seen you typing away?"

"All the nights I couldn't sleep, I went downstairs and wrote before dawn. Your business trips were prime times to make my scribblings. During your trip to Switzerland, I finished and edited my second book." Mimi shrugged. "I had to do something to keep me occupied. My body decided to forego adventures, but my mind travels the world."

"Why did you hide this from me?" Hamish whispered.

"You're never interested in novels. Any I tried to get you to peruse, you said no thank you. Outdoor adventure conquests and French cheese are your passions. I thought writing was a silly little hobby and didn't want to bother you. Besides, it kept my mind off my health problems. Turns out, I adore writing." Mimi ran her hand over the book's leather cover she held. "You can be married to someone and have different interests."

"You published a book?" asked Carter.

"Yes, first in a series. Second one is written, and after today, I have ideas for a third." The novelist smirked. "I've done loads of research. My computer would look like a criminal's."

Hamish reached out, embraced his wife, and she melted into his muscular arms. "No more secrets?"

They pulled back and looked at one another. Mimi's warm smile emerged. "Agreed. There isn't anything else?"

Her husband grinned. "No."

Flora walked into the room with Penwarden and Henslowe. She clutched her handkerchief, balled up in her fist. "Am I in trouble?"

"No," assured Carter. "I need to verify something regarding Mr. Spooner and his whereabouts last night. Has Penwarden filled you in?"

"He did. I can't believe it. I feel like a fool."

"Don't, Miss Fairchild." The DCI shook her head. "That young man manipulated many."

"I could've stopped him from touching the tea." Flora gasped. "I could've saved her." Tears flowed down her face.

"He would have found another way. Please don't do this to yourself." Carter put her hand on the head housekeeper's shoulder. "This was not your fault. Mr. Spooner is responsible."

Flora's renewed weeping caused the lump to rise again in

Cassandra's throat. She wiped the sweat from her forehead with her trapped hands. "Will you please take these off me?" she begged. "You know what happened."

Carter took a moment and then gave a nod to Penwarden. The DCI continued to speak quietly to Flora.

Cassandra stood shakily as the handcuffs were unlocked. She rubbed her wrists.

He reached into his pocket. "Excuse me, Miss Haywood. Mr. Chamberlain asked me to give you this." Penwarden handed her a piece of paper. "It's his mobile number."

"Mr. Chamberlain?" Cassandra accepted the paper. "Thank you. May I go and see him?"

"No. The ambulance took him to hospital. Two lacerations on his scalp were deep and needed additional care. Nothing serious, and he should be released later." Penwarden smiled. "He wanted to reassure you he's fine and asked if you would text him later."

"Absolutely." She ran a finger across the hastily written number. "Thank you." Cassandra slipped the paper into her pocket.

"He wanted to apologize to you about his advice for wanting to see the photographs. He knew you weren't pleased but was concerned that viewing photos of your aunt would upset you. He's a thoughtful fellow."

"He is," said Cassandra. *I got angry with him for that?*

The front door opened in the great hall to reveal the fire chief. He was enveloped in the heavy smell of smoke and sweat that carried into the parlor. "Detectives?" He removed his white helmet and clomped into the room. "DCI? May I have a word?"

"Most assuredly. Pardon me, Miss Fairchild." Carter asked the chief, "Status?"

The firefighter viewed the crowd. "The blaze is out. One team will stay another hour or so to assure there are no flareups. I've given orders for the other brigades to return to their stations. Two have done so already. The building is a total loss, I'm afraid. It doesn't appear much can be saved."

Mimi raised her finger, capturing the chief's attention. "How does a hothouse burn? It has water and hoses everywhere. And dirt. Dirt doesn't burn."

"You'd be surprised, ma'am. Bark chips, pallets, dry peat, plastic, mulch, and even plants can ignite relatively easily," answered the fire chief. "Chemicals for soil additives and gasoline for mowers are also usually around, too. All burn well."

Mimi tapped her fingertips on the book held up to her chest. "Interesting. I didn't know that."

Cassandra rubbed her shoulder. "What caused the explosions?"

He eyed Cassandra. "I've briefed the DCI. We have a theory and will conduct further investigations after the area has cooled. If you'll excuse me, I need to button things up outside." He tipped his head toward Carter. "Ma'am."

"I'll be in touch. Thank you, Chief." Cold air swirled into the room as he opened the main door.

"Pardon me, sir," said Jenkins, passing the firefighter. The detective hurried to his superior. "Mr. Spooner is secured and on his way."

"Thank you, Jenkins." Carter took out her notepad and pen. "Mr. Birch, I'm sorry for the loss of your work. Any idea what could have caused an explosion?"

Birch glared at Fartworthy. "I have several," he snarled through gritted teeth.

Fartworthy returned the scowl. "I told you outside I had nothing to do with this, Birch. You were too busy shouting to listen."

The head gardener crossed his arms. "I saw you on the hothouse surveillance cameras. You were prowling around today. As usual."

"I was trying to find you." Fartworthy stood taller. "We were to be in the manor. What were you doing?"

"Setting up heaters for my beauties. We had an ice storm last night, remember? It was too cold in there, despite the heating system. Not that it's any of your business."

Carter raised her finger. "Stop! This is the same argument you two had outside. Hold on a moment. How did you set up the heaters?"

Birch waved his hand around. "How? I plugged them in."

"In one spot?" she asked.

"No, all over. Some in tandem. What does this have to do with anything? Fartworthy set fire to the place. I'm sure of it." Birch raised his voice and paced. "He's been trying to get rid of me, or he's working for someone."

Fartworthy straightened his black-rimmed eyeglasses. "Nothing of the sort. I want you to do your job without having to be monitored like a child assigned to chores. I'm always having to check up on you."

Carter held up her hands. "Gentlemen. Please."

"That isn't true, Mr. Birch." Cassandra chimed in. "After you were fired last night, Mr. Fartworthy desperately attempted to get Aunt Lily to change her mind. I was witness to the conversation. He didn't want to see you sacked."

Birch stopped moving and turned to the head butler. "Really?"

Fartworthy smiled. "Yes. I don't know why you believe I have some vendetta against you. The manor would be deprived of your talented work if you were released." He opened his hands with his palms to Birch. "Lady Lemington was wrong to fire you. Miss Haywood wants you to stay. As do I."

"Truly?" Birch stared at his brown shoes. "My deepest apologies, Fartworthy. One can't be too trusting nowadays." He looked up. The scowl left and his shoulders relaxed. His face transformed, as if he were a different person.

The DCI took a step toward Birch. "See? All we needed was some cooler heads to prevail. After yelling at Fartworthy earlier, you stormed in here, Mr. Birch. Why?"

"I was looking for Miss Haywood. She's the only one who cares what happens to me."

"Doesn't seem to be the case." Carter shrugged. "The fire chief informed me outside that the cause of the fire looks to be due to an electrical malfunction."

Cassandra gasped. "The heaters?"

"Yes, Miss Haywood." The head detective pointed. "The preliminary findings, he said, showed that the ones set up in tandem were the problem."

Birch groaned. "I overloaded it?"

"The burning wires would have caught anything nearby on fire," added Jenkins.

"And then, eventually, the bags." He scratched his goatee.

"Bags, Mr. Birch?" Carter shrugged.

"Of fertilizer. Ammonium nitrate. All you need is a flame and those things can detonate. I don't allow smoking around the hothouse and suspect that's where the first explosion came from. There were several bags in the storeroom on the far end. I had another few out on the other side. Used them yesterday morning. Probably the second small explosion came from there." His head dropped as an exasperated breath escaped his lips.

"That was the chief's theory, too. Good to know you concur." Carter scribbled notes. "I'll inform him of your thoughts. I'm sure that will help speed up his investigation. Anything else?"

"Not that I can think of." Birch looked at Fartworthy. "Sorry I thought it was you. It was all my fault."

Fartworthy grimaced. "At least we know what happened."

"I'm curious, though. Why does a hothouse need surveillance?" Carter continued to write.

"Thieves will steal anything." Birch smoothed his goatee. "Some flowers for my heirloom seeds are cultivated over a long time and are expensive. It could tempt anyone."

"I see." The DCI flipped a page on her pad. "I noticed debris from burner mobiles in the lawn after the explosion. From the looks of it, you had numerous phones in there. Why?"

His fingers raked his brown-and-gray hair. "I run the hothouse and the groundskeeper crew. I plan everything and need to be in constant contact with my team."

The head detective watched him. No one spoke.

"Ah." Birch touched his goatee again. "I provided the phones for them. It's easier that way. Not everyone has the latest mobile like me." He slipped his gadget out of his tweed trouser pocket and waved it in Carter's direction.

"You give them ones like that? Lucky workers." Jenkins smirked, eyeing Carter. "That's the newest model."

Birch chuckled. "They don't get this, Detective. This is my personal one. And yes, it's the latest with all the bells and whistles." He reached into his other pocket and pulled out a burner phone. "They get these. It does the job. I text their assignments, so they can't claim ignorance." He put the phones back in separate pockets.

The silence resumed. Carter crossed one arm and with the other hand held the pen by her mouth, staring at Birch.

Cassandra's eyes darted from one detective to another. *Why isn't Carter saying something? What are the rest of them waiting for?* She caught Mimi's eye. The women looked curiously at one another.

"I had a stash out there to give to new workers. My team constantly evolves." The grumpy gardener shrugged. "Hard to keep good crew members. I didn't notice the pieces on the ground. That's my money lost."

"Your money for the mobiles? Not Lady Lemington's?" asked Jenkins.

"It was to make my work easier. I didn't want to trouble her." He looked up. "The losses today are almost unbearable."

"You cared very much about Lady Lemington." Carter tilted her head.

"I did," the gardener whispered, setting his jaw. "She meant a great deal to me. She believed in my work."

"That's why you proposed." Carter squinted. "Plus, you had a nice living here."

"Yes." He breathed out a heavy sigh. "Asking her to marry me was crossing a line. I didn't anticipate her firing me for it. It was a mistake."

The head detective shrugged. "Would there be any other reason for her to fire you?"

Birch tapped his brown-loafered foot. "No."

"What if she found out about your second occupation?"

He chuckled and shifted his weight. "Detective Chief Inspector, Lady Lemington knew I sold the heirloom seeds online and flowers from the hothouse to locals. It's sources of income for the manor. No secrets there. She even encouraged it."

"I'm sorry. I misspoke." Carter smiled. "Your third occupation. The real reason you need the mobiles. Did she know?"

Birch's eyes widened, and his nostrils flared for a moment.

"Mr. Birch loved my aunt. What are you accusing him of?" Cassandra whispered, "Mr. Birch?"

"No clue what she's implying." The gardener's scowl returned.

"Come, come, sir. This day has gone on long enough. There's plenty of evidence." Carter sighed. "Apparently, your activity alerted others, and you've been under surveillance for months. I made a call after observing the destroyed mobiles in the lawn. They have a case against you."

"For what?" Cassandra shook her head.

"Want to tell her? On second thought, probably a good idea to remain silent." Carter sucked in a breath, looking at Cassandra. "He's been dealing in local drugs for a long time."

"From my aunt's manor?"

Carter nodded. "The deliveries his crew were making for the legitimate hothouse businesses were often drug drops. They were none the wiser about their role. This will get sorted by the narcotics team. We only need to bring him in."

Cassandra's heart sank. Her eyes caught the drug dealer's. "Why?"

Birch didn't answer his former employer, was handcuffed, and read his rights among incoherent, stammered excuses. Two constables escorted him outside. Carter returned to the parlor.

"This is too much. I trusted him, too." Cassandra pulled her ivory scarf off her head and ran her fingers through her long hair.

A disturbance erupted across the room.

Von Pickle pushed his way through the crowd. "Carter! Enough of this waiting. You have the killer *and* a drug dealer. Two for one! Time to let the rest of us go."

Carter turned to him. "We're wrapping things up."

"I'll believe it when I see it." Von Pickle groaned. "I demand you release us." Arabella took his arm and whispered into his ear. He pouted and yelled, "I don't care about proper. They're wasting my time."

DS Jenkins grumbled, "Stop stirring up trouble, sir."

Arabella stroked his upper arm. "Darling, it will be over soon enough. Please." She leaned into his shoulder.

Cassandra's stomach lurched as she watched her former best friend. Arabella's eyes focused on the floor.

Von Pickle shrugged out of her grasp and stormed forward. "Who is going to compensate me for today? Hmm?" He pointed his finger around to the cluster of law enforcement. "Somebody owes me."

"Rupert, shut it." Mimi's voice dripped with disdain. "No one owes you anything."

Arabella sneered. "Don't talk to my husband like that, Mrs. York. Keep your sickly opinions to yourself."

Cassandra put her headband scarf back on and moved away from the sofa. "Arabella, you need to be quiet. Mimi is right," she said, her voice laced with resentment. "He need not speak, nor should you."

The DCI held her hands up. "Ladies. Gentlemen. Enough. Baron, we have some loose ends to tie up. We should have everyone on their way soon."

"Loose ends? You got the man who snuffed out Lemington. Why delay us?" The baron adjusted his cuff links. "I'm glad the old crow is gone." Most gasped. "What?" Von Pickle sneered. "With her dead, most of us will be better off. Admit it."

Cassandra clenched her jaw. "You said that earlier. No need to repeat it." Her eyes and anger locked on Arabella. "All the insults directed to him, the jokes at his expense, were so I didn't know your true feelings? That fake horror about him stealing my QR idea was to throw me off? It was right after I looked at the photographs. You were afraid I would see a picture of you together and discover your relationship."

Arabella held her forehead and studied the floor.

Cassandra's mouth puckered. "For years, you've said how much you appreciated me telling you the unfiltered truth about anything. If only you did the same for me. How could you deceive me so, Bel—Arabel—Miss Dalton? No. Mrs. *Von Pickle*."

Baron Von Pickle groaned. "Grow a spine, Cassandra. She chose wisely for a great life. I won. Your friendship meant nothing."

Arabella turned to her husband. "That's not true." She faced her former friend. "It did mean something." Her voice cracked. "But I needed . . . well, I don't know what I needed."

The braggart threw his hands up. "Please, get your sentiments in check, Bella. You know I don't tolerate emotion."

Arabella bit her lip.

Cassandra shut her eyes, holding in her internal tempest. *How can I get him to be quiet? Wait.* Her eyes popped open. *Aunt Lily had something on him. She said it was in the papers.* "Who plundered my bedroom?" She turned to Carter. "Was it someone from your department?"

The DCI frowned. "What are you talking about?"

"I left my room in order this morning. When I went there this afternoon, someone had opened drawers, ripped blankets off the beds, ransacked the closet, and torn through my desk." Cassandra's hand cut through the air. "Someone was searching for something."

"My detectives weren't authorized to perform that search and wouldn't do so in the manner you described."

"Then who did?" She drew in a calming breath. "*Mrs.* Von Pickle?"

Arabella crossed her arms. "Don't look at me. I did nothing to your room."

"You were in there with me, and that phony shower you took makes me think you wanted to save your—"

Arabella waved her hands. "You're right, I didn't shower. I was texting Rupert. You have me, but I didn't vandalize your bedroom."

Robin Turner stepped forward and coughed. "That would be me. I rummaged around, Cassandra. My apologies."

"But why?" asked Cassandra.

"It wasn't out of spite." Robin tugged on her red, silk dress. "I was searching for something to help my son."

"Perhaps the paperwork for me to sign concerning the ownership of the company? I mentioned they were in my room when we were together in the library." Cassandra folded her arms. "You wanted to stop me."

"I did." Robin shuffled her feet. "After we were told to go, I peeked out and saw you walking down the hall. I waited until you turned the corner and I slipped into your room. I thought I could stop what Lily wanted if I destroyed the legal documents."

"Mother!" Roland strode forward. "Why would you even consider such a thing?"

Mrs. Turner's mouth dipped downward. "I know. Irrational. I wanted what was best for you. I did that before you told me of your future hopes."

"I'm not changing my mind." Roland stuffed his hands deep into his trouser pockets.

"I know you won't. Your idea still sounds ridiculous to me. You must understand I did what I thought was right. I wasn't going to accept a new direction in your life. And then"—Robin looked at Flora—"we found Richard's daughter hiding in plain sight. It changed everything."

Flora smiled. "Aunt Robin, I'm so sorry for the deception."

"Please." Mrs. Turner crossed the room to her niece and touched her shoulders. "We've wasted enough time."

"It was my wish to remain hidden. I demanded she keep silent. I thought you would. . . ." The head housekeeper paused, staring at the floor.

Robin shrugged. "I would, what?"

Flora wiped her eye. "Hate me for killing your brother."

Without a word, Robin took Flora's chin in one hand and raised Miss Fairchild's face. She held her niece's hand in her own. "You didn't kill your father. Richard always had health issues, even when we were children. Our decisions teach us about life, and some of those choices, we regret. Everyone carries heavy parcels of lessons. You're no different."

Flora wiped a tear off her cheek with the back of her hand and nodded.

Robin continued. "I argued with Lily about many things, last night and anytime I saw her. I was wrong. She's gone, and I cannot apologize. I must live with that. We need to learn from our mistakes and move forward. Guilt doesn't help anyone heal."

Robin turned to her son. "Roland, if you desire to be a puppet guy . . . puppet person—"

"Puppeteer," Roland corrected.

Mrs. Turner grimaced. "Puppeteer." She coughed. "I don't want to lose you because we disagree. For you to leave with no contact would be a torment I couldn't bear." Her voice cracked, but she shook the emotion away. "If you wish to pursue that, I won't stop you. I don't like it, but I won't interfere."

Roland's face erupted in a wide grin. "Thank you, Mother! I won't disappoint. It will be an amazing experience that—"

Robin held her hand up and tutted. "Accepting your desires and showing excitement for this path are two *very* different things."

"I'll take what I can get." Roland pulled his hand and puppet out of his pocket and clutched the felt friend to his chest. "Thank you."

Robin rolled her eyes.

Von Pickle laughed. "Good gravy! Can we end the sappy, 'We're all family, I'm going after my dreams' nonsense? Bella, time to get our bags. We're leaving." Von Pickle and his wife turned toward the hall.

The DCI held up her hands. "We're not finished."

"I am. You're dragging this out for your own enjoyment. I have an international company, and the rest of these losers are drowning in their terrible decisions." He locked eyes with Cassandra.

She glared and remembered. "Mr. Fartworthy? Where are the papers from my room?"

"Right here, ma'am." He removed the packet from an interior coat pocket and walked toward her. He whispered, "I believe page three is what you seek."

"Thank you, Mr. Fartworthy." She took the stack and flipped through. Her eyes scanned the words. She stopped and smirked.

"Miss Haywood?" DS Jenkins sniffed. "Do you have something for us, or can the DCI continue?"

The young woman breathed in deeply, looking at Von Pickle. "You'll want to hear this." Cassandra covered her smiling mouth for a moment. "Baron, you've said your company is flourishing."

"I'm leaving." Von Pickle resumed his walk toward the great hall.

"Dealing on the black market has consequences." Cassandra waved the papers.

"Black market?" Carter's eyes went wide in astonishment. "Hold on, sir."

Cassandra continued. "Yes, selling Casu Marsu. Importing that cheese from Italy is completely illegal."

"That?" The braggart stopped and stared over his shoulder. "You have no proof. Besides, that would involve a minor fine."

"It can be proven. And yes, there's a fine. Pretty sizable since it has been going on for years." Cassandra strode closer. "However, there's the little matter of bribery to let cheese crawling with live maggots into our country. *That* comes with a mandatory jail sentence."

Von Pickle's face blanched.

A loud gasp came from Arabella, the lines on her face deepening. "Cassie, what are you talking about?"

"Don't call me that. You lost the privilege," she said through gritted teeth. She took a breath. "Casu Marsu is the maggot cheese I told you about in my room. Your lovely husband has been importing that vile product to sell on the black market here and abroad. He also bribed a certain port health officer, who happened to get caught in an Interpol raid on another matter. To take a lesser sentence, the officer ratted him out yesterday afternoon. There should be a warrant for your arrest soon, Baron."

Arabella's hand covered her mouth.

"No," he seethed. "Impossible."

"It is possible, and you knew. This was what Aunt Lily spoke to you about at the party when you got angry and told her she couldn't do something to you. I imagine she said she'd have you arrested when the constable came for Mr. Savage. She wasn't going to turn Owen over to the authorities—it was you. That's the real reason you can't wait to leave." She turned to Carter. "Here, look." She showed the head detective the papers in her hand.

Carter studied the information.

Mimi chimed in. "He's doing business around the world and must have global bank accounts. Shutting down access to his money might be time consuming and too late. He's a flight risk, could leave the country tonight, and likely has plenty of currency stashed somewhere. Extradition would be impossible."

Hamish turned slowly to Mimi. "How do you know all this?"

Mrs. York smiled broadly. "No worries, my love. Research for one of my villains."

"Impressive," Hamish murmured, his eyes dancing as he gazed at his wife. Her eyebrow flicked upward.

Arabella rushed to her husband's side. "He's been frantic all day. Tell me this isn't true, Rupert."

The baron bit the skin on the side of his thumbnail. "No, Cassandra made it up. There's no proof."

DS Jenkins laughed. "That paper right there is enough to have you come with us. This is an Interpol case. We can hold you until they come to chat."

Von Pickle's eyes shot daggers at the detective.

"My aunt told me she knew your world was about to collapse. You have no one to blame but yourself. I think she wanted to have the pleasure of telling you your days as a free man were numbered. She probably didn't realize you would attempt to run and hide like a weasel."

Von Pickle scoffed. "You don't know anything."

Cassandra moved closer to him. "Ambition has led to your amazing, successful life, you said. You told me I'll never embrace that and, therefore, would fail again." She crossed her arms. "But who am I? I failed business school because I assisted my aunt during her legal battle. She didn't need a diploma to prove my competence. And she was right. I can manage reptilian competition like you."

The DCI handed all but one of the papers back to Cassandra. "You're in a bit of trouble, sir."

"You can't prove a thing." He took a few steps backward. "Your aunt was a crazy, old bird. You're trying to get me to incriminate myself. I'm not falling for it."

DS Jenkins gave a quick nod to DC Baker and stepped closer to Von Pickle. "You'll come down to the station with us, and we'll get this all sorted. I'm sure it's a big misunderstanding."

"No, I have things to do." He moved to the parlor doorway.

Arabella piped up, her chin jutting out. "Things to do? Like the flight you need to catch to Italy without me?"

Von Pickle stammered, "D-d-darling, it's an overnight."

"So you said, *darling*. Not the case, is it? You were going to flee"—Arabella pursed her lips—"leaving me to be hauled off to talk to constables or detectives or Interpol or whomever about your indiscretions." Her voice rose in pitch. "Let me be interrogated while you sip wine at our favorite villa?"

"Bella, how did you know I was going there?"

"You idiot. I booked the flight and accommodations for you last night, remember? You never said you were in trouble. What kind of man are you?" Arabella turned to Carter. "I had no idea about any of this black market business or the bribery."

Carter motioned to Penwarden. "Let's wrap things up here. There are phone calls to be made to higher-ups."

Jenkins blocked Von Pickle's way. "Come. Time to go to town for a little talk. You, too, Miss Dalton."

The baron's eyes grew wide. "No!" He shoved the officer back and turned to run.

A gaggle of detectives swarmed, rushing past Cassandra. In a flurry of bodies and shouting, Von Pickle's hands were soon clasped in front of him in handcuffs.

"Get off me! Get off me!" The baron struggled against Detectives Jenkins and Henslowe as they flanked him, holding his upper arms. "You have nothing! You can't arrest me! I have an international business! Immunity! Immunity!"

DCI Carter chuckled. "Immunity from what? You're not a diplomat. Quiet down. I'm placing you under arrest." Carter and her team escorted the corrupt businessman to the front door. Arabella darted after them.

Mimi hurried to Cassandra's side. "Are you all right, Cassandra?" Flora and Fartworthy joined the two women.

Fartworthy touched her arm. "Miss Haywood?"

Cassandra nodded and massaged her wrists.

Mimi tossed the book onto the sofa. "I can't believe it." She pointed to the group of detectives with Von Pickle. "Rupert shouldn't have pushed that detective. That gave them a reason to arrest him and will add to the charges."

Cassandra looked at her and said, "Right." She exhaled. "What a day."

Chapter Twenty-Nine

Cassandra stood with the DCI alone in the great hall. "We know Mr. Spooner added the medication while her cup was in the kitchen. I'm unclear how the tea killed Aunt Lily."

Carter put on her black overcoat. "Lady Lemington consumed her evening drink in her bedroom. For someone like Mrs. York, the pills strengthen her weak cardiac muscles. For your aunt's healthy heart, it may have been too much and, we believe, induced a heart attack."

They walked to the front door, Cassandra holding the side of her head. "Why was she found in the water closet? And what about the—blood?"

"She could have felt nauseous or had a sudden severe headache. She may have thought cold water on her face, or something from the cabinet, would make her feel better. There's no evidence anyone else was in the room at the time. The damage to her watch and bruises on her arms indicate she blacked out."

Cassandra stopped and shut her eyes tight for a moment.

Carter whispered, "The blood resulted from hitting her head. The coroner didn't believe the wound was the cause of death. Her teacup tested positive, and the remains of your cup, as I said, were negative for the drug. He was telling the truth about your coffee. Are you all right?"

"Yes. Everything makes sense now. Thank you."

"You're welcome." Carter placed her hand on Cassandra's upper arm. "Mr. Spooner acted alone. With him in custody, I believe you're safe. A final report of your aunt's autopsy will be sent." She buttoned her coat. "It'll take a few weeks."

Cassandra opened the exterior door and the cold blew in. They stepped outside into the twilight and walked across the gray stone landing.

"The hothouse inquiry will be a separate case. Narcotics division will be in contact with questions about Birch." Carter pulled out her card. "My mobile is on there. If you recall anything else about Mr. Spooner, please call me directly. I'll stay in touch with the progress of the cases."

Cassandra stared at the card in her hand. "I understand." The wind picked up, whipping the long, floral skirt around her bare legs.

The head detective tugged on her own neck and sighed. "I'm sorry I suspected you. Sometimes we . . . I . . . am influenced by my own viewpoint and make the wrong conclusions."

Cassandra nodded.

"With my team, the fire brigade, and the guests all gone, you and the staff have your house back." Carter closed her coat's top button. "On behalf of the department, we're very sorry for your loss."

"Thank you." Cassandra shivered in the bitter air.

The head detective descended the gray steps into a waiting auto. Blue lights continued to spin from the top of her unmarked, parked vehicle, adding a cold cast to the January evening. The car pulled off the semi-circle turnaround and onto the long driveway. The taillights receded as the car moved down the hill between the bare, ancient oak trees. A single, black vehicle with tinted windows remained running near the house on the gravel.

Carter must have been mistaken. Cassandra hugged herself. *Someone still needs to leave.* Icy rain began to fall.

She walked to the wooden doors, her lilac and ivory scarf tails floating like ghosts in the wind. The head butler opened the door when she reached for the handle. "Thank you, Mr. Fartworthy." She stepped inside the warm manor, slipped Carter's card into her skirt pocket, and shuffled across the hardwood floor. "There's still a ride out there for someone. Please find out who the driver is waiting for." She heard the door close behind her as she headed for the main staircase.

"Miss Haywood? I need to speak with you."

"I'm retiring to my room. I'll talk tomorrow. I'm sorry."

"This matter cannot wait," pressed the butler.

Cassandra's shoulders slumped with one foot on the bottom step. "Whatever it is, we'll discuss it in the morning. I'm knackered." She gazed at the grandfather clock against the wall. It read *7:34. Twenty-four hours ago.* She resumed climbing the steps. "Please tell Mrs. Forest I'll take a tray in my room. Nothing fancy. A sandwich, some cheese—*anything* but Stilton—and a cup of tea will do."

"You gave me those instructions before the guests left, ma'am. I believe Miss Fairchild should have it all in your chamber when you arrive."

"I did? I don't remember." Cassandra stopped, turned around, and sighed. "More proof I'm not myself. It was a late night and a long, terrible day."

"I'm so sorry, ma'am, but it's most imperative we talk."

"What is it then?" Her body slouched, finding support from the curved handrail.

He moved away from the door, closer to Cassandra. The crispness of his steps fell in time with the loud ticking of the tall clock. He stopped at the foot of the staircase, silent.

"Please, Mr. Fartworthy," she begged. "What is it?"

"Miss Haywood, I'll cut to the chase." Fartworthy's green eyes focused on her from behind his black, squared-rimmed glasses. "Considering today's events, I must hand in my resignation."

"What? Why?"

"It's for the best, I'm afraid, ma'am."

She descended the steps, reviving adrenaline surging through her fatigued body. "I understand as a PI you might have other things to do. I'm fine with your side occupation. That shouldn't cause you to cease your employment here. No, I don't accept your resignation."

"I'm sorry. You do *not* have a choice in the matter, Miss Haywood. The car waiting outside is for me. I have a flight departing from Heathrow Airport in several hours and need to go immediately so there's enough time to get through security."

"You're leaving? Just like that?" Cassandra stepped closer to him. "Saying goodbye because you don't want to work for me?"

"No, ma'am. It's . . . more . . . complicated than that." The head butler walked to the closet under the stairs and opened it. "Circumstances dictate I must go," he said as he retrieved a rectangular, black duffel bag, and a long, dark-gray, woolen coat. "I wish I could give you more of an explanation."

Cassandra crossed her arms. "After what we've been through today? You cannot do this." Her voice rose in pitch. "I want you to stay. I need you to stay. And what's this? You planned to leave all along?"

"No, this was a new development." Fartworthy walked back to her, set his bag down, and draped the heavy coat over the handrail. "I'm sorry it's another shock for you. I packed while the detectives were wrapping up. All I need is in here."

"This is sudden. Is it because a murder occurred on the premises?"

"No."

"You agreed to work for Aunt Lily, and this means your contract is up?"

"No, ma'am."

"You dislike your coworkers?" Cassandra moved closer.

"No. Birch was not my favorite chap, but he won't be here." He backed up a step.

"You're ill?"

"No."

Cassandra threw her hands up. "What then? You detonate a bomb and expect to waltz out the door without an explanation? And I won't continue to play twenty questions. You *will* tell me." She paused. "Please."

A grin spread across his face. "Miss Haywood, you certainly have grown into your role as a PI."

"I'm not a detective." She crossed her arms again.

"Who solved this case for Carter? It wasn't me." He laughed and stepped toward her. "Who eavesdropped on the team's discussion in the library and discovered who they suspected? Who deduced Miss Dalton was giving information to the baron?" He moved several steps closer. "Who viewed the party photos and connected it with Spooner going to the kitchen? Who put the pieces together? Yes, Miss Haywood, many other secrets were discovered, and your aunt's killer is in custody because of *you*."

"Still doesn't make me an investigator."

"You're a natural for detective work, ma'am."

She chuckled. "You won't distract me with flattery. I'm not accepting your sudden departure without an answer." She lowered her voice to a murmur. "Why are you leaving? I'll miss you terribly if you go."

He sighed. "I have another missing person case. It's imperative I leave." He threaded his fingers together in front of him.

Cassandra stared at the head butler and said nothing.

"I won't be back."

She crossed her arms, narrowed her eyes, and remained silent.

"I must go." Fartworthy chortled. "Miss Haywood? What is it? You're practically staring through me."

"I find your explanation wanting. What's the real story? No. More. Deception."

"Miss Haywood." Fartworthy tossed his head back, slapped his hand to his chest, and laughed. "What have I done? Between my training and watching Carter interrogate, you have learned quickly."

"So, what is it?" Cassandra's hands went to her hips. "Out with it."

He paused and breathed out. "I'm MI6."

She stepped back and exclaimed, "You're a government spy?" Her mouth flew open.

"Shh!" he commanded. "Yes. I'm with British International Intelligence."

"You're here in the UK. How is that international?" Cassandra whispered.

"Sometimes an imminent global threat is right under one's own roof."

"Clearly. Why does that mean you need to leave?"

"My job here is finished. Birch has been apprehended, and his arrest completes my assignment."

"Wait a minute." She twisted an ivory tail from her headband scarf. "You said MI6 deals with international threats. Birch was only a petty drug dealer in our literal backyard."

"True, he operated right here." Fartworthy ran his fingers through the wavy front of his jet-black hair. "But there's more to it."

She shrugged in silent expectation.

He leaned in. "Birch's operation was expansive. He's an international drug lord."

"Our gardener is a *what*?"

Fartworthy continued. "International drug dealing is a complicated world. It takes a great deal of work to discover the sources of these empires. Birch ran a global wholesale network. His tentacles threaded through every continent. Well, not Antarctica. To stop him, we needed a long-term plan. If we removed Birch when we first uncovered his domain, other cartels would swoop in and break up the territory. Nature abhors a vacuum."

"This makes little sense."

"I know." Fartworthy picked up his coat and slid one arm into a sleeve. "By leaving him in place, and having me embedded as a butler, I could glean information and help destroy his enterprise, slowly and methodically. Not too much at once to raise suspicion or have him go back into hiding." He put the other arm in and shrugged to straighten the lapels. "Birch needed to feel safe here, and his operation could flourish. It did for some time. It was ideal for the cartel and for busting him."

Cassandra held a hand to her forehead, holding the sudden infusion of information in her brain. "Are you joking?"

"I wish I were. He has fierce competition in his occupation. Albanian gangs are number one in cocaine distribution in the UK. We're working to eliminate that, too. For Birch, we dismantled his web in stages, over an extended period. Our intel informs us he believes the Albanians are responsible, and that was our goal. He has little left under his control. That would explain why his outbursts and general grumpiness increased as time went on."

"But didn't you tell Carter you uncovered this today?"

"The lie was necessary. By pointing out the busted mobiles and handing her enough surveillance info, the other work my division did in secret could remain hidden."

"The smashed mobiles. How did that clue her in?"

"Drug dealers often use burners for their contacts. Not traceable. At least, not easily traceable. But having a stash of them is a good indication of illegal activity. Carter believed me that Birch was up to something when I pointed it out."

"I see."

Fartworthy smiled. "Dead giveaway, what happened in the parlor. If someone has an expensive, latest model mobile and, in addition, carries a cheap phone, it's another sign they're a drug dealer—and a high-level one. Not always, but much more than criminals realize. That was exquisite. Jenkins picked up on the possibility then."

"But she made the arrest. Wouldn't you have liked to do that?"

"I never do. I love to complete my work and fade off like smoke. They can't connect me."

"If you knew he was such a dangerous man, why did you live here with him for three years?"

"If I hadn't, all the information obtained would evaporate, and we would have to start over."

"But still . . . you left him here to operate in my aunt and uncle's house? Three years?" She clutched all four scarf tails together. "Wasn't that an enormous danger to everyone?"

"There are other national security issues connected with this, too. I can't go into that. It was necessary for that time period to be here. When I discovered Lady Lemington on the floor of the bathroom, I thought Birch might have changed his MO and been responsible. I needed to find proof one way or the other before Carter did."

"He has an MO?"

"Other kingpins are ruthless and play a large role in terminations to keep their empire. Drug charges can be hard to make stick. Many of these individuals who have been caught were convicted of murder." Fartworthy tapped his fingertips together. "Birch is wickedly intelligent. He used other tactics to maintain control and has the reputation of minimizing collateral damage. He also operates as a wholesaler and avoids direct contact. There is less chance of someone ratting him out." He neatened his overcoat. "I cannot go into all of what he did. He didn't have any issues with the residents here. His flower and seed businesses were legitimate and the perfect cover when he needed to receive and make deliveries." Fartworthy glanced at the clock. "I really must go."

"*Finish* the story. And it's not settled you're leaving."

"It *is* settled, ma'am. Besides completing my assignment, there's another reason to depart." He tilted his head up. "People in my profession need to remain unattached for the work we do. Yesterday and today proved I failed twice."

"How?"

"Friendships, especially like the one I have with Flora and you, are discouraged in my line of work."

"I don't understand."

"When I was talking to you about grief in the dining room, I wanted to comfort you. I dropped my guard."

"You could relate because of your missing little brother." Cassandra grimaced.

"No, that was made up for Birch's benefit. He could understand my hobby from that. The circumstances of an abduction I did contend with . . . for a significant other." He cleared his throat. "Anyway, Greenfield read my lips with ease. As a member of my organization, to do that in a different situation could have deadly consequences. Not in this case, but the potential is there."

She stepped closer. "A significant other?"

"I don't wish to discuss it, Miss Haywood." Fartworthy pressed his lips tight.

"Oh."

The clock ticked several times as they stood there, silent.

Cassandra breathed out. "You said there were two times you dropped your guard. When was the other?"

"Lady Lemington was getting too comfortable with Birch. It's my belief he wanted to remain after his drug business folded. It's a nice life here at the manor. In addition, if they had married, your aunt wouldn't be called on to testify against her spouse if charges were brought up against him. However, he might not have realized his illegal actions before they tied the knot would not fall under that protection. Birch pretended to be romantically interested and did so many things to convince her. Ironically, I believe *he* actually fell in love."

"I think so, too. The way he lamented about her in the library was genuine." Cassandra shook her head.

"My desire to protect Lady Lemington and Miss Fairchild got in the way of my work. I wanted to put her on guard around him and told Lady Lemington I suspected Birch was doing something with drugs. There were consequences I didn't foresee but should have. Her counter-action was to shield Flora at all costs."

"That's why Aunt Lily sacked him!"

"Yes. A poor choice on my part to reveal that information. Firing him would have been disastrous for my mission." He frowned. "Years of work. Our ability to arrest and stop him once and for all would have vanished if he did."

"You argued with her to reconsider his firing after he proposed."

"Precisely."

There was another moment of silence.

Cassandra walked to the antique grandfather clock, grappling with the new information. "Was Aunt Lily or Uncle Richard aware of this?" Her finger traced the intricate, curved line in the mahogany wood.

"No. They knew me as a PI they stumbled upon in their quest. That was also not by chance. You're the first in this household to know my identity. You'll be the *only* one. My safety and my very life depend on you remaining silent. Do you understand?"

She turned to him. "Then why tell me any of this if it is such a great secret?" Her face pinched tight.

"Miss Haywood." He breathed out a heavy breath and his shoulders dropped. "You've had enough deception today for a lifetime. As your friend . . . as your true friend . . . I couldn't add to the stack of lies anymore. You deserve the absolute truth from me and can, emotionally, handle my burden."

"What about Flora?" Cassandra's scarf tails resembled a rope.

"She does not and can never know. I said my goodbyes to her downstairs. Alone. She was understandably upset. Miss Fairchild started out as an assignment but developed into a deep friendship."

"You told me you were a professional, and yet you said before everyone you were not."

"Again, I lied when talking to Carter." He grinned. "Birch needed to believe the destruction of his empire and my PI work had nothing to do with one another. It was imperative that I convince him my other 'job' of finding Flora was a hobby. When I saw Miss Fairchild downstairs, I explained my earlier actions. She knows I'm a professional. She trusts me implicitly, figured there was a reason for what I said, and went along with the story earlier. Believe me, deceit is not a part of the job I enjoy."

"Then why do this at all?"

Fartworthy stood taller. "For God and country. Someone needs to defend humanity from unseen threats. Miss Fairchild was told what I tried to tell you—that I needed to depart because of another missing person case. She accepted my explanation. In a way, that's true. *I* must disappear." He tilted his head back.

"I don't understand."

"I blew my cover. Birch knows me as an amateur PI. If he connects the dots and can see that, in fact, I'm a professional, my life is in danger. I can't take that chance. I need to vanish and become a new person. After tonight, Archibald Fartworthy will be no more."

"I can't believe what I'm hearing." Cassandra removed her lilac scarf from her neck and balled it in her hands. "You'd give up your name and your home and your friends?"

His eyes twinkled. "I did that years ago. 'Fartworthy' is a pseudonym I created. I must admit, every time Lady Lemington shouted that name, it amused the five-year-old boy in me. Ah . . . I shall *miss* this name"—he looked around and back at Cassandra—"and this manor, and the lovely people here."

"Can we communicate with you?"

"No, it isn't safe for either of us."

Her mouth hung open. She moved closer to him. "Ever?"

"No, I'm sorry. Please remember the words your aunt repeated so often. You're stronger than you think and can handle whatever comes your way. I know this to be true. You proved it today."

The young woman breathed in deeply, forced back the lump in her throat, and attempted to square her shoulders. "Go do what you must. I will always treasure our time together." Her voice quivered, straining to sound professional. She reached out mechanically, and they shook hands for a few moments.

This cannot be our goodbye. No. This won't do.

Cassandra tugged Fartworthy close and they embraced. "I'm going to miss you," she murmured, her mouth next to the folds of the scratchy, dark-gray wool, the scent of cedar filling her nose. "I don't want you to go." She shut her eyes against his shoulder, willing him to change his mind.

"I must," he whispered to the top of her head, squeezing her a little tighter. "I'm so very sorry." His soft voice quavered. "I *really* am." He drew in a deep breath.

She swallowed hard and took a half step back from his strong arms. She gave several pats to his lapel. "Go. I don't want you to miss your flight."

He picked up his black duffel bag and turned away. When he opened the door, the cold air blew in, dropping the hall temperature in an instant. He cleared his throat. "I'll keep a weather eye out for you—and Miss Fairchild. You can count on that."

"I'm sure you will. Thank you. Goodbye, Mr. . . . *Fartworthy.*" Cassandra smiled. "The best of luck. Please stay safe."

"That's my goal. Thank you for the privilege of serving." He grinned. "Goodbye, Miss Haywood." Fartworthy pulled the antique door closed behind him.

The ticking echoed in the empty great hall. Golden lights twinkled on the enormous Christmas tree. The silver ornaments sparkled.

Cassandra drifted to the curved staircase. Pressure on her chest threatened to suffocate the young woman, and her legs turned to gelatin. She sank on the second step. Her lilac scarf dropped from her hands and coiled in her lap. Volatile emotions resulting from the day's events mixed and slammed together, combusting.

She could no longer hold back the deluge. Dejected, quiet sobs rattled Cassandra's whole being. Her palms covered her face while her elbows dug into her thighs. A culmination of images flashed in her head, squeezing pain from every cell. For several minutes, she remained bent forward, lungs screaming for air between gasps and salty water dripping on her skirt.

Icy hail tap-danced on the panes of the long hall windows. Wind howled through the poorly insulated window frames. The towering clock continued to tick.

When every tear held in check all day by propriety and pride had flowed, she let out a breath and straightened her spine. She whispered to the universe, "I can do this. I don't know how, but I'll manage." She sniffed. *Aunt Lily would expect me to.* Cassandra stood and relaxed her shoulders.

I want to do this. I shall.

While wiping her eyes with the back of her hand, she climbed the steps. On the landing halfway up, she turned to take in her favorite sweeping view of the manor.

Something caught her eye.

There, at the bottom of the stairs, her scarf lay in a lavender puddle.

Not again.

She clomped down the staircase, picked up the scarf with a sigh, and pulled it behind her as she resumed the climb to her bedroom.

Chapter Thirty

Four months later . . .

A stocky taxi dispatcher, working the sidewalk at New York City's JFK International Airport, held open the yellow cab door for Cassandra. "Here you go, ma'am." He called out, "She's going to be heading to The Plaza on Fifth in Manhattan."

Another man, a skinny, middle-aged driver, took the plum-colored suitcase from her hand and placed it inside the trunk. "Plaza. Got it. Thanks, buddy."

Lines painted on the ground attempted to control empty yellow vehicles with cabbies waiting for fares. Interspersed with the for-hire transport, other cars jockeyed for position to pick up relatives or friends. Voices of multiple dispatchers spoke, while an impatient New Yorker leaned on the horn and added to the noise. Weary travelers with their rolling, black suitcases populated the crowded outdoor space and stood in a long queue, eager to get to their final destinations. A roof overhang protected pedestrians from the spring rain that fell a short time ago. The fumes from the cars and the smell of wet asphalt slicked with oil made for an interesting olfactory American greeting for Cassandra. The cabbie got into the left driving side.

What's he doing? He's getting in the wrong—Wait. There is so much to get used to here. She chuckled to herself. *I can do this. Other Brits come here all the time.*

"Have a nice stay. He'll take good care of you." The dispatcher smiled again at the young woman.

"Thank you." She pulled up the end of her long, A-line skirt and lifted her leg into the vehicle. He closed the door and double-tapped the roof.

Cassandra used the strap to buckle herself into the black bench seat. "Hello." She removed her royal-blue, gossamer scarf, placed it in her lap, and tugged on the back of her neck. Tight muscles from the long airplane ride concentrated near her right shoulder. Taking a deep breath, she sighed.

"Haya, miss." Her cab driver, with straight, short, black hair and olive skin, pulled his vehicle forward toward the line of departing cars. "Welcome to New Yawk. First time here? Where ya from?" His thick, regional accent poured out of his smiling mouth. "What ya in town for? Vacation or business?" He turned to talk through the closed window to a driver on his left. "Can't be kind and let me in? Moron." He peered in the rearview mirror. "So sorry, miss. Not calling you a moron. I still think if I talk to other drivas through the window, they hear me."

Jolly good. Sounds strange. "Whatever you need to do. I'm just along for the ride."

"I asked ya a question and didn't let ya answer. Not helpin'. I'm tryin' to get rid of the New-Yawkers-are-rude thing. There are plenty of decent folks here. The idiots are the ones who make the news. So. Where ya from?" The car swung into the lane with a jolt. "Be nice," he said, pointing to a shouting driver in a red Ford Focus.

"I'm from the UK and here for an international cheese conference." The vehicle inched forward in the new lane.

"No kiddin', no kiddin'. Cheese, ya say. Like Swiss and chedda?"

Cassandra chuckled. "Yes, those and more. Discussions and panels about processing, distribution, and other business items. I'm giving a talk on marketing during the week."

"Seriously? Good for ya! Cheese conference. Ha! Didn't realize that was even a thing. Ya learn somethin' new every day. I tell the wife I love this job for exactly this reason, exactly this reason." He pulled into the next lane and hit the gas.

By sheer physics, she sank into the black bench seat, instinctively grabbing the armrest on the door. It shifted in her hand since it was held on by duct tape. A quiet gasp escaped her lips.

"The name's Ahmed. Pleased to meet ya, miss."

She caught her breath. "I'm Cassandra. Likewise. How long have you lived in New York?"

"Born here. So were my parents. Love it. I can't imagine—" He turned to the taxi on his right that edged forward, attempting to cut him off. "Ya gotta be kiddin' me, ya yellow idiot. Such a rush. Go, go!" Ahmed laughed. "I have many conversations with myself every day. Twenty-one years as a cabbie will do that to ya. Anyways, I can't imagine livin' anywhere else. So much to do. The food. The food here is outta this world. Ya can have anythin', anythin' at all. All the cheese, I'm sure!"

"I look forward to that." Cassandra noticed the traffic surrounding her taxicab. No one seemed to be in any one lane, but somehow the chaos evolved into a mechanical ballet troupe performance. "Is it always this crowded?"

"Nah. This is nothin'. I could tell ya stories of some epic traffic jams I've been in. Epic. Like hours and hours no movin' crazy. Soon as we shift outta these lanes, it'll clear up right quick. We'll get on the L.I.E. in a few, and I'll get ya to the city in no time."

She pointed out the window. "I thought I landed in New York City?"

"Yeah, ya did. You're in Queens. One of the five boroughs that make up the Big Apple. Manhattan is another one. Anyone who lives in the boroughs that are not Manhattan call Manhattan 'The City.' I live here in Queens. We also happen to technically be Long Island. Yet, if ya goin' to the beaches or someplace farther out that way"—he pointed in a meaningless direction to Cassandra—"ya goin' 'out the Island.' Just a heads-up on the lingo if ya gonna be around for a bit. A friendly service I provide for my outta town passengers."

"I appreciate the information. It's my first time in the US."

"Welcome to America, then! Ya know what? Ya talk like them people in my wife's favorite movies. Ya know, them Jane Austen, fancy-pants ones. Same accent. She has them on all the time. I don't like admittin' this to my cabbie buddies, but me and the wife watch them together. I don't mind. I like the banter. Cracks me up. So sophisticated. And those collars! The thought of wearin' one of those? I can't deal with a scratchy tag in a T-shirt. Ya ever been in a manna? She loves them giant houses. I can't imagine the taxes on those things."

She chuckled. "Actually, I own and live in a manor."

He slapped the steering wheel and smiled, catching her eye in the rearview mirror. "No kiddin', no kiddin'? Ha! A real, live English lady who lives in a manna! I gotta tell her about ya. She'll be thrilled! She wants to go on one of them big house tours if we ever get to Europe. On a cabbie's and a nurse's salaries, I don't know when that'll happen. Ya can dream, can't ya? How's it like livin' in a big house like that? Gotta be different than a regular place."

"It is. I didn't grow up in a manor. I inherited it after my aunt . . . passed away."

Four months later, and she still couldn't bring herself to say the word 'murdered' out loud or even in her head. A wave of sadness washed over her. She shut her eyes. For a moment, she wasn't bouncing along in the back seat of a taxi in America. Alexander's smug face close to her own, threatening her life, filled her thoughts. Her stomach dropped. She still endured nightmares about him. *At least Spooner took the plea deal and is in jail. So thankful I didn't need to endure a long trial.*

She opened her eyes and played with the delicate, royal-blue scarf in her lap. *Snap out of it, Cassandra.* She cleared her throat. "You're right. The taxes and upkeep are expensive." She forced a smile onto her lips. "It's funny you should mention the Jane Austen movies. I recently signed a contract with the BBC. They'll be using the front of my home, the dining room, and parlor for a new production of *Persuasion.* They begin filming in about a month."

"Seriously? That's great! I gotta tell the wife. She'll be so jazzed to hear that." He merged onto a road with several lanes and rapid-moving vehicles. She admired how he maneuvered around the slower ones, gliding like a speed skater on ice. A hot-pink sports car cut out in front of their cab, causing Ahmed to slow down for a moment. The driver and Cassandra lunged forward.

She was grateful for the sturdy seat belt and the duct-taped armrest.

"Ya gotta be kiddin' me, Pinky! Ya look like a Barbie doll drivin' that thing! Get ya license on Amazon?" He pointed at the brightly colored vehicle that again switched lanes without signaling. "These drivas are nuts. Who buys a car that color? It looks like a toy. A giant toy."

She chuckled. "It's almost a car rugby match. Sorry, more like your American football?"

Ahmed laughed. "Yeah, yeah, ya right. Drivin' here is a full-contact sport."

Cassandra's mobile buzzed in her purse. *Who would be calling me?* She popped the snap on her bag and dug blindly into the fashionable

abyss. Her hand found the device, and she checked the caller ID.
Frederick Chamberlain.

She grinned at his picture as the phone vibrated again. *He's
calling me.* She took the photo when they went to an art show together
a month ago. The handsome man's smile still dazzled her. *I'm glad I
got that international plan.* "Excuse me for a moment, sir," she said to
the cabbie. Her fingertip swiped her phone. "Hello? Frederick?"

"Cassandra! Hello. I got your text you landed safely. Flight
good? They . . . ah . . . feed you well?" asked the young man across
the ocean.

Her cheeks flushed warm. "Yes, everything is perfectly fine.
I'm in a taxicab on my way to the hotel. I didn't expect you to call."

"Oh, I know. Um . . . I needed to . . . hear your voice that you
were fine. I miss you."

"I miss you, too." Her stomach bounced. "It's only for a week."

Frederick laughed. "One extremely long week."

Cassandra's smile grew wide. "I'm still nervous about this
presentation. Thank you so much for your help. It's always better for
me to practice with someone listening."

"My pleasure. You'll be fantastic. You're brilliant, and they'll
love you. And bonus—Von Pickle won't be there heckling."

"They said he dominated the conference last year. I'm sure
others will be happy he'll be missing." She smoothed the scarf tails in
her lap. "Maybe he would bribe someone to get out." She stared out
the window at businesses going by on the large boulevard. "He said he
has enough money to be free."

Frederick sniffed. "Not likely. He has a full two years on his
sentence for that exact thing. That judge threw the book at him, and
I doubt he'll talk his way out of this one. If he thinks he can, he's
a sandwich short of a picnic. Even better, Arabella won't be there
to upset you."

Cassandra's shoulders dropped at the mere mention of her former best friend. "That's true. I'm not ready to face her. It would be easier to forgive if she expressed sorrow for her actions against my aunt." She blew out a breath. "And yet, she remains angry at me for contributing to her husband's incarceration. I don't know how to fix the relationship. I'm not even certain I want to."

"You tried, and here's a thought. You don't have to be the one to repair the friendship. It's on her. Maybe she needs more time to realize how terrible she treated you. Von Pickle landed in jail because of his illegal actions. He chose poorly. So did she."

"I suppose you're right, Frederick."

"I'm sorry I mentioned her. This is a happy trip. Did you hear if Mr. and Mrs. York will be there?"

She smiled at his thoughtfulness. "The Yorks are definitely coming. I'm looking forward to seeing Mimi. Her latest book was delightful. I can't wait to tell her in person."

"And you like that she consulted with you about the next book, set in a manor, of all places." She could hear the teasing grin in Frederick's voice.

"And you were tickled she consulted you because it's a jewelry heist!"

They laughed in unison.

Frederick continued. "Anyone else you're acquainted with?"

"Others from the industry in Europe should be there and some from several US companies."

The taxi's wheels hit a pothole. Hard. The metal from the undercarriage scraped the asphalt, and the whole vehicle rattled and bounced. "Ah!" shouted Cassandra as she sprang airborne for about an inch. Her safety tether functioned correctly, keeping her head from smacking the ceiling.

"What! What happened? Are you okay, Cassandra?" Frederick's panicked voice came through the phone.

The driver chimed in. "Sorry about the pothole, miss. No way to avoid them around here sometimes. We just got on the L.I.E., and this road is terrible in places."

She nervously laughed. "I'm okay, Frederick. The cab drove over a large pothole. Nothing else."

"Be careful over there." She could hear him breathe out. "You sure?"

She smiled again. "Yes, I'm fine, dear." She gasped. That sentimental term had never passed her lips before with him. "Ah .. . no problem here." She bit her lower lip. "It'll be safe. Please don't worry about me." *Maybe he didn't notice. What did he think?*

"I should let you go. When you get a chance, let me know how things are progressing. If you need any more help before your presentation, I'll be here for you." He paused and whispered, "Cassie."

Cassie. She squeezed her eyes and mouth tight with joy. *He noticed.* Her whole body was electrified. "Thank you, Frederick. I'll let you know. And . . . I'm over the moon that you called me Cassie."

Frederick added, "I'm glad. Been wanting to do that for months. Text me later?"

"Absolutely." Her cheeks hurt from smiling. "I should go."

"Jolly good. Enjoy your time in New York. Bye."

"Goodbye." Cassandra tapped the end-call circle. *This trip got off to a magnificent start.* She sighed. *Frederick.*

An exhaust pipe rattled on a truck that passed too close. The bumpy expressway, the smell of the vinyl, black bench seat, the duct tape, and blurry scenery out the window jolted her back to New York.

"Boyfriend? Husband?" asked Ahmed.

"What?" She blinked hard.

He glanced at her in the rearview mirror. "You look 'perfectly content,' as one of them fancy-pants would declare."

Cassandra's mouth hung open.

"Sorry about that, miss." Ahmed smiled, turning his head over his shoulder for a moment. "What can I say? I wanna make sure everyone has an enjoyable ride."

"I see." Cassandra nodded and played with her scarf tails. "He's a dear friend I have been spending a bit of time with lately. Not officially a boyfriend."

"One of those." He chuckled. "Don't string him along. Us guys don't like that. Is there another that ya can't make up ya mind?"

"There's no one else. We're taking things slowly. My life has been terribly busy over the last few months. He's special. He once got hurt protecting me from flying glass due to an explosion. Thankfully, his injury was not serious and there was no lasting damage."

"Ya don't say? And what are ya guys doin' in England blowin' up things? Wow. Good guy. He's a keepa."

She smiled and looked out the window. "I think so."

Large billboards dotted the sides of the expressway, facing the constant stream of vehicles. One sign, saturated in primary colors, advertised the location and performance time of a puppet production. Cassandra pointed. "They advertise puppet shows on those?"

Ahmed waved one hand. "Not like them regular library ones. That's some new, Off-Broadway musical thing, and the hottest ticket around. Some passengers saw it said it's witty for grown-ups and great for kids. I always got my ear out for recommendations. They told me adults won't want to rip out their eardrums from the show soundtrack. That's a good endorsement."

"I have a friend currently enrolled in puppetry school in London." A succession of bumps bounced the vehicle. "He loves it." She tugged on the seat belt to make sure it would still hold.

"I suppose they gotta get trainin' somewhere." He leaned on his horn as a lime-green taxi on his right slid partway into their lane. Ahmed flicked his hand in the air as if swatting away an insect. "Get over, ya snot nose. There ya go. Stay there."

"I must tell Roland about this production. He'll be thrilled." She pointed at the other car. "There are green ones like this? I only ever saw yellow taxis when they want to show New York City on the telly."

"Yup. Borough Taxis is what they call them. Those things can't do pickups at the airports and certain sections of Manhattan, which is a blessin'. When you're tryin' to get around while you stay here, that lovely puke color lets ya know they'll take ya to the other places outta Manhattan without givin' ya a hassle."

"So out of *The City*." Cassandra grinned.

"Ya a fast learna! Excellent. Before they had those, some of my yellow predecessors used to give people a real hard time if they wanted to go to Queens, Brooklyn, or the Bronx. I won't even mention Staten Island. For us cabbies, stayin' close to the action is the money-makin' ideal. I never mind travelin' farther. When you need to trek someplace else around Manhattan, hail one of those green beauties. They could have picked a better color, ya know? What genius chose that pneumonia-phlegm shade?"

Cassandra burst out laughing and held her sides. "You don't seem to be a fan of the other kinds of taxicabs."

Ahmed joined her in the merriment. "I guess they're not so bad. New Yawkers enjoy their rivalries."

Up ahead on the road, a series of red brake lights gathered. Ahmed tutted. "Bah. What's this slowdown? Come on, come on." He tapped his GPS. "New backup all the way to the Midtown. Plan B. We'll take the Fifty-ninth Street Bridge. Hold on." He took the exit off the expressway. "Good thing is you'll get the view this way and no toll. Usually I find the tunnel is quicker. Gotta be flexible livin' here."

For the next few minutes, the cabbie deftly maneuvered down side streets, around double-parked cars, through a series of traffic lights, and pedestrians with heads bent over their phones, ignoring crosswalks. They made their way through the urban maze, then up a long, curved ramp.

As they veered right, the New York City skyline came into full view. "Wow," popped out of Cassandra's mouth. Directly across the river, the skyscrapers lived up to their reputation.

Ahmed nodded in agreement. "I know, right? I love this place. Love it. It's crazy here. The traffic is the pits. The crowds can get to ya sometimes, but this!" He pointed with his open hand. "This is amazin', and ya can't get this view anywhere else in the world. Wait until ya see it after dark. It's like the best holiday light display ever. I never get tired of it. Never."

"I'm looking forward to the night view. It's something I've always wanted to see."

"Ya won't be disappointed. We're about to cross the East River." The vehicle jostled as it merged onto the bridge. "It'll be a straight shot across." A black SUV in front of them braked. "Move, ya slowpoke. I got to get this lady to her destination. Let's do this." The SUV moved over as if understanding his command through the closed window. "Thaaaaat's what I'm talkin' about," said Ahmed as he sped up. "Sometimes the morons listen."

Cassandra chuckled.

After crossing the bridge, they made their way along the width of Manhattan, and the cab driver pointed out other places she should see while in town.

Her brain failed to absorb the information.

A cluster of trees came into view at the end of the block. The taxi emerged from the concrete canyon of East Sixtieth Street and followed the road as it curved to the left. A line of horses attached to carriages waited to take passengers. "The wife wants to go on one of those sometime through the park. I blame those English movies! Just jokin'. Someday." He pointed to the corner in front of them. "There." The Plaza Hotel loomed.

She marveled at the size and French Renaissance chateau architecture.

He gestured to the foliage on their right. "Central Park is here. The beautiful, green, heart of Manhattan. It's great and takes many visits to explore. Make sure you look around there at some point. Do yourself a favor, though, and don't go walkin' alone there at night. Not smart." Ahmed tapped the side of his head. He crossed Fifty-ninth, pulled in front of the iconic building, stopped, and punched buttons on his meter. "And here we are."

She removed the US currency from her wallet and counted the bills. "I thoroughly enjoyed our ride and talk, Ahmed." Cassandra handed the wad to him over the seat. "My welcome to the United States and New York City has been extraordinary."

"Glad to hear it. Ya know, my sister works here and sometimes I drive her home. Ya might see me around." He quickly thumbed through the money. "Thanks for the generous tip. My wife will be tickled to hear about your manna. Absolutely tickled. Good luck with your cheese conference."

"Thank you. It would be pleasant to meet up again."

The hotel doorman pulled the taxi door open and smiled. "Welcome to The Plaza." His bleached-blond hair, which almost matched his skin color, poked out from under his Pershing hat. "This way, miss."

"Thank you." Cassandra shouldered her large, multicolor travel purse and stepped out of the taxi and up to the sidewalk.

Ahmed got out, retrieved her luggage from the trunk, and handed it to her. "Here ya go. Enjoy your stay. Remember, yellow cabs for the city and ugly, green ones for the outta boroughs."

Cassandra grinned. "I'll remember that. Have a lovely day." The friendly cabbie hopped back into his vehicle. She grasped the handle on her suitcase and turned to walk up the blue-carpeted stairs to the lobby."

"Miss Haywood, I can get that for ya," said a voice behind her.

She pivoted to see the doorman, wearing a long, uniform jacket, who addressed her. "I appreciate it." *What did he say?*

"Yeah, no problem. Part of my job," said the man in a New York accent. "And ya dropped this." He held her royal-blue, gossamer scarf in his hand.

When am I going to learn? "Thank you." She looked at his gold-plated name badge. "Thank you, Marcel." She stepped forward and retrieved her dropped item from the man. "Do I know you, sir?" She let go of the handle to her suitcase to drape the delicate fabric around her neck.

He shrugged. "Got one of those friendly faces, I guess." He tugged at his ornate, gold leaf-and-vine decorated lapels. The cuffs to his jacket and the vest underneath displayed the same intricate, affluent design. "Several other heads of companies have already arrived, and some are currently in The Palm Court if ya wish to visit with them. You'll find the schedule of events for the week at the front desk when ya check in." Marcel smiled. "Ya talk on marketing will be first thing Wednesday mornin'. Enjoy the cheese conference."

Ice ran up her spine while she touched the handle of her bag. The hubbub of traffic vanished. She eyed the hotel employee. "You knew my name."

"The cabbie musta told me." He reached to take the plum-colored suitcase from her hand.

Cassandra didn't let go. "I'm new to this city and never told him my last name. How do you know so much about me and my plans?"

"Didn't ya ever hear that a good doorman can predict the future?" His green eyes twinkled.

Cassandra stared into his familiar yet non-bespectacled face and released the luggage into his hand. She gasped in sudden recognition. "Mr. Fartworthy?"

"I'm sorry, miss. Ya musta got me confused with someone else." He smiled and tapped the gold name badge. "The name's Marcel. Marcel Cassoulet." He winked, leaned in, and whispered, "For now, Miss Haywood."

MRS. ROSE FOREST'S
BLEU CHEESE SCONES

Ingredients:

2 cups + 1 tbsp. flour

3 tbsp. sugar

1 tbsp. baking powder

½ tsp. salt

.28-.30 lb. (approx. 1 cup) Stilton Bleu Cheese

¾ cup of half and half

3 tbsp. of melted butter + 1 tbsp.

Directions:

1. Preheat the oven to 350° and spread parchment paper on a baking sheet.
2. Mix 2 cups of the flour, sugar, baking powder, and salt together in a large bowl.
3. In a small bowl, mix the half and half and 3 tbsp. of melted butter.
4. Make a well in the middle of the flour mixture and pour the wet mixture into the well.
5. Mix the wet and dry ingredients together until a smooth, round ball forms.
6. Spread 1 tbsp. of flour on a table and turn out the dough in the center of the flour.
7. Flip the dough over to coat both sides in flour, then roll out into a 12-inch x 20-inch rectangle.

8. Crumble the cheese into a small bowl, then sprinkle evenly over the rectangle of dough.

9. Pat the cheese to help it adhere gently to the dough.

10. Roll the dough into a tight log along the long edge.

11. Press the center of the log out to form a 12-inch x 3-inch rectangle.

12. Slice the dough into 16 triangular scones using a crisscross pattern.

13. Transfer the scones to the prepared baking sheet and brush with half of the remaining 1 tbsp. of melted butter.

14. Bake for 15-18 minutes, rotating the pan and brushing with more butter halfway through the bake.

15. Remove from oven when the center of the scones spring back to the touch and the bottoms are lightly browned.

Enjoy! When the scones are baking, the pungent bleu cheese smell will fill whatever space they are baked.

Acknowledgments

A big thank you to the family and friends who participated in the murder mystery party: Abigail Burns, Anne Burns, Benjamin Burns, Christopher Burns, Daniel Burns, Elizabeth Burns, Henry Burns, John Burns, Joseph Burns, Kathleen Burns, Luke Burns, Nichole Burns, Rebecca Burns, Sarah Burns, Susan Burns, Joseph Frissora, Kevin Mathy, William Mathy, Chad Miller, and Annette Vandervort. Thank you so much for playing along with our bit of silliness. Your performances inspired many of the character traits and ideas for the chapters I created afterward to flesh out the remainder of the story. I have been told it is an adventure coming to our house for a party. That January 2015 night was no exception. I appreciate your willingness to jump into my nutty creation.

To Debra and Justin, from the Old World Cheese Department at Wegmans in Corning, NY. Your insightful knowledge about cheese was inspirational and, unwittingly, encouraged me to eat a frightening number of new cheeses as I wrote this book. My taste buds also thank you.

To the Corning (NY) Area Writers' Group. This work you hold in your hands would not have been possible without the enormous encouragement, assistance in the craft of writing and editing, and the business end of creating a book from this amazing group of talented people. I appreciate all of you who participated in our weekly meetings and helped my manuscript in some way. The knowledge I gained from listening to the interesting, strange, and wonderful stories and poems from the group is something that would have taken a decade to learn on my own. A special shout out to the people who went above and beyond to help this newbie feel like she belonged from the very beginning. Dear friends, you have encouraged me when I doubted myself or my writing, sincerely cheered on my successes, and sustained me in so many ways during gloomy times. I'm looking at you, Aleathea Drehmer, Anna Hoyler, Christy Jackson Nicholas (author, the Druid's Brooch Series and *Time Travel Outfitters*), G.H. Monroe (author, *That's My Story!* and *The Hanley Chronicles*), Mattea Orr, A.V. Rogers, Patrick Thomas (author, the Jack Gardner Mysteries, the Mystic Investigators Series, the Murphy's Lore Series, and the Babe B. Bear Mysteries for kids (as Patrick T. Fibbs), Melora Johnson (author, *Sanctuary Built of Words* and *Earthbound*), and Tarren Young. You are all wonderfully quirky, funny, brilliant, and helpful. I adore the time I spend with you, in person and otherwise.

To Joseph Gary Crance (author, The Ryland Creek Saga series). Everything I said above about the CWG applies to you, too. You're also responsible for me finding out about the group in the first place. In addition, I sincerely appreciate the time you spent away from your own writing projects and your terribly busy schedule to walk me through endless vital topics concerning writing, editing, and publishing. My deepest gratitude, my fedora-wearing friend.

I am so grateful for my team of beta readers. Your insight into characters and many comments, plus corrections, places to cut, and additions improved the content and flow of this book. A giant shout out to Marie Burns, Nichole Burns, Rebecca Burns, Joseph Gary Crance, Meg Derick, Jennifer Dolgoff, Maya Dolgoff, Rachel Martonik, and Mattea Orr. Thank you to the bonus beta readers:

Christy Nicholas, G.H. Monroe, and Michelle Wells who, in the last week right before the manuscript went off to my editor, helped tweak my beginning chapters.

Thank you to my copy editor and proofreader, Joyce Mochrie, owner of *One Last Look* (www.onelastlookcopyedits.com). Your professionalism and skills with the pen are amazing. I'm so glad we had the opportunity to work together, and I look forward to future collaborations.

To my book cover designing team at JD & J (www.jdandj.com), thank you. You took the rough concept I had and turned it into an amazing cover. It's perfect, and I absolutely love how it turned out.

Thank you to my family and friends who, in person, on the phone, or through social media, supported and encouraged me through this journey. It meant the world to me when you asked about my writing.

To my offspring, I thank you for listening endlessly when I would chatter on about plot points, clues, symbolism, cover art, marketing, and other topics necessary for my writing. I love you and thank you from the bottom of my heart. To publish a book has been a dream of mine for some time. However, one of my greatest joys in life has been, hands down, being your mother. Big, squishy hugs and kisses for you all.

Sarah: Thank you for your assistance with the party chapters, and especially for all the music insight, as your suggestions helped create the changing mood I needed. Your help with remembering details from the actual party was terrific and saved me so much time.

Rebecca: After my early morning writing sessions, you listened to what I wrote to see if it made sense as you got ready for work. I appreciate how you listened, provided wonderful advice, and excellent additions with poise, and graciously didn't tell me to go away. Thank you for your verbal kick in the pants when I needed to get moving, either in the words for the book or physically.

Daniel: Thank you for being the original "sounding board" for the creation of the characters and the web of secrets for the party. I'm grateful for your calm and quiet manner, the awesome name you created, your contributions to the plot, and your ability to remain silent on the subject, no matter how much your siblings bugged you before the party night.

Christopher: Thank you for the male perspective when I was writing the middle to end of the book. I'm grateful for your insight after reading several chapters when I needed it the most. Your comments regarding several pivotal scenes helped add to the tension I was searching for. I appreciate all the times you reined me in when Von Pickle went too far. Good call.

Benjamin: A heartfelt thank you for so much source material for the character you played. Your lightheartedness, and your famous "Attila, the Hun" way of calming me down, made me laugh when I was stressed about this manuscript or anything else. I also appreciate the work you did to help with the marketing for my book.

Abigail: Thank you for providing the reason to write the party and, subsequently, the book. It was so great that you took on creating the lovely bleu cheese scone recipe. Your clear opinions on who Cassandra was as a person, not just a character, made it easy to write and put through the "Abby test." Sometimes I didn't agree with you immediately, but ultimately, your radar was spot-on for her personality.

Elizabeth: Thank you so much for field testing the scone recipe. Your baking skills for one so young are impressive. I also appreciate your diligent and thorough handling of the family laundry while I edited this book. Knowing you had the daily job under control gave me peace of mind that everyone would still have clean underwear and socks in their drawers, despite Mom's project.

Luke: Thank you for the (at the time) nine-year-old sage insight as to "what guys fight about." Your answer, that quiet Sunday morning when just the two of us were awake, was great. It changed the trajectory of several characters and added meaning under the surface. Well done, Lukey-man! After that, your comment of "What are we working on today?" made me laugh many early mornings when you were the first to show up at my side at the computer.

Henry: My ER buddy! Your one visit for the squished, bloody finger added a realistic description to the manuscript after I observed the semi-dried drops of your blood on the floor upon our return. For the second visit, your explanation of what it felt like and how you could think after you broke your nose changed how I originally wrote that chapter. Life imitated art. The collision with your twin brother's head turned out to be extremely helpful for the novel. Thanks, Master Henslowe, for the physical assistance.

Mary-Clare: Thank you for your sweet hugs and kisses all the time. Your adorable excitement the morning I typed the last word on the first draft made it all worthwhile, my little Gingersnap.

To my husband, Kevin. I appreciate your support of this silly, little project that morphed into something so much bigger than when I started this novel-writing journey two years ago. Thank you for nudging me when my alarm went off at 4:30 or 5 in the morning and I wasn't getting up quite yet. You knew how much happier I was getting in my writing time before the minions descended the stairs at their ridiculously early wake time. Thank you for taking the youngest four children to Wegmans most Saturdays to do the weekly shopping so I could extend the morning writing hours. A quiet house and time to pursue my dream of writing a book were priceless gifts. Thank you, honey, for all the small and big ways you supported me. I love you.

And thank you to God. You knew I needed to write to keep sane, and I'm grateful. Thanks for the push into this hobby.

Author Bio

Michelle Pointis Burns juggles mothering her ten children, homeschooling (the oldest five have now graduated college), living her Catholic faith, and writing. She loves to research topics of all kinds, read British authors (especially Jane Austen and Sir Arthur Conan Doyle), quote movies in regular conversation, and drink hot chocolate from elegant teacups. When asked how does she manage it all, she has been known to reply, "Prayer, caffeine, and a sense of humor."

Michelle has been a dedicated member of the NY Chemung Valley Mothers of Twins Club (she has two sets of twins), and the Corning Area Writers' Group. Born and raised in Queens, NY, Michelle currently lives in Upstate New York on a working goat and sheep farm with her husband and more than half of her children. This is her first novel.

CPSIA information can be obtained
at www.ICGtesting.com
Printed in the USA
FSHW010709151020
74753FS